*R*ouhi Shafii was born in Kerman (Karmanieh as Her mother came from a middle class, educated father was a tribal chief. When she was eight, her pare town in the remote part of south east Persia, where her father ruled the Shafii clan. Rouhi finished primary school in Jiroft. Since there were no secondary girls' schools in town at the time, she was sent away to Bam, where her aunt and grandmother lived. Rouhi moved to Tehran in the late 1950s to go to the university. In the mid-1980s, she migrated to England where she now lives with her two children and grandchildren. Apart from working on women's issues, which is her speciality, Rouhi has published her autobiography, which is a social history of women of her time. Her work gets its inspiration from the Kerman province and the deserts that surround it. She says she owes it to her maternal grandfather, Ebrahim Sa'id (Paysepar), who was a poet and writer, to make Kerman known to the outside world.

For my children and grandchildren

Pomegranate Hearts is a work of fiction. While none of the characters or names had ever existed, they have lived through historical facts.

Published in English by Rouhi Shafii:

"Scent of Saffron"

Three generations of an Iranian family

Also

Translated from English into Persian:

"A complete history of women's movement in more than 14 countries, throughout the twentieth century"

"Argentina and the Peron Dictatorship"

"Chile and the CIA Coup"

"Women of Vietnam"

Also

Translated from Persian into English:

"Migrating Birds"

A collection of Poems

Written by the acclaimed contemporary poet Jaleh Esfahani

Pomegranate Hearts

Copyright: 2006 Rouhi Shafii

First published by

Shiraz Press

First published in paperback in 2006

A CIP Catalogue record of this book is available from
the British Library.

ISBN: 0-9544481-4-6

Shiraz Press

www.Shirazpress.com

Email: info@shirazpress.com

Cover design by: KeeScott

Printed and bound in the UK

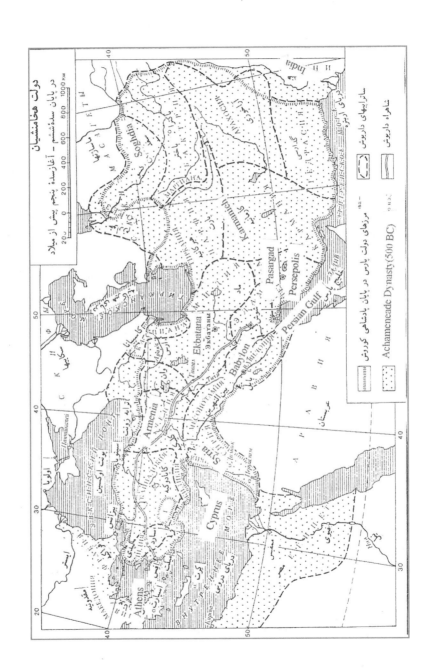

دولت هخامنشیان

در پایان سلطنتِ آغازندهٔ پنجم پیش از میلاد

0   200   400   600   800   1000 KM

مرزهای دولت پارس در پایان پادشاهی کوروش

Achameneade Dynasty (500 BC)

سازمانهای داریوش

ظاهراء داریوش

India

Sogdia

Pasargad
Persepolis
Persian Gulf
Ekbatana
Babylon
Armenia
Syria
Cyprus
Athens

Pomegranate
Hearts

Part One

One

Copper, gold, mustard, gleaming, floating in the mirage of long, hot days. An expanse of torrid land. Hills in the middle, range of mountains out on the horizon, subterranean waters resound harmoniously. Thorn bushes amassed here, scattered there, scorpions in courtship, rattlesnakes playing in an orchestra, stranded birds dozing off under the shelter of an arid rock waiting to fly away. A cyclone curling up, a caravan of loaded beasts struggling solemnly across the endless path. An occasional emerald oasis, refreshing the tired eyes. At night the universe leaping forward, stars hanging upside down. The moon indulging in the heat of the day and the cool of the night. Dawn emerging with morning dews evaporating swiftly, the air heaving with the approach of sunrise. A myth exists that God herself monitored the genesis of the deserts of southern Persia. Otherwise, how could the sequel of beauty and total serenity in that barren plain have come into existence with such precision and professionalism.

And there you see an ancient city bordering the deserts. My parents' hometown and their ancient industry; the carpet weaving workshops. Karmanieh, the beating heart of the desert populated by kind and friendly people. Kind at heart and gentle in manners. People who have survived centuries of troubles but have locked their pains in their broad chests.

Each year, spring arrived from faraway lands, dragging clouds impregnated with heavy bursts of rain, which would pour down suddenly and awaken the nature with wild desires. Then a new chapter would begin. Time for the 'Ustads', whose expertise had transcended centuries, to sketch new designs or stamp their approval on the old ones. Time for the buyers to be dispatched to the villages to buy wool. Time for the skilled hands to treat and colour the wool and turn it into the finest yarns. Time for the army of workers, aged six to sixty, to start afresh, to immortalise the nature. Sitting on the rows of trellis from dawn to dusk, ears to the chanting of pattern-readers echoing from a corner: red, blue, green, yellow...., eyes fixed and fingers moving swiftly across the hanging threads, dragging each to knot, creating: gardens of Shiraz with their plentiful peacocks and nightingales, butterflies, roses, tuberoses, narcissus and begonias; lovers kissing under a magnolia tree, falling blossoms motionless; Khayam sipping wine from his turquoise woven goblet offered by a saghi girl with half-closed, intoxicated eyes; King Khosro Parviz playing Polo on the plain, the Queen of Queens, Shireen, watching from high meadows; women musicians resounding the harp eternally. Persian carpets as a unique work of art have lived in Persia as long as memory goes.

* * *

And so it happened that early in the twentieth century, a delegation of elders negotiated the marriage of my mother, Ashraf khanum to my father, Haji Amir, which took place after much wheeling and dealing and deliberation. One day the city woke up to the most monumental coalition between the two most influential carpet industry owners.

Like the melody of a poem, my mother's traditional beauty caught everyone's eyes. Her skin was soft as velvet. She had a narrow waist and her firm breasts resembled sweet lemons of Shiraz. The tendril of her hair, were waves around the moonlight over water. Her long lashes surrounded her huge eyes and she had a small nose and full lips. Her voice was the singing breeze of one summer's night as she recited Hafez and Saadi's poetry. Her fragrance, sparkling roses and jasmines of southern gardens. And apart from all her earthly beauty there was no handicraft she had not mastered; flower embroidery, knitting, needlework and so on. And. And apart from that, in an age where women were deprived of formal education and illiterate en masse, upon the instruction of her

12

enlightened father, Haji Morteza, an Assyrian governess had taught my mother reading and writing.

Alas! Despite all her credentials, my mother was destined to wed the son of a notorious wealthy widow; whose name brought fear to the mind of those who had done business with her at some stage in life. They say your destiny is carved on your forehead before you are born. My mother believed that she would carry an ill-fate to her husband's house along with her alimony. Future sat in waiting.

Unlike my mother's family, my father's family had a troubled history. Some twenty years earlier, my grandfather, Abdol Hossein khan had contracted smallpox and had died a painful death, leaving four young children and a big business behind. Naturally, my grandmother, Alieh khanum, who was in her late twenties, was devastated. But soon she put her grief aside and prevented the household from disintegration and the business from bankruptcy. She trespassed the boundaries and ignored voices heard from all corners and forced her way through the division of the andaruni and the biruni; met business partners and traders; inspected the accounts and negotiated deals; visited the factories and talked to the carpet-weavers and labourers and saw to their welfare. As the elder son, my father, Amir, a young lad at the time, trailed his mother obediently until he completed his apprenticeship some years later. Finally, Alieh khanum entrusted the trade into his capable hands and ordered the two younger sons, Abbas Mirza and Naser Mirza, to assist him, and she retired to the andaruni. There, as the mistress of the harem, she was in full control of the household. Her commanding voice left no space for objection as she dictated her policies. Once a week, sitting on her usual cushion in the grand living room, smoking ghelyan, drinking tea and listening to her audience of sons, daughter-in-laws and their children, she was briefed on matters at hand and then issued orders. All in all and thanks to Alieh khanum's dictatorial regime, my father's family lived in stability through many years. My first recollection of my father, Amir is this stocky man with sinking eyes and a beard that reached down to his prominent abdomen. A few strands of grey hair peeped from under his turban, which hid his balding patch. Every morning as he walked past through the corridor leading to the biruni I looked at him from the corner of my eyes with caution. He never noticed this creature that was his own child. Yet as sworn by those who were close to him and unlike his mother, Alieh khanum, he was a man of gentle character and generous nature.

Contrary to his brothers, who married young, Amir dedicated his time to the trade and running the family business. A bachelor throughout his twenties, he sometimes spent some evenings in the company of young men after the close of business. Everyone was discreet about such nights. The close circuit of an all-male world; the bazaar or trading compounds and the religious madrases, where the young Talabehs studied for many years to become Akhunds were natural breeding grounds for employing young men and seducing 'pretty boys' to the attics and quiet corners. Later, a mature man, Amir travelled to Mecca, the house of God and then asked his mother to find him a bride. The pilgrimage to Mecca and his few strands of white hair gained him the respected title of Haji.

In old Persia, worlds apart, men lived in the biruni, which were the outer buildings in each household compound and women were confined to the andaruni, which was protected by high walls. The andaruni had a vibrant life, the lives of women, half the population of every city and town but all concealed from the outside world. Living the first part of my life in the andarun of my father, Haji Amir, observing that lively and intelligent crowd, I wondered how they could remain such imaginary silhouettes, ghosts, non-humans, rumours. Shadows moving under the cover of night, their voices never heard, and their faces covered from the sun, the moon and the male fish in the pond. Captive birds caged and hidden. For centuries Persia had lived as a one-sex nation. It must have been merely the power of imagination that led women into the world of poetry and prose.

Naturally, inside the walled andaruns there was an abundance of adventures and scandals. The neighbourhood had just settled for the heated negotiations to match my mother to my father, when Mirza Mustafa's first wife, Nargis khanum, neglected and left alone after Mirza wedded his second wife, decided to approach a matchmaker, who convinced the deprived woman to court men in Mirza's own house. In Mirza's own backyard! The famous merchant, whose name rolled off everyone's tongue with respect! Well, it seemed the safest option. So, dressmakers, hairdressers, fortune-tellers and finally amateur musicians crowded the compound. Unfortunately, one early autumn afternoon, Mirza finished his business earlier than expected and returned home. The sun was shining, children were playing in the courtyard and apart from Nargis khanum's quarters, the rest of the household was in siesta. She had tasted the forbidden fruit with much satisfaction when suddenly a deep, familiar voice echoed through the courtyard. The departure of a stocky figure in a woman's outfit in haste from Nargis khanum's quarters and the sight of an instrument left behind erupted into a volcano which spread fire and ash. Yet the walls of denial were high and Mirza could not prove a thing. Nevertheless, people's imagination travelled far beyond. For days, women puffed and panted like boiling pots, children went astray, lunch was delayed, housework cancelled. Sitting around, cross-legged, nibbling nuts, drinking tea, all ears and sweat; adding, deducting, spreading and ruining. Lives and reputations. Unfortunately, you can shut the gate to an enemy but you can not shut people's mouths!

The matchmakers! Women of no social status but the town's inner heartbeat. Making a profession from the stockpile of intelligence, touring the andaruns, carrying the web of gossip, capable of exaggerating, adding, deducting, extracting, negotiating and finalising deals; talented in painting descriptive pictures of the unseen, and skilful in convincing the most difficult tastes. Matchmakers were not only the catalysts to marriages but they came to have the solution to another social problem. Inside the enclosures of the andaruns, an army of young women lived without men. Their movements were scrutinised and controlled by elder guardians. Their urge to step out often led them through dangerous paths. Among them were women who could not bear sons, or those who did not perform satisfactorily in bed. Women, whose husbands took a second and third wife or frequently went to the Wine Houses and mixed with the loose women. Women who had the courage not to sleep with their husbands because they had intolerable body odours. Widows and maidens who had no way to burn off their suffocating desires. Matchmakers had the key to all. Women paid them well. Men paid them well. To find safe havens so they could rejoice the company of each other without facing dangers or bearing obligations. Matchmakers were skilful in spotting the candidates and teaching them to avoid the scandal of facing their own husbands or male relatives should it happen as it had on rare occasions.

The city centre and the main square were a smiling onlooker, dusty faced and panting for a cool breeze, shops surrounding their planted heart, traders inviting the wriggling crowd to examine and taste their products, errand boys seeking passage through, females walking like sacks of potato with two holes on the top, yet freshening the torrid air. Window shopping from behind their rubandeh, seeking the potential suitor. Spotting him, approving, approaching and rubbing their perfumed body against him in a flicker of a moment, then sneaking through the maze of narrow streets to wash off the boredom. God herself was a go-between and facilitator. To pronounce a temporary marriage of a few hours sanctioned by the holy religion would wash off the guilt and the sin alltogether.

16

Two

Every year as spring approached, life began afresh. Snow melted on the rooftops and icy streets turned into sticking mud; migrating birds encircled the city, their black and white wings glowed across the azure sky; poplar and cypress trees shook off their trunks from the long, crisp season. The buds peeped out; the undergrowth resounded with rhythms as the desert came to life. Roads opened and the convoy of merchants set out for the journey of many months. The only means of transportation were mules, camels and horses. The southern roads were not asphalt, nor were there any trucks to transport the merchandise. The caravanserais en route sheltered the convoys but the travellers took sufficient provisions in case they could not reach them in time. At any rate, the length of the journey left a shadow of doubt to the merchants' safe return. Passing through towns and villages, deserts and mountain ranges, facing armed bandits, getting caught in wild storms, collapsing from fatigue, contracting typhus or cholera....until ultimately they reached their destination. Worry stayed behind and lingered in the air.

At the hour of departure, families would gather to say farewell. Women in the andaruni, men in the biruni. In a festive atmosphere, food was prepared and rapidly consumed. Stocks of bread and bundles of dried fruit were loaded on the beasts; the mullah would arrive in time to read passages from the holy book and fold written prayers into the men's pockets. Saturated emotions would reach a new height. Agitated children would get in the way and frequently smacked and pinched and sworn at. Women would cry and wail, some would even faint, others commiserate. The mullah would console. The promise of a short-lived freedom would tickle an undetected pleasure in a few. This continued until the dust settled and died down and the line of men on horseback and servants on foot became smaller and then swallowed by the sandy hills into the vastness of the desert.

A few miles further the convoy had to choose its route. The southern route stretched into the deserts of central Persia while the northern route joined the Silk Road. The southern route passed through villages and towns at the edge of the desert until it reached the shores of the Persian Gulf. There on, the merchandise was transferred into commercial vessels and continued its way through the southern seas, reaching India and beyond. The Silk Road began from China, stretched across Russia before it zigzagged through Persia, then into Turkey and finally into Eastern and Western Europe.

Before such journeys, as the head of the family was about to leave, there always bubbled the question of the Chastity Belt. That polluted relationships as husbands, backed by the mischievous mothers-in-law favoured the act but wives refused it vehemently. It was a disgrace, the manifestation of total lack of trust. But if the wife was furnished with the Belt, the key was kept with a trustworthy person, usually the mullah at the local mosque. These were respected members of the community as well as religious authority. Unfortunately, sometimes the thread of trust was too thin and broke by the force of seduction.

The biggest episode of this kind that remained in memory for some considerable time but never proved credible was the story of Haji Eskandar who, in the spring of 1912, left his two hostile wives behind, to accompany his merchandise to Damascus. The issue of the Belt crossed Haji's mind but he found it impossible to take such a heavy measure against one or both women. However, their constant hostility was assurance enough that none would jeopardise her position. The first wife was much respected by Haji as the mother of his three children and the younger was dearly loved because of her beauty. In normal circumstances the journey would last about four months. This time, his convoy travelled through central Persia, passed the cities of Yazd, Isfahan, Hamadan and Kermanshah before it reached Iraq and Syria, by which time the month of Haj was round the corner and Eskandar gave in to the insistence of his fellow travellers to visit Mecca, the house of God. Although he had already gone there and gained the title of Haji, it would be a blessing if he went the second time. That in all took him nine months. Upon his return, his second wife Zarin Banu was expecting.

Wow, wow! Oh, dear God! How could that happen? When was the last time he…? If not him, who could have been the….? What was he supposed to do? How could he pull words out of closed mouths? Ironically, Haji had arrived at a territory far from what he had left behind. In his absence, the two wives, worn out by constant fighting entered a treaty of conciliation, divided the territory under their rule and so the household breathed peace and tranquillity and the women blossomed in harmony. As with the case of his young wife's pregnancy, Haji had to be very careful. Had suspicion been raised to his suspicion, rumours would have spread and ruined his total life. So, he swallowed his pride and admitted that he had made his wife pregnant right before departure. Yet when the baby was born, the rose-scented, chubby young mullah Hussein, who was appointed the executor of his will, sometimes enquired about Haji Eskandar's 'andarun affairs', which were none of his business now that Haji had returned. Still Haji kept his silence but from then on, he stationed the firmest Belt on his wives and kept the key in his own pocket. News of such an act soon reached the outside world. News gathered momentum and rained down the andaruns, where women devoured the juice.

* * *

All this aside, negotiations went underway between the two most famous families of Karmanieh and occupied the headlines and filled the gossip columns, pushing other stories to the back pages. The grandeur of my mother's wedding remained the hottest topic for many, many months.

For a whole week, every afternoon, Amin Sultan, Haji Amir's elder uncle as the chief negotiator, accompanied by his aides arrived at Haji Morteza's house to seal the deal. Alieh khanum aspired to accompany the convoy but the gesture of Amin Sultan of total refusal choked the words in her throat. How could a woman accompany men in such an important mission! Yet Alieh khanum could not be ignored and so they had to report back to her every day and listen to her suggestions and advice.

Sitting in Haji Morteza's reception room, leaning on a cushion, smoking ghelyan, Amin Sultan would patiently listen to the terms and conditions put forward by my grandfather, respectfully, yet firmly with his delicate choice of words. With his charismatic smile and tactful manoeuvring, Amin Sultan would nod, pause to think and then react. Both delegations wanted to tie knots and so were cautious not to break the fine thread of negotiations. Both were adamant not to give way to extra concessions. A twist of calculated words would refuse, then reduce and finally adjust Haji Morteza's demands; the amount of gift money, the variety of jewellery and the place of residence.

Finally, an agreement was reached. A date next summer was set. Haji Amir, jubilant at his forthcoming marriage, rushed buyers to Russia for the latest furs and fashions, to Bukhara for rubies, Bahrain for pearls, Yazd for gold, China and India for silk, satin and chiffon. A month prior to the wedding, his caravan of gifts packed and sealed in gold boxes and mahogany cases set out for the bride's home. The whole town sat watching. No one had witnessed such a grand procession in years. The bazaar closed its front stalls and gave way to the group of eunuchs, who carried the goods over their heads and musicians who danced ahead. Women gathered at the edge of rooftops, their household chores unattended. The children jumped up and down, some fell off the rooftops into the crowded alleyways. Had it not been for the promptness of the passers-by, a few injuries would have flavoured the wedding presents.

A few days before the wedding, my mother's dowry, collected over many years was dispatched to her future home. Cases of china and crystal, silver and copperware, hand-made quilts, duvets, curtains and mattresses and special carpets, the unique work of Haji Morteza's personal Ustad. The consignment, sealed and packed, accompanied by Fatima the trusted maid and her family, left for Haji Amir's household, as part of my mother's dowry. The sun had spread light across the city, streets were broomed and people kept away from the roads. Musicians entertained and the whole neighbourhood was offered sweets and sherbet. It took the convoy half a day to reach a destination of a few miles. From the vicinity of my father's house, a separate group of waiting musicians met the oncoming caravan half way and competition took a high velocity. Alieh khanum was present to receive the goods. Cases were put in place and opened for the clerks to begin the task of listing the contents. As the sun fell behind the horizon and dusk rose, they delivered a copy to each party; one to Alieh khanum, the other to Haji Morteza's younger bother. Celebrations continued through the evening.

* * *

Of the three sisters, the younger siblings Parvin and Zohreh were playful and unruly. They filled the andarun of Haji Morteza with their laughter, put their noses into everything and formed an ungovernable contingent of devils. A few years older than them, my mother, Ashraf had taken after her mother, Ismat khanum and grew into a quiet and reserved girl. Against her astounding beauty and sound education, she sometimes sank into a state of melancholy and depression. She would hide in a corner, embrace her knees and a waterfall of tears would rush out of her beautiful eyes, fill the room, soaking everything and overflowing onto the veranda. At such times, sadness would engulf the andarun, poplar and cypress trees would put their heads together in grief, nightingales would stop splashing lyrics over tuberoses, sparrows' giggles choked in their throat and swallows brought their choir to a halt. The Indian parrot would sit beside Ashraf, getting nostalgic for her hometown, Calcutta, constantly wiping her eyes with her feathery handkerchief. Ismat khanum would be dragged along to console her daughter.

In her early teens, accompanied by her aunt Monir, my mother had visited a fortune-teller and palm-reader, which predicted an ill fate in her future life. The thought of that lurked around and mingled with her other thoughts, leaving a persistent anxiety in her. Ashraf resorted to God to relieve her of the distress and remove the curse from her. She had begged and pleaded with God to lead her through the path of a smooth life, but God was too busy with Her own domesticity and did not spare time for this silly girl who stalked Her at odd times.

* * *

My mother, Ashraf was the last one to be officially informed of her forthcoming marriage to my father, Haji Amir. Near the time, her mother, Ismat khanum took her to a corner and told her of the agreement and spoke of the arrangements. Ashraf blushed and lowered her eyes and stamped her approval in a broken voice. Elders knew what was best for her! Curious though, she opened her heart to her aunt Monir and asked her to make enquiries about the groom's looks. Not much was gained except exaggerations of Gelin khanum, the matchmaker, who was on the groom's side.

In the summer of 1910, after a week-long wedding celebration, at the age of fifteen, my mother set foot into my father's andarun, which was a compound of inner and outer buildings among acres of mature gardens. As was agreed, she was allocated separate quarters, away from her mother-in-law, Alieh khanum and her widowed sister-in-law Moluk Azam. Upon the advice of elders, she maintained a distant but respectful relationship with her in-laws, where even a short visit to each other's quarters was made by prior arrangement. Although that did not deter my grandmother, Alieh khanum from intrusion.

For the first ten years, Ashraf found little time to return to her old blues. Too much was paid for her. Too much was expected of her. Running Haji Amir's household and bearing children every other year, she lived a busy and happy life for most of the time. Yet her blues waited patiently to return.

Three

Time passed and my mother had her third female child. Gradually, my father and his family changed attitude. A male grandchild was long overdue and of this Haji Amir was reminded at every opportunity. Yet my mother was not the woman to be disposed of easily. She was the daughter of a wealthy and respected family. Besides, my father loved her dearly and the thought of departing from her devastated him. Yet he was not sure how long he could wait for a son. Subdued, he distanced from the issue as much as possible. The birth of the fourth female was the final straw. There on, everything and everyone changed direction and my mother's status was lowered from its high position to that of a woman who had brought four females into the family. Dark clouds were gathering momentum, heavy with ill omens. A storm was rising from under the dunes and the tide of events was turning against my beautiful mother, Ashraf.

Gradually, my father absented himself from the andarun. No more was he the tender, loving husband, who showered my mother with love and affection at every opportunity. Instead, he turned into a sullen and bad-tempered man, who would creep into the house late at night, or worse, would head for the 'Wine House', where he drowned himself in wine and the company of loose women, or young boys. His return in the early hours of the morning would not be ignored by his wife or his mother, who stayed awake in their solitude, each thinking their own thoughts. At the break of dawn, without a hint of the nightlong absence, Haji Amir would set off for the morning prayers and then settle for work in the biruni. Haji Amir spent his nights, drinking wine with Setareh, an eastern beauty of the Kavir, the seducer of men and the talk of town. Who would have imagined that after years of respectable family life, Haji would resort to such sinful acts?

Setareh worked in the 'Wine House' at the outskirts of town, where men spent generously on her. Yet she chose the men she liked, drank with them, danced with the music across the smoky, low-ceilinged hall and entertained whomever she wanted. She was powerful, daring and beautiful. But she was not respected. She had a profession as old as time itself. She was condemned by society despite the fact that the male population sought utmost pleasure in her company. Women in the andaruns were fascinated by Setareh's recklessness. She entertained Haji Amir proudly and became a potential rival to the most respected and beautiful woman in town. Setareh and my mother happened to share the same man for a period of time. My mother's heart ached but she was unable to prevent her husband from self-destruction. Nor would she complain to anyone. She covered her dignity with silence for that moment in time.

Soon it came to Ashraf's attention that Alieh khanum was encouraging her son to take a second wife. After all, who would stand the shame of having a sequence of daughters and no son? While Alieh khanum was hunting a suitable girl, the horror of a rival shadowed Ashraf's life slowly, relentlessly, with a heavy pace, the string of life was loosening from her grip. Ismat khanum smuggled in fortune-tellers and sorceresses to help her daughter. They gave advice, wrote prayers and prepared magical potions. But to no avail. None stopped my father, Haji Amir from going to the Wine House and my grandmother, Alieh khanum from hunting the second wife.

My parents grew distant in the down-stream of time. Cordial, yet far apart, a sand-bed separated them for that time span. A wall of silence prevailed. Both avoided the unspoken and hid behind the sand stones. Despite my parents' differences, my siblings were raised properly as was required at the time. A live-in governess was teaching them reading and writing and supervised their manners and upbringing. Then, the last daughter before me had grown to be a two-year-old toddler.

Surprisingly, particles of the lost love surged across the divide, intense but short-lived. It was May 1919 and the weather was mild. Surrounding snowy peaks had melted into streams of parallel lines, speeding and roaring into the vastness of the desert. The undergrowth had long awakened from the winter siesta. Swallows were giggling, sparrows singing. Wild flowers turning the city and the plateau into a paradise, their aromas mingling with the cool breeze, wafting across the domes. Delighted at such abundance, my grandmother, Alieh khanum and her daughter Moluk Azam decided to go on a pilgrimage of a holy shrine in the outskirts of the city and with the swing of their good mood decided to stay in the countryside for the while.

A unique opportunity had arisen. My mother's sixth sense whispered a conspiracy. Having the whole andarun to herself, she thought she might be able to bring her estranged husband back. She was right. My father closed his trade early and came to the andarun. My mother's fresh and delightful fragrance danced through the ripple of her silk dress. Lost desires awoke driving my father to near madness. He rushed to his room, opened the holy book, read a passage and consulted with God and concluded that it was a favourable moment and so approached my mother with both guilt and ecstatic desire. She pulled herself away, and then shyly agreed to his demands. Haji Amir sowed the seed of a prince whom he saw on an Arabian horse passing through deserts, conquering territories. Love smiled on the blossoms and happiness danced in the air. The andarun breathed normality for that moment in time.

* * *

My mother knew that she should not waste anytime. She had to use all available resources in her favour. Learning from experience, she was certain that resorting to God directly was of no avail. It was best if she worked her way through Her messengers. Out of the one hundred and twenty four thousand saints scattered around the globe, a few had crossed the seas on flying horses and embarked on the deserts of southern Persia. Some had reincarnated in people's dreams, and so shrines had been erected here and there. These saints were the only source of consolation to the female population of Karmanieh. Women missed no opportunity to consult them, confide in them and demand mediation, prescription and solution to their problems. Finding proper husbands, taming an untamed man, locking the mother-in-law's tongue, scaring away the matchmakers who brought second and third wives into a household and bearing boys instead of girls were among many matters under constant contention. On Thursdays and Fridays, these holy shrines were swamped with females, who opened their hearts and unleashed their yearnings. The domes would become saturated with low cries, sweat, anger, moans and groans. Thousands of secrets floated around and scattered away. Some spoke loudly, others whispered and the rest kept their lips tight, believing His Holiness knew what their pleas were about. Sometimes weeping turned into thunder and ornaments of the tombs, presents of loyal worshippers floated out and hid in the desert nearby.

The saints knew for most of the time how to handle the matters and advised the females not to approach God directly. 'Here we are, ready and willing to settle the matters. We are experts in every area and you can trust us as the go-betweens'. In private, they confessed that if clients were not satisfied with their services, 'they would remove the bolt off the God's gate'. After all, if relations between the saints and their clients broke, the whole state of affairs would spiral out of hand; husbands would go astray; mothers-in-law would throw their daughters-in-law out into the street, new brides would swamp households; newborn girls would out-number boys and chaos would reign in the town.

My mother drafted a long list of all the saints in the neighbourhood. Day in, day out, Fatima, her trustworthy maid was ordered to prepare cookies and halvahs and accompanied by a relative she roamed the four corners of the universe in search of a solution. Upon arrival at her favourite shrine, she would open her heart and leave no space for speculation. Apprehensive that she might be betrayed by the saint, as well as begging, she threatened she would take her own life if her wishes did not come true. Clinging to the iron bars, she would whisper: 'my dear Imam, I am talking about a son for the wealthiest man in town and I will not take no for an answer. You know what would happen if I bear a female for the fifth time. You yourself married four times and took many concubines before your last wife gave you a son and so you can not blame Haji Amir if he re-marries for the sake of having an heir to his throne. I'd rather be dead than go through the shame of a rival at my doorstep'.

And so for nine months and nine hours and ninety minutes, my mother rushed in and out of the tombs and confided in their holinesses who, awoke intoxicated by the fragrance of her body. Sometimes seeing her determination, which manifested in the tone of her voice, her favourite holiness would get scared. Pale, bony and yawning he would emerge from his tomb and sit at the doorstep beside her and listen in anticipation. He knew very well that his hands were tied and his authority limited. Yet he was sad and did his best to mediate between his client and God.

In addition to such visitations, my grandmother, Ismat khanum and her sister Monir, as special advisors, took my mother to an attar that was known to have cured all girl-bearing women. After taking the potion of herbal mixture, she turned pale and vomited for two whole weeks and almost lost me, the baby. Yet that did not deter her from seeing other attars and seeking further advice. In addition to that, throughout the nine-month pregnancy, fortune-tellers and palm readers spent hours surfing her palm, reading the lines and confirming the arrival of a young lad who would soon roam around the household, and order the occupants to obey him. At such moments, my mother's face would brighten up and happiness would spread across the andaruni and spill onto the biruni and the outside world. Was there a conspiracy or pure bad luck? All worked to create me, a female.

Four

In the midst of winter, suddenly, an early spring showed on the horizon. The sun stood at the equinox, the heat woke the nature from her deep sleep, the heap of snow slid down the domes, forming layers of ice over muddy streets which crunched under footsteps, melted and streamed down the brooks. Nature was yawning, stretching, brightening, birds were singing, flower buds rippling, farmers ploughing. All unaware that winter had not yet departed, but waited in the shade of the moon planning his next move. Should he suddenly decide to return gale-force winds and snowstorms would regain life and an embargo would put the city under an icy siege.

Winters disfigured Karmanieh. Barren, lifeless as far as the eye could see. Cold, crisp as much as the skin could endure. Gardens and orchards were stripped of their glamour turned into skeletons. Frozen brooks lined alongside frozen streets. Hungry wolves howled at nights. Crows shrilled throughout the days. Beneath the ancient trunks of poplar and cypress trees in the gardens encircling the andarun of Haji Amir, the wave of multicoloured shrubs and flower beds, which in spring and summer mirrored an oceanic paradise, turned into piles of dead, grey compost where worms crept over each other and snails dreamt in their shells of a life which would some day stream out. Woven tightly to last longer, crows' nests at the top branches barely protected, initially remained undamaged but eventually were scattered by further storms and high winds, urging the birds to rebuild on love's arrival.

Stretching forward a generous hand, in the year 1920, the mild weather encouraged the household to greet the spring earlier than expected. My grandmother, Alieh khanum turned a blind eye to the winter's possible return. A Commander in Chief, she tightened her chador around her waist, rolled up her sleeves and supervised preparations. From dawn till dusk. Extra hands were called in to assist with the extra work. First, curtains were brought down, cushions were uncovered and sheets and towels were all piled in the laundry room. Constant hot water was boiled in copper pots stationed on stoves in the adjoining kitchen. And three women squatted on the floor, soaking, scrubbing and squeezing for three consecutive days. Then, it was time to rinse the mountain of washing in the central pond. Hammering on the ice did not break it but frightened the tiny gold fish beneath who rushed to safety. Alieh khanum reluctantly retreated from the ritual and silence resumed. The fish returned to bed and the washing was lined up on the hanging ropes, dancing with the breeze, drying in the sun. China and silverware were unearthed from the trunks, crystal lamps and chandeliers giggled noisily while receiving brilliance. Dust, mud and dead leaves were brushed aside, giving way to a broad smile which sat at the gate. Waiting.

On the other side of town, Leila, the renowned baker, postponed her routine and along with her aides and the armoury of pots, pans, metal moulds, copper trays and portable steel ovens arrived one early morning. A room and part of the kitchen were allocated to her. A jovial woman and knowing that it was to be a joyous occasion and that she might find some time to spare, Leila had brought her famous tambourine with her so as to please and entertain.

In the neighbourhood, the pace of housework had slowed down. Neighbours were devoting long hours to the occasion. They would walk into Ismat khanum's house, squatted in the kitchen ready to assist in any way they could. Or, they would take part in conversation, nibbling disfigured cookies and enjoying the occasion.

For a whole week, the air was saturated with aromas of roasted coffee and roasted dried seeds as the rhythm of heavy mortars echoed in the air and scents of fresh cookies intermingled. Every hour, on the hour, a set of cookies, perfect in texture, taste and mould was taken out and set aside to cool, then stored in tight-lid copper pans, which stood side by side in rows. Fresh dough blended in rosewater and orange extracts swelled under white muslin, getting ready to be shaped into flowers, stars, moons, hearts and shining eyes, decorated with cardamom and saffron. Apart from the cookies and various nibbles made in abundance, bottles of sherbet and distilled extracts of herbs and green leaves were secured in wooden cases. A heap of knitted and tailored baby clothes, hand-made quilts and embroidered sheets all wrapped in keshmiri fabrics, waited patiently to be dispatched to Ashraf's home.

As the day progressed, Leila found time to brush her 'charaghad' aside, clear some ground, let out a big laugh and announce the hour of leisure by raising her tambourine, playing forcefully and singing loudly, no fear of being heard in the biruni;

'I have a golden-hair boy on the way,

worth one million, two million, even more.

His small dudul is priceless.

Only if the daughter of King Jamshid

does come along and beg,

I might consider

getting him a bride.'

And as she turned and twisted her big rump, women and children joined in a frenzied dance, bending forward, shaking backward, jumping up and down, twisting their waists, shaking their bosoms and heavy bellies until sweat and tears rolled down their faces and their laughter died into sighs of contented exhaustion. There, they spread on the floor for a minute of meditation before work resumed all over again. Smells and scents, the rhythm of the tambourine and women's laughter escaped the kitchen, stretched out of the chimney, divided equally among the low domes and eventually crept down the neighbourhood's wind turrets.

Ismat khanum and her recently married daughter, Parvin, stood witness to this madness, their hearts filled with pride and happiness. At noon, as the muezzin chanted invitations to the devotees to rush to the neighbouring mosque, women sat at lunch. Niereh, the old maid prepared ghelyan for Leila using quality tobacco she took from her mistress's stock. Rugs were spread on the veranda for women to enjoy the break while the sun's generosity warmed the courtyard. Soaked in the pleasure of the treat, Leila would lean on the cushions, smoking ghelyan slowly, letting the smoke out with delicacy and professionalism, pausing between her sentences, raising her voice at times, or softening it into a whisper, putting emphasis on a word or mumbling to gain the audience's full attention, and continuing with her saucy jokes. Leila's never-ending stories enriched the moment with enjoyment and framed the occasion. Women cried out their laughter, wiped their tears and occasionally herded the youngsters away from Leila's explicit language. The girls hurried into the adjoining rooms, sticking their ears to the doors, trembling with fear and excitement, yearning to hear it all.

Early in the morning, throughout the week, neighbours assembled for a quick exchange of information:

'God knows why such a fuss over a fifth pregnancy!'

'Are they certain it will be a boy?'

'What if she delivers yet another girl?'

'How will the two families cope with the shame?'

'Let's pray to God that this time it will be a boy.'

And so women's comments travelled back and forth. Their worries stretched and expanded from house to house, street to street, into the bazaar, then mirrored back into the andarun. Having known both families all their lives, they were aware of the importance of my mother's latest pregnancy. Exhausted by speculations and touched by the feverish bustle, neighbours resorted to God in private. Some took a step further and visited the holy shrines to urge the saints to mediate, so that 'Ismat khanum and her daughter emerge victorious out of this 'experience', which God has imposed on them.'

Life was lived differently in the biruni. From early morning, men sat at business. Servants offered tea from the steaming samovars; clerks entered, took orders and left for the bazaar. Money changed hands and deals were sealed. Politics, economics, social constraints surfaced, were discussed, decided upon and set aside. Until noon arrived. Important men accompanied by unimportant aides rushed to the mosque from every direction. But prayers would not resume until my grandfather, Haji Morteza, occupied his place by the side of the Imam, who then would chant out prayers, while followers humbled themselves and knelt on their sajadeh. Out of fear, or habit, on negotiating or demanding terms, or otherwise, they worshipped God's sovereignty. Then upon their return to the biruni, lunch was served and men prepared to go home for the afternoon siesta.

While in the biruni, Haji Morteza's mind dealt with the outside world, his heart frequently trekked into the andarun and filled with much affection, returned to his broad chest to rest for the while. A sigh of relief would escape and a delighted smile would sit at the corner of his mouth as he heard in the distance noises of joyous activities. Assured that he had allocated enough resources, Ismat khanum was free to spend generously. The rest was out of his control and under constant negotiations with god. The outcome was yet to arrive.

Each day, as the sun set to rest behind the mountain ranges far from the desert, Leila's cooking stopped and Haji Morteza's trade came to a close. He would announce his arrival by shouting 'Ya-allah' and coughing loudly and pacing slowly to allow the women to disappear behind their 'rubandeh'. Then he would walk straight into the washroom, change into a Kashmiri robe and a thermal cap and arrive in the family room to sit at the top of the Korsi, where dinner was served. The nights were cold enough for the 'Korsi' to remain. Haji Morteza's feet beneath the blanket enjoyed the warmth of the constant, slow burn of coal in the brazier. Ismat khanum and the remaining three children, Zohreh, 15, Alimardan, 13 and Darab, 10, would occupy their places around the korsi and relax to an evening of eating, drinking tea, nibbling nuts and fruit, chatting, and conversing.

Haji Morteza loved his family passionately, enjoyed their company immensely, engaged himself in their interests constantly and gave them valuable advice, whenever he found it necessary and in all, devoted his entire life to his wife and children. When at home, he was a mountain of tenderness and attention and the household rested under his care, which he accommodated with all his heart. He seldom took worries of his trade and the affairs of his business home, except when he was alone with Ismat, in which case he spoke his heart and let his true feelings flow over and be shared with his wife, now in her early forties.

Ismat khanum had arrived at grandfather's household a thirteen year old child bride. He was sixteen. They grew up together, learnt to share their sadness, pains, and happiness and so a long-lasting love plaited itself around their relationship as long as they lived. Domestic and docile, yet dignified and efficient, Ismat khanum knew no world outside the gates of her house. Nothing existed beyond. Yet the neighbourhood turned to her for advice in cases of financial hardship or for consultation on matters of great importance.

One evening after dinner as they were about to go to bed, and Ismat was sitting cross legged in front of the mirror, unplaiting and combing her long, greying hair, Haji Morteza's tall figure approached her cautiously. He looked at her in the mirror for a long time she smiled back tenderly, a tremble of joy rushing through her veins. Then he sat beside her and held her in his arms and asked her delicately the question that had lurked in his mind for quite some time. 'What would happen if the new comer was born a female?'

Reddened with fury, Ismat pulled herself free and shouted at him so loud that her voice cracked the walls and travelled beyond: 'why do you speak of misfortune, man? I hope you bite your tongue hard. Do not send a bad omen at this crucial time.' She hid her face among her hair to let her tears flow from the root of her long lashes. May God be kind enough to spare them this one time.

Five

Soon, winter re-emerged and icy grey clouds began to rise from the lines of rocky mountains indicating a storm underway. Inside and out. The pain started in the early afternoon and continued throughout the night. My mother, Ashraf ignored it at first but when it escalated and the time between contractions shortened, she sent for her mother, who, accompanied by my aunt Parvin, and aunt Monir set off in a doroshky. The gallop of horses echoed in the crisp air of early dawn. The gate opened and the visitors were rushed to our quarters, waves of anxiety clinging to them. Exchanging pleasantries, enquiring about the state of affairs, reassuring and consoling took them well beyond the hour of the evening prayers. A deep concern pinned its marks on the pace of their walk, the tone of their voice and the pupil of their eyes, as they looked at each other or glanced at Ashraf. Even silence bore some anxiety.

The Korsi had been removed temporarily. The braziers filled with burning charcoal warmed the air. A mattress had been spread, away from the draft with sheets and pillows and a hand embroidered quilt the edge. Close by, a smaller one covered in bright satin and fine muslin, beside which glittered a wooden carved case, swollen with undergarments and knitted baby clothes, a dozen cotton nappies, bottles of oils, liquid shampoos and other small items. A snowy white chest contained herbs and organic medicine. The adjoining room which had an entrance to the delivery room through a wide walnut door with its floor covered with Kermani carpets and alongside its walls rested blankets covered with white sheets, and propped up feather cushions. Hand-carved walnut tables at each corner bore the weight of silver bowls, filled with cookies, ghauts and nuts brought from my grandmother, Ismat khanum's house a few days earlier. Winter fruits, products of the orchards in the outskirts of city, glowed in the fruit baskets.

In the kitchen, the nerve centre, preparations had continued for days. Doors had opened for the butcher to deliver slaughtered lambs and the farmers to bring in sacks of fresh vegetables and the fruiterers boxes of fruit. Bread came out of the oven and cooled in the basement to store. Aromas and scents interlaced and danced in a circle at the kitchen's apex. The household was cautious not to excite Soghra, the cook who was utilising her maximum energy and expertise. On important occasions, she worked under Alieh khanum's supervision but now the latter had absented herself to be in the delivery room. Soghra was agitated and nervous, jumped from one corner to the other, put her nose into everything, issued orders and nullified them all at the same time and swore at the maids, who would become frightened and in their confusion made extra mistakes.

* * *

The sequence of pain indicated the baby was due any moment. Yet for thirty-six hours, waiting air lurked inside the household. Swinging clouds high in the sky encircled the courtyard. Shrilling crows sat at the top of the bare trees. The grumpy family cat dozed on the veranda, opening her eyes occasionally to see her kittens playing nearby. Waiting women were killing time. Eventually, my father, Haji Amir informed his fellow traders and partners that he would not be available for the next few days. All matters to be dealt with by his assistants. He stayed in the biruni, to-ing and fro-ing. A secret from his mother, diamonds and rubies waited in a satin box. Dreaming of friendly hands, gold coins peeped out of their hideout as Haji Amir rose from the propped-up cushion to pace. The first to reach him with good news would be the luckiest. The midwife could have a chance of a lifetime.

A boy it must be. A boy it had better be. Riding an Arabian horse, the surreal picture of a prince was painted all over the walls. Upside down. Inside out. Becoming increasingly heavy with a boyish smell the air was hard to breathe. Hanging from the edge of thoughts, the tip of silent tongues, the surface of worried looks, a penis with various shapes and sizes, fresh and uncircumcised, cut and ready to use, potent and impotent floated in the air, threatened the population and laughed straight into space.

At noon, the sun penetrated the clouds, but was short-lived. Soon, it was sucked into the darkness. Thunderous clouds were approaching and putting the city under siege. Soon an icy rainfall raced towards the domes and hailstorms followed. Pedestrians quickened their paces and rushed to safety. Farmers herded their bulls into stables and themselves slid through the doors of their huts. Hail turned into drizzle of light snow. The day ended and the night fell. Oil lamps flickered at every corner and illuminated my mother's quarters. My father retired to bed but ordered that he should be awakened at any time. Apart from my mother's occasional cries, and the whispering voices, silence submerged the household. Parvin stayed at her sister's side, whispering amusing remarks in an effort to ease her agony. Other women tended to her, returning to whisper among themselves while drinking, nibbling, and smoking. Alieh khanum had ordered the maids to soak ample tobacco. Hope hid dormant inside fresh tobacco and optimism danced in the bubbles, then burnt to ash, was inhaled and gone. Throughout the night, the pain intensified but birth did not take place. Instead, it cut through to my mother's bones, reaching the root of her soul. The source of her worries had stiffened her muscles. She moaned and groaned. At times she cried out and swore at the entire world for having been born a woman.

By dawn, the third day, the city was covered under a white shroud. Anxious looks appeared on women's faces and Ismat khanum spent a long time at her sajadeh, head down, begging for God's mercy and a desirable outcome. Exhausted with the long labour, my mother's endurance was near an end. Yet every once in a while, her cries were interrupted by a remark from Alieh khanum:

'Now, now, dear, enough of screaming and making scenes. Why are you fretting so much? Try to breathe deeply and relax your muscles. After all you are not the first and only woman giving birth and this is not your first delivery.' And then she would turn to the audience, rolling her eyes upwards, trying to gain their approval: 'In our time we bore children year after year and no one was around to spoil us, why then?' Her high pitched voice coming through the exhaled smoke cut through my mother's nerves.

As the shivering rays of sunshine started to touch the surface of the garden, penetrating through the lace curtains, the maids, who had sat all night waiting for orders to come from the labour chamber, turned off the oil lamps. A snowy day stretched beyond the morning. My mother's pleas to be released from the unbearable pain cracked the air and continued on. Observing her daughter's agony, Ismat khanum's own bones and muscles felt torn apart to give passage to the newcomer. She would tip-toe to her daughter, put a hand on her forehead and murmur in a pleading, low voice: 'darling, try to push when you think the time has come. Sweetheart, don't think about the pain. It will wither away once the baby moves out. Remember, by God's will, you will shortly have a prince in your arms'.

On several occasions, the midwife, who had previously delivered my mother's four children, examined her for a good long time and rubbed her hands across her swollen belly. Concluding that she had been summoned prematurely, and annoyed that her night's sleep had been ruined, she made herself comfortable in the adjacent room, paying no attention to Ismat khanum, who would rush to her once in a while, shaking her and pleading with her to do something. Accustomed to this over-reaction and with half-opened eyes, the midwife would mumble reassurances then doze off.

* * *

Passing through, the pale frail sun was reaching the equinox, the muezzin's chant was echoing through the neighbourhood. My mother was seated on a high platform, under which a heap of ashes spread to suck the flow of blood away, her legs parted, screaming. A copper bowl was in place with plenty of warm water in china basins. Towels ready at hand. Moluk Azam and Parvin were holding her from behind. Three days of labour had sucked away her strength and she could no longer push the baby out. Rivulets of sweat trickled down her pretty face, running through her thick black hair and onto her swelling breasts. A worried expression was frozen on their faces as women were hypnotised at the gate. Ismat khanum rushed to the prayer room, awakening God from Her siesta. On several occasions, an angry voice replied: 'Stop disturbing me with your silly blubbering. Pray to me later when you are satisfied with the outcome.'

Ismat khanum did not detect the mocking tone in the God's last words. Kneeling, she apologised and promised she would obey Her orders. But still, pleadingly, she murmured: 'dear God please relieve my daughter of her agonies.' Then taking courage from her own words, she added: 'after all, You know how difficult it is for a mother to see her child suffering!' And in her bewildered mind she wondered how God would cope with Her own pregnancies and whom She would pray to, in order to gain absolution and comfort?

Waves of dark clouds once again on the attack gathered strength near the peak of the snowy mountains soon to send storms of hail for the punishment of sinners. A piercing flash from the fading sun struck at the purity. Layers of snow thundered down into the plateau and landed at the door of the delivery room. My mother was clattering her teeth with such intensity that the noise frightened the wasps buzzing around the fruit baskets. They ran for safety and disappeared from sight. Under the beams of the holy shrines, the saints whom my mother had befriended during the previous nine months sighed in despair and washed their hands of the whole matter. Forgetful as they were, they glimpsed at her, yawned and turned away their hollow eyes, shutting them to the dream of a deep sleep. The muezzin had long finished his chants and midday prayers had come to a close. The congregation was hurriedly searching among the rows of waiting-shoes at the exit. The deafening shriek of the crows ceased. The beggar dervish, who routinely passed through the street at that time of the day, chanting forcefully, asking for charity stopped abruptly. On the veranda, the mother cat who moments before was daydreaming under the fading light, opened her eyes, raised her head in alarm and heralded her kittens to the nearest shelter. Silence flashed through the andarun, spilled into the biruni and whirled out, encircling the city of Karmanieh, my new home.

* * *

In that day of the year 1920, a rough hand pulled that tiny body of mine out and for that I screamed and screamed but no sound came out of my throat. The passage was dark and frightening, the road narrow and I was gasping in the darkened silence. The midwife held me upside down. My arms were dangling and my legs were wide apart. My lashes were drawn by the impulse of curiosity and I saw through a blurred screen, frozen flames and the intensity of gazes fixed upon one spot. Instantly the midwife entered a state of frenzy and I was dropped from her clasp. I was snatched in mid air. Silence spread its wings over the moment and floated through time and space. Silence and I became one interlaced entity, though I did my best to move away and enter the world of noise. Suddenly, something shaped in my head and my brain registered the first reflection of my arrival into this world. Thought entered my brain and stayed in me and never left me not to think. Not until such time that my brain would cease to exist. Ever since, thought, instead of the interaction of words has decided on the emotions that have lived in me, love, joy, sorrow, fear, pain. Tied up and moulded into a process called life.

I opened my eyes for the first time and focused on the frosty faces. I scrutinised, examined, evaluated, and decided to shut them quickly, hoping I would return to my warm and reassuring watery bed. But that was bygones. I was denied the comfort of floating weightless, thoughtless, painless. No more rolling, kicking and sucking at my own pleasure. The rejection occurred without my knowledge and consent. I did not know then but I was made aware of it later, that that would happen again and again. That I would be denied the pleasures and joys of life, no matter how desperately I tried to cling to them.

I opened my mouth to raise my voice in objection but to no avail. The murmur of groans, the uproar of sighs, and the thunder of rage, soon the shrill of a roaring waterfall pierced the labyrinth of my ears, replacing the soundlessness in me. My eyes saw their sad faces, frowning foreheads, fuming eyes, shaking heads, boiling tempers, bending backs; staggering bottoms, and tottering legs. Clouds of despair had landed on their troubled minds and had incised from them their living spirit. My newly shaped thoughts concluded that I had not been welcomed to this world.

At the delivery room, Alieh khanum turned her face towards my mother in disgust and left the room. That was the last time she looked my mother in the eyes. My aunt, Moluk Azam, marched to the bed to drag me out of my mother's arms but the firm hand of my mother drove her to the door and out. My aunt, Parvin was weeping hysterically, while my grandmother, Ismat khanum was nowhere to be seen. In the biruni, my father, Haji Amir was engaged in negotiations with god. Suddenly, he stood guard as he heard the shrieks and felt a shiver in the ensuing silence that shrouded the household. He walked away from the house and the occurring incident and disappeared from sight for a long, long time.

A familiar smell, moistened by the sweet incense and the warmth of an arm entwined around me and a deep sleep landed on my tired body. I returned to my own territory, filled with passion and craving. Outside, the world was coming to an end. An unleashed energy had lifted the earth up and splashed it into the sun's eyes, almost blinding him. The light was confusingly looking for a corridor to pass through and its rays clashed with each other. The blast poured over the city and buried the inhabitants under an unprecedented snowstorm. A number of shanty dwellings collapsed, chimneys fell and narrow alleyways filled with snow, doors and some houses were blocked from the outside. The tornado of the winter of 1920 was the hallmark of the day I, Suri set foot in this world.

Six

The train of my childhood rushed through the tunnel of time, quick as a sandstorm, swift as the passing of time itself. My recollections of the first few years, a mirage of khaki deserts one summer noon, covered in dust, yet vividly filled with detailed memories of a child swinging between two worlds. Rejected by my mother and separated from her long before I experienced the taste of her scented body, I was handed over to Fatima, who became my foster mother. My life began among Fatima's odours and the stench of her ever-after soaked-in-milk clothes. She took me to her care and so I stayed close to her and loved her as my own mother until such time that forces of tradition separated me from her.

I followed Fatima everywhere, first crawling, then tottering and toddling. I often held my hands to her and pleaded with burning eyes for a hug or a feed. Looking at Fatima from the ground, where I was mostly laid to kick and roll, she resembled a giant and the thought of reaching her nipples seemed impossible unless I had a gigantic ladder. Yet when hunger approached, I spread myself on her lap and climbed those two mountains of reservoir with no effort at all. Along with sucking hastily the flow of milk, which gushed out, my orange-sized head felt the burden of her breast. Had I paused between swallowing gulps, rivulets would have formed and flowed down, soaking the wrapping around me, making a milk puddle in which I would float. The unspoilt, unrefined rural love I received from my red-faced, rich voiced, giggly 'dayeh' and the never-ending resource of nourishment, sweet, reassuring and on offer, diminished the solitude in me and replaced and repaired the world of fear that otherwise ruled me. Frequently, the nipples, swelling, dripping and inviting stuck out of Fatima's village garment and I, with half closed eyelids to the startling world of a mute child, clung to her flesh and dragged myself up into her bosom and indulged in my childhood dreams.

My half brother Ali, Fatima's natural-born child never resented me for taking his share. There was enough to be shared and enjoyed between the two of us. We were both aware of that fact though we played rivals. Ali and I were one soul in two bodies. Separated, yet inter-linked. Only a full calendar of a month separated Ali and I. Nothing else. Not until we reached the age of maturity, of seven years old.

* * *

I was the last child in the family and my mother was much shunned for having me, despite the fact that we both had no hand in my gender, and bearing in mind that having had a say I would have opted for my present sex all the same. Over the years, the andarun of my father yearned for a male child who was never born and that built mountains of humility in my sisters' inner selves, who grew up envying an absent brother who occupied much space in everyone's mind. My situation was different from my siblings. I had Ali as a brother and so did not share their feeling of envy. My luck hid inside Fatima's milky skirt, where Ali and I were growing up to find the happiness of brother/sister relations all through childhood. Ali, the red-nosed, narrow-eyed naughty baby, who dried Fatima's heavy breasts with wolfish gulps and kicked me to steal my share and I, the bony, fair-skinned, silent doll, who had many hidden tricks under my sulky expression. Even for once he did not succeed to rob me of my share. I would kick back, roll over, pull his long coarse, black hair and even bite him with the one or two newly grown teeth, until he would burst into tears and back off. This rivalry intense, yet hollow of hostility resided beneath our deep affection for each other. While growing up, our bond kept me sane in the solitude of coming years. Yet over and over again and as I matured to see the world from all angles, one unanswered question constantly whirled in my mind. Why a male child was so important to my family?

I lived in Fatima's quarters for most of the time; two rooms in all, which for me were a magnet of tranquillity and comfort. There, I was not expected to sit properly and behave. I was not exposed to the flow of chatter and the pollution of noise that I could not be a part of. I was left on my own to spend hours climbing the mattresses and cushions Fatima piled at a corner, hiding myself playfully in their layers, indulging in daydreams. Fatima's children loved me unconditionally and never expected me to do what I did not want to. Fatima's coarse voice and rough affection divided equally among us children brought calmness to my tormented soul. I was growing up with silent wings to fly the world around. The world of Ali and I was a happy and carefree one for that moment in time.

While infants, we were wrapped in a bundle and put at a safe corner to loll still as the kitchen moved through the bustle of food preparations. In later stages, Ali and I crawled wherever Fatima worked. We were vigilant to the time she was ready to feed us. When the hour approached, she would suddenly squat at a corner and bring both breasts out and yell in a thunder of love, which whirled and rushed us towards her with the broadest smiles.

'Come you devils, I do not have the whole day to wait. Come and dry the life out of me you little brats.'

We would race, tingling and excitement in our throats. Milk dripping from the side of our mouths, looking at each other from the corner of our eyes and as our bellies swelled, kicking and eventually ending up on the floor, rolling and wrestling until someone's patience would run out:

'Stop those devils or I will throw them to the dogs to be eaten.'

'I have a better idea. If they make one more move or even blink I will roast them alive in this hot pot and put them on the menu for the day'.

That would be the final ultimatum. Not believing a word they said but keeping the side of caution, we would creep to a corner, hug each other and wait for the moment to start afresh.

Apart from Ali, the youngest and Sakineh, the eldest, Fatima's other children, two girls, Soghra and Kobra, and a boy, Abbas aged 6, all worked at my father's carpet weaving workshops. Fatima's husband, Mashti Mohammed, knew no world but my parents' household. He put his children to work when each reached the workable age of six.

Dawn began with muezzin's chanting from the nearby mosque. Regardless of snow or heat, dust storm or tornado, the muezzin would climb the minaret and invite the believers with his deep, rich voice to perform their duty to God. Before such time arrived, men would rush to the public baths to clean themselves of last night's pleasures and then hurriedly turn up at the mosque's gate. The sense of guilt at knowing each other's secrets carved on their faces and the taste of relishing hours boiling in their bright eyes. Women washed and cleaned in private before standing for prayers.

Every day, we woke up before the sun found time to rush through the curtain-less window. Fatima was up at work by the hour of prayers. Preparing a hasty wrap of bread and cheese for the part of her family soon to leave for work and then attending to the remaining children. Her young son Abbas was always the spearhead of trouble. He would beg, he would plead, he would scream just for a few extra minutes to stay in bed. Minutes that had already been swallowed by the brightness of dawn. If they were late, the foreman would have allocated their place to someone else. Even if Mashti Mohammed could be given an assignment, the children would most likely be sent home, empty handed. Frequently, the episode came to a close by a slap on the bum or a forceful drag to the cold latrine located at the end of the servants' courtyard. Abbas had to pee amongst tears, moans and groans and the strongest objections.

In the main building, my siblings led a regulated life, preparing to become dutiful aristocratic housewives; well behaved, well spoken and shiny clean, waiting for wealthy husbands queuing on the line of horizon to pick them up. I was growing up with a peculiar sense of elation, away from that dominant Order. I was learning the unsophisticated manners of Fatima and the rest, who took me to their hearts without pity. I was so used to sleeping close to Fatima, that if I was taken to my mother on rare occasions and stayed with my natural siblings, I would wake up and crawl over the beds, looking for Fatima while sobbing hysterically. The loss of her smell agonised me to such an extent that forced my mother to send me back, where my heavy lids would shut immediately. Fatima was my real mother. The household had got used to this little mute creature that preferred to be left among the maids, whose humble dwelling swamped with rugged things, left-over clothes and an army of lice of different shapes and sizes.

* * *

The kitchen at my parents' mansion was situated at the far end of the andarun, near the gate to the biruni. It was a long chamber with stoves at one side and cupboards and worktops on the other and stock rooms in the back, where provisions, enough to feed an army, were kept all year around. Through seasons, the air, intermingled with aromas of vegetables, spices and herbs that hovered at the apex, then travelled down, wandered through my narrow veins, sought a place of their own, clung and waited to be remembered years after my brain had expanded and my veins had widened and I was living far away from that familiar domain.

By five years of age, I was well familiar with most scents and smells. I could guess the type of food about to be prepared by the size, shape and the number of pots and pans that were taken out from the shelves beneath the white-tiled row of worktops. Too much emphasis on the menu and extra formality meant the guests were my fathers' at the biruni.

The kitchen was a busy territory all year around, preparing food for the large population of the andarun and the biruni. But if I cross the borders of time and take you to the days prior to special occasions such as Ashura and Tasua, the martyrdom of Imam Hossein, when thousands of mourners were fed, or Norooz (New Year) preparations, where for a whole month tons of cookies and sweets were prepared, your head would spin around and the dizziness would hamper you from travelling into the daily routine of our kitchen; the centre of the universe. There, happiness interlaced and braided the most precious memories in my mind.

Each woman declared to be the absolute and undisputed commander of our kitchen. This manifested its importance at the annual ceremonies, when from China through Asia to the Americas there was no other place to be associated with than the kitchen of the andarun of Haji Amir, my father, whom incidentally I do not remember to have known as my father until I reached the tender age of seven.

The division of labour in the kitchen was prompt and direct. Otherwise, Soghra believed the work would never be done to its perfection. Within the ladder of hierarchy, my grandmother, my aunt and my mother had come to an agreement. Alieh khanum supervised the big occasions such as commemorating the martyrdom of the Imam Hossein, the Prophet's grandson, who was killed by his rival in an unequal battle in the deserts of southern Iraq, near the River Euphrates. Without her command, I must admit the kitchen would not have been able to feed so many thousands of people. Customarily, at noon the tenth day, the crowd of thousands of mourners would reach our estate, flogging themselves with chains or beating their bare chests while chanting religious songs. Slowing their pace, they would pass through our street as the last leg and assemble in the nearby square, where lunch would be brought to them by teams of volunteers. Moluk Azam was responsible for the New Year feasts and my mother saw to the daily routine and my father's special guests at the biruni.

I grew up with a mixture of abilities and one disability. Muteness. My eyes were huge resources to see, to notice, to witness, to assess and to calculate. I was gifted with the ability to separate and distinguish all smells and fragrances. In passing from infancy to childhood and beyond, I knitted firm threads with the herbs and vegetables that were carried by mules from the villages nearby and delivered to the kitchen in the early hours of each morning. As the unloading began, my nostrils would expand to take in the aromas of bunches of dill, parsley, coriander, spring onions, garlic and spinach. The heart of lettuces would open and invite me to a feast as they were trimmed, washed and set in rows on copper trays, along with heavenly delicious syrups later to be taken to the andarun for afternoon nibbling. Ali and I had our shares set aside. I indulged in dipping the youngest leaves into the syrup and chewing them with the utmost pleasure.

My friendship with greenery and vegetables never wavered, nor did my hostility to onions. Onions were an enemy to be destroyed on the spot. I prayed to God to spare Fatima from touching the round shaped, thousand-layered monsters, the source of her uncontrollable weeping. Every morning, before frying, roasting and cooking began, Fatima would squat at a corner with a heap of those brutes in front of her and a knife ready to cut their throats and slice them into tiny pieces, as they deserved. I sat impatiently to watch rivulets bubbling, swelling and overflowing from her narrow eyes. And soon before we knew it, the kitchen was drowned in a flood of tears, with Ali and me, clinging to pots and pans, looking desperately for a place to hide. No one else ever volunteered to slice the onions and the devils knew how to make Fatima weep her head off. I sometimes found the courage to approach her and give her a hug of reassurance but she even rejected that and would send me away. Happiness filled my heart when Fatima finished with the last onion and wiped her eyes. We were saved and sorrow was whisked off as she, being her own self once more got up heavily, shook off her skirt, and limped towards the tap to wash her face. The end to her weeping was often announced by an ironic remark she threw at one of the girls:

'Your skin looks fresh today and you have formed firm breasts. Tell me, was it good last night? Did you enjoy the....', and then she would burst into laughter, leaving her immediate target speechless. Everyone was aware of her sudden attacks as a ritual to the end of the onion slicing. But no one was ever prepared to get involved in a counterattack. There on, Fatima would drive her attention into a folk lyric she murmured to herself and if Soghra didn't voice her objection, she would tune up her voice. In such cases, the girls would find the courage to join in, slowly but continuously moving their rumps side ways, their bosoms jumping alongside. Ali and I were at the forefront clinging to Fatima's skirt, swaying and transfixed in the moment. That would have been the state of affairs until thunder would strike as my grandmother, Alieh khanum would appear at the door, rays of sun hiding her face from behind, making her more frightening. We had learnt by experience to quickly sneak under the shelves and close our eyes, hoping she would soon disappear and leave us in peace. The commander-in-chief of the army of evil would pack happiness away by shouting, criticising and ensuring that her comments left marks on the brittle happy moments in the kitchen life for the rest of the day.

Apart from Soghra and Fatima, three maidservants lived in the compound. These were sent to Alieh khanum at a very young age. It took many years to transform such rural girls into delicate maidservants with social manners of the city, who could serve tea to the ladies, cook different meals, make sweets and cookies, set tables, dress neatly, speak eloquently and raise children properly.

My parents' household was famous for educating these girls and there always stood a chance that through the matchmakers, a secretary at the bazaar, a retailer and even a junior merchant would marry them at last. I must admit that not all maidservants were as lucky as the ones who lived with us. In some andaruns, maidservants were an easy prey to the master or his sons, who expected sexual services at their own pleasure. In such cases, no sanction was required from the mother. It was an unwritten agreement understood by all parties. These girls were unprotected and unchallenged, apart from possible rivalries between fathers and sons, who sometimes divided and sometimes shared between them. The episode would begin by an innocent flirting, a squeeze of the bosom at the corner of a dark room, a kiss here and there awakening passions. Mothers often provided the space for their sons, while narrow was the scope for the husband. As for the girls, the future was a path they walked blindfolded. Sometimes, the girl would be rewarded by marrying a decent man who would pay a dowry and take her away. The story would turn a different page should the wife discover her husband's promiscuity. The trail of adventures would turn nasty should a child be conceived of such relationships.

The ancient city of Karmanieh with its shimmering sun and scorching hot winds and stormy rains caused the greenery to grow at a wild pace. It also gave rise to an extraordinary craving for forbidden pleasures. Despite restrictions and limitations, which had woven an everlasting web and had suffocated peoples' living spirit, things still happened. Extraordinary things! There existed a universe of incidents and tragedies barely finding their way out. Clouds of secrecy surrounded everything and not much seeped out.

Seven

Going through childhood, things were beginning to shape in my mind. Having lacked the power of speech, I concentrated on seeing, observing and evaluating in the solitude of my own world. Judgement formed in my mind without consulting with others. I decided for myself whether to like or dislike, to be wary of, to distance myself or to approach, to love or to hate the world around me. My emotions were clean of pollution and free from infiltration. I could not share them with others nor could I speak them out. Everything was filtered through the wires of my own mind, which worked extra to fill the cavity of interaction. Sometimes people or things hovered in uncertainty because I could not decide. For example, Fatima's husband, Mashti Mohammed was the one I did not know whether to like or to dislike. In general, I did not hate him but sometimes seeing him and Fatima close, jealousy overpowered me. The way Fatima whispered to him and gave him the best portion of food and especially at night, when Mohammed came between her and me. I never knew why Fatima would let Mohammed, the stocky-built figure, who sometimes restrained and frightened us children, climb on top of her as soon as she spread her body to rest. Frightened to move an eyelid, yet watching, I got used to the idea that this was the way Mohammed went to sleep after his long day of uninterrupted toiling. I grew up believing that the rough movements of Mohammed's body, breathing through nostrils, groaning, and Fatima's whispering pleas to finish quickly was the only way she could put him to sleep. To me, he was a bigger child in the family, who brought more trouble to Fatima because she had to use extra force to put him to sleep and to nourish him with more food from the ration she received.

Fatima's children had their mattresses spread at the far end of the small room and I assume that they pretended to be asleep as soon as Mohammed mounted their mother. Some of them were beaten up in the middle of the darkness should they sit on the bed or aim to go to the latrine. Ever since, something has clutched among the wires of my brain, a shred of undesirable memory, bloodied by that never-ending ritual. My recollections, though vague and hazy had stayed in my mind until years later when I was able to put them down and give them meaning.

* * *

Ali and I were growing up as mischievous as possible. Daydreaming, we often sat at a corner, nostrils swallowing smells of foods, waiting to have our ration. Through time, Ali and I had constructed our own language, my language, which he interpreted to the audience. When a thought appeared on the surface of my mind and words shaped inside my brain and concepts waited patiently at the tip of my tongue, then coiled and dried down and I was pressed to make myself understood, Ali was swift to clarify my intention. I never knew how he read the words and took meanings out of them but I was reassured, confirmed and wrapped in the lace of safety whenever Ali was by my side. I was often frightened if Ali was at a distance and someone approached me. To separate me from my twin brother, to live apart from him who complemented my cut tongue was beyond my imagination.

One can never imagine my horror once my small world collapsed and I was parted from my other half, Ali. I was forbidden to associate with him, or to be with him or to see him and to even think about him. I was told that I was reaching the age of reason. I never saw in my wildest dreams that I would be separated from my own brother. There on, silence fell upon me and stretched its heavy wings on my speechless tongue. It lasted for years until letters tore the shield apart to let the light in. There sat a long time between my separation from Ali and the time that the dark chapter in my life came to a close. I painted the tragedy with all the details on the canvas of my memory and sometimes still feel the pain, fresh as it has remained.

In the afternoon of one hot summer's day, as the household submerged in siesta, Ali and I tiptoed to the back orchard, where branches of cherries, peaches, plums and apricots had lowered their succulent bulk and our hands could reach them easily. It was the best of times since intruders, who would often disrupt our world were not around. I could only see my mother watching us from behind the lace curtain as we played hide and seek. She smiled and waved and at times wiped her beautiful eyes with the back of her hand. A bird was singing, the breeze was dancing amid the upper branches rays of sun were shooting light from among the shade of ancient trunks. Ali and I were swinging from one branch to the other, giggling light-heartedly, I silently, he aloud, picking ripe cherries, munching their skin, swallowing their juice and throwing their stones at each other, our tongues full of fresh red juice, our eyes searching among heavy branches. I could not see my mother anymore. Suddenly, she appeared at the window and summoned me in. Unable to sense the malice in her voice and accompanied by Ali, I stepped into the house. Standing at the door, she took my hand and guided me through. All at the same time, Ali was ordered to return to the servants' quarters. Alarmed at my mother's tone of voice, I raised the flag of objection by pulling Ali along but my mother's firm hand pushed him aside and out. He turned into a stone. His eyes widened and his mouth stiffened in utter bewilderment. Whether he was worried to leave me alone or hurt by my mother's sudden change of mood was never known to me. Thereafter, I endured the pain all by myself. Never were we allowed to be together in public or in private and the flames of our innocent childhood melted away into the deep sands of the nearby desert.

I was declared to have come close to the age of reason, of seven years old. Old enough to live by the rule of elders and prepare myself for adulthood. My life was decided upon, sealed and registered in the book of time. Whether I approved of it, accepted or rejected it did not count. A rope round my neck ended my short-lived happiness along with my childhood. There on, I had to talk to my brother Ali and consult with him inwards into a mind unable to speak out even through her agonies. I opened my eyes to the morning of restrictions, limitations and deprivation. I was denied the blanket of love and the unconditional freedom I had with Fatima and her family. Worse, I was deprived of a brother, whom I had grown up to believe was no one else's but mine. Not knowing how the world came to a stop, the gates of my innocent dreams shut one by one, slowly and meticulously, and my days stretched into weeks and swelled over years until I reached the age of suitability. Passed over a decade of my life. Old enough to become an adult and have a husband of my own.

In the years of solitude, I concluded that my birth was an unnecessary burden on all. My existence had no association with real life. Although a normal child with natural sense and sensibilities, my mother, herself sinking in an island of loose sands, had no affection to spare me. My father had come to the belief that I occupied the place of a son he should have had and totally deprived me of fatherly attention, even that little amount he gave to my sisters. I often saw him passing hurriedly by me ignoring my existence. I could not adjust to the andarun life and refused to do what was expected of me. I hated my grandmother and my father, so much so that I prayed to god to send them away from sight. When I grew older I took great satisfaction knowing the fact that despite desperate measures my father and my grandmother took, my father's wish of having a son never materialised. Over years, the andarun of Haji Amir staggered through thunders of arguments, suggestions and recommendations until they reached a final destination. By then I was nine years of age.

* * *

The day has registered in my memory in bold, dark ink. The prediction of many years was materialising from covert wheeling and dealing and conspicuous whispers to overt talking of my father's second marriage. It was the matriarch, Alieh khanum and the web of conspirators, who believed Haji Amir, should finally have the chance of producing an heir, that Ziba, daughter of Amin O-Zarb, a wealthy merchant, was nominated. In his late forties, Haji Amir married this fourteen-year-old child-bride with proper negotiations, wedding ceremony; music, feast, dowry and so on. There on, she lived a few yards away from my mother's quarters.

My mother imprisoned herself in her compound and finally returned to her father's house, leaving us to witness the arrival of her rival. God knows how she coped with the humiliation and pain. She never cried or complained in public, nor did she open her heart to her own family who took her in and consoled her on those gloomy days. She was no more different from any other women whose husbands took second, third or fourth wives. Her father's wealth and social status, my mother's astonishing beauty and grace were unable to gain her nobility. She preserved her dignity by leaving home and taking refuge in her parent's house but she had to return a month later. There were no other avenues to be taken. She could not stay there for long. Five children wanted to have their mother back. And besides, no one had ever heard that a woman would abandon her husband and children because of a second marriage, especially Haji Amir, who had every reason to make such a decision. The whole world backed him. However, my mother returned home and took control of the daily routine and life resumed as if nothing had happened. But being the daughter of Haji Morteza she never permitted my father into her bedroom. She also broke relations with my grandmother, Alieh khanum and ignored her presence until the day she died.

My father's second wife was a young, frightened girl, who cried day and night. So much so that when my mother heard her sobbing, with her kind-hearted nature she felt more grief for her, than her own situation. Ziba resembled a bewildered, little chick, parted from her nest. She was petrified of my grandmother. When she arrived into the hostile environment of our andarun, Ziba was the same age as my second sister, Pari. While Pari relished her early teens and enjoyed the luxury of a foreign missionary tutor, who taught her and my other siblings at home, Ziba's belly swelled thereafter. Gradually, as the dust settled and my mother began to accept her, she decided it better to make an ally of Ziba than an enemy. She had no ill intention towards her, whom she called my 'child' and spoke of her with deep sympathy and motherly affection. At the beginning, everyone thought that my mother had a snake hidden in the corner and that Ziba was jumping from the frying pan into the fire but time proved that my mother's genuine concern for Ziba as a child-bride was the best protection she had in the maze of the andarun's polluted alleyways. So, over time Ziba became totally dependent on my mother and tied herself to her. Gradually, her confidence gained pace as she saw no danger and her soul rested under my mother's protection and the two women with the army of females who sprang from one man pushed the matriarch, Alieh khanum, aside and isolated her from their lives.

Eight

Spring of 1931 had arrived and departed. Long, idle summer days had just begun. Migration had approached. During the day, we would move to the big, shady 'howzkhaneh' chamber with stony platforms at every corner. There, the scorching wind changed into a cool breeze while travelling down the wind turret and whirled round the high ceiling and brushed across our dozing bodies in the afternoon siesta, then creeping out of the tunnel into the back garden. There was a shallow pond in the middle of howzkhaneh, which was bubbling with underground waters reflecting its azure bed into the dome's apex. Water splashed sideways and over-spilt onto the pond's borders in search of a breathing space, under the weight of melons and watermelons. Ignored by all, I often sat at a corner watching. All through the day, the chamber was saturated with heated conversation, arguments and comments which swayed back and forth until after lunch when siesta quietened the noise wave.

In the evening, shortly after dinner, we would travel up the rooftop and spread our mattresses horizon to horizon. Karmanieh is famous for its blue and cloudless sky across which the sun reigns throughout the day for most of the year and a universe of stars assemble at nightfall. The moon swims lazily in her silver costume, first in the shape of a rainbow, then in full, sailing away, leaving the cosmos all to the stars to twinkle and tweak. Stars lower their heads, leap forward to witness with exploratory eyes, flames and flashes of human activities, heaving in the heat of the summer nights. As night deepened, whispers turned into moans, and then died down. Sighs travelled up and around then quietened. Chuckles choked where they had begun and cries were heard out in the distance. The cool breeze, floating above our heads relayed messages of the nearby desert back into our sleeping ears. Up until dawn when prayer time approached.

One such early summer morning, while sleeping with my siblings and as the eye of the last twinkling star was about to shut, I experienced my first menstruation. A line of warm liquid, dripping down my sticky legs woke me to discover blood all over the sheets. A phenomenon which frightened me to the point of hysteria and sent me straight to Fatima for clarification. All around, bodies were rolling across mattresses, seeking shelter from the approaching sunshine which would soon rise from the desert bed. Beneath, the kitchen was getting ready to serve breakfast. Soon breakfast would be served in the family room. My mother would sit at the top of the sofreh, my father on one side and Ziba on the other. Then the army of females would sit with no order of seniority but me, who was placed at the end. There arrived trays of hot bread, cheese, butter, honey and jams, surrounded by the aroma of boiling milk and fried eggs. That colourful scene, the smells and the steam rising from the Russian samovar curling up to the ceiling and mixing with the particles of light and penetrating the deepest corners of our awakened appetite. Cups of tea, glasses of boiled milk travelled around and rested at someone's hand.

Ignoring the fact that I had been forbidden to go to the kitchen area, I rushed down the stairs to reach Fatima for clarity. She was standing near a stove, stirring. Steam rising from the pot, hiding her upper part. Her big silhouette seemed to have no head. The aromas of fresh vegetables, onion, garlic, roasted meat and baking bread blended together and travelled into my nostrils and for a flicker of a moment, I was the child I had once been. Jumping straight into Fatima's open arms, clinging to her, tears gushing out uncontrollably. The long wooden spoon was lost into the deep pot as she saw my situation. Not knowing the cause of my sudden outburst, she began to console, the sight of blood then alerting her to the incident. Lifting me with difficulty, she rushed to her room. Put me down gently and tried to find suitable words to soothe and reassure. I was sobbing. Her rough hands entwined around my body, her gentle voice travelled down my bewildered brain: 'dearest, dearest, this is a sign of you becoming a woman and there is nothing to worry about. Sooner or later, all girls pass through this stage into womanhood. You have to celebrate the occasion instead of being ashamed and frightened. Wipe your tears my child and let me clean you. She took me back to the andarun to my mother, who unaware of my situation had prepared herself to scorn.

* * *

Migration would end by the approach of autumn. We would travel down from the rooftops to settle in our rooms. Life seemed to be streaming slowly on its normal path when suddenly extraordinary events diverted the routine. Upon the instigation of Alieh khanum, with the approval of my father and the silence of my mother, and in a formal family meeting, it was decided that the time had come to reduce the female population. By then, seven girls were born into the household and my father was apprehensive, feeling that controlling such a contingent would soon get out of hand. Reaching an agreement, the weight of developments landed on my shoulders. The fact that, customarily, elder sisters were the first to marry played little part in this decision. Rather, I was to be dispensed of, got out of the way for my sisters to marry suitable men. Knotting ties with a family that had a deformed child was unfavourable. So, matchmakers were called in. Heavy tips were promised and news floated across and travelled through town. Finally, a list of suitors was presented to my father. Muteness had blocked the way for prosperous candidates.

Meanwhile, I lived in my own solitude which often took me to a quiet place, where I would embrace my knees, longing to see Ali and talk to him in the language of our own invention. Though a few yards away, our distance had stretched to infinity. I knew by then that our reunion was impossible no matter how much I yearned to be with him. Ali had long started work at the factory and was nowhere to be seen.

Shortly, a suitable candidate was approved and the family in question were informed. Then, a group of women came to visit my mother. In normal circumstances, my mother rarely spoke to my grandmother, Alieh khanum but now she was present at these meetings. On one such occasion, and to my astonishment, the army of sisters were sent away and ordered to stay away and I was the only one to put a clean dress on, to have my hair combed and to be commanded to greet the women. To me, these women were my mother's tea party guests, whom before then I was never allowed to meet. Now my mother reminded me to behave like a young lady and in her confusion, emphasised that I should answer politely if asked a question. I was too young to understand, too timid to enquire and to have a say in the whole affair.

The sun was bending towards grey mountains. Rising from flowerbeds, scents and smells mingled with the evaporating dust, which was departing from the newly washed veranda. Awakened from their lazy siesta, gold fish in their abundance were dancing playfully around the heart of the courtyard pool, waving water to overflow into the pond's borders. Waiting to take orders from the reception room, maidservants had their best costumes on. All the chandeliers were lit. Baskets were bearing autumn fruits and silver bowls were glittering with home-made cookies. The formality of the occasion had taken the room by surprise. Waiting air had choked its cough for the right moment to spit out. The elders, including Alieh khanum were sitting at the top, my mother beside her.

Trembling, I entered and sat at a corner. Eyes turned. Quizzically, they exchanged glances. I understood from their focus that I had a strong presence in their purpose. They were examining me, turning my petite body around, bending, straightening and bargaining over my price. I felt the density of shame and humiliation filling me and wished the earth to open up and swallow me in total. I was melting in despair and ran out of the room, into a dark corner, bursts of tears gushing out, drenching my clean dress, filling the room and overflowing onto the veranda. The women took it to be my shyness and praised my behaviour.

A few days later, patriarchs convened in the biruni to negotiate the most important subject, my price. The matter of my muteness was put out of mainstream talks and my father did not demand a high price. Surprised that a matter which was the most difficult part of negotiations had been resolved fairly quickly, they pressed for a date to be set. Satisfied with the outcome, the andarun was ordered to get prepared.

And all of a sudden, I, who in normal circumstances was an ignored child, became the centre of the universe. My sisters were briefed and advised to pay more respect to me because 'I was now a temporary guest and would soon leave the household'. My mother, with sighs which preceded her words, and eyes which were moistened now and then, sat with her daughters and admitted to them that, 'one day by God's will, you will have to leave your father's household. It is Suri's fate to be the first, although against the customary practice of wedding the eldest daughter. What could she do against the wish of God? The family had chosen Suri for a bride and they would have a better chance if I was out of the way.'

* * *

The autumn of 1931 was gradually moving in and the sun was losing its intensity. In the garden, geraniums, marigolds, gladiolas, mimosas, jasmines and tuberoses were preparing to embrace the winter. At the top branch of tall trees, birds were watching their chicks practising their newly acquired flying skills, soon destined to warm climates. My senses were standing guard to quiz and comprehend the situation, my eyes wider than normal, ears ready to catch snippets of conversation, my mind puzzled, yet quick to assess. No avail. I could not grasp something my mind had not yet encountered and experienced.

Then the hustle and bustle started, intensified and continued as my wedding day approached. One cool afternoon as the household had settled for siesta, Fatima, who had understood from my expression that no one had explained to me what it meant to be a bride and have a husband, drew me to a corner away from curious eyes and sat me on her lap. In the middle of down pouring tears, of hugging and kissing, she told me that: 'I was about to have a man by my side, whom I would have to love and take care of, that that man would be my husband and guardian.' And though she had never seen the groom, she painted a nice picture of him: 'he is very handsome you know. I have heard that he loves you very much and is waiting for you to step into his house. In a few years' time, he will appreciate you so much that you will be the envy of all. You will become a lady at your own house and have plenty of beautiful children and live a happy life.' She assured me that: 'although I might face unexpected events, there was nothing to be frightened of. I should not be resentful of him if I was left alone with him. He would probably want to touch me as Fatima's husband, Mohammed did. It was God's will and I must accept my fate and obey my future master.'

Sobbing silently, I was storing Fatima's smell and her gentle voice in a long lasting memory, where I could reach out easily whenever the urge prevailed. I nodded and promised to behave. Many, many questions lurked around and stumbled over each other but answers were nowhere to be found. Did I have to put him to sleep every night like Mohammad? Strangulating was the thought of someone mounting me. What if he was too heavy and I suffocated under his weight? Could I scream for help? I was already imprisoned in a strange place. Shadows were gathering around me. Fear was getting stronger and closer.

Through the stream of conversation, I had discovered that my future husband was the son of a retailer, who was my father's business associate. Sometimes, in the solitude of my mind, I imagined him a boy of my own age. A brother I had lost in the maze of the ancient order. A duplicate of Ali. I was then filled with a soothing sense and consoled myself. 'We will play together, running around the garden, having fun.' Then I stumbled upon the fact that he was much older by almost twenty five years.

Time flew as events took momentum. My wedding day approached. And without a soul caring for what went on inside my head, I was soon handed over to the beauty specialists. Curling my hair, shaping my eyebrows, intruding between my tiny legs, despite my violent objections and rubbing off the newly grown pubertal hair from my thighs and then, accompanied by a group of women, musicians dancing and singing, their tambourine and drums deafening the ear, herded through the streets to the 'hamam'. Inside the steamy chamber, shampooed, scrubbed, decorated with henna patterns, massaged all over with aromatic oils. I no longer endured consciousness, fell asleep and had to be carried onto the carriage, into the andarun and on my bed until the next day, the wedding day. I was awoken by noises far away, which none-the-less had forced their way into my head. The grooming woman had arrived. Taking me to a secluded room and shutting the door behind her, the shadow of fear spreading, tears running at every direction and her commanding voice bringing me to my senses: 'don't you start young bride. I have to prepare you for the night. The prettiest bride for Agha Javad Khan. Please, don't spoil my good fortune'. Not knowing whether she was begging or threatening, yet trying to overcome my fear and preventing tears from overflowing and drenching everything and finally, exhausted by all that was happening against my will, I lifted myself from the ground. Watching. To my childish eyes, the ceremony was substantially grand. Yet it bore no resemblance to the weddings of my sisters some years later.

Later, sitting motionless, sweat running down in every direction, reflecting in the looking glass, a painted image carved out of a skeleton, growing into a woman: eyes widened with 'sormeh', cheeks reddened with 'sorkhab' and lips thickened with lipstick. The noise. The deafening noise of the drums and 'sorna', the coming and going, children screaming and running, pinching, punching and swearing. The neighbourhood had placed itself on the rooftops, anxious to have a glimpse. Every piece of news, exaggerated and engrossed, circled around and travelled back and forth. Over-excited women. Eventually, the music and singing taking the crowd to the highest momentum:

'Flowers are blooming, nightingales singing,

our bride is a beauty, where is the groom,

the king of grooms to welcome her,

with a garland of precious stones.'

All joined the festivities and the singing continued:

'Shirazi girl, oh my dear Shirazi girl,

show me your lips so that I kiss them,

and become satisfied.

Why do you want my lips, you shameless boy,

haven't you seen the silk thread in the bazaar,

mine resembles that but more precious?.

Shirazi girl, oh my dear Shirazi girl,

show me your bosoms so I squeeze them with passion.

why do you want my little bosoms, you wicked boy?

Have you not seen sweet lemons in the bazaar?

mine resemble the lemons but firmer.'

And lyrics flew through space, music rose and bodies became a whirlwind of sweat and vapour. From time to time obscene remarks were thrown into the air:

'Lucky her, she will be enjoying it enormously. We hope that Agha will have the energy to endure such a young body. How many times do you think he will do it? Let's hope she won't be frightened the first time'.

Slanderous comments accompanied by laughter and shrieks of excitement. Explicit sexual language was a standard method of enjoyment for women at every wedding. Mine was not an exception. Finding out through the flow of conversation that I would soon be taken to my husband's home and handed over to him, questions were raised in my mind, lurked around and froze. Fear stood close by. One question that kept returning to my mind was the fate of the household cat. Would he kill the cat at the doorsteps of 'hedjleh'?' I had heard the story time and again.

Some time in the past, a bride was handed over to the groom by an elder who said: 'she is all yours and it is your duty to control her and take care of her'. Then the couple were left alone in their decorated 'hedjleh'. The groom approached the bride. Frightened of the move, escaping from his grip, she began running around, him chasing. Suddenly, the family cat slid through the door and stood in between. A ball of excitement and anger, he ordered the cat out. Rubbing itself against his legs, the cat refused to leave. Picking it up and throwing it to the wall, smashing its scull and thereafter, the bride tamed as a lamb. I was determined to find the family cat in the first instance and beg of her to make herself scarce for one night in a thousand years.

* * *

The arrival of the mullah put a temporary lid on the deafening noise. Women craved for the mullah's authoritative voice, full of lust and undetected passion. They had the pleasure of seeing him via holes in the curtain, pleading with him flirtatiously to speak louder. As trusted people, women often sneaked out of the andaruns and into the mullahs' 'hojrehs', where they would partially remove their veil, open their hearts, confide, confess and plead to them to be directed. Each with several wives of their own, mullahs were trained to enjoy the company of women and knew well how to 'advise' the army of blind enthusiasts. Now, sitting behind the curtain, deprived of seeing the women in the flesh, yet getting his excitement from the power of imagination and female odours, the mullah began the ritual.

Everything was ready for registration. Almost fainting under the intensity of the moment, I sat motionless to witness a child becoming the wife of an unknown person, officially and in the presence of many onlookers. When asked whether I would agree to be wedded to Javad Khan, son of Haji Hassan Khan, my mother responded in haste. Swaying between consciousness and a tired mind, I was not in a position to consent nor to object. I opened my eyes to the uproar of noises, the wave of congratulations and the rainfall of kisses and presents which pronounced me a married woman. At such a moment, the presence of the mullah was forgotten; singing and dancing began and continued.

Soon midnight approached. Time for departure. My possessions, what was mine and were prepared as dowry had already been dispatched to my husband's household. I was the last piece to be taken in full ceremony. I was leaving my home and my family forever. Not being given the opportunity to say farewell to Fatima and her family hurt me immensely. Hurt remained and took rein from fear and exhaustion. Finally, under the heavy veil and the craze of women, I was escorted through the corridors of the andarun and into the biruni, mounting a six-horse carriage. I looked around; a lump blocked the path to my breath, my eyes blurred with waiting tears, I caught a glimpse of Ali, standing in a dark corner, pouting.

The horses, excited at the sight of the crowd, galloped through the stony streets. Then, upon the command of the coachman slowed down their paces. The sound of their orchestrated feet echoed in the darkness, broke the silence and awakened the neighbourhood, whose men, unaware of the happy event, rushed out, lanterns in hands, to enquire the nature of the intrusion. Seeing decorated horses and the army of eunuchs walking alongside the carriage, they wished the couple happiness and slid inside, locking their gates. Accompanying me, were my Aunt Moluk Azam and two maidservants. I could no longer endure the drums of my heart pounding. I went to sleep with the movement of the carriage. My aunt's orders to keep me awake were of no avail. In my inner mind, I could hear the horses' cantering, taking me away further and farther from a portion of my life, which had experienced pain more than anything else. I wished the journey would never end and the movement would never stop. Just rocking and rocking, alleyways duplicating, the road stretching to eternity. In my sleepy mind, a question formed and died down, then surfaced again. What was expected of me down the road? What was I supposed to do? What was expected of me?

Nine

Haji Hassan khan's house was located on the west-side of the city, about five miles from my father's estate. The closer we got, the narrower the streets became and houses changed into small domed-shaped dwellings. My aunt was tired and her patience was running out. Under heavy makeup and the thick veil, her eyes were swollen. Yet concerned about my state, she removed the veil from my face. The sides of the carriage were open and midnight air was breezing through, brushing over, sliding out of the other end. It comforted me. I could breathe the moist of the night, yet my mind had shut itself to reality. The night was stretching beyond imagination. Me, being pushed towards the unknown. Fear had kept a firm grip. It didn't matter how long this journey would last as long as it didn't come to an end. I was not sure whether I would live to see the dawn breaking, the sun shining and the birds singing once again.

At last we reached the neighbourhood. The street leading to my new home was lit with lanterns and colourful decorations. At the gate a group of women stood on one side, men on the other. As our carriage approached, drums and tambourines tuned to welcoming lyrics:

'The bride has come, furnish her with flowers,

get her all the silk and decorate her hair with prettiest roses,

where is the groom to celebrate and welcome such beauty?'

Lyrics flew over the sleepy town and awakened the whole neighbourhood, who rushed to their rooftops to witness me, descending. I woke up fresh. An unknown sense of gaiety prevailed and replaced the state of melancholy. The noise, the crowd and the midnight chill brought to me particles of hope, of a new life. Aunt Moluk, seeing my change of mood was all smiles. She suddenly felt an urge to kiss and cuddle me. 'Come dear, come. Sit here beside me.' Tears filled her eyes. Did she remember her own wedding, as she was taken to a stranger's house? She must have been the same age as me. The difference was that she had a mother like Alieh khanum, who watched over her and made sure that she was not badly treated. I saw that a rush of pity flew over my aunt's painted face and made her aware of my pain. A thought must have crossed her mind: 'this child cannot even complain. Yet she has encountered the same destiny. Why do we women keep repeating ourselves through time? Will there be a time when we can break this pre-determined chain of travelling from our father's house, to our husband's, to our graves?' And surprised at her sudden revelation of questioning a phenomenon which had always existed, Aunt Moluk pulled me towards her, held me tight and assured me that there was nothing to worry about. To her astonishment, I pulled myself away. A stubborn thought came to my mind forcing me to refuse my aunt's hand. 'I have come this far by myself. I can travel the rest on my own.' Anyway, I didn't expect to live long. The certainty that I would choke under my husband's weight had set firm roots in my entangled mind.

The carriage was surrounded. I descended. The music rose higher and higher. Everyone cheered. The eunuchs waited at the gate to receive their tips. Our party was hurried through a corridor, a circled courtyard, up the stairs and into a smiling reception room. A sense of warmth was slowly replacing the fear. We were offered sherbet and cookies. I refused. Someone walked to me in a slow pace and lifted my veil with much delicacy. Her eyes looked at me with affection; her hands touched mine with tenderness, her lips kissed my forehead with care and a scented voice whispered in my ear: 'you must have been tired my dear child. You should drink the sherbet and eat the cookies. I will not take no for an answer.' The reassurance made my heart pound with a distant promise. A flower representing the future, smiling in bloom.

Tambourine players entered. They began a mystical dance around the room; their skirts made an oceanic colour. They soon left and another band entered. They began playing the most beautiful lyrics with their 'Tars'. Everyone looked at me with affection. The whole procession was different from the earlier ceremony at my parents' house. My tenseness was gone and my muscles were relaxed. I even found the urge to get up and accompany the young girls in their jolly dance but my aunt's serious look nailed me to my place. Suddenly, everything came to a close as it had started. Women began to disperse. A few remained. My aunt did not know what to do. The unfamiliarity and awkwardness irritated her. More than anything, she wanted to leave and that showed on her face. A gracious woman -my mother-in-law, Ghamar khanum- who had previously persuaded me to take some food, approached Aunt Moluk Azam and spoke firmly but with utmost respect: 'you must have been tired, madam. Do you want to wait at the 'hejleh' or go to your room to rest? Do not worry about Suri. She is now under my jurisdiction and there is no cause for worry.'

My aunt was caught between the urge to rest and her duty to stay awake. Finally, duty prevailed. She said she would not leave her niece the first night; meaning that she had to stay to witness and verify my virginity. Otherwise, nothing could be proven later. My mother-in-law, pleased at this decision, led her to a room close to the 'hejleh'. Then I was escorted among cheers, dancing and the tambourine players, out of the room. Up the stairs. To the left. To the right. And a door opened and I was rushed into a magnificently decorated chamber. A chandelier and few candles were burning here and there and lit the room brightly. The scent of fresh, smiling tuberoses, spreading on the bedspread and sitting at every corner lifted the spirit of anxiety from my heart. A sense of elation touched my heart in haste. Was happiness waiting at the mouth of the buds? Or, had it hidden itself among the lace of the white curtains?

I walked to the middle, then halfway across I stopped and looked around, not knowing what was expected of me. I noticed that a young woman, whom I later knew was my sister-in-law, Batul, had stayed behind and waited those agonising moments to approach me. She came close, opened her arms and shielded me from anxiety, kissed me on the forehead and reassured me that there was nothing, nothing to worry about. Then I was left alone. Sitting at the edge of the bed, wondering what to do. My suitcase, the only familiar object from my past, was waiting at a corner. The curtains were drawn and I did not know how many doors opened to that room. Everything seemed locked, sealed and secured. A fight broke out between sleep and anxiety, each pushing the other away. I looked at the golden-framed looking glass, which stood alongside the wall, reflecting the bed and a frightened girl against the lights coming from every direction. She was covered in heavy make up and her tiny body was buried under the white dress. I tried to collect my senses and my ears, tired of the hanging gold, concentrated on the voices in the distance. Butterflies were about to take charge, though a straw of reassurance existed but not strong enough to block shadows of uncertainty. I was in a mysterious terrain trying to find solace to set my mind at rest. I stood before the mirror and examined myself. I hadn't seen the wedding dress on me. I looked pretty by my own judgement. I walked a few steps, the dress following from behind. Who was this girl who seemed familiar and at the same time a stranger? Could I hide her inside the multiple of laces never to be found again?

Suddenly, the echo of footsteps put my whole body on alert. I sat at the edge of the bed as quickly as possible. Fright shielded the entrance to my vision. My mind was wondering, my eyes were searching but not seeing and a door sliding open silently. The silhouette of a man appeared on the opposite wall and reflected in the mirror. The smell of a strange perfume rushed forward as he tip-toed towards me in slow steps. I collected my body, rolled into a ball. I shut my eyes and in a flicker of a moment, begged God to make me disappear, to melt me away, to vanish and to evaporate me. Then the shadow stopped at my feet and looked down. A voice breathed in my ears: 'my dear, why are you coiling yourself like that? Do relax, do relax. I am sorry I frightened you. Please forgive me. I am Javad, your husband. I thought you had been told that I might come around to meet you.' The voice was warm and reassuring. Still I did not know whether it was safe to open my eyes. He stood in front of me and that blocked the light. Slowly, I opened one eye, then the other, raised my head and looked up. He smiled at me: 'please forgive me. I am not here to hurt you. You must have been tired. I had to come because everyone expected me to do so but I will leave you to yourself. Just let me look at you and make sure that you are fine.'

I was puzzled. This man, my husband, did not fit the description everyone had portrayed. There were no cats to be killed. I did not need to put him to sleep! I raised my head and my muscles relaxed. My legs dropped from the edge of the bed and my hands went to my face to cover it in relief. I rushed to put the veil down but he understood my intention and began to talk in his soothing voice: 'listen my dear, we are going to be husband and wife and between us there will be no veils. You do not have to cover yourself from me but if you would like to do so, before you get used to my presence that is fine by me.' He put the white veil down with a delicate gesture, which was amusing at the same time.

'I am going to leave you to this big and comfortable bed to have a nice sleep. Please dream of pleasant things and drive fear away. You are going to be fine. Just fine. Now if you do not mind, I will see you in the morning. Do clean your face from these colours. You probably look prettier without them. I will ask the women not to disturb you. Only the maid will bring you water and some fruit and leave you to yourself. Good night my dear. Sweet dreams.' He patted my hair and left. The trail of his perfume followed reluctantly.

Unable to collect my thoughts, I looked around and wondered if he was hidden in a corner and would climb on top of me all of a sudden. Time passed. An hour? A few minutes? I was not in a position to count. Slowly, cautiously, I got up from the bed and walked around, looked behind the curtains, put my ears to the doors and listened. Nothing could be seen or heard. Darkness had surrounded the room. Far in the distance, voices were dying down. Someone was calling on the maid. The empire of sleep, more powerful than my fearful mind, invaded my body and before I knew, I indulged in dreams, weightless, thoughtless, and floating. I fell asleep on the floor and later a maid put me on the bed. My wedding night passed smoothly into dawn. I opened my eyes to the rush of sunlight dancing across the lacy windows, to find that my first day as a married woman had just begun.

Ten

How I have been able to remember details of the first few years of growing up to become a real wife to my husband is not so much of a mystery. The clue is hidden among the journals I have kept since the day I learnt to write. How did it come to my mind to register what I had not been able to speak out and keep them safe from intrusion? Well, I do not know. I only remember that once Javad taught me writing, I developed this urge to put my thoughts down and to quickly hide them in fear of discovery. Whether I was frightened of the exposure or it was simply a childish act, is not known to me. Yet I know that when I began my journals was not a day or a month or any specific time. It was never meant to begin the way it did or to continue as it did. There was never a plan for me to be or not to be what I was years later. A woman deeply in love, who wrote poetry and prose and became distinguished in her own right.

That pyramid of a tender love between Javad and I began to build up steadily, softly and in the passing of ten years. Brick by brick, stone by stone, moulded in, and interlaced by the essence of human dignity, carved deeper into the life of a girl, who eventually grew out of her muteness.

In the first four years, Javad ignored the fact that I was his wife. He made it clear from the very first day that he had no intention to act as a husband, rather he saw himself as a tutor, an older relative who wanted to drive me out of the shell that had imprisoned me. I grew up to decide for myself to fall in love with him and take him into the deepest corners of my soul. I grew up to see that he was my mentor, my husband, my world and the arch of my existence. Finally, I became his wife just as I reached fifteen.

My new home was a compound belonging to my father-in-law, Haji Hassan khan. Though it was not as big as my parent's mansion it was big enough to leave space for everyone. My husband's parents occupied the northern wing, which consisted of four big rooms and a number of smaller rooms for stocking necessities. Two of my sisters-in-law, Minoo and Manzar, occupied a bigger room adjacent to their parents'. Initially, when I arrived, Manzar was moved to one of the rooms my mother-in-law kept for herself and I was given her place with Minoo, who became my mentor, confidant and best friend. My husband Javad lived in the southern wing separated from the rest of the compound by a thick row of Shirazi cedars. There, he lived in five grand rooms, with a modern toilet and a private bath, two changing rooms and a kitchen of its own. Upon his request, a door had been installed to the back street to give Javad freedom of movement. The compound had wide verandas in front of all the rooms and like most houses in Karmanieh encircled the big courtyard in the middle. At the heart of the courtyard stood a shallow pond full of gold fish, around which, vases of geranium bloomed all through summer. The rest of the space was an orchard of more than fifty trees, which in summer bore fruit in abundance. The howzkhaneh or summer chamber with its high wind-turret stood on the eastern side. There was also a payab of subterranean waters at the end of the orchard. Women walked some hundred steps down to reach its depth and wash clothes in its warm waters. Payabs were unique to the desert. They began from outside the city limits and ran through some houses in Karmanieh. People built a wide corridor travelling down to reach the stream. I was terrified of the shadowy steps and the payab itself until I reached adulthood and was taken down by my mother-in-law, who laughed all the way down to give me courage. There, I stood away from the dark stream listening to the lyrics of nature, which came from the heart of the earth. The family kitchen was located near the door to the outside and the two servants and the gardener and their families occupied the outer buildings that were separated from the main compound by a long corridor. I moved in with my husband some four years later and transformed the place to a love nest for us to enjoy.

After the wedding ceremonies died down and I was moved to Minoo's room, located at a quiet corner of the compound, I spent most of my time coiling on the bed, pretending to be asleep but mostly daydreaming, thinking my childish thoughts and crying myself to sleep. I was feeling like a lost child. I was frightened of everyone and everything. Minoo, a teenager herself, did her best to get close to me. Initially, my muteness blocked our road to friendship.

It took me a long time to tear the veil of terror and suspicion and get accustomed to my husband's family and their way of life. Eventually I began to love them more than I had ever loved my natural family. They were patient with me and offered me reassurances at every step. Ghamar khanum would often take me to the kitchen and let me help with the cooking. There, I was immersed in the aromas of coriander, dill, parsley, baked bread and boiling stews. I prepared the right amount of herbs for her to chop for each specific dish. I often closed my eyes and returned to my parents' kitchen, the busiest place I had ever seen. I would sit with Ali to have our ration of delicacies. I still considered onions as an enemy (to be killed on the spot) and avoided them without being able to explain the reason. Soon Ghamar khanum found out that I had a good sense for every dish and sometimes let me cook a simple meal or bake a cake, which she would praise in front of others who ate with much delight. Minoo took me to the hamam where we would wash and scrub each other and splash soap and water over us and giggle until totally exhausted. She would dry my hair and braid it carefully while telling jokes and tickling me at the same time. Haji Hasan khan used to sit me down after supper and tell me stories of the old days in order to prepare me for a peaceful night.

Whenever Javad was home and I was around, his eyes would follow me, looking for ways to gain my trust and get close to me. He treated me like a lost child found in a desert storm. He bought me presents; dolls to play with, painting books and coloured pencils to draw and express my feelings. Sometimes he sat by my side, cautiously and told me to draw and then paint my drawing. He took to himself to educate me and help me to communicate with the outside world. He knew it was hard for me to express my feelings, so he started teaching me elementary words, then sentences and finally writing and reading. At first, I did not understand his intention and did not trust him. Later, it was as if I was put on fire. I was racing to catch up to read, to write, question and inquire. My enthusiasm gave him the courage to intensify his efforts and finally, at the age of thirteen, I finished the elementary stage and pressed to move on. A year later, I sat the examination for the secondary school and got good grades. Slowly, slowly, my tormented soul began to rest. I saw all eyes on me in admiration of my beauty whenever I arrived at a family gathering. I devoured the attention and was not afraid to show off. I was growing up. I was falling in love. Years later Javad told me that he was already in love with me but had restrained himself until he made sure that I wanted him by my own choice.

The day after my fifteenth birthday, which Javad celebrated with a grand feast, we went on a picnic to the outskirts of town. Under the shade of falling blossoms he took me in his arms for the first time and looked me in the eyes and asked me whether I had any feelings for him. He did not know that I write poetry. I took the notebook and scribbled the fire I had kept in me for a very long time.

Something in me set rebellion

as time sailed in time and

hallucination of old fears

were set afire.

Time lost its way forward

and sat still to witness love

throw arms around me

and lock me in the lace of

ecstatic moments of purity.

Rebellion at bay,

fire hidden in the ashes,

time found its way

under the guide of a shooting star

deep into the planet of lovers'

* * *

And so, eight years passed and I was no longer the child who was pushed out of the enclosures of her familiar comfort; first from her nurse's arms and later from her mother, into an alien territory called 'husband's home'. Through time, muddled wires were re-arranged, put in order, cleansed of fearsome dreams. Memories, bloodied with pain faded away and by learning how life should be lived, I threw the pain away, not to be reached and remembered. Eventually my soul rested in peace and my hand was raised to hold a torch to the pilgrimage of love, inviting the worshippers to look for it and when found, to safeguard it by all their means.

I arrived at Javad's home a child-bride. But under the intense affection and care, gradually grew into a young and assertive woman. The imbued fear that had previously spread over me and confined me and kept my soul in constant torment had vanished. I, a child who had strayed away from home, was found by this family who were determined to give me all necessary assurances for me to stay sane. Slowly and tenderly and in the course of moving to adulthood, with Javad's patience and determination and his family's concern to see to my welfare, I began to live as a normal person and through reading and writing, express myself. Gradually, thousands of words and phrases, exclamations, questions and expressions, strangled in my mind for years, jumped out into the tip of my pen onto the whiteness of paper and finally found their way into the outside world. My pauses, indecisiveness, mistrust, and my ignorance of the world were gradually replaced by the knowledge I had gained through the windows Javad Khan opened to me. He, as one entity, replaced all that was lacking in my young life. At the end of the first four years, as I reached sixteen, and through the condensation of love, I concluded that against all the odds, being married to Javad was the best thing that could ever happen to me.

Javad Khan on the other hand, found solace in his creation. His teachings were so intensely combined with his love that they broke the shell of intimidation, which had over-powered my spirit. In the course of the first four years, not only did he teach me reading and writing, and so communicating, and opening to the world, but he was the force behind me blossoming like a flower that grew in its own space. I was Javad Khan's pride, his project; fully implemented and finished to the best of his ability. I was a living witness to the power of love and the majesty of will. A projection of the capacity of humans to show that wherever the will was strong the way could be found. I sufficed to replace what Javad Khan had been forced to abandon, his youthful ambition to change the world, single-handedly. Sadly, I was made aware of his high ambitions years later when he was no longer at my side.

* * *

In the summer of 1939, under the haze of a sleepy sunshine, with the world at our feet, Javad and I were sitting on the veranda, pouring ideas, shifting from a philosophical discourse to conferring over a minor incident, frowning at a serious thought that surfaced on our minds, blocking our happiness momentarily. Driving that away, giving way to the joy of our mutual companionship and the delight we shared in the passing of time. We often used to choose secluded spots to wrap ourselves in heated debates. Javad loved to drag me into conversation and I devoured the moments of togetherness and total closeness.

On that summer day, his remarks had a particular significance. I have often dragged them word by word out of my fading memory to read through them in hope of finding clues to the puzzle that surrounded my life thereafter. The household was submerged in silence. He was sitting beside me, trying to make me conscious of something without raising an alarm. Why wasn't I alarmed at his tone of voice and the seriousness of the subject? Why didn't I read between the lines and let the matter rest for that moment in time?

Javad had his eyes closed with my hand firmly in his grip as his tender voice trailed on: 'my dear love, isn't it wonderful to sit in peace, breathe this air that mingles with your fragrance and talk about whatever comes to our mind? I wish the world to cease, the moments to freeze and Now, caught between the past and the future be the only time left in the universe and Us the last persons on earth, immortal'.

A soft music began to tune by the movement of poplar leaves against the breeze. A tuberose lazily opened its mouth to yawn; a butterfly dipped her head into it and began sucking. Her belly shone under its thousand coloured wings. Ali and I emerged from among its wings. We had just finished Fatima's milk and had become heavy with swollen bellies. I felt a sense of sweet numbness. I shut my eyes and listened to something which I had heard over and over again and devoured it every time: 'Suri darling, do you know that just before our wedding, when I found out that you were so young, and were not allowed to have a say in the whole matter I was ashamed of myself and the cruelty of this society with a tradition that allows parents to give their children away at their own discretion? Do you know that I wanted to send you a message of assurance, explaining that I was not going to hurt you, that I had been forced to choose you by the same tradition that had forced you not to choose me? Whose fault was that to match us together without our consent? Our parents, the matchmakers, or these ancient traditions? You know, I hate these matchmakers and their cunning methods and the way they portray people, full of exaggeration, void of any life and spirit. But when my mother told me in delight that my bride was yet to become a 'ripe fruit', and so I would have to be careful on the first night, I shuddered with disgust. Yet I had to keep my appearance and decide for myself to take action, to protect you from your internal anxieties. From me. I wanted to assure you that our wedding night would be postponed until you become my bride by age and maturity and accept me by your own choice. My heart fills with happiness when I think that those are the bygone days and that in future we will not impose our views on our children and that they will be free to make their own choices and the labyrinth of the andaruns' and old-aged traditions will not torment them. Traditions, traditions. Dark silhouettes creeping under the mind's skin. Rotting everything, contaminating the essence of human dignity. When will be the time we do away with traditions and create a tradition-free society, where the soul can wander around, explore, discover, examine, and choose! Can you imagine a world, free of the constraints of everyday rules, regulations, taboos and customs? '

'Oh, stop it darling, you have spoken of this over and over again.'

But Javad ignored my scribble and his eyes looked at me absent-mindedly as if hypnotised: 'do you think that you have enough conviction not to be influenced by the forces of darkness that rule our lives? You have to promise me that you will continue with what we have agreed regarding the upbringing of our children in case I will not be around? Please my love just reassure me. My dead body would not bear oppression on our children. My soul would wander around this house bewildered with anxiety.'

Tears were falling on his clean-shaven cheeks, finding their way onto his neck, slipping down and hiding in his summer shirt. I remember sitting upright. Lines began to gather on my forehead. I noticed that my husband's remarks carried a message he was not able to give me directly. Did he want to tell me something but couldn't spell it out? I felt a chill running through me while scribbling: 'have you gone out of your senses dearest? Why have you suddenly become so worried about a non -existent occurrence? What revelation has come to you to talk of death at this moment of tranquillity? Why do you want to grow seeds of torment in my otherwise peaceful mind?' I paused to think and looked around in anticipation.

Words filled the whiteness while Javad was rubbing his hands together looking into the space. Then he grabbed the paper from my grip. As always, he first moved his eyes across it in one glance then returned to the beginning and read carefully, giving him time to absorb. Finally, he put the writing aside, turned to me, took both my hands, and went on in a low, stern voice, as if he did not want the butterflies to hear or the breeze to take away what was said between the two of us on that summer day: 'you never know my darling. Maybe a catastrophe lands at our doorstep and we do not find time to say what we should have said. A farewell, a last advice, a last glance. What if I separate from you by forces beyond my power and would not be able to pass you a message, a kiss?' Then he flavoured his sentence with a softer, amusing tone: 'maybe I get amnesia and lose part of my memory and cannot put my thoughts into words. Imagine you have all these thoughts in your head but find no structure to let them out, to make people understand you.'

Javad stopped abruptly and silence fell heavily between us and shielded the heat of our love. I had been in that very same situation before he helped me to discover ways of letting the words out. Trapped, I often choked with anger not being able to respond, to express and to make myself heard. Fortunately, for me those dark days were gone. The past belonged to the past. I was reluctant to stain our present happiness and crack our future life by reviewing the past. So, I lowered my eyes not to meet his. Javad sighed, half his breath evaporated as he was immersed in his thoughts. There were thoughts he shared with me and thoughts he kept to himself but on that day, I felt that he had decided to open all his heart to me: 'sometimes I feel the weight of great worries mounting on my shoulders. A question needs to be answered. Why is the world moving and we are where we have been centuries ago? How can we change ourselves to become better humans, create a better world for all to live in peace and harmony without prejudice and empty of ignorance? I believe we need to gain more knowledge about the world around us. The more we learn, the better we would be equipped to encounter the complexities of our society and the changing world. My darling, you need to get more insight into things. Never, ever be content with what you know. Never, ever be complacent. I have to remind you that should you lose my support, you will be left on your own to carry an impossible mission. My logic tells me that you have to be vigilant. Our children must live as free as possible and follow their own path. How? I do not know. I even wonder if our secluded happiness counts. Sometimes questions pile up, doubts gather and answers are far to reach. I know that we have moved a long way and set aside moments of deep ignorance but how many will follow our path? Are there many bends around the corner, dark, deep, and treacherous that we do not know of until we reach their vicinity? Is this the right path we are taking, distancing ourselves from the established norms to create a world of our own? And what if you have to continue on your own?'

I smiled at Javad and decided to write him a piece to end our conversation.

'My heart beats heavy drums

as you walk to me with

garlands of crimson thoughts.

Twirling in delight,

streaming through my veins.

Torches in hand,

I open the gate of passion and love

for you to embroider yourself

needle by needle

in and out.'

Javad read and re-read the piece. His mood changed. He raised his eyes and smiled, stretched his hands to reach mine, caressed my fingers one by one until I managed to take the pen and make him wait for more clarification. My thoughts were travelling further and farther: 'you know my darling, maybe you are right. Our power is immense, but we do not utilise it. I know that the world is changing as we are sitting, a silent witness. Sometimes I think ignorant people live a happier life. The more I know, the more I know that I don't know. This is a fact that frightens me. Maybe the knowledge I have acquired is not enough, or is working against me. At this moment you are the only advocate of my quest. By teaching me how to doubt and question, I have broken the laws of history, moved away from the norms and transformed myself. You have taught me to think differently and I am a woman with broad imagination. But moments of doubt and an explosion of thirst are melting together, creating a mould of their own. What will I do if you vanish from my life? How can I move away from tradition in a society, which recognises no other path? Now, we join forces searching for a clue, or feel our hearts beat slowly but steadily, reminding us that meddling with the beating and urging a backward society to suddenly move forward, may result in declaring the death of the beat. Look! The butterfly is moving away. We have each other, two hearts that beat the same tune. This moment, my darling is precious. We are here together, in love. We have the future on our side. We have each other.'

Javad read in haste and let the paper slip through his fingers on the veranda. Delicately as his style was, he held my head between his two hands. His fingers dipped into the rolling curls. Some struggled to loosen from his grip and to peep out. He was looking into my eyes with such intensity that I closed them to the flames. He kissed my lashes, my mouth as I slid into his arms. The door closed to the passage of an unforeseen future. Our hearts coiled together, labouring an everlasting love. Our eyes shut to the world, to the future with dark clouds lurking. The Two of us became One.

Part TWO

Eleven

Some three thousand years ago, Persia was a vast empire and the cradle of ancient civilisation. During the Achameneade Dynasty (5th century BC), the empire stretched from Greece to Egypt in the west, to borders with India in the east and China in the north east. Cyrus, the founder of the Persian Empire was the first ruler in history, who issued a decree which in today's terms is considered as the first declaration of human rights. During his reign, peoples of different origins and faiths lived in harmony and peace. Due to her geopolitical importance and over two millennia Persia became the target of many invasions by the Greeks, the Romans, the Arabs, the Mogul and the Turks, who killed, robbed and set ruin to her towns and cities. Some invaders stayed longer and ultimately assimilated in the indigenous population. Others were driven out after long, hard battles. None left traces directly towards new horizons. While the Western world woke up and left the Dark Ages behind and passed through the Renaissance, Enlightenment and the Industrial Revolution, Persia, the symbol of the oldest civilisation did not find a space to move on and join in. She was enshrined in the secret world of religion and superstition, motionless, eternal. Immortally still.

It was only at the onset of the Twentieth Century that Persia rose from her long hibernation. At the time, the country was a gathering of tribes and warlords ruled by the Quajar Dynasty, who were of Turkish origin. A revolution, guided by a number of urban intellectuals and western educated elite and some nationalist elements took place and as a result the last Quajar Dynasty, whose corruption had drained the country's resources, was removed from power. This revolution was not a widespread revolt and few cities took on active role in the uprisings, Tehran, the Capital and Tabriz in the northwest of the country in particular. From Karmanieh, a handful of educated men got involved. But women, who until then were kept inside the walled andaruns went on the streets supporting the men. Some died in the battlefield in the guise of men. For a very short time, Persia experienced political freedom. Apart from the downfall of the corrupt Dynasty, structurally little changed in Persia. Yet this incident drove the country out of centuries of hibernation and into the light of political activity. Like a sleepy lizard, she woke up soaked in turmoil. She opened her eyes and saw the world transforming and moving away from its past. Puzzled, she yawned and looked around and was blinded by the forces of the enlightenment. Constitutional Revolution was a blink in the passage of time. Fundamentally, nothing changed. A few years later, Persia had another dictator.

Javad was born just when the Constitutional Revolution was taking shape. Then he was too young to understand the impact of that historical incident on his future. His father, Haji Hassan khan was a wise man. A man who saw the country had awakened from her deep sleep. He believed that it would not be long, maybe in his lifetime that Persia would join the rest of the world and build herself afresh. To start with, the country needed a contingent of educated men to run her affairs. Haji Hassan khan had high ambitions for his only son, Javad who was growing up rapidly. He wanted his son to become a party in the making of modern Persia. He was determined to put a stop to the repetition of a life-long tradition, of sons replacing their fathers. What was the use of sitting in the 'hojreh', dawn to dusk, day in day out, selling herbs and dried vegetables? His young lad had to open his mind, to travel, to experience, to stretch beyond this yellowish, dusty city. Travel expands the mind, gives wisdom and makes a man ready to challenge life. As Persia was moving towards the contemporary world, and upon the advice of his close friend and confidant, Haji David, he decided to send Javad then, aged 15, to Russia to study.

Javad's mother, Ghamar khanum was devastated by her husband's decision, and cried day and night to deter him from such an act, though she was convinced that it was a wise decision. But Russia was far, too far away a place. Her only son, the apple of her eye, whom she wished would wed in a few years' time and produce grandchildren, would be separated from her. More than anything, she was frightened. To Ghamar Khanum, the outside world was a mystery, dangers were waiting at every corner and disasters loomed on the horizon. What if she never saw her Javadu again? How could life be lived without her teenage boy, who had just grown a line on his upper lip? What if something happened to him? By disappearing from sight, he might be gone forever. She might be dead before he returned. She could not sketch a clear picture in her troubled mind and that brought her immense pain. Yet her husband did not waver in his decision.

* * *

On a sunny day in April 1915, a caravan of merchants left Karmanieh for the borders of Russia through the deserts of eastern Persia. Among the river of tears and the rainfall of farewells, taking with him bags of advice, a head full of worries and a mind swelled by ambition, Javadu's handsome figure, riding on a Turkeman horse, holding his sobs aback disappeared into the haze and dust of the desert. Accompanied by Haji David, his guardian and protector, it took him three months of travelling on horseback and a vessel that sailed through the stormy Caspian Sea and a rattling train, that whistled through Central Asia, to arrive at the gates of Moscow, the giant Russian capital. Soon Haji David disappeared from the scene and Javad was left in the care of a local friend, who promised to oversee his development. As Persia moved far away, Karmanieh, a distant spot in his memory and his family, in the vicinity of the horizon, Javad decided to listen to the voice of reason and to put a halt to his past and immerse himself in the life of a country which would be his home for years to come.

Arriving in Russia at the best time, Javad had a few years before he witnessed and then joined the greatest event of the early twentieth century. In the first few months he was a confused, bewildered child, bearing an ignorance that almost paralysed him. He could barely cope with this ocean of people and the river of events. Russia was beyond Javad's limited vision and he found an urge to see, to understand, to learn and to absorb everything that went on around him. He had come from a country whose populace, having not travelled outside the vicinity of their own four walls, had queued along the stretch of a single line, life after life, generation after generation throughout centuries. Their daily conversation went no further than family affairs; births, marriages and deaths. Asleep through time, were the people of his beloved country.

A few years later, a continent stood between comrade Javadov and that young lad, Javadu, who from the age of six, used to obediently accompany his father to his herbal shop at the heart of the bazaar. The lad, who used to take orders from customers and sometimes delivered to their doors across all areas of town, soon grew into a handsome young man with eastern looks and western manners. One must not forget that Javad went through a lot of agony to transform into that young man.

How different he saw Russia from Persia! Sometimes he wondered whether Russia had come to existence just for his bewilderment! Yet he was convinced that she had been there long before the birth of time. From the beginning, Javad found little time to switch on his mind's machine. It began working by the tide of developments. Initially, the wires entangled and the trains of his thoughts derailed. The enormity of their task, sorting out, giving them dimension and comprehending the concepts that were absent from Javad's vocabulary was a hard task. Shortly afterwards he managed to find his way into the heart of that wonderful country.

But that was years later. Initially, as the train reached the main station in Moscow and Javad followed Haji David out of the carriage and down onto the platform, he suddenly noticed a group of young girls walking hand in hand, talking and laughing. His mouth went ajar, his eyes burst out and his mind swelled. His heart pounded violently. He blushed. He sweated. He went numb. Then he began shivering uncontrollably at the shame of what was pressing to peep out through his trousers. How could this be possible? Where is this place? Eden on earth, where Huris walk around the Garden, serving milk and honey to the devotees? Well worth a lifetime of prayers and devotion. Javad reached Moscow with the innocence of a newborn child, believing the world would come to an end and he would be sent away to hell to burn forever, if he were not able to keep his gaze away from the unveiled women. Haji David, the learned man of all seasons noticed Javad's bewildered look. He had experienced the same the first time such a scene emerged in front of his narrow eyes.

'Come on my dear boy. You will get used to it. This is not Persia, where women are chattels kept tight in the stables. Here, women have a life of their own and they fight alongside men and demand equal rights. You will see a lot of them, especially here in Moscow and St Petersburg.' Haji David paused for a while to let his words sink in. Then, as they were walking out of the station, he continued in a slower pace:

'I wish there would be a time when women of Persia would be treated as humans. Have their own space and walk on the streets free of walls and veils.'

Women of Persia? His own mother and sisters? Walking on the streets unveiled? Are these words coming from the mouth of Haji David, who had his place in the front line, shoulder to shoulder with the Imam at the grand mosque? Has he had these obscene thoughts and yet given advice to his family on different theological issues! Why has he not spoken of his observations abroad and of his true beliefs?

Caught between respect for Haji David and what he had just heard,

94

not able to comprehend, questions arrived and hid in Javad's dry mouth. Answers delayed arrival.

* * *

Russia of the early twentieth century was herself in turmoil. An earthquake was shaking the foundations of her vast entity. A giant had woken up from centuries of deep sleep. The energy gathered through thousands of years had spat out. The energy of not one mind but that of millions of insects, mammals, birds, man-eaters and fish-hunters had been unleashed. Everything was moving, changing, transforming. People had woken up because it was time for them to awaken. There was no plot behind that. Their minds began working round the clock to manufacture new ideas, to flourish political parties, to bloom their innovative capabilities. And as a result the Tsar abdicated his reign and a new government took charge. It was at the beginning of the century that Russia was engaged in an uprising, which eventually led to the socialist revolution. Communists and socialists, anarchists and libertarians were clashing over political power. Finally, the Bolsheviks headed by Vladimir Illich Lenin, a genius communist and fervent supporter of the Proletariat Dictatorship managed to stage the October 1917 revolution. The Bolshevik Revolution was the greatest political event of the early twentieth century and cut the heart of history in two halves.

At the time of the revolution, Comrade Javadov had long taken leave from that young boy he once was. Transforming from a raw teenager into a well-kneaded, well-cooked entity in the space of three years. Swept away by the whirlwind of events, he walked away from his old-self and grew into a young man no one would have recognised, had they come across him on the street. A year after his enrolment at school, he found a huge energy unleashed in him and became an active member of the students' movement. Dedicating passionately most of his time to the oncoming revolution, participating in demonstrations, learning the art of shaking sleepy minds, inspiring and directing the masses towards that final goal, he turned into a comrade in support of the Bolsheviks. Pride and strong-will lifted his spirit when, for the first time, he was called by his official name, Comrade Javadov, member of the students' brigade.

Javad did not join the rank and file overnight. He walked the stretch of a long road to become a comrade. At nights he was in the core of uninterrupted debates; hot-headedly, light-heartedly, drawing strategies, sketching plans. During the day he roamed the city searching, learning, absorbing and over months he moved on, laying bricks, moulding and cementing and building his utopia. In crossing the road to knowledge and cultivating the seeds and flourishing in the spirit of comradeship, he joined hands with his Persian comrades, who promised to build heavens on earth. There on, gradually, with determination, they became socialists in the true sense. Building a socialist utopia. A utopia so it remained.

Forming their own group of activists, a number of Persians who had been sent to Russia to study, were heavily involved in the political activities and were enchanted by their new titles, given to them by no one but themselves; Comrade Javadov, Comrade Ehsanov, Comrade Joseviov. Javad's gaining this title bore a resemblance to the first day of school in a new uniform; a prize won; the taste of a first kiss; an encounter with the opposite sex leading to the loss of one's virginity. Their titles had a strong resemblance to that of their fathers', whom after pilgrimage to Mecca, the house of God were granted the title of Haji. Soon the Marxist Hajis, clean-shaven, smartly dressed, not in the least resembling the silhouette of a Haji back home, drafted a manifesto for a Socialist Persia. A state they hoped would be born out of the rubble of dictatorships and ancient dynasties. Javad's mind had geared towards one goal: 'that like the Russians, Persians deserved to rule their own destiny; that upon returning to Persia, he would awaken the inhabitants from their thousand-year sleep and teach them how to take control of their lives.'

So, in the process of three years, comrade Javadov's conviction to the Bolshevik cause took root and he was immersed in the tide of events, which led to the revolution. The picture of the first time he attended a rally and shouted 'Viva Revolution, Down with reaction', in Russian with a Persian accent carved itself in his mind as an unforgettable experience. It was his voice. Loud and clear. A voice he never imagined would rise in protest. Whether he knew the concept of 'revolution', or 'reaction' was not the subject matter. At that juncture in time, having the power to shout was the centre of importance. There on, he could be seen at the forefront of clandestine meetings packed with all types of people; students in their combat outfits, workers and sailors in their ragged clothes, and the intelligentsia with dark suits and narrow cravats; the vanguard of a sleepy-minded people - the oppressed - who were about to wake up. Lines of speakers stood on the platforms. The listeners were mesmerised. Messages were arriving from four corners of the world and read out to the noisy audience, whose stench of sweat and cheap tobacco and vodka mingled with the polluted air, hovered at the apex and rained down over the oppressed. Not able to drag meaning out of the words, and just weighing their importance against their own confused judgement, the crowd listened.

'Their world would soon peel off its old skin'. They were told. 'New Order would shape things on their behalf.' They were reassured. 'Their rights would be restored, taken back from tyrants.' They were promised. 'Power would be transferred to them; workers and peasants, the oppressed.' These were confirmed. All that was required of them was 'To Unite'. There was no time for questions. Answers arrived before questions formed. At their doorstep readily packed, in smart Bolshevik and Monshevik clothes. Hopes were rising, energies unleashing, mountains were being moved by the power of speech. Action sat dormant in the bubble of future to bear stillborn children. That was how Workers of the World United, not in the land of Karl Marx and Fredrick Engels, the original messiahs but in a country least expected to rise and unite. And Russia opened her womb to deliver a child, who shook the world in ten days.

The day Lenin returned from years of exile, the Young Persian Socialists were among the first groups to welcome the prophet at the platform of the railway station. Thousands had packed to have a glimpse of their leader, who was about to liberate them from oppression. Alexander Kolontai, the revolutionary woman, the pride of all women, stood a few steps away. Comrade Javadov had the honour of waving a red flag. When Lenin was approaching, he shouted Viva Revolution and detected the glint of genius in Lenin's eyes who, smiled absent-mindedly but in satisfaction. Then the tide took him away, further, farther into the human sea. Along with others, comrade Javadov prepared himself to die for the freedom of Russian workers. That would baptise him for the task he saw for himself once he returned to Persia. During these stormy periods, sometimes comrade Javadov was confused as he compared and contrasted his homeland with his adopted one. There were times when he felt deep humiliation for being a Persian. For a short period in time and after a long battle against his old convictions, comrade Javadov, re-born and baptised, concluded that he had been born at the wrong moment in time and the wrong place; that anything and anywhere apart from and before that moment and that land, Mother Russia, was a misunderstanding of history. That would have been then.

* * *

Finally, in 1917, Lenin and the Bolsheviks seized power and the first socialist state was born. The capital and capitalists were deposed and the proletariat became master of their own destiny.

Socialist ideology was declared as the official ideology. Unfortunately, the ideal of a socialist state and the proletarian dictatorship worked marvellously on paper, in practice, it never materialised. Proletarian dictatorship created barriers to advancement, to initiative and creativity. After all, dictatorship was dictatorship, no matter by whom and against whom. Shortly after the establishment of the socialist republic, the inexperienced revolutionaries awakened to the horror of their inability to govern that vast country and more than that they could not hold on to their socialist promises. As time went by, Russia faced enormous opposition from within and without. Civil war broke out and cut Russia into pieces. Anarchy and famine of the early 1920s, a by-product of the situation followed afterwards. Millions of people were dead or displaced. Millions of children were abandoned by their families and rampaged towns and villages. It seemed that Russia was falling apart. Yet the miracle of revolution carved its way ahead. The Bolsheviks managed to overcome the civil war and the famine and brought the country under some kind of control. But then in 1921, Lenin was shot in a crowded gathering. It was a woman who fired the bullet into his heart. Comrade Javadov wondered for many years the irony of a bullet piercing the flesh of a man, who claimed to be close to women's hearts. Gradually, Lenin's ill health gave power to Stalin, who later replaced him after his death in 1925.

* * *

The day Lenin died lonely, though Stalin and the whole Central Committee at his bedside, Kropskaya, the faithful, devoted wife of this unfaithful husband was kept away in a corner of the Kremlin to mourn by herself. Lenin found no time to warn the central committee not to appoint Comrade Josef Stalin as his successor, but history has registered that he raised the matter on several occasions. Whether he knew that the man would bring catastrophe to the

Soviet State or he simply did not agree with Stalin's leadership is up to history to judge.

Comrade Javadov was browsing around the Red Square, thinking red thoughts. Red flags were dancing with the breeze, singing a red song. It was not a bright day. The clouds had already surrounded the buildings and birds were seeking shelter. Suddenly and for no apparent reason, Javad's heart had sunk into his chest as if a stone of sadness had fallen on it. He saw people walking in haste, apprehensive and sombre. Then the flag stood erect. People froze. Comrade Javadov heard someone shouting. His voice transcending over space. He turned his head towards the voice. The bewildered man, holding a telegram in his hand, running along the streets in no direction: Lenin is dead. Lenin is dead. As if the world had come to a stop. Finished.

Thereafter, people, Workers of the World United, patiently formed a queue, the length of China wall around the Red Square, throughout months, seasons, years and decades to get absolution from Lenin's calm mind and saw their dreams of a utopia caught in that glass box. A dream that ever since, has been dreamt through his glassy eyes. Since then, Karl Marx from Highgate in North London and Fredrick Engels from his remote village in Germany had raised their heads to see whether their own dreams have come true but every time, a heavy hand decorated all over with a 'C' -Capital- has pushed them down into their graves.

* * *

October 1917 marked the birth of the first socialist revolution and the dawn of a socialist state in Russia, a country least expected. The Capitalist World bewildered and in shock could not tolerate this occurrence. A red revolution at the heart of an old empire sent shivers down the spine of capitalism, which came short of nothing to crush it from inception. Socialism had the capacity to mobilise millions around its ideals. It was a powerful tool in the hands of the peoples of Africa, Americas and Asia to free themselves from imperialism and capitalism. It was too soon for anyone to know that that was yet another yoke in another guise and even more brutal than capitalism. The West could not tolerate this, nor waste any time to let socialism spread. From supporting the anti-revolutionaries, to enforcing economic blockade, to staging an orchestrated propaganda machine and acts of sabotage. Analloutwar was declared and maintained against the Soviet Union and her allies. Well after the purge of the first generation of revolutionaries in Russia, in and out of the Second World War and Stalin's Iron Curtain, behind which he rebuilt the Russian Empire. While Socialism and its humanistic ideals were sucked away in the horrors of labour camps and the killing fields in Russia, in the West, socialist ideology remained a metaphor for waging wars and coups and invasions. And until all traces of those grand hopes were washed off, the West did not let go. Yet for seven decades and five years, millions lived the dream of a world free of exploitation until they found out that the whole world had long been conquered by capitalism as a sole trader.

Today, if you tour Russia, now dressed in the latest fashion, holding a bottle of Sherry mixed with Scotch Bourbon in one hand and Smirnoff vodka in the other, in celebration of the abandonment of her disobedient bastards, the Republics of the Soviet Union, you will see the queue around the Red Square, still stubbornly resembling the wall of China. You might even see Lenin jumping out of a Big-Mac, looking sideways at the onlookers with bewildered, opaque eyes, rushing towards the steppes outside the city square, to deliver a speech to the waiting Workers of the World.

* * *

However, comrade Javadov stayed in Russia a further five years. By then, Stalin had set a firm grip round the neck of the newly-matured revolution, choking it slowly and systematically. Comrade

Javadov peeled off the Ov from his name and decided to return home. No need to stay in Russia anymore. Lucky as he was, he did not witness the catastrophe of shattered dreams and waste of lives, of Stalin's Stalinist politics replacing the early humanistic ideals of the Bolsheviks and of the gradual death of Socialism. By then, Lenin was far away in his glass compartment enjoying a quiet evening in the presence of his Collection of Works, which had become the bible of millions allovertheworld.

Javad was informed of his father's illness and as the only male-child he was summoned back in case his father departed. He concluded that he had done his share in the materialisation of the World Revolution, to the Unification of Workers of the World and at the end of the first decade of the Revolution there was no space for worry. The birthplace of the first Socialist Revolution, young and ambitious in her designer clothes, then the Republics of the Soviet Union, under the heavy breast of the Mother were the beating heart of the world. Nowhere in the muddled pages of history had it written that the union was a forceful drag into the grieving earth, that her soil would soon be stained with the blood of her own children, that the memory of the dead and the disappeared would remain long after the pages of history have turned yellow, that its comrades would one day become the smartest smugglers and organised crime squads in the whole world. Comrades who would gain profit by exporting human flesh abroad and train strippers in their colleges of Striptease at the heart of the Motherland, St Petersburg, which changed name into Leningrad, into Stalingrad, into St Petersburg at long last. Then, it was too soon to become disillusioned and despair over Mother Russia. The Young Persian Socialist had in mind to build a similar paradise in his beloved Persia once he returned home.

Twelve

Javad left Russia in the spring of 1930. En route to his hometown he stayed in the capital Tehran for a few weeks and visited the friends he had made in Russia, who had long established a socialist party in Tehran and were deeply engaged in politics. Naturally, the country had transformed since his absence. Reza Shah had long seized power and declared himself the King of Persia, now officially Iran and with his dictatorial style was pushing the country towards modernisation. He had successfully silenced many of his opponents. There were lots of activities going on although the new dictator wanted everything done his way. Javad had long discussions with his comrades. They persuaded him to stay and work with them. Had it not been for his father's illness, which made him leave Russia in the first place, Javad would have loved to stay in Tehran. That was his dream. But he knew that his presence was much needed back home and so, he set off shortly afterwards.

As he neared the Kavirs of eastern Persia his hazy memory was brightened up and pictures emerged with much clarity. Sandy hills and rocky mountains stood as they were; a green oasis emerged here and there, and then moved away as the caravan headed towards the city. Then, Karmanieh came close, static, changeless, holding its majestic coppery mould. The curtain of dust rested on its domes, a dense layer of mud on the streets underneath. Minor improvements were detected as Javad's convoy passed through the main road and rushed into the narrow alleyways that welcomed and embraced the traveller. New office buildings had risen at strategic points. There, the contingent of young bureaucrats, sons of merchants and retailers, had opted to work for the local government. The aged, long-term governor had been replaced by a young, short-term man whose ideas of governing the city were not much different from those of his predecessor.

* * *

Javad reached home and the stretch of long, lonely years of separation came to a close. His arrival was celebrated in style. For six nights and six days. Clearing itself of rainstorms and sudden hails, the sun had taken charge. Leading into Haji Hassan khan's house, the alleyways had washed off the mud. Decorated with a wide smile, the gate sat open. Lanterns were waving high on the poles. Glittering with fresh, cool water, the fish danced down under and up into the air. Harmonising in an orchestrated tune, the samovar's steam and the gelyan's smoke whispered joyous moments Javad's return had brought into the household. Turning into a ball of fire, a band of merry songs and the spirit of living, Javad's mother, Ghamar khanum and his sisters had spent weeks making preparations to welcome their beloved. Fleeing from sight, Haji Hassan khan's illness of many years had granted him a wide breathing space. Walking in and out, shouting, ordering, laughing. His heart warming, his eyes shimmering. Hope, hope raining. Love, love arriving. Javad, his son arriving.

Yet the first few days left little space for his parents to touch their son, to feel him, to have him. The household turned into a Mecca of visitors. From dawn to dusk, the merchants and the retailers, the mullahs and the authorities, relatives and acquaintances. People arrived and stayed, leaned back, ate and drank; all ears and eyes fixed on the young, handsome product of The Republics of the Soviet Union. Furnished with the title 'khan', given to him by his father, clean-shaven with European attire, Javad khan would sit at the top of the room, remembering, re-telling and portraying fifteen years of his life in Russia.

As the initial phase of excitement passed and Javad khan came closer to knowing everyone, contradictory sentiments began to interact simultaneously. People were constantly asking questions but

Javad understood that he had to economise with his narration. It was advisable that he did not include details of his experiences and the values he treasured. His audience was far from reaching the battles he had won, the mountains he had climbed and the hills he had trotted down, walking his thoughts through turbulence and storms until they approached maturity to become a socialist. Yet the young enthusiast of the World Revolution had made a covenant with his comrades to act as the Messiah, the Messenger. Hot-headed, light-hearted and strong-willed, Javad khan saw it best to feel the people's pulse and to wait for the right time. He was determined to reach his listeners and to carry out his mission. To reveal his socialist revolutionary ideas and to convince the people to follow him. As he was scrutinising the visitors, at a corner of his brain planning was underway to put his strategies in motion. He aimed to transform these static figures into active humans in his ideological factory. Along the assembly line, socialist ideas had to spread through the wires of people's brains. If they were aware of their strength, people, Workers of the World would Unite against the oppressors and free themselves from centuries of injustice. It was not an easy task. They had to be convinced of the necessity for unification and change. An Old Order whose depth reached the heart of mother earth and whose vastness travelled across the globe had to be eradicated and ancient footsteps erased. Roads had to be built afresh for the new ideas to walk on. Millions had to pour their blood over the fresh path. Javad khan, the socialist enthusiast was ready to give his own blood for the cause. A cause, which undoubtedly was nurtured on blood. But he waited for the right moment.

There were major barriers to break. Geographically, Persia had thousands of miles of borders with her northern neighbour. Russia had repeatedly invaded Persia and forced the country into signing humiliating pacts. Turkemanchai and Golestan Treaties, according to which, the Quajar Kings gave Russia parts of northern regions were still fresh in memories. Historically, people were well familiar with the Tsarist Imperialist policies and suspicious of anything that had a Russian brand name. Now, Javad khan had to convince the people that Russia had entered a new era. She intended to enter a new phase based on mutual respect and friendship. In reality, the cancellation of Persia's debt to Russia was among the first orders signed by Lenin after he took office. He could argue that the Tsar's successors were deeply committed to an ideology, a humanistic cause. A revolutionary cause that had no intention to invade and conquer by force.

All at the same time, socialism was transcending the boundaries of Russia and seizing the heart of the twentieth century. It had even reached Karmanieh. Its essence, peculiar though had some fascination. People queried about it and weighed Javad khan's responses against their own limited knowledge. Why did such an historical incident occur in Russia and not in Western Europe, where socialism had originated in the first place? Did people, ordinary men take power into their own hands and dismantle the Tsarist regime? How could those rugged peasants and workers overthrow such an empire? And Javad khan explained and the audience travelled back and forth with his explanations and asked the same question time and again. Did it really happen the way the narrator narrated the events?

As days passed and conversation moved further and deeper, Javad khan decided to make his move. Hidden under his searching eyes and pleasant voice, inflammatory seeds of rebellion, of revolt, a Red Revolt was surfacing and reaching the mesmerised. Javad khan was a ball of fire, a spinning moth. No longer soft and calculated, his words were contaminated with flame, a burning flame. Soon, they moved beyond, cracked the space and disturbed the silence. His narration took the audience to moments of high excitement. People sat around, all ears. Javad khan's words were new and flashed across sleepy minds. Some woke up terrified. But somehow it was reaching their ears, not their minds. Javad was far from convincing. And people's curiosity did not travel beyond the ordinary. As he developed his notions of demolishing the existing order and creating a Russian-model revolution throughout Persia people became terrified. Some slid away through the door, others were dismayed. That was the end of the beginning. Javad's dreams were shattered by the reality and went in the abyss of his mind.

One has to remember that Karmanieh had always been governed by the unwritten, and unspoken, yet strong codes imposed by the long-bearded, turban-headed leaders. Those men who came to visit Javad khan and sat listening with glassy eyes glued inside their stony faces. Soon voices were heard all around. In exasperation. In protest and caution. The governor general and the religious authorities were prompt in detecting the danger underneath the words that sped out of Javad's mouth. They found it hard to swallow Javad khan's dangerous words. Elders spoke first. How dare this young man, who had just returned from a foreign country criticise the state of affairs and speak of change! Question tradition and the rule of law! If he were not silenced from inception, he would even find the courage to raise his voice against the authority of holy religion. News of disapproval spread like the plague. People slowed down their paces. And the flame died down as quickly as it had risen. Finally, the oppressed and the oppressors were united to reject Javad's notions of social change. He found himself alienated and squeezed out. Dismantled. More than that, he entered the list of suspects, the saboteurs. A profile of him was in progress. Haji Hassan khan became vigilant. He was devastated. The poor man wished he had never sent his son away to study. If he had kept him in his trade, he would have made 'something of himself'. He would have married and settled down. Haji Hassan khan did not understand what had caused his son to turn into such an irrational and tactless person. A distanced, far-reaching young man, who spoke of nothing but revolution and the act of change; who criticised his mother and sisters for being slaves to the andarun. Javad's parents were trying desperately to pull him towards normality. Inside the life of Karmanieh. Static. Calm. Ordinary.

* * *

Since his return a few months earlier, Javad khan was in the state of self-denial. His father, old, fragile with one wish to come true was pushing him towards the familiar road. He wanted him to apply for a job, to get married and establish a family. But Javad's eyes were blind to the world of desires. He had been trained that way. Revolution had left no space for family life and normality. As time passed, he was further isolated from the people. Gradually, a mountain of despair landed on his shoulders. He understood that his strategies for change and revolution were premature and the city was far from grasping the essence of his preaching. Between him, the messenger and the people who were supposed to receive the message stretched a long, dark road, which travelled down the history line. Javad was quick to assess the situation and distance from the portrait he had painted of himself. And distancing from ideals and revolutions, he found a heart within his heart for loving his family, for not being so blind to the sea of love that surrounded him in the enclosure of his home. His parents offered the world on a simple plate, for him to take.

In that time and age few people from Karmanieh had sent their children abroad to study. Yet Haji Hassan khan had done so, hoping Javad would return an educated man. Others who returned from abroad had quickly reached high positions in the newly established nation-state Reza Shah was building. Javad could become one of them. Then he understood that planting a Russian ideology in the heart of this religious-stricken land would not take root no matter how many people gave their blood to nurture it. The fact was that this land did not need any martyrs for any cause. Thousands of martyrs had already painted the pages of her history, yet not much had changed. Even if Javad joined the queue and gave his blood for a red revolution, would anything change? Anyone dedicate a word of tribute to him? A sentence, a dot? Would it not be advisable if he joined the rank of the bureaucrats and worked his way through slow reforms instead of a sudden revolution? A decision that kept him tamed at that moment in time was then reached against his strong beliefs. His political life ended where it had begun. Marriage came at this time of confusion and resignation.

* * *

As the outside world shut its doors to Javad and revolt and revolution seemed a million years away and the earth swallowed dirt to spit dust into his eyes, his young bride, Suri turned up to become his goal, a spark in the distance, a hope to live for. Changing Suri meant wrestling with the hostile world, well worth the effort. His child-bride had years ahead of her before becoming his wife. In the crack of time between now and then, Javad decided to dedicate his long reserves of intellect to transform Suri into a Project. A Model Village. Slowly, painstakingly, he succeeded in gaining Suri's confidence, in pouring the heat of reassurances and his good intention into her young heart. Slowly, he gained her heart and her love. Her love for him seeded and sprouted and flourished as his attention to her intensified and transformed Suri into a woman, whose ability to communicate grew every day, whose knowledge of the world expanded at the speed of sound. At times, Suri's sharp tongue and stimulating thoughts splashed across the paper and spilled over Javad's amazed and amused face. Sometimes the bliss of his success scared him. How could she be his making? This beautiful, young woman with a head on her shoulders! Javad carried in him a mountain of pride, a sea of contentment, well-satisfied with his product.

As time passed Suri transcended the boundaries and became more able than the abled and the envy of town. That little mute girl, covered in rouge and sormeh, shivering and coiling, crying and despairing soon vanished away, and out of the odyssey of learning emerged a young woman, who walked her way with determined steps. No longer hidden from history, Suri could read and write both in Persian and Russian. In her late teens, Suri wrote the most ebullient poetry, argued most articulately and took control of her life most confidently.

'A slice of time is mine

in this forsaken earth.

The seal of the window has cracked,

a needle of light

has slid through and

set my brain alight.'

For almost a decade, the household paced gently and joyfully through life. Haji Hassan khan, contented at the equilibrium in his family gave himself up to the illness which had long waited to take him away. He was lucky enough not to witness the malignant tumour that was growing inside the womb of the future. The womb of the future.

Thirteen

The euphoria of the constitutional revolution faded in the second decade of the twentieth century as the revolutionaries were not able to keep to their promises and sustain their power base. In the vacuum created, the British Empire increased her presence in Persia and the country went under the grip of yet another appointed dictator, who took office by way of a coup de'etat.

In 1921, Reza Khan, the Commander of a Cossack Brigade, assisted by the Commander General, the representative of His Majesty, the King of the Great Empire of Great Britain, against the will of the governments of the Socialist state of Soviet Union and France, all rivals in the region, attacked the Capital Tehran and took the power from the coalition government that had ruled Persia for almost two decades since the overthrow of the Quajar Dynasty.

A few years later, Reza Khan, who until then was the army's chief commander, declared himself the King of Persia, now officially Iran. Simultaneously, in the neighbouring Turkey, the Ottoman Empire disintegrated and Kamal Ataturk, the founder of modern, secular Turkey became the champion and vanguard of social reforms. Ataturk's ideas of modernisation and Russia's notions of socialism reached Iran in time for Reza Shah to utilise them to his advantage.

Reza Shah was clever enough to see the need for reforms. A Cossack with three wives and a military-feudalistic vision, his ambitions were higher than expected. Scholars who have studied his reign are perplexed at such contradiction. As soon as Reza Shah seized power, the state of affairs changed direction. Whether he took his inspiration from neighbouring Turkey, socialist Russia, or demands set by the Constitutionalists early in the century, or suggestions made by a number of Western-educated individuals, who co-operated with him to build a modern Iran, is not clear. Yet ten years into his kingship, it was certain that Iran was heading for and shifting towards an all out modernisation programme. Top to bottom, inside and out. The country was moving away from her static past.

The new king/dictator was a determined military man who imposed his reforms by way of military discipline. He knew no other way to fulfil his dreams. The majority followed him obediently. Reza Shah's reforms cut through the fabric of Iranian society. Although people, especially religious leaders were opposed to Reza Shah's ideas they did not show strong resistance to his authority.

Within a short period the country was restructured all the way, roads, railways, universities, army, navy, police force and banking systems were established. Students were sent abroad to learn new skills and foreign personnel were recruited to get projects off the ground. It was hoped that Iran would soon come out of the Dark Ages and like Turkey would join the New World. Establishing modern institutions was only part of the strategy. Iran needed a profound facelift, paramount for displaying her to the outside world; reborn, modern, well-groomed. And that could not be possible unless the hidden half of the population was declared human and brought out into the public arena. Women. Up until then the majority of women were kept as chattels inside the walls, hidden from sight, non-existent, deprived from the process of life. Reza Shah decided to bring them out of the andaruns and use them as the last finishing touch to his projects; a gloss over, the fine art of decoration.

So, plans were set in motion to unveil women, to free them from harems and to enter them into the education system and the workforce. The publicity machine began its huge task. Women were encouraged to raise their voices and demand some rights. More schools were established and women teachers were employed. Feminists, men and women who, during the constitutional revolution, had campaigned for women's rights took advantage of the situation and established independent institutions to further women's cause. There already existed women's societies and associations that published magazines and periodicals. Now they found ample grounds to flourish. These were in total agreement with Reza Shah's universal unveiling project. Yet apart from a handful of intellectuals the populace was not ready to approve of such an outrageous act in the land of the holy religion. Social reforms in the area of family and women were vehemently opposed by the religious authorities. Their opposition was crushed and many were sent into exile or silenced all together. Reza Shah knew that he was playing with fire. Nevertheless, he herded the women out and ordered them to stay out for history to register its new-born child. The New Iranian Woman. At that time, Javad khan and the dictator, though worlds apart, shared similar views on this specific issue.

* * *

Appearing in public was a historical moment that required officialisation by way of celebrations. In the winter of 1935, Karmanieh prepared herself for the Big Occasion. The first reception for the emancipation of women. At the forefront of those who had received invitations were government employees, teachers, army officers and civil servants. Unveiling as a project was unpopular among men and women alike. No woman in Karmanieh was prepared to take such an unprecedented step as to walk outside without the veil. So, when invitations arrived, not too many showed up at the reception, although none declined it officially. Refusal meant sabotage. Some became sick on the day and sent apologies. Ten army officers and twelve in the police force, having heard of the forthcoming reception, divorced their wives. Their children, forty-five in all, were stranded among torn families for years to come. Some civil servants resigned and returned to their fathers' businesses in the bazaar, where they began their march backward down the history lane. And all in all, for the compulsory event, some hundred and fifty people showed up at this first Reception for the Emancipation of Women in Karmanieh.

Javad khan was among a handful which stood firm in support of the unveiling. He lobbied his colleagues vigorously. As a senior civil servant he was among the first to be invited. Cordially but firmly he was asked to bring his wife along. 'The Banu would accompany you we expect'. Of course, he would take his wife, his Banu. He was a fervent advocator and campaigner for women's rights. He had been waiting for this moment impatiently.

* * *

On balance, one could say that out of sight is out of mind. Hidden. It seemed that beyond the moment of being unveiled, uncovered, thus discovered women were non-existent. Women's space was hollow, a cavity in the brain. A hole in the history of humankind. Left abandoned. Waiting to be filled. Their features, sacks of potatoes with holes at the top. For as long as memory reached, the outside world was occupied by men. Now, history rendered women an opportunity to experience life outside the harem walls. But how? Women had to push men aside and claim a place, a window of their own to look at the world. A road of their own to walk on and march forward. March and leave the dark ages behind. March to a future glittering on the horizon. But was it glittering on the horizon? Shadowy, shaky, no footprints to follow the new path, women were pushed out in that moment in history. In the uneven road to women being unveiled, uncovered, thus discovered, the Iranians were divided into two groups. Men were

Agonised, because to them, the idea of displaying their honour in public seemed absurd.

Frightened, because they were conscious of the possible breakdown of ancient structure, which meant loss of control and authority.

Hatred filled their hearts and overflowed into their veins as they saw themselves incapable of reacting, rejecting and refusing.

Disobedience was not a possible option. Reza Shah's machinery was well equipped to deal with overt objections. So, they sat waiting, patiently, precariously in the box of history for the right moment to take their revenge.

Women did not walk far from men. After all, men held the key to the doors and women saw the world through men's eyes. The majority of women denied their own interests and rejected the idea of the unveiling because,

Frightened they were of themselves and the reaction of men in general.

Lack of experience kept a sound judgement out of reach. Experience was a male product, repetition, and reproduction, female. Men had crossed the outside road since time began. Women had been absent from this process.

Overwhelmed, because they suddenly saw the chains removed, the doors opened and a fresh breeze came through. Nonetheless, they had no torch to see farther than the tip of their noses. No one knew where women were being led to and what was going to be gained by the act of unveiling. Even the architect of the unveiling, Reza Shah was ignorant of the final gain. Uncovering women did not simply mean allowing them to go outside the house and be seen by strangers. Grave implications were to follow. When given the opportunity to flee from shadowy corners, women would end up denying the corner and seeking refuge in a wider world. If they found the key to open the doors and break the boundaries, they would experiment and learn, make errors and correct them in the process. They would demand the space they had always been denied. So, a battle began inside the tranquil andarunis and disrupted the 'birunis' and spread throughout the town and over-spilt into the desert and woke the undergrowth up from its thousands year sleep. The history was turning its pages in haste. This battle was portrayed in Suri's fist poem on her experience of the unveiling:

'Boiling, boiling, the ferment of earth.

bursting, bursting bubbles in the air.

Marching, marching my feet ahead.

Breathing is made easy a task.

Today is all mine,

and tomorrow belongs

to the future.'

Getting ready to leave for the reception, Javad khan could not keep his eyes away from his wife, his beloved, the apple of his eye, the beauty of all beauties. He would not leave the room, tiptoed around her and made comments, sent a kiss, sat motionless, only to stand up and fold Suri in his arms, inhaling the scent of her body, taking kisses from undiscovered curves. Suri would object and shy away, smile and push him aside, hide her elation between the lines of a frown to discourage her husband from seducing her at such a crucial time. She had recently cut her hair to shoulder length and in a painstaking process of five hours, sitting motionless, the hairdresser, selecting, soaking, rolling and at last, ringlets pouring down. Wave, after wave, after wave, surrounding her face. The middle connection of eyebrows was removed, her beautiful eyes, standing out decorated slightly by a line of sormeh; the hidden line of her cheekbones rose-colored by sorkhab, two lines of white teeth glittering inside her full lips. Her reflection in the looking glass. The looking glass reflecting her beauty and a melting agony of what to wear to demonstrate her charm and grace. Displaying her newly-

116

tailored clothes, for her and Javad khan to choose from. Green, black, dark grey, rustic brown, copper, gold, platinum; a mixture of nature's colours caressing their eyes. The collection of hats of matching colours brought from abroad by special order. Walking around, sitting down, holding a dress to her body, begging the looking glass for advice. And finally, Javad khan came to his senses: 'it will be late darling. We have to make up our minds.' He whispered to her as his eyes were transfixed on her belly, slightly standing out.

'A life will soon be moving inside this beautiful body, hers and mine. Shaping, developing. Growing into a human. A child. A beloved who is much loved even before its time has begun. Oh, dear God, what part of its tiny body is taking shape now, at this moment? A finger? A toe? A cell in the brain? The brain, the brain. The centre of the universe. When will the brain become a brain? How does mind enter the brain, taking the soul inside? Whose soul will it be? Mine, Suri's? Is soul separate from the chemicals of the brain? When is the moment that the foetus will opt for maleness or femaleness? Oh, dear God, how ignorant I am to all these, how can I demonstrate this immense love that is boiling inside me for this body that has accepted me inside her and is nourishing part of me to produce our child? Oh, my dearest, I am an outsider, ignorant to so many things, yet a party to your being. My darling, part of my existence.'

The foetus, unshaped, undecided and unwilling to enter the world of questions and expectations coiled itself into a tiny ball and remained undetected. Suri took advantage of Javad khan's meditating state, which he sometimes engaged in, and put on a long, black skirt, a copper-colour jacket with stripes of gold and cat-walked in front of him to get his approval. He smiled in satisfaction, rose to his feet and held enveloped her in full. My darling. The centre of my universe. Javad was in a three-piece European suit of grey gabardine, a stiff-collared shirt and a striped black and white narrow cravat tailored for his handsome figure. His clean-shaven face with the tiny moustache atop his lips gave him an air of poetic know-how. In all, when he put on his hat, Javad resembled a European ambassador to an eastern country. Suri was trying to remember the manners her husband had taught her. Her eyes were unsettled. Making final touches to their outfit, checking to see if everything matched, hand in hand, they set out to capture history in the making. Then, the horizon was bright without a hint of gloomy clouds. Clouds were hiding mischievously behind grey mountains.

Fourteen

The reception to mark the unveiling of Karmanieh women was held at the governor's grand mansion, located in the middle of a well-kept Persian garden, outside and away from the heart of the city. From the veranda facing the gate at the far end of the garden, two wide lanes paralleled each other, led into a wide marble staircase at the foot of the hall, along which flowerbeds were displaying their blooms. Embraced by the two lanes, the source of a brook of cool, clear water streamed rhythmically into the wide rectangular pond; in the middle of which, a contingent of gold fish were playing as fountains were sprinkling high in the sky. Shirazi emerald cedars were touching shoulders with dancing cypresses and poplars alongside the high walls, shielding the insiders from intruding eyes. Guarded by two men standing at either side, the gate was opening slowly to the guests and shutting quickly as they slid inside. Torches and candles were lighting the pathway.

The grand reception hall sparkled in its mirrored walls and hand-carved painted ceilings. Wall to wall were Persian rugs, hand-made furniture alongside the hall and chandeliers in their majestic glitter. Servants in formal costume waiting nearby. The governor's wife, a tiny, slim-built lady of fifty years, with searching eyes, a once well-shaped neck, now sunken into her shoulders, carrying the experience of years living abroad, standing at the door in her stylish velvet evening dress and feather hat to welcome the guests. She and the reception hall kept their smiles until the last guest arrived and the party started.

The hall was panting with anxiety, screaming with excitement as the reception began and continued and finally came to a close and calm returned. Lights sparkled over the group of women, who formed a colourful bunch, stood at a corner in total awkwardness. Sweat running down. Stiff, stern and void of expression. Men shied away at the very far, denying the existence at the other end. History looked down and released an aching sigh. How long would it take for these creatures to get used to their own presence in public and reclaim their space? That microscopic space which had forcefully been allocated to them?

Mrs Etesam al-Saltaneh, was walking through the hall, doing her best to put every one at ease. She introduced each to the other, smiled and conversed, released the tension. She knew all too well the sense of awkwardness and anxiety, which over-powered the self. A self that was about to emerge from infancy and create an identity of its own. A self that was far from making an independent personality, claiming its own space now that history had rendered her an opportunity to come out of anonymity. In the absence of the perception of ownership to space and with the built-in inferiority of body and soul, how could one expect a sudden confidence on the part of women? How could they claim and reclaim their existence equal to men? One had to travel over years into the future in order to see real change in the situation of women in Persia. They would have the future to themselves but for now, women were nothing but an extension of men hidden from history.

Mrs Etesam al-Saltaneh was a wise woman who had seen the world over and was aware of women's anxieties and their lack of self worth. Earlier in the century, accompanied by her diplomat husband, she had travelled throughout Europe, had attended receptions in Paris and London, where she had been overtly avoided and covertly pointed at by the European Ladies, who raised their eyebrows at 'this Oriental woman in Western outfit'. Initially, her weakness, and her alienation and lack of experience and this hostile world outside the confinement of Persian harems impaired her. As time passed and she learnt foreign languages and western manners, she was quick to put the ladies in their place by her sharp tongue.

As the ambassador's wife, she had to attend receptions and parties. There, women would approach her and ask questions only to amuse their audience, who would gather around, watching: 'do you still ride camels in your country my dear? How many of your husbands' wives have remained behind in Persia and why did he choose you to bring with him?'

Fury boiling, yet contained, Mrs Etesam al-Saltaneh would often reply sternly: 'no, we ride horses just as you ride them on your Saturday racings and annual Ascots and yes, sometimes we ride camels as well. Is there a problem with that? I am the only wife and my husband has not left any behind.' And then the women would smirk and walk away, leaving her bereft and bewildered.

* * *

Suri was amongst the few who were at ease throughout the reception. Over years and whenever there was an opportunity and as part of her education, Javad khan had talked to her, showed her photos and sketched full pictures and descriptive details of life outside the enclosures of Persia; where men and women walk hand in hand on the streets and nannies take the children out in their prams and ladies dress up to accompany their husbands on social occasions. As a mark of respect, men touch the tip of their hats as a lady approaches and passes by them. There would be an exchange of pleasantries if the person is known to them. Javad khan repeated the gestures at home, making Suri choke with laughter. With patience and pleasure, he taught her to walk straight, to raise the tip of her long skirt with her gloved hand.

Now, self-awareness and confidence poured out of Suri's figure as she walked in and smiled at the governor and held out her hand to shake his. Gone were the days she was taken into the town square to look at the world through the holes in her 'rubandeh'. A small sack of potato, rolling, halting, wondering, looking. That looking glass had long been broken into a thousand pieces.

'Today for the first time

I saw myself

in the looking glass that hanged

from the bend of the road.

All heads turned

mine included

to look at this beauty

which had been deprived of gleam

since time began.

The looking glass turned and smiled

in approval.

Time sat witness

to frame me as I was.

And there I stood

in the memory of

an everlasting mind.'

Fifteen

Long before the order for the unveiling was issued, Karmanieh witnessed a swarm of foreign presence. The Americans and the British had already established churches and schools to cultivate seeds of Christianity. In the autumn of 1933, Reverend Jackson, the new head of the British Missionary school; broad-shouldered, tall, cold-eyed, with a deep, commanding voice and a dry smile, accompanied by his petite, nervous wife Jane, Sister Elena, short, round-figured with a coarse voice, shiny cheeks and lines of kindness on her face; and Sister Rose, firm, maiden, subdued; all from Southampton, travelled from Britain to Iran across high seas and treacherous lands until they reached the Persian Gulf. Their final destination was, of course, the city of Karmanieh.

On the southern coasts of Persia, the Great Empire of Great Britain had a full presence. To assist the missionaries, as was their duty, Colonel Smith from the Empire's Navy took with him a brigade of trained commandos and accompanied the convoy from the port of Bushehr through the dangerous mountain peaks which sheltered armed bandits, across the deserts of south east Persia, down to the city of Karmanieh. Their predecessors left through the same route and returned safely to a life of rain and routine in a quiet village somewhere in their home county of Essex. Shortly after their arrival, the missionaries took over the church and the school which catered for non-Muslims. The church had a congregation of a handful of Christians.

Monsieur Jackobsin, the representative of the French government, was a pleasant, good-humoured man and his wife Madame Brigitte, puffy, scented with a radiant face and an-everlasting warmth, had lived in the town for many years. Comrade Tamarov, comrade Rustov and comrade Binacov, representatives of the Republic of the Soviet Union, were there as well. And the Germans in their abundance. Although Reza Shah was a British choice, it was said that he had a strong tendency towards the Germans. Coming from the 'civilised world' these Europeans carried with them an illusionary air of supremacy over the natives and intense rivalry amongst themselves, which was manifested at every opportunity. Their games often affected local politics and drew innocent Karmanians in a labyrinth of thrills, treachery and double-dealings. Such was the state of affairs as Reza Shah, himself a by-product of such policies, began his programmes of modernisation.

* * *

One hazy afternoon of the Autumn of 1934, as Karmanieh people woke up from their lazy siesta and noise filled the streets and shops reopened and the bazaar overflowed with passers-by, shoppers and errand boys, and dark clouds ambushed the sky while lights were frantically carving a passage through, an incident sent shock waves through the town. That was well before the official reception for the unveiling of women of Karmanieh had been announced.

Suddenly, two female foreigners appeared on the main street in well-tailored suits and matching hats, enjoying the stroll as if on a Frankfurt Strausse. The sight of these women initially froze people in their place. Then a childish curiosity took over and a circle formed around them. Un-alarmed, they continued walking with a slow pace, conversing with their male colleagues as the circle moved alongside them. Reaction and opposition was delayed until the group reached the end of the street and curved its way into the entrance to the grand bazaar. Then some rushed to the grand mosque to inform the Imam of such an outrageous act in the land of the holy religion. The round-faced, rose-scented Imam was sitting at the top of the chamber engaging in a heated debate on the necessity and the best method his congregation use to wash their anus after they emptied themselves. How many fingers should they use, two, three? How do they start the ritual, top to bottom or vice versa? The thought of playing with their genitals had already aroused much excitement. Suddenly, interrupted by the angry mob, the Imam was taken away from the joyful moment of authority over such an important issue. He looked deep into the eyes of the most agonised elder, who waited patiently for an answer. Scratching his beard he sank into meditation. Caught between two dilemmas; his duty to the mob, who sought his guidance, and his inability to lead them into protest. Was the matter related to the Order that had been issued by the central government to put into effect women's unveiling and he, as the Imam of the grand mosque was made aware of it before it had reached the governor's office? Did the Germans know of such an order and so acted upon it without an official inauguration?

The Imam knew that when the document had finally arrived at the governor's desk, he had not paid much attention to the broken seal. He had been shocked by the tone and the directness of the Order. 'Raise people's consciousness to the necessity of the unveiling, yet carry it out regardless.' The governor spoke of his concern to his wife, who in normal circumstances gave him ample advice but on this occasion she did not offer much consolation. It did not matter that he was in agreement with the order. To put it to the town's religious authorities and to get their support was a paramount task. Either had to resort to force and intimidation or abandon the project altogether.

The Imam sat still with closed eyes. He knew that the avenue of objection to what the foreigners had done was not easy to walk. His far-reaching sight saw that the country was on the road to modernisation and that the unveiling of females was high on the agenda and would be carried out regardless. Life in exile to a remote corner was not a desirable option should he raise his voice in protest. So, he mumbled a few crushed words to the waiting mob and excused himself to a hasty exit. By the time the people returned to the scene of the crime, where the infidels had been strolling, their footprints had faded into the darkness.

* * *

Reverend Jackson accompanied by his wife and the two Sisters, arrived on time to find a proper place, muttering among themselves. Madam Brigitte, wearing a bright coloured dress and matching hat, walked across the hall, trying to get close to the local ladies and make friends with them. Her charm distinguished her amongst the foreigners, who distanced from the Karmanians. The few Persian words she spoke with a native dialect helped her to make her way through. She and Suri fell for a deep and lasting friendship the minute they shook hands. Javad khan explained in his broken French, that his wife, Suri could not speak but could write her thoughts in Persian and Russian. 'She would be delighted if Madam would later spare the time to teach her French.'

The Russian delegation, Comrade Tamarov, Comrade Rustov and Comrade Binacov felt at home as they conversed with Javad khan and listened to his Muscovite accent in admiration and delight. As night fell, the guests loosened up, the reception grew warmer and the chime of noise, the clatter of knives and forks swirled around and danced with the lights of the chandeliers. On that January evening of the year 1935, this international gathering convened in Karmanieh to mark the unveiling, uncovering and discovering of women.

But despite all precautions it did not go as planned. When the guests arrived and just as the gates were about to shut, a high pitched roar was heard from inside the garden and shouts from the outside. A group of people had gathered on the dusty road that curved and disappeared into the desert. Under the silence of the night falling heavy upon the city, a coup de'etat was waged by the desert weather and the garden inhabitants and the mob outside in protest to the occasion of the unveiling in the land of holy religion. The tall Shirazi cedars having no previous experience of such perverseness and outraged to the point of rioting, saw it their duty to protect the populace. After much roaring and relaying threatening words they blocked the way to the curious eyes of the stars, which had gathered in the Milky Way to watch the proceedings. The moon, shining in full and in total agreement with the occasion, slid the curve of her slender body behind a cloud just as a cyclone swept through the edges of the city. Flowers, astonished at first, ashamed then and humoured later at such an act of stupidity, giggled and mocked the cedars for their macho attitude and hoped they would shortly come to their senses and unblock the road forward. The chief cedar, with its long needles, demanded an immediate stop to the giggles. The cyclone roared and darkness fell on the garden. Scents and smells were no longer splashing over. Bewildered, little gerberas turned their heads and looked away. Geraniums opened their mouths in protest but were silenced by the horror in the eyes of the tuberoses. Roses, braver than ever, closer than others stuck their thorns into the cedar trunks but these were not impressed. A willow that was combing her hair in the dancing breeze a minute before broke into tears seconds later. Weeping for a nation that had lost the way forward and wanted to march into darkness. Finally, the fountains, now reaching high, by the force of the subterranean waters turned direction and splashed in full force over the cedars and their instigators, who had gathered in their hundreds at the gate, shouting in protest. In fear of being shot by the armed soldiers, people dispersed. The Imam of the small mosque heading the protest slid into obscurity and fled in fear of being beheaded in the process. The cyclone hurried into the abyss of the desert and the unveiling, uncovering and discovering of women went ahead thereafter.

* * *

Six months later, receptions turned into ice-cold gatherings. Tired of receptioning the mass of unbearably hard-headed populace, whose women took their veils off once inside the venues and put them on once outside, the governor's wife issued an ultimatum. The governor sent a telegram to the Capital begging the authorities to be rid of the receptions. 'Excellencies, please try to understand. It is of no avail. Women arrive unveiled but once on the street they veil themselves as they have done for thousands of years. Centuries veiled they have been and now they wonder why they have to be forced to unveil. Force, force is all they hate. Nothing has ever been gained by this coercion. Nothing. Mrs Etesam al-Saltaneh has lost her patience and has threatened to leave me. The mark of her smile has frozen on her lips and she is quivering uncontrollably.'

A few days later, a confidential telegram arrived: 'Never reveal to anybody that the Capital was made aware of this. Do what you think is best but pretending that the order is still in place.'

Thereafter, the streets had a quasi-colourful scene of some unveiled women who, like Suri, refused to bow to pressures and walked forward with an adamant air of self–awareness derived from the encouragement they received from their menfolk. But unveiling as a project faced defeat. Seeds of hatred at such an outrageous act in the land of the holy religion, where the ulama were the ultimate authority, planted itself at every corner. Martyrs lined across history to be martyred in order to save the faith from corruption. The earth held the seeds until some decades later the buds sprouted out of the compost of time and the fire rose from their bloom and burnt the unveiling, the uncovering, the modernisation, the advancement and the bones of the architect of that all. History walked backward and slid down an abyss where finding a way forward was an impossible task.

Sixteen

Suri's belly was expanding, bringing into life what Javad khan and she were waiting anxiously to embrace. The winter of the unveiling of women in Persia had sailed into spring and summer was about to arrive and take charge. Being pregnant at such young age, Suri was struggling to familiarise herself with the existence inside her body. It was increasing its size and volume, influencing her temperament, working its way into her soul. She was experiencing an amazing phenomenon; growing another life out of her own. A child soon to become an independent person. At times Suri was apprehensive, then marvelled at the act of nature as she was getting used to her new body. Every step of pregnancy enlivened her spirit and enriched the nature of her experience. Every day was a new beginning, a road to discovering how she was the maker and the creator of another life. At night, she awoke and listened to the movement of her cells now transforming rapidly. During the day, she often hid from sight and sat in a meditating state, measuring the changes in her body.

Once in the fifth month of her pregnancy, she woke up with ecstasy, shaking Javad, who opened his sleepy eyes and jumped out of bed only to notice that Suri had felt the baby's movements in its waterbed. Perhaps it woke up and demanded food. Perhaps its brain had just received the first wavelength informing it of an outside existence and wanted to communicate. Perhaps the incense perfume of its mother had just reached it and it was trying to store and remember its particles. Then silence. Javad rushed to his mother, Ghamar khanum and dragged her in, only to be informed that from then on, the baby would live a full life, would wake up, kick, play and grow faster than expected. There, Ghamar khanum held Suri in her arms and reassured her that there was nothing to worry about. The baby listened to the noises filtering through layers of flesh and kicked in delight. 'So, there was an existence beyond its waterbed!'

Meanwhile, Javad khan's world was expanding from the body he adored so much. Many nights he woke up to watch Suri's sleeping face, soon to be a mother. And he wondered and worried. Had he given her all the love he could stretch out of himself? Was there any left for their shared product, the fruit of their life, taking shape inside his beloved? What more could he do? What else could he offer? He knew that pregnant mothers would love to talk to their unborn babies and hum lyrics to get them used to the ancient songs and ancient tunes. Babies relish moments of solitude when they are still in their waterbed, eyes closed, blood giving them enough nourishment and the sound of lyrics reaching from the unknown. Javad khan would often put his ear on Suri's belly and listen to the baby's movements. He would put his mouth close to where he thought the baby's head was located and sing with sweet pleasure, lyrics he knew Suri would have yearned to sing. The baby cherished these moments. Its little hands waved, its little feet kicked, a well-shaped head on the shoulder with a brain that had already formed its own thought. 'I am loved outside the enclosure of my waterbed.' At such moments Suri would look at her husband with flames in the pupil of her eyes and stroke his hair and kiss him gently: 'Sing your songs my darling. This is our world. Far from worry, soaked in the warmth of our love.'

One day at such a moment, Suri wrote a few lines in celebration of their joy and handed it to her husband, who relished every word of it:

'You set sail in me

and carried in your hands

a torch for me to see

the beginning and the end.

A breeze is mellowing

through my veins,

the elation of

passion and love.

A seedling is growing

from my flesh and

love is too light a word.

to portray my jubilation.'

* * *

All these set aside, most of the times, Suri was possessive of her baby. She understood that it was her body, her flesh and blood that was making the baby and no matter how much she loved her husband or him, her, this new life was hers exclusively. She was rejecting interference from the outside though advice rained from all sides. Gradually and as her pregnancy developed, she was drawing lines between her world and the outside. Invisible, hidden, yet distinguished. She spent hours on her own examining the changes in her young body, wondering how she was growing in volume. Looking at herself in the looking glass: her breasts filling, the nipples getting darker, the line of her slender waist disappearing, her flat belly, enlarging and her pelvis widening. She would measure round her belly and write the changes down. She wondered from which of them the baby would pick its looks and temperament. What would be her feelings once the baby was out in her arms? Suri had become secretive with her motherhood. She talked to her baby inwards and promised that she would take care of her with her wild passion and eternal love.

Javad yearned to talk to the baby but as Suri's pregnancy progressed, she rejected him and warned him in commanding words: 'I am going to make it clear that there would be some secrets between me and my baby that would be kept as secrets. I will not share them with you, or anyone else.' At such times, Javad would hold her in his arms and murmur in her ear: 'how do you know my darling that secrets exist between you and your baby? This is ours, a shared product. It is a mutual experience we are going through. Please, my darling, don't shut me out. I want to be part of you and stay in. I want to live in the enclosure of your heart. Oh, my darling what has come over you to treat me as an outsider!' But Suri would become adamant and then retreat to her room. At such moments Javad's eyes swelled with tears and jealousy filled his heart as he withdrew from sight. Yet there existed showers of love in a singing voice, strokes of tenderness rushing through their blood. Suri and her baby were shielded by the intensity of this love. No place for worry at that moment in time.

* * *

It was dawn and the cool air was melting into the early heat and the strip of lines dividing the darkness over the mountains surrounding the city were breaking by the lights rising from behind, informing the inhabitants that the sun was about to majestically emerge from the horizon. The midwife, elegant, professional, with a bag full of surgical materials, arrived in time to help Suri deliver her first child. Although Suri had stated and emphasised that she wished to have her husband by her side, an army of women pushed their way through the delivery room, to witness the birth of yet another child; an occurrence which repeated itself over time and space. Against both their wishes, Javad was kept away and ordered to stay away. No one had ever seen a man present at such a female experience. Decades later, the philosophy of childbirth changed direction and men's right to stay in the delivery room was asserted and emphasised. It was believed that men would be more responsible, should they witness the pain mothers go through while giving birth. Then, time was behind such change of heart. Javad was desperate, furious, and afraid. He was the only one who had travelled into the depth of Suri's heart and knew her fears and her loneliness. He had promised not to leave her during labour. It seemed impossible that she would pass through so much pain all by herself. The answer was no. He was not allowed. He was ordered to patiently wait outside the delivery room for women to do their job. Javad khan hid from sight, toed and froed, banged his head against the wall, sobbed and cried and wished Suri could endure the pain and deliver the child safely. 'Oh, dear god, my darling, the light of my eyes, my love, how did I betray you! My promise is broken and you are parted from me when you most needed my support.' And unable to express the severity and the intensity of bursting in flames, Suri gave herself up to the command of women.

And finally, the earth opened up; a head appeared, two bright eyes looked around, the well-shaped body of a female rolled into the midwife's hands. Looking up at the crowd, finding them at odds with her taste, she released a loud cry. Her voice travelled through the glaciers and melted the ice away. Javad rushed inside and against all the warnings held Suri in his arms and they both cried out of joy and the fear of an incident, which had not occurred. Tears rolled down Ashraf khanum's eyes as she saw the love between her daughter and Javad. Bitter was the day Suri stepped into this world. Sweet is this moment that her child is being born. Suri held the baby in her arms and rested her head on Javad's shoulder. She was in jubilation, at peace with herself and the world. Content!

* * *

Suri's experience of the birth, her fears and her doubts were piled in a series of scribbles she kept in a hidden box. She had actually kept a journal from the first day she learnt to write. First, her notes did not make sense, scribbles of childhood experiences, of things, events; feelings with no organised form or context. Later, she obtained a meticulous method and a sophisticated style, in rhythm with the thirst she developed for reading, writing and learning, reading and comprehending, memorising and writing. 'Reference for the future and the past', she wrote on the margin of a page. No one was aware of this hidden records office. Yet it grew in volume and size as time went by.

On the first night of Sara's birth and as the house went to sleep and dawn was yet to arrive, Suri woke up to register the moments of agony, of uncertainty about the baby's health, of its looks and sex and whether she would be mute like her. At the beginning of this chapter it read, 'When one speaks, words vanish into the air, one can deny them, add things to them, erase them or change them altogether. Once one puts the words down, they stay there forever. Now I wish to put down my feelings and understanding of this unique experience. The experience of giving birth to a female. I might be too young to truly grip the complexities of the universe but I know that I went through unbearable pain to give birth to her. There would be no barriers between Sara and me since she is an extension of me, made of my flesh and blood. I will try my best to open her eyes to the joys of life and take her away from the pains of life. I know that as a female she carries the burden of history on her shoulders; silenced, concealed, shrouded. Yet I hope her universe would be different from mine, and she lives in a better world and makes the world a better place. I know that through her I will live to eternity. From this moment I aim to register life in this cosmos for her to trespass and grab its intimate moments, relish in it and cherish the first reflections of her arrival and my resolution at her birth.'

And Sara at sixty four years of age, who then lived in a cottage in a tranquil green village in the orbit of London, a few yards away from a church, which in its yard buried the eight hundred years old bones of the Saxons, and attracted a congregation of non-believers by way of Bach and Mozart concerts, and where its handsome priest flirted with married women and kept young boys at hand for rainy days; opened the case of her mother's private thoughts sent to her by special mail and walked some sixty four steps backwards to witness the fate of a family she was once a part of and later left behind by forces of undetected disasters.

Seventeen

Suri cherished her motherhood with pride and excitement. Yet no one expected her to rear the baby on her own. She lived in an extended family and there was an army of volunteers to see to the baby's physical needs. But unlike most women of her time, who gave their babies to the wet nurses and in-laws and themselves tended to their husbands, Suri was a natural mother and aimed to care for her baby by herself. She did not want to be deprived of the pleasures of motherhood and so she firmly took responsibility for Sara's upbringing. On this matter she had already negotiated with her husband and they both agreed upon the subject. Javad khan was the backbone of Suri's strength. With his backing, she stood up for herself and demanded what she wished. Javad khan himself was sharing the parenting; an area that until then was a women's only domain.

In those days, fathering in its modern context was unheard of. Men used to plant a seed and go astray only to return and demand full ownership once the child reached an age to be separated from the mother, the carer and nurturer. Cruel as it was, fathers had full rights to a product grown out of women. Women were not counted as full humans and had no rights to their own children. Women were the fertile farmlands for planting seeds in order to reproduce children. Later, they had to hand them over to others, males to the outside and females to the inside world. One, springing outwards, the other sliding inwards into the obscurity of yet another household. To the world, women were men's property, their subject. Men themselves were the king's subjects and together they were the God's flock of sheep. A chain of subjectivity stretching along history, its knots tying across time, choking the first subject, the flock of females. There was much talk of women as humans and half the population and a source of extra workforce in the capitalist system. Yet females were far from having their own voice. They were little dots alongside each other, hanging loose. Whether a time would come when they would walk on the same road, shoulder to shoulder with men was out of reach and out of mind.

Suri thought a lot about these dilemmas and talked to her husband. Sometimes she saw her own situation and wondered whether Sara would have to follow the path of a thousand footsteps into the obscurity of a husband's house? Suri knew that Javad khan was an understanding man. A rarity in a community, where men were men and women were women. On the other hand, Javad's aspirations of making revolutions and changing the world had long been summarised in enlightening Suri and making his family a model for others to follow. Javad khan had promised to assist Suri to raise Sara as a free woman. On the night of Sara's arrival, Suri assured her little baby to sleep sound and let the future take care of it all. She should rest assured for that moment in time.

Future proved that there were rules one had to observe, customs to follow, and elders to listen to. Cracks here, gaps there separated Suri and her husband from others but they could not create a continent of their own and live in a wonderland. Family and traditions, society and the unforeseen incidents barricaded them at every step. Future sat witness in a crystal ball.

* * *

Five years later in 1940, Suri delivered her third and last child. Her health was affected by the last pregnancy and as a result the couple decided to bring the chapter of reproduction to a close. They had two daughters, Sara and Shireen and a baby boy, Sasan. Triangles of love at the heart of the universe. Javad khan lifted Suri's spirit once she was well enough to sit with him on the veranda and enjoy the lazy sunshine of one winter afternoon. 'No more children my darling. What we have is more than enough. Thank God you have gained your health. From now on, we will focus on our children's education and their upbringing.' Having three children had changed their relationship to some extent simply because little time was spared for them to spend together as they used to. Suri had grown out of her teenage years and mothering had shrunken pleasurable moments they used to share in uninterrupted conversations followed by anecdotes Suri painted over the pages, so eclipsing the occasional blues that appeared at the corner of Javad's deep eyes. Gradually, Suri's playfulness and cheerful character was squeezed out and replaced by her parental role and responsibilities. Javad khan was still madly in love with her. She was an excellent mother to his children and the loving wife he adored. Javad's heart followed Suri all the time; from one corner to the other, one moment to the next and the blaze of his affection filled their loving hearts.

They talked about their children most of the time and painted a clear picture in their minds how to raise their trio, the source of their jubilation. They planned in advance and in great detail to raise them with much love and care but let them have their own space as well. No way would they let their children live their lives in the confinement of Karmanieh. They wanted them to leave the small city and explore high seas and blue skies, surf, and fly. Experience the world with their parents at the start, on their own thereafter. Future would fulfil their dreams and they would see their children grow up and make something of themselves. Yet at times they moved through waves of worry because they were not sure whether they were building a dreamland or real foundations. In making decisions and putting them to practice, both their past lives played an important role. Suri remembered and referred to her own childhood, a blend of sweet and sour memories; the liberty of growing up amongst the servants and the unrefined love she received from them on the one hand, and people's attitudes to her disability and the harem's strict rules that had injured her heart, on the other. She had pressed for her views right from the beginning, pressed and emphasised. So, time glided through hours of questions, arguments and experiment. Away from worry, concealed from disasters.

* * *

The trio were growing up forming their own distinguished personalities and that showed in their daily routine as Sara chirped, Shireen thundered and Sasan crawled on his plump hands and feet. Sometimes, Sara would appear at the door, dusty, muddy and in tears, her voice afflicted and Shireen would follow head strong, defensive, and unrepentant. Every moment was filled with the excitement of fights that would break between them and others and then assemblies of peace that would convene, agreements that would be signed, sweets and cookies distributed in celebration of peace as they rolled over each other and started alloveragain. The cyclone of noise rose at dawn and curled up through the day until darkness would set rule to the universe and night would fall heavy on the household. Then the elders breathed a sigh of relief only to be awakened at dawn to a fresh round.

Gradually, Suri had become a distinguished young woman in her own right. She had the breath of life in her soul and that reflected in her manner as she walked with gravity and exuberance. She was at the heart of the high society and the talk of the town. Her presence at the parties and gatherings with her fashionable outfits and latest hairstyles brought much delight to the audience as she held her husband's hand, smiled and exchanged pleasantries and then joined her friends, especially Madam Brigitte who was close to her like a sister. Yet her lifestyle and the upbringing of her children were a betrayal to her aristocratic and conservative roots. In the eyes of her parents, she and her husband were eccentrics who lived out of norm. She knew that as a non-conformist she would never be spared the scorn and the blame should anything go wrong in her life. But she had the support of her husband and the security he had provided for her had made her a very confident woman. Besides, Madam Brigitte was always present in the scene to fill the gaps Javad was not able to fill. Suri and this friend and confidant were together at social gatherings, out on the street or at each other's homes. They exchanged views and talked about the life they lived and the restrictions that tradition put in the way of advancement and the necessity of change. They complained about the constraint women were experiencing although Reza Shah had sanctioned their integration into the society. Madam Brigitte travelled to Paris every once in a while and brought Suri cases of Parisian fashions. By then, she had lived in Karmanieh for twenty years, spoke Persian with a sweet local accent and considered herself a native. She believed that traditional practices, which had deep roots in ancient culture, would have to give way to modern ideas. There was no other alternative. She assured her friend that aristocratic classes that kept the class society in place were a breed on the verge of extinction.

Suri and Javad khan never doubted Madam Brigitte. Nevertheless, the class system and inequality existed in society, even in their own household. Their children had privileges far greater than their playmates, whose mothers worked in Javad khan's household dawn to dusk and stood at the door, hands crossed on the chest, ready to take orders while food was served; and male servants walked alongside Javad khan's horse as he rode into the countryside on hunting expeditions.

It was obvious that Javad, now a man of important social responsibilities, had distanced from his youthful aspirations of changing the world single-handedly and making it equal to everyone, but he still held on to some of his socialist ideas and enlightened Suri to some degree. Suri had read about the October Revolution and the French Revolution. Besides, the Iranian

Constitutional movement still lived in memories and people talked about it and intellectuals recited revolutionary songs that were written during those exciting years. Songs which had entered folk culture and travelled across mountains, where mothers repeated the lyrics to their unborn children.

Suri often read Iraj Mirza's comics portraying veiled women as poor creatures shrouded in darkness and knew Aref's inflammatory poems by heart. Yet Javad knew that they had to wait a long time for the society to mature and his dream of a modern country to materialise.

* * *

And time was passing and happiness was stretching to the horizon. By the early 1940, against objections from Suri's family and the education authorities, Sara was attending the English Missionary's school. Madam Brigitte had taken to herself to teach her French. The three children were growing up rapidly, Sara turning into a thoughtful, calm soul, Shireen, intense, volatile, and headstrong, squeezing her way through life, changing every moment in time. Javad khan had received a big promotion and was appointed the head of the Education Department for the whole province, which required long hours at the office, travelling, visiting and inspecting. In recent years, he had often travelled to the Capital Tehran to receive further training. Had it not been for the sake of their small children, Suri would have accompanied her husband.

For almost ten years, Suri sojourned through the euphoria of a contented life and a peaceful existence wrapped in love. Safe, sound, assured. Asleep, hidden from sight were worries. Gods of happiness, of calmness, of soothing nights and cooling days had stationed their headquarters nearby, just close to the door.

Eighteen

And further down across the city, deep in the desert, throughout the country and in the vast world, a hidden terror had begun to surface and spread. A horror that was secretly conceived in the womb of the twentieth century. Twentieth Century. Twentieth century was the century of delinquency and gruesome revelations in human history. From the onset, it stumbled on an uneven road, which took the earth and its inhabitants not by surprise but through the erupting volcanoes of wars, upheavals, revolutions and coups. Far from centuries before, the impregnated twentieth century had in its womb greedy babies thirsty for money, for power, for blood and for war. While memories were still fresh from the trenches of the First World War that killed millions and set ruin to towns and cities and the bloody Proletarian Revolution in Russia was passing through its infancy to become a rival to the world of capitalism, rumours travelled mouth to mouth, house to house and across the globe of yet another war. A hidden terror was emerging in full force, sweeping across, sparkling fire and burning millions alive, destroying nations and civilisations.

The Second World War, the by-product of greed and blind racism, was creating the plague of a giant rising from the land of Beethoven and Schiller. From inside the time capsule, a giant was rising with a thousand tongues. Hitler. Hitler emerged and took power with the intention to set the world ablaze. Stalin was yet to replace him as a mass murderer. Other dictators were yet to emerge and replace Stalin or walk alongside him across the terrain of the twentieth century. Hitler, Stalin, Pol Pot, Pinochet, leaders of all shades and races, faiths and sects.

Europe, the civilised world, the cradle of human dignity and human endeavours, unaware of the catastrophe, awoke too late to halt the disaster of the Second World War. Suddenly, the globe was pulled into a gothic novel. A ball of fire was spinning around, its particles falling down, engulfing everything. Hitler was born to instigate hatred and war. In the span of a short time, he managed to create enemies from obscurity, to divide races into superiors and inferiors, to colonise countries and sub-divide and rearrange territories. Social Nationalism, hand in hand with Capitalism, as opposed to Socialism and Communism took roots first in Germany, then further and farther and beyond. The advancement of technology in the war industry, the invention of well-equipped flying machines and the aggressiveness of Hitler's propaganda machine drove the world into a frenzy of killing fields. Initially, the capitalist world appreciated Hitler's intention to destroy the first socialist state and even encouraged him and co-operated with him to some extent. Gradually, they themselves became victims of his aggression as he attacked neighbouring countries and annexed them to his empire. In the process of creating the most horrifying empire history had ever seen humans were divided into those who were to live and those who had to be exterminated by way of forced labour, displacement, prison camps and ultimately gas chambers and death squads. So, humankind experienced human unkindness and years of typhus, years of cholera and years of ultimate misery registered themselves in memory.

In the span of a short time some countries joined in and sided with Hitler, others became adversaries, the majority fell victim to his atrocities. By the early 1941, World War Two expanded and moved outside Europe. Oddly enough, Iran declared her neutrality. Neutrality! That made sense to no one. Iran's geopolitics; thousands of miles of borders with the Soviet Union in the north, thousands of miles of shores along the Persian Gulf in the south, Turkey to her west, Afghanistan and India to her east. Sitting at the apex of a torpedo and declaring neutrality!

By the early 1940s, flames of war had already engulfed Iran's borders from all sides. The cradle of her kingdom was crumbling and Reza Shah was about to be swept away from power. The west suspected that Iran's policies of 'neutrality' favoured the Nazis; the country was invaded from all sides. The army that Reza Shah had built with much pride and passion did not last long to resist. Like paper soldiers, it disintegrated and dispersed within days. Iran fell into the hands of the Soviets in the north and the British in the south. Reza Shah was forced into exile and his young son Mohammed Reza replaced him. The country plunged into chaos, shortages and disease.

War reached borders of Karmanieh sooner than expected. Shortages brought the poison of war closer to home. Along with the population of Karmanieh, who sat witness to the madness spinning around them, Javad khan was specifically concerned about the catastrophe. The Soviet Union was his second country and over the years, he had kept contact with his Russian friends at the consulate, who were often present at the lavish dinner parties he held at his house in the presence of his beloved wife. More than that, Javad did not approve of the Allies' invasion although he was aware of the underlying reasons to prevent Hitler invading Russia through Iran. Yet one would think that these developments did not crack the wall of happiness that shielded Javad's family.

Nevertheless, an undetected worry was creeping into Javad khan's household. Suri could not put her finger on it but its presence was there from dawn to dusk. Suddenly, it was rumoured that the Russian representatives in Karmanieh had left the region. Suddenly, Javad was receiving letters from Tehran and Russia. Letters from comrades who had not written to him for almost a decade; of whose whereabouts Javad was not aware. Or was he not? Gradually, Javad's behaviour began to change. He was apprehensive, kept to himself and avoided his wife's inquisitive eyes. Letters came with bundles of newsletters and pamphlets depicting heroism of the Russian people and their resistance. Mother Russia was fighting fiercely. Russia's front cities were caught in the crossfire and the ill-equipped Red army was losing ground. Part of the country was in ruins. Thousands of factories, the pride of Stalin's plan to create an advanced industrial state, were forced to close down. Yet men, women, young, old, children were fighting side by side to push the enemy out. And a call to the Internationalists to join in and do their duty. International solidarity. Suri was informed of this unknown link between her husband and the international solidarity slowly and over a period of time. A secret pact, an oath of brotherhood in times of hardship and threat.

* * *

Suri had never trekked the depth and the extent of Javad khan's involvement in the October Revolution, neither had he spoken of it in detail. Here a word, there the description of an incident, all in the passing words. In all, it was a secret well hidden for fear of becoming part of their daily life, too tempting to be left aside if all came out in the open. Suddenly, a new chapter opened in Suri's life and she was not prepared to read it through reason. Initially an upsurge of dialogue erupted the calm. Javad would sit with Suri at every opportunity and talk to her about the October Revolution and his involvement in the socialist upheavals. He would prepare lectures and seminars and deliver them to his young, bewildered wife who had no choice but to sit and listen. He would portray Russia as the bedrock of socialism, the heartbeat of human ideals. He would talk of the paradise socialism aimed to build at every corner, given time and opportunity. He would assure Suri that should Socialism be defeated, the whole world would plunge into the malice of Capitalism and Fascism and humanity would perish all in all.

Up until then, Suri was convinced that Javad's past was dead and buried in the past. Now, he was a devoted father, a loving husband and a public figure. How can the dead rise from their graves and claim what they had already left to history? How can a hidden enemy creep inside the breath of air, spreading its wings and slowly and meticulously occupying her husband's brain and awaken his forgotten memory? How would Russia's fight against Fascism, once remote and in the distance move into the neighbourhood and station outside their peaceful household? Suddenly, fear forced itself on Suri and she did not know how to absorb these revelations or react to them. Every corner of the house was standing guard.

Suri had never seen her husband in such swing of moods. One day he was high with passion, the next, serious, deep, inaccessible. Sometimes he would read extracts of the letters he received and analyse them with much heat. Gradually Suri was exposed to a new vocabulary, which by itself increased her knowledge but the price her family paid was far reaching. Commintern! International Socialists! Internationalists! Why did these words bear such heavy meanings? Had they come into existence and fed under the breast of history to tear her family apart? Suri was sitting witness to see her loving husband moving away with every word he spelled out and every letter he received, further and farther. She saw her inability to pull him to herself. The thread of daily life was loosening from the grip of Suri's firm hands. Suddenly, a powerful enemy had surfaced from obscurity and Suri needed much skill to deal with it in order to defeat it. She was frightened. What could she do? Where should she start? She consulted her husband's family and friends but no one came up with a firm resolution. The enemy had landed at her doorstep and Javad had allied with it.

On the other hand, Javad discovered that his only audience, Suri was moving her attention from the concept to the consequences of what she heard. Javad was mesmerised in his old dreams. International solidarity called upon him and asked him to leave his present life and save the first socialist country from the terror of fascism. Javad was swinging between diversified thoughts. Suri had to battle with this hidden enemy. If she denied its existence it was not going away and if she was too harsh on it, that would drive her husband farther and encourage him to totally side with her foe. If she was lenient to it that might as well encourage Javad to join in. The earth was shaking under her feet and she was stumbling while walking. Meanwhile, more letters arrived, telegrams arrived, people she had never met arrived and stationed themselves in her house to snatch her beloved, the arch of her existence.

These revelations did not happen over-night. In the first few months of the year 1940, Javad was still his own self and Suri was almost convinced that she should not let these developments darken their happiness. At times, Javad would become the loving husband and reassured his wife that all was well: 'darling, please try to understand, these are the ideals I held when I was involved in the revolution in my youth. Do you think that these are powerful enough to make me leave my family, you and the children and fight in the Russian fronts? Please my darling, rest assured that my love for you is stronger than anything else in the whole world. We will not be separated. Not now. Not ever. I am staying here with you and we will get old together.' At such time, Suri would swallow her choking tears and look at him intensely and kiss him head to toe. Yet her scribbles manifested the anxiety of her sleepless nights and the pretence she used to veil during the day.

Somewhere in the vicinity of the skin,

I see a malignant tumour,

swelling, suckling

the blood of tender love,

The breath of my brittle veins.

Down, hidden, down under

a scorpion has raised the tip of

his poisonous tail

to recoil, then suffocate

the velvet of earth's moisture.

The holocaust of my cloudy days

rain tears of pain and affliction.'

* * *

And letters arrived, begging, encouraging, inviting, and demanding. No one knew which one of the concepts was more powerful in convincing Javad khan to leave his family and join international brigades to fight in the Russian fronts. Did he know about internationalists from around Europe, who joined forces to save the Spanish republic? Did he know how many lost their lives to keep the Republic alive? Had it not been for his ties to Karmanieh, would Javad have packed and gone to join his comrades when the first letter arrived? There were no easy answers to these questions but it was obvious that Javad khan was wavering in a whirlpool of doubt. In the months ahead letters were hidden from Suri's keen eyes the minute they arrived. Finally, subdued, Javad stopped his lectures as quickly as he had started them. He pretended to live a normal life. Suri kept her calm on the surface pretending the intruders had not intruded, but at the same time she was searching for more clues to the situation and possibly prepared for the worst. Sometimes she would start a conversation about unimportant issues in their daily life. On one occasion she plunged her aim directly referring to the pile of correspondence she found accidentally. She would scribble her comments and concentrate her blazing gaze to read Javad's mind, tears on full alert, and her heart pleading violently not to get the truth out. 'Don't tell me that you are not tempted to leave us and join your comrades in the fronts? I bet you see the children and me a burden to your youthful aspirations and if I give you the go ahead, you would pack and leave at once.'

And Javad would hold her in his arms and whisper in her ears as he always did: 'my beloved, please do not let worry darken your life. We have many years ahead of us. We have so much to do. The future is ours. I am here beside you and will not leave you on your own'. Then suddenly, he would be entwined in silence, the weight of a hidden worry heavy on his shoulders. Suri would be removed from his mind's eyes and red flags, red songs, blood everywhere and war fronts would stretch horizon to horizon, his comrades and him standing upright, rifles aimed at the enemy and shooting the Nazis in their thousands. Mother Russia needed sacrifice, the cause had to nurture on blood. His family was a small price for such a grand goal. Then Suri would fall from his grip on the stony veranda and he would march forward to pass through the next steppe near the southern frontiers.

* * *

As time passed into the year 1941, pressures intensified. Javad was caught up in the middle of two extremely difficult positions; his family whom he loved and cared for immensely and a revolution, which he had helped to materialise and which now needed him badly at such crucial time. How could he choose between the two loves? Two contradictory, yet similarly demanding duties? Internationalists were called in to uphold the cause and save the land of socialism and communism from destruction. This return of the old ideals was too tempting to be ignored especially when he understood that many of his comrades were preparing to join international brigades. Remembering the days they planned to turn the earth up side down, to make revolutions, to change the world for every mother to deliver a revolutionary child. Russia as the cradle of Marxist ideology held hopes for millions, who were dreaming to be led into paradise. Russia and her socialist regime must be protected from extinction. Had Comrade Lenin been alive, Javad would not have hesitated to sacrifice everything at his feet. But now he was not sure. His soul was disintegrating and he was not able to pull himself together.

Yet in the course of this internal battle, Javad came across the revelation that his ancient passion, his love for socialism had not died down or withered away but it had matured and grown into a well-shaped, well-kneaded entity waiting patiently at the corner of his forgotten memory to be embraced and given priority over other loves. A dormant urge had arisen and taken control of his soul. Gradually, his blood was running hot, youthful dreams were re-emerging, the present was moving further and farther and yesterday was catching up with the future, holding him in its grip. He was entangled in convulsions of anger of being caught in a dilemma with no easy way out. As a man of action, he expected to be able to make a decision a long time ago. A cry from within called on him: you are a man, do not listen to women's pleas. Do act as a man. Follow your instincts. Do what you think is best for you.

And indeed in the final analysis, Javad khan was a man, a man of his time. Being a man, as he was, he saw himself the centre of the universe, as all men do. He believed the world should revolve around his aspirations, as all men believe. Identifying himself with an ideology made matters worse. His attachment to his family was binding him to this earth and he despised himself for that. Had he not bowed to pressures and not engaged himself in daily life, he would have been free to disentangle himself from the town and its people and join ranks with the comrades and travel the world over. He knew that if he left this army of dependants, they would not be able to pull through rough seas and God knew what would happen to them in his absence. How could he explain to them, especially to his wife, that those high walls of hope they had built under the guise of the stars and the promises he had given, to stand between life and Suri and to protect her from hardship, were giving way to other aspirations? Questions hovered with no answer to tie them to the ground. Was he able to break the chains and free himself without breaking many hearts?

* * *

Finally, Reza Shah the mighty dictator/king, the architect of new Iran and the saviour of women, was forced to abdicate his throne. The Allies had a strong suspicion that Reza Shah had pro-German tendencies and was co-operating with the Germans. They believed that Iran would soon be used as a direct route to the south of the Soviet Union. So, in a well-planned secret agreement between Stalin and the West, Iran was occupied from the north and the south and Reza Shah's young son was sworn in as the new king of Iran. Escorted by the Allied Forces, Reza Shah set sail into exile, where he was transferred from remote islands to remote towns, to strange cities until he died a few years later, a lonely death.

Perhaps allegations were true and the expansion of fascism had to be stopped. Perhaps Reza Shah had to pack and go because his policies were pushing the world into further disaster, but what did it all have to do with this tiny unit of happiness in this remotest corner of the world? How was Suri able to solve this dilemma inside her weeping mind, now standing guard, watching?

* * *

As winter was coming to a close, Javad khan withdrew from public life. He sent his resignation to the education authorities without a word of explanation: 'Excellencies, please accept my resignation from my post as of next month.' Thereafter, he imprisoned himself inside his room. Awake at night, pacing up and down. Up and down, talking to himself. His hair turning grey, his unshaven haunted face drawn with hollow eyes, his handsome figure, shabby in his loose suits. Moving away, leaving love behind, distancing from life. The father who embraced his trio all in one, gradually turned into a sullen, impatient man, who would not hesitate to shout at Suri had the children made extra noise. Pacing up and down. Talking to no one but himself. For weeks, then months. A decision was not easy to reach. Strands of white hair ambushed his broad forehead, the deepened lines of concentration sitting on his feature, tears waiting at the tip of his long lashes speaking of long hard battles. And Suri and his mother, Ghamar khanum trying in vain to enter his soul, to attract his attention to his immediate responsibilities, reminding him that he was needed, he was loved. Now the children sensed the change in their father's behaviour and were in total confusion. Sara was the one who could read her mother's explanations, so she turned into a messenger for Shireen, who impatiently demanded answers. Suri would have to sit them down and take them through the adult world by means of children's logic: 'My darlings', she would write, 'do not pay much attention to the change of mood in your father. He is in much trouble with himself and I promise you that he will soon recover and return to his old goodness.'

'What is going on, mummy? How can you promise, mummy? Papa does not even speak to you as he used to. He does not take us riding and does not play with us. You are crying all the time.'

'I do not know my precious souls. I only know that we have to keep ourselves together and pray for your father's soul. I know he loves us very much but it is difficult for me to explain why he is behaving like that. Just wait for a while and do not worry.'

'Will he ever be our father again, our old father?'

'Yes, my darlings he will. I hope he will.'

And tears would run all over her cheeks and soak the girls and fill the room and overflow into the garden. Sara was not convinced. She was old enough to grasp the gravity of the matter. She had the task of explaining to her younger sister what she herself could not comprehend. Sara never recovered from this hard task.

* * *

New Year arrived and passed through piling anxieties. Finally, the moment of decision arrived. Between the two loves, Javad khan abandoned the one he loved less, just a particle of an atom less, and chose the one he loved more, a particle of an atom more. Gods of happiness were about to leave the neighbourhood. Departure was close and long, lonely days were about to stretch to eternity, cold, frowning, and dark. Waiting at the curve of time with much patience.

One day in late spring, swallows packed their chicks on their backs and flew far away. Poplars and cypresses, frightened of a coming sandstorm, embraced each other, shivering uncontrollably. Two owls in a frantic attempt tried to raise the alarm but no one was alarmed. A group of weeping willows along the main brook, which passed through the garden, wept for days, then months while combing their hair in the water. Their tears filled the garden and spilt over the pond, forcing the gold fish out, which gasped for breath and finally choked. The mother cat, grumpy and reluctant took her newly born kittens by the teeth into the safety of the unknown. No one ever heard of her thereafter. Gods of happiness left hurriedly, leaving no traces to be followed. Silence fell over the shoulder of time. Fear put his new costume on and arrived in style as Suri registered the moments of agony in her hidden records office:

'Hidden from the breath of a passing breeze

I hear footsteps approaching,

then grabbed by an eye

and stood against a brick wall

spiders set at work

and your hands were far away to reach

the density of the threads

woven

around the tendril of my existence.'

* * *

Javad khan, remote, withdrawn but determined, packed and left. No amount of pleading, reasoning, warning, and wailing put a distance between him and his decision. Hypnotised, following instructions given to him over the wave of words. Wasn't that the fate of thousands of idealists who lost their loves and lives to keep the International alive? With him was the photograph of a tiny twelve-year-old child-bride, taken on her wedding day, eyes widened in fright. Sara's features in another photo which Javad had taken on the last New Year he spent with his family looked identical to her mother's when she had set foot into Haji Hassan khan's household all those years before. Shireen and Sasan had their arms around Sara's shoulders, smiling to the camera. Along with the photos, scents and smells, memories of good times and bad times, wrapped in a bundle, hidden at the corner of his mind and vanished. Into the thin air of the desert sky. Quietness arrived, sadness arrived, grief arrived. Lots and lots of them. Bags full of them.

The path that separated Javad khan's dreams from Suri appeared at the bend of a dark tunnel. Whether he was emptied of his emotions and his mind sought new avenues in other lands, among other people remained a question that hovered in the air after Javad khan was gone and his footsteps were washed from the town's memory. The World Revolution succeeded in taking him away from it all.

Part Three

Nineteen

Suri's life had been a trail of grotesque ups and downs, on the vessel of many years, slowly, steeply crossing troubled seas. A life that gradually slipped from the tip of a pen into the whiteness of paper. Suri carried in her the history of human beings as they drift forward, walk backward, transcend time, journey forbidden territories and make pages of history. The history of bygone times as they trek from the abyss of the past into the present and paddle towards the future. A mass kneaded in the colour of pains and joys, folded and wrapped in the memory of time at every dimension. Our lives. History is our lives recreated by the historians.

Remember! We all bear within us a sea to surf and a territory to discover, a story to tell and a history to write. Each one of us can be a history, a historian. The decision is ours. If we decide to add ourselves to the future it only takes a few steps and then a large amount of determination to break the existing boundaries and to register ourselves. No one but us knows how we lived our lives, of days that went by with or without, and seasons that changed colour from spring to summer, to the autumn and the uninterrupted winters that stayed and settled through years. No one but us knows how the joys of life as well as the pains and sufferings are tattooed on our skin needle by needle in all shapes and colours. If we trek back the alleyways of time, reality peels off its ancient wrap for the history to come into creation. Then we are registered. Yes, we could have existed in the mouth of a rose bud or the eye of a petunia or the lines of a love song, under the skin of a rattlesnake or the teeth of a dragon. If we are determined to register ourselves we can stand along with the kings and the queens, the dictators and the cannibals. We can register our existence. But I must warn you of one consequence. Writing one's life history is not as easy as it might sound. The minute we decide to take up the pen and settle our dispute with time, we declare war. By writing our life histories, we unravel the ugliness as well as the beauties of life. Sometimes the pain is immense and it clouds the way to our vision and so we drift through darkness and the agony of remembering. Yet if we have to break the laws and register ourselves and leave our mark and make a statement, so be it. I am. I want to be included in history. And yes, we have to do it. We must. We have to leave our mark on history, simply because we have been a party to it. If history pours out of our own pen it paints the pain, the joy of our existence as we have experienced it. Otherwise, outsiders would invade our boundaries, cut the edges and who knows how we would be portrayed through the eyes of someone who writes from without?

Don't forget! If Suri did not settle her dispute with time, who would have put the record straight in this stonehearted age? Who would have known better than she the reality of being left on her own in a frosty zone to swim or sink? And at the end of the day when reality shows itself in the surreal mirror of life are we not all left on our own to excavate the life we have lived and loved and died for? Do we not sometimes gaze at the looking glass only to see our dreams up in smoke? And would we not land at this crude fact that the reality of life is in the mirror of life itself and the value we give to the process of life, nothing less, nothing more? There is no end to reach. Life itself is the aim, not passing through it to reach an end. The end is nothing but a finishing line to eternal hollowness.

Imagine the years that passed until Suri reached the decision that she had to register her pain. She knew that she could not swim up-stream to the beginning or put a hold on time but she could saturate it, squeeze it and give it density, and grant it more value by writing it down as she passed through it. She had descended high mountains and ascended low hills to reach the point where she found the necessity to register herself. I am. I was. I will be.

* * *

Suri never knew how her dreams shattered in the downstream of a wild river that thundered and drowned her completely. Dreams that were dreamt in the middle of one summer night as she and her husband slept on the rooftop, heads on feathery cushions, fingers locked together, eyes staring at the sky, counting the stars in pairs until the moon charmingly shielded them in fear of being lessened by their count. There, they smoothed their bodies into one, blessed with two twin souls. One became part of the other, a stretch of two in one. Sailing the night into dawn, building mountains of hope, away from snowy winters and rainy autumns, climbing with ease, sitting at the peak, looking over the day their children, the fruit of their love would have grown up and life would have pushed them away to form their own territories and they, Suri and Javad, would have grown old together, together. Two lives in one.

Suri's heart tore into pieces and then scattered across the dewy desert, aching, panting, burning. A big hole like an entrance to hell, deep as the base of a barren well in the middle of the desert, replaced her tender, loving heart. Javad had departed and had left her alone, the phantoms of events had surfaced and the seriousness of the situation was revealed. Suddenly, she realised that her husband, her lover and the arch of her existence had deserted her, had drifted away and left her on her own to cope with a hostile world. Devastation was a word short of Suri's situation. She froze in total darkness. Stood at the edge, a bundle of ice. Her icy eyes could not see, her frozen brain became empty and her estranged mind left thought behind. There was no one to hold her and keep her away from the frozen glaciers. There was no strength in her to pull her through, to let thought enter her brain, no helping hand. A blank sheet in front of her mind's eyes with no traces to follow. It was as if time was caught up in a static moment and she was thrown outside its zone. A long road stretched to eternity and she had to walk on and on and on. If one defines a boundary for human mind to function, hers fell beyond. She hovered between life and death for days that never wrapped up and nights that never dawned. Eventually she crashed under the thunder and lost the power to communicate from her hallucinatory world. Once in the middle of her volatile agonies she rose from her bed, a mad woman, breaking everything she got hold of, ripping Javad's clothes one by one, by one, shredding them across her broken heart, cleansing the room of his physical existence. Then she returned to her frosty enclosure and hoped to join her beloved. A sorceress was called in to encapsulate her mind, to put sanity back into her. But if sanity returned, she did not know how to live the life on her own and how to endure the loss.

Had Suri's husband died a natural death, she might have broken down in the same way but her mourning would end. With time, she would have accepted his death and declared herself a widow and behaved like one. But going away on a journey, where he might be alive, he might be dead, where she had no way of reaching the warmth of his hand. Suri stood in the icy zone for a long, long time. No one told her how long. Time did not matter when one fell outside its boundaries. Time travelled slowly through days then months. There were a lot of people around; her mother-in-law and Javad's loving sisters, her own mother Ashraf khanum and her children. But no one knew what to do or how to bring life into Suri's dying heart. Everyone was waiting for a miracle to happen and bring her back to life.

* * *

Summer and autumn gave way to a harsh winter and Suri was yet to overcome her grief. Then, a year to the day Javad had departed, suddenly, the ice began melting and her memory sliding back. Something extraordinary must have happened. Suri was fighting for her life through days and months of despair until her cells called her back from the depth of depression as she was returning to her senses. Her young body was rebelling life was returning as the lid was removed from her daunted eyes and saw half a dozen curious eyes filled with love fixed on her as she lay on an ice ridden bed. The rebellion inside her was exasperated by the fragrance of the small bodies floating over her, a sense of lightness was throwing the gloom away, her energy came to a level for her to sit up.

Gradually, Javad khan was moving away from reality, confined to her fantasies, became the creation of her mind. Now, she could see those small bodies moving around. Her mind's eye, blurred and dusty, concentrated on one, then moved to the next and finally rested on the last. A sense of gaiety brushed the clouds of stubborn melancholy aside and a blazing light gleamed into the corner of her mind. Her heart pounded violently, her mouth widened ajar to spell a word. Sara and Shireen's hands stretched, their burning eyes watched their mother intensely. The pair of small but firm bodies locked into hers and the icy particles melted away. Her mind was awakened. Thought returned. And she was filled with an urge to look herself in the looking glass. She saw that her former beauty was obscured by clouds of grief and a mad woman stood and looked her right into the eyes. No. This cannot be me. This must not be me. She rushed back to her children. Her portrait embracing the three of them all at the same time remained in memory for years to come.

* * *

Suri came back to life after months of severe depression, during which time, her life had changed dramatically. Her mother-in-law, Ghamar khanum, though grief-stricken herself had taken charge of the household. After a long absence from her life, her parents re-emerged, demanding a share of control. People, gave themselves the liberty to spread opinions, to invade her privacy and to watch over her shattered life. Gradually, she understood that in the absence of her husband, her autonomy was taken away. What she had built in the enclosure of her happy years was no more valid. It did not matter that her husband had taken her out of ancient practices and injected modern ideas into her head and made her a woman different from the mainstream. It did not count that she had acquired a reasonable knowledge of life and proved to be talented in languages and writing poetry and prose and made a reputation for herself in the intellectual circles. That did not count. Reality was not her lifestyle. Reality lived in the layers of traditions, which had remained ancient and rejected her credentials. She was declared invalid and a guardian was appointed for her children and she herself was put under the direct rule of her husband's family. Her parents, hand in hand with the army of tradition preservers and custodians of archaic norms unleashed their attack on her lifestyle and forced her to walk backward into the road of family traditions and its inhabitants had never bowed to change and modern ideas. Her father, Haji Amir, who had often expressed his dissatisfaction with Suri and her husband, advised his wife, Ashraf khanum, to pull the children out of the missionary school. The infidels, he believed, would certainly poison their minds. Across this line, Madam Brigitte, Suri's only friend and confidant, the remains of her past and the only one who had empowered her to stand on her feet again, was politely but firmly advised to lessen her visits. In her grief-stricken mind Suri had no choice but to take her complaints straight to her beloved, the one who was miles away from her heart. Oh darling! Where did you go? Why did you go? Who took you away from me? How could you leave me all by myself? How can I ever forgive you for the crime you committed? And grief embarked on her and sadness settled in her heart until there were no more tears to run and no more questions to ask.

Inevitably, Suri's grief fed the power of invasion and a terror that crept under her skin tightened the chains of long, deep traditions. Was her loss lighter if these intrusions had not occurred at such a fast pace? Would she ever find the courage to stand up and raise her hand in protest and reclaim her life? Would she ever live a life, free of rules and traditions? One day in time a window opened up in front of her curious eyes and she saw the horizon. She walked a short distance on the road towards it. There, at the corner of her grieving heart stood an urge to open that window at the first chance.

'One day in time

there flew over

my silent thoughts

a wild bird with

broken wings.

I saw myself hanged by toe

upside down

from the branch of a dead acacia.

One day in time

through the crack of a window.

I watched an ant climbing up and up

her shoulders fallen,

her heart beaten,

her eyes brighten,

to the top,

to the top.'

Twenty

Between 1941-1943, the catastrophe of World War Two had widened its scope. By then half of the globe was engaged in the madness of the war. No news of Javad had reached home. Ever. Through word of mouth and the censored news that occasionally reached Karmanieh people were made aware of the developments at the war fronts. But the full scale of the horrors was yet to be unearthed.

Later, years later, the world opened its eyes to the killing fields, gas chambers, and prison camps that stood erect to witness the degradation of human-kind. Gradually, nations tore apart the web of terror and a sea of resistance emerged from every direction. Hitler's military machine slowed down in the vast snowy steppes of Russia, and the French, the Polish and the Czech Resistance took shape and brought the aggressor to his knees. All through the war, Iran remained 'neutral' though virtually under occupation of the Allied Forces in the south and the Soviets in the north. During this period and thereafter, no one knew where that lone internationalist was fighting and whether he was still alive somewhere out in that tormented world.

At the home front, after two years of grief, of idleness, of watching her children growing up and her life sailing away, leaving her behind, Suri finally accepted that her husband was gone for good and there was nothing she could do about it. Her mind was clearing itself of the mist of ambiguous hopes. But would she ever forget her beloved and stop yearning to catch his warm hand and beg of him to hold her tight? Would she ever know what made Javad leave home and wander across the steppes of that foreign land, away from those who needed him so badly and wanted him back to be theirs forever?

Two years passed before Suri finally found the courage to seal her lamentation and take charge of her shattered life. Now she understood that up until then, she had lived her life through her husband, had thought his thoughts and followed him wherever he took her. Javad had not prepared her to live independent of him. The fact that she was left on her own brought fear to her mind. She was at a loss. It seemed that her children had lost both their parents and unless she did act decisively she would not have any role in their life. She had to reinvent herself, to recreate a father and a mother from the rubble of her broken soul. She was there and the aspirations she had for her children had not died down but were hidden under the ashes of grief. She must stand up for them. She must. She must. So, she decided to brush her grief aside and to think rationally. If she was able to connect her situation to the wider world. If millions of people were fighting against the occupation of their land and resisted aggressors and struggled to retain their human dignity, then she must stand up to take back her small territory.

Suri knew that at every step she would be confronted by opposition but if she could find allies and break the army of invaders in part and if they were convinced that she had recovered from the breakdown and was aware of her responsibilities and if her inability to speak could be set aside, then she would be in a position to take charge. There were mountains of thoughts to be climbed and rough seas of responsibilities to be taken into consideration. She had to deal with them one by one, day by day. A key had to be found to unlock the blockade. For days, she sat silent, watching everyone's movements and weighed their reactions to her recovery. Her recovery came in slow paces. Finally, Suri's eager eyes found the key to the first lock.

* * *

It was one early morning of July 1943. The heat had taken them to the rooftop, where they slept under the blanket of the desert. Dawn had just broken in the desert. The eastern breeze was splashing dews over the mosquito nets. The sun was yet to swallow them in his thirsty mouth. The muezzin had finished chanting. Rolling on the mattress, Suri's eyes caught the last bright star fading into the mist of azure sky, her hands rolled over her body, examining every inch she had missed for the past two years. And she felt an urge to look in the looking glass after such period of neglect. Cautiously, she got up and walked down into the hallway and watched the ghost of a woman who had aged a thousand years. The pair of lifeless eyes staring at her and a shower of sorrow pouring over her mutilated mind. If anything, she had to negotiate with life again, to break from being what she was, an extension of her husband, his creation. She had to remould, to rebuild the ruins and transplant herself to life. Perhaps he was her tongue and the power behind her mind but the mind was hers and by determination she could reconstruct it afresh. She yearned to invite herself to a hot shower but going to the hamam was a tiring ritual and she could not endure it at that moment in time. Instead, she put on a nice dress and some make up and rolled her hair loosely into a bun. Looking deep in the looking glass. Turning around, tip-toeing, letting the breeze flirt with her skirt. Coming out into the living room, Suri noticed that Ghamar khanum's tired and grief stricken figure was bending, her voice whispering complaints she hardly spoke of, hoping God was in the vicinity to hear it all. She caught a glimpse of Suri and her mouth went ajar. A sense of gaiety filled her heart and forced her to rush and embrace her and hold her to her bosom. 'Oh God, I thank you a million times. Oh, dear God forgive me if I complained. My prayers have been answered. Life is coming back to this child and I am grateful for that. My dear child, I am glad to see you in good spirit.' Suri kissed her on the cheeks. Something reminded her of Javad, her smell, the texture of her skin? Tears filled her eyes but her lashes swallowed them before running on her face.

Breakfast was consumed in a contented silence. Both women avoided unnecessary conversation. Suri left the room to get ready and Ghamar khanum followed her curiously. The sun had already spread over the city domes, penetrating the curtains. A man was chanting from a distance, listing his commodities, his voice getting closer as he was approaching. Suri put on a light jacket, hiding the flowers of her dress, wrapped her hair in a scarf and prepared to exit. By then, the majority of Karmanieh women had returned to the veil after the initial fever of the unveiling in the late thirties. Ghamar khanum was watching her with eager eyes and noticed Suri's determination and so broke the silence:

'Oh my dear child. I am so glad that you feel well enough to go out. Let me call the maid to accompany you. It won't take a minute.'

'No mother please, I wish to go on my own. I want to visit my mother and stay there for a while. It has been so long since I have set foot outside the house.' The scribble landed on Ghamar khanum's palm.

'But my child!'

'No mother please, let me try it on my own. I will be all right. You need not worry about me.' Suri was choosing the words with care and before her mother-in-law prepared herself to object, she was near the gate and out. Empty, without him holding her hand.

Walking on her own and Javad not being there to throw an anecdote at a passer-by or say hello to another and bow to an elder. Would she ever be able to walk the road ahead? But she must reach her destination. She had an important business to attend to and her future depended on this initial visit. If she retreated now, she would remain in disintegration. So, her mind pushed away dark thoughts as she advanced, as the sun sprinkled on her cheeks and warmed her skin and dripped from the faint smile that sat at the corner of her mouth.

Streets had washed the dust off their surface to welcome her arrival. Shops had their shutters up and the pavements lifted the scent of earth up into the air. Shopkeepers were putting their commodities on display and the first customers were queuing to take the best pick. Passing through the main bazaar, heading for her parent's home, Suri walked the two-mile distance through the noise and the crowd, without recognising anyone as if hypnotised into a mission. Suddenly, from the far end of the bazaar a group of teenage girls in school uniform were heading her direction. Suri quickly moved aside to watch those free souls. Their laughter was loud as they passed by her. A few years ahead, she could see Sara and Shireen among the group. As she moved on, curious eyes turned towards her unveiled figure, swallowing words of disapproval. Men were gazing harshly. Women, more in admiration than blame. She avoided confrontation and passed by adamantly. At the end of the bazaar, a doroshky spotted her charming, elegant figure strolling and stood in hope. She waved him away and continued. Did she deprive the poor man of his first customer?

* * *

Suri's unexpected arrival created a lot of excitement. Everyone rushed to look at her, to greet her and to enquire about her health. Questions were pouring while Suri was trying to scribble the answers. From the vicinity of the kitchen came the familiar voice of delight. Fatima, old and bending rushed towards her. In her arms, Suri found peace and comfort and they cried together until Suri's mother sent her scolding looks and so they separated. But Fatima's presence soothed and consoled her.

Suri was well aware that over years, her mother had not bothered to care for her as she did for her sisters and half-sisters. She had left Suri at the mercy of her husband's family altogether. Haji Amir had virtually forgotten this daughter. Her sisters avoided her as well. She had scarcely visited them. Now she had to negotiate with them her life and the future of her children because it all depended on their decision. But why should they bother? Just because her

167

husband had abandoned her and gone away? What if she told them that Javad was about to return? Would they believe her and leave her on her own? No, she could not tell lies. Yes, she had to be frank and bold and leave fear behind. And if they gave her independence and she failed, would she be able to return and ask clemency?

Tea and cookies were brought in and consumed. Children, nieces and nephews were playfully running back and forth. From a far distance a bird was cooing, a sparrow flapping its wings among the trees, the mother cat was mewing at her kittens. The kitchen was preparing lunch, smells and aromas were clouding the air, reaching Suri's nostrils. None of them knew how to begin real conversation. There seemed a deep sympathy for her. Yet it was hidden under the guise of formalities, and none were able to express their true feelings. Would Suri's parents wish to mend the road and get close to her? Would they ever understand who she really was and what she wanted? She was their flesh and blood, yet so far apart. Did that make a difference, if one is made of one's flesh and blood? Unfortunately, at that moment in time, Suri had no option but to cling to them for protection and financial support.

However, after the initial phase of excitement died down and calm returned and children dispersed, Suri sat crossed legged, opened her notebook, took her time to begin and break the ice, scribbled her feelings, her pains, and talked about her plans, aspirations and hopes for her children. She wrote not in hidden words but bold and clear that her mourning time had come to an end and she was able to take care of herself and the children and it would be best if she did so. She brushed aside worries and gave her parents assurances and told them that now she was a woman grown out of that crippled child bride, who left this house in a white dress and was told to stay in her husband's until being carried to her grave in a white shroud. She pictured the harshness of the first few years of exile and the horrors and sufferings she had endured. That little mute creature had ceased to exist. She told them how she found happiness and love, and lost it in the most unusual circumstances. No hard feelings but since they didn't bother about her then, why should they bother now? Why have they arrived in her life now? Just because her husband has gone away? Why should that matter to them? Do they really want to help her, or do they think it is their moral duty to intervene in her life?

'Please mother, try to understand me for once. I am not complaining. All I want from you is my own life and that of my children. Your interference does more harm than good. Javad's family have taken advantage of the situation. My children's future will be ruined if this continues. I want you to trust me all the way through. I know what is best for my children and I will not leave here until I make sure that you are supporting me.'

And then she stopped, handed over the notebook, gave her mother time to read and reach the depth of her worries. Oh, god, please help my mother to understand. She sat motionless, touching Fatima's hand, weighing the possibilities and impossibilities of her parent's decision. Then lunch was brought in and consumed and Suri sat with a few of the sisters reviewing life, talking about ordinary matters, while Asharaf khanum went out, summoned her husband, Haji Amir from his office and handed over the notebook.

Suri needed her parents' support. Her husband had not left much money and she was in no position to earn a living. Her father's financial support was the only lifeline of survival. If only she could maintain herself, she would be free from the grip of both families but in that day and age, there was no work for any woman let alone her. From her father's point of view, Suri was a negative equity and he was not the man to easily bow to pressures. He had already threatened to deny his support, should Suri decide to opt for an independent life. She had to live under her father's control, something she did not want to do. Meanwhile, Ashraf khanum and

Haji Amir talked and quarrelled and threw harsh words at each other. A decision was yet to be reached.

Evening approached. Hours of scribbling, arguing and nerve-racking disagreements came to a close with no apparent conclusion. A doroshky was called and Suri headed home, accompanied by a servant. The household rested for the night, heavy with thoughts. Haji Amir wanted to make sure that if Suri was given her freedom and they pulled away from her life, and told Javad's family to leave her alone, she would do her best not to tarnish the honour of both families. Suri returned home with a head full of looming questions. She locked away the memory of a husband, who had abandoned her in such a cruel world. She did not wish to remember him for now. Not until she settled her dispute with life. And that was just a first step to a long, hard battle, which took Suri on the road to forcing both families into retreat. And as time passed, the gentle, kind-hearted Ghamar khanum saw the depth of Suri's desire to live her own life and shifted sides and eventually ceased to interfere in the daily affairs of her daughter-in-law and the children.

It happened like this. One day, the two women sat and spoke of terrible times that had passed and the hardships that stood ahead. They cried and consoled their broken hearts. Then they put sadness aside and talked of matters in a practical way, tied their responsibilities together, separated each from the other and prepared a package for Haji Amir to decide upon in due course.

* * *

The page of history turned to the year before World War Two came to an end and the globe began to reconstruct itself from the rubble of human destruction. For Suri, the strain of learning and harbouring difficulties, living life as full as it could be through the years of hardship, dragged on and on. For her husband Javad khan the pages were bloodier than expected.

Decades later in a stormy night Suri saw a handsome, white-haired man, resembling Javad at that age, waiting at the gate of her distorted dreams. He was carrying a broken banner, which was burnt in the middle, making it difficult to see the writing. Suri's heart trembled and a question hovered in the air. Was it worth leaving so many broken hearts to trot to a wasteland, following a whirlwind? History proved it was not.

Twenty One

Gradually, Suri found more courage to persistently negotiate her situation with her parents and finally sealed a pact. Haji Amir approved financial support without much interference, provided Suri would act reasonably and took responsibility for her children's education and their upbringing and Ghamar khanum would oversee matters. Haji Amir left no space for possible whimsical activities, where his family's name might be tarnished. In reality he had no choice. He was reluctant to bring Suri and the three children under his roof. He had never approved of Suri's lifestyle and the way Javad used to treat her. Besides, modernity and unveiling brought much chaos into town and spread its infectious germs into Haji Amir's own household, where his remaining daughters were demanding freedom from the veil, something Haji vehemently opposed. Suri had a big impact on her sisters. During the unveiling era, the whole town talked about her and the way she was coached by her husband, then a prominent civil servant. She had learnt foreign languages and took foreign friends. Suri's lifestyle was marvelled at by some and hated by others. It raised people's jealousy, specially her sisters. How come the little mute had so many advantages but they were kept inside the walls like caged birds? Happiness stationed itself where least expected. Ironically, most of Suri's sisters were married off to wealthy men and moved to wealthy households only to be caged in yet another golden enclosure.

So, life returned to normal. The course of events turned Suri into a quiet, thoughtful woman who seldom spoke of her husband. She spent a lot of time with the children as they were growing up quickly, demanding the world ahead. Her memory of the happy days when her husband's handsome figure stood by her and her soul searched him for reassurance at every step had now faded away into the abyss of time. Though her rosy dreams were stopped abruptly in the middle she was determined to do what was best for her children.

'They must stretch in every dimension and reach the world across. They must. They must.'

* * *

Ten years passed and ashes covered the town's memory of Javad khan's sudden disappearance. Ten years that went through bumpy roads and sharp bends as Suri walked and stumbled, fell down and got up until the year 1951. Suri kept herself up to date with the world by reading magazines and newspapers and listening to the radio and writing poetry. Her poems were kept from sight only to be shared by her children. Sometimes they urged their mother to send a selection to the press so that people could read and enjoy them. She opposed the idea. She was afraid that people might reach the depth of passion for her dead love. Yet in time her poetry flew from the enclosure of her notebooks and spread across the land. She became a distinguished poet in her own right.

By then, Sara had a year to graduate from high school. She had become a copy of her mother, patient, dignified, and far-sighted. Her eyes were looking deep into the future, her head full of raw ideas, her ambitions walking ahead of time. Sara had familiarised herself with Persian and English poetry, read the works of French poets as well and often engaged in heated debates with Madam Brigitte, who had remained close to them as ever. Sara sometimes thought of her father and cherished little memories she held of him, though slowly fading through the haze of time. Suri confided in her elder daughter and the two reminisced at every opportunity in fear of losing their memories in the process of life. Yet Sara was not a romantic type. She aimed to fulfil higher ambitions.

Shireen had grown into a passionate, hot-headed, volatile beauty, who took nonsense from no one. Her sharp tongue and commanding manners were said to have taken after her great-grandmother, Alieh khanum, who had departed long before she was

173

on her feet. Shireen terrorised the household by putting her foot down whenever she saw it necessary. Academically she was above average and that gave her mother lots of hope for her future.

Sasan had taken his handsome looks from his father and his calm, thoughtful manners from his great-grandfather, Haji Morteza. When they walked and as they talked the three of them showered Suri with pride and ecstasy. At times Sasan's tone of voice opened an ancient wound which had never stopped bleeding.

* * *

World War Two had long ended, leaving its ugly marks on the face of the earth. Europe, Africa and parts of Asia had gone through the war, occupation and devastation. But the burden of destruction fell on Europe, as it was the breeding ground of Hitler, Mussolini and Franco.

After the war, crimes and criminals came to the surface. People's accounts of war crimes all bore significant resemblance to each other; survivors had seen too much misery. Every nation at every corner of the globe had a story to tell. The holocaust was the hallmark of the war. The Nuremberg Court was convened to try criminals and bring them to justice. But the majority fled to safe havens though some received long prison sentences. Victims' lives never gained normality. They remained victimised for the rest of their lives. The idea of establishing a united assembly for the prevention of such crimes and protecting the weak nations finally materialised and the United Nation's organisation was born to pursue such goals. The establishment of the United Nations with the aim of uniting nations and putting an end to wars and further catastrophes was a grand idea. Unfortunately, to this date the aims have remained to be accomplished.

World War Two put the re-division of the globe on the agenda. The old order collapsed and the world was re-arranged according to the new geopolitical manifesto. In the post-war era, some countries were annexed to their strong neighbours a few were wiped out from the map. New nations emerged here and there. The Soviet Union declared itself the victor, the saviour of other nations because it had resisted and fought the Nazis with full force. Its empire expanded in every direction with Comrade Stalin the ultimate commander. In years to come, the Soviet Union became a powerful rival to the United States of America. The Soviets had to use their resources to rebuild their ruined country while the United States of America became the post-war most powerful country because it was far from the war zone. The US assisted Europe to rebuild itself. There followed the crumbling of the old colonial Europe and the revival of the two powerful blocs; America and the Soviet Union. In the post-war era, Europe lost most of its colonies while America and the Soviet Union emerged as modern imperialists. The Soviet Union annexed parts of Eastern Europe and Middle Asia to her empire and increased her influence in other parts by way of a global ideological campaign in the name of socialism and socialist brotherhood. The United States strengthened its influence in the geopolitics of the world by waging more than two hundred and fifty coups de'etat and bringing puppet dictators to power. This rivalry resulted in the Cold War and the race between the West and the Soviet bloc to build nuclear arsenals and the anti-communist hysteria in America.

The Second World War had an ironic benefit for the Jews since they were the main victims of Nazi ideology. For the sake of those Jews who were exterminated during the war, the rest were promised a state of their own so to find a collective identity and never to be stranded around the globe. Unfortunately, this could not be done unless another nation, the Palestinians were driven out of their lands to clear the way for the Jews, who claimed Palestine as their promised land. Shortly after the war, the world witnessed the irony of yet another catastrophe. The refugee crisis in its modern form took shape and had continued to this date.

Three million Palestinians were made homeless for three million Jews to be relocated and re-housed. The Jews founded their state on the blood and bones of the Palestinians who were butchered in the refugee camps of Sabra and Shatila. Some forty years later, sitting outside a camp in Lebanon, an old man held the key to his house in Jerusalem, waiting to return. If asked, he would give you details of his orange groves, then occupied by a Jewish family, who had emigrated from Russia to the Holy Land. For decades to come that region swayed and swam in blood, never to see a day of peace and reconciliation as was promised by the architects of the Jewish state.

* * *

After the end of war, waves of revolutions and liberation movements, stretched from China to India, to Latin America, Africa and Asia. Nations under the colonial rule rose, revolted and fought to take control of their territories. The movement for freedom and independence spread rapidly. In the post-war era, socialist ideology and socialist movements sprang from every corner. No one was aware that the socialist system in Russia did not hold up to its promises, the paradise that was promised, was built on the skeletons of millions who were systematically killed in Stalin's labour camps and prisons. Decades later the extent of this holocaust was revealed and humans were made aware of what humans can do to their own kind.

Iran was not spared the geopolitics of post-war. She remained under the influence of foreign powers; mainly the British until America took over. By the 1950s, Iran was one of the biggest oil producers in the world. Her natural resources brought her wealth and misery all at the same time. Oil, the golden liquid and the lifeline of building a new Europe was then controlled by British Petroleum. In the early 1950s, a national upheaval in Iran put the nationalisation of the oil industry high on the agenda and the industry was taken back from British Petroleum and nationalised. But disagreements between the Shah and the national government emerged and consequently the Shah flew the country in protest. There he signed a pact with the Americans and sold Iran to the United States of America. The 1953 coup that was masterminded by the CIA overthrew the patriotic government Of Mohammed Mosadeque in Iran and made the Shah an authoritarian dictator. Western Europe and America, full of greed, two world wars lined behind them, forced Iran to sell her oil as cheaply as possible.

There followed the transformation of Iran from an agricultural based economy to an oil-dependent one. Iran became the battleground of post-war politics. The Shah sold his soul to the Americans and in order to stay in power opened the doors to foreign investment and foreign banks and high-speed technologies. For the next three decades, the middle class Iranians copied the West, while the majority of the populace were yet to come out of the middle Ages. The Shah had no strategy to build anallout modern state; just a western gloss over eastern cracks. From the 1960s onwards, and thanks to the oil money, Iran was driving on a fast-moving track to become westernised.

The Shah, the by-product of post-war politics, was a puppet dictator with the style of all dictators. Political suffocation and repression. During his reign political parties were banned and politicians and group leaders were sent to the gallows. An American-style secret intelligence was established and terror took firm roots. If Javad khan and his comrades were in Iran, they would have been among the first to have their tongues cut. Thousands like Javad had their throats slashed in the process of 'stabilisation', 'open door' policies and entering Iran into the world market. By the early 1970s, Iran was declared 'Gendarme of the region' and 'The Island of Stability'.

In 1952, shortly after the coup in Iran, Suri wrote in her notebook a poem, which was hidden from sight for years to come.

'Under the shroud of night,

mosquitoes falling pregnant,

bearing children of malignant thoughts.

As time goes by

across the swamps of earth,

the fish gasp for breath

and depart with a last look

on their glassy eyes

and open their mouths to ask,

when would it stop raining acid

the sour of earth

when would this earth come to a end

and life begins?'

* * *

By the late 1950s, and all through the sixties and the seventies, Iran was operating this fast-moving train towards no direction. The modern dictator with no ideas to dictate was planning a future with no shape, no size and no weight. Iranian oil was constantly seeped into the pipelines, out onto the tankers, onto the sea, into the depots of western countries. In return, wasteful goods were put into the containers, onto the ships and in the shopping trolleys of the Iranian elite. The ordinary people with bemused eyes saw the Shah riding an oily horse, trotting across the globe, showing oily dollars to the onlookers. On the surface, Iran was heading towards compatibility with the West underneath she remained incompatible with the modern world. The Shah, adamant, full of shallow pride and empty of a thoughtful mind, unable to see the realities of the country he was ruling, constantly delivered dictatorial promises to a nation, which was sitting aside watching its wealth slipping away from its grip. Future was green and orange. Future was whatever the oil money could buy from the shopping malls. Future was foreign seeds cultivated in a native land, cropping hatred.

The rot of history hid behind Iran's glossy paint. It sank back. Waited for the right moment to surface, to crash the rails into each other, to derail the fast-forward carriages. Fermentation of the soil bubbled up and cracks opened some decades later. Ancient wounds opened, blood dripped and oozed and the stench of human degradation spread across the globe. News of the crash were broadcast in time by the fastest mode of communication; of those who were charcoaled inside a modern cinema compound, while moments before, their lively eyes were filled with lively hopes as they were watching a modern comedy; of people who saw their new Messiah in the moon soon to arrive on the wings of a flying machine to save them from the dictator; of prisons equipped with modernest equipment to empty brains of thought, to cut hands and fingers, to force those who were broken to the point of repenting, shoot their comrades in order to prove their loyalty to the Messiah; of streets littered with clowns, black, brown, black, dark, dark, dark. The modern dictator was quickly extinguished by the fire he had started by oil. His 'achievements' went up in flames and many ancient dictators, big, small, tiny, fat, and foetuses in the wombs, rose from the compost of history. And the world sat witness with bemused and astonished eyes.

Twenty Two

Suri saw her three children as one entity of pure love and devotion, though from birth they had different personalities and Suri had no choice but to deal with each of them in their own way. Yet her love for them, immense, condensed and pure never took sides with this one or that. Javad khan's mother was tender and caring and in that household violence and coercion was out of norm. Suri had learnt Ghamar khanum's tender way and in the absence of her husband, a single mother, even at times of frustration resorting to harsh codes rarely crossed her mind.

Sara and Shireen were far apart by character and temperament. Unlike Sara, who was soft-hearted, and serene, Shireen had a fierce temper. To move against her wish meant to collide with the fire head on. From early childhood Shireen had her own mind set on things. No amount of pressure could force her to abide a matter she did not approve of or believe in. While Sara admired her mother passionately, Shireen was closer to Sasan although they were different in character. Together, they fought over matters which at the time were the most important world affairs, discovered friendship, ganged up against intruders and disentangled themselves from the orders which were constantly issued by the elders; out of love or worry. Suri relied on Javad khan's advice in dealing with difficulties of child rearing and how to control her temper, how to take them under the wing of love and give them reassurances and the safety of a deep bond that entwined and pulled them into the future so that they could stand on their own two feet. In the absence of Javad, they were the main purpose of Suri's existence and took her through the road to recovery, to picking up the pieces and rebuilding her life.

Among the children, Shireen seemed to have resolved the matter of a fatherless life quicker than the rest. Sara had the heavy hand of loss on her shoulders because she had more years behind with her father's love plaited into every moment. Sasan was too young to understand the gravity of the situation. He had accepted that his father had gone on a long journey and would one day return. The memory of their father as he used to take the girls mountain hiking, horse riding, desert discovering; playing hide and seek, making them snowman with a funny nose as the snow reached the top of the walls and people carved tunnels to walk to the bazaar and their father made breakfast out of fresh snow with grape syrup poured over it and showed them how to enjoy eating it; as he tuned the gramophone, danced with them Russian dances until they spread their delighted bodies on the rug, panting in exuberant exhaustion, in which case, he would take Suri in his arms and continue till she begged of him to stop, was gradually fading away, leaving a blank space.

Time was travelling fast and the children were growing up, pushing through life with Sasan blindly and Sara, admiring, following Shireen. There was not a moment Shireen's life empty of episodes. Suri had her motherly anguish as to the consequences of her daughter's boldness in a world which was too narrow for women to move. On occasions she was filled with pride seeing Shireen throwing herself into the universe giving no way to fear and caution. But most of the time she was apprehensive. Nonetheless, Shireen was not the girl to walk into the darkness without knowing the dangers and finding solutions. Rather, she had a thoughtful mind and a strong sense of reason to her actions.

Suri spent much time reading and writing poetry. She had subscribed to almost every magazine published in the land and bought every book that came into print. She listened to the radio and often went to the only cinema in town. She absorbed the plots and they remained with her long after the pictures lost colour. Above all, 'Gone with the Wind' and 'The Grass is Green', aroused an old flame in her and kept her silent for months to come. Radio was the magic box. Music, previously confined to special circles, was now broadcast from the radio. Radio Iran, the nationwide network was expanding rapidly. Every once in a while a new singer bewitched the hearts and aroused much passion among the listeners. Poetry, story-telling and weekly contests were Suri's favourites. She also listened to the news broadcast on foreign radio stations and matched their authenticity against the national radio and the press. By then, her own poetry now in its maturity had squeezed out of the enclosures of Karmanieh. They decorated pages of magazines and were recited inside intellectual circles. People's imagination travelled beyond this anonymous poet, who had found the courage to open her heart and speak of her dreams. Initially, Sara had sent a few of her mother's poems to some national magazines, which published them immediately and demanded more. Suri was angry at her daughter for exposing her. Sara argued relentlessly against that and then Shireen backed her sister.

'Why are you so stubborn mother? Listen! People love your poetry and it would be mean not to share it with them.'

'But why my darlings? These are my yearnings, the flames of my broken heart. Why should I share them with strangers? What good does it do if people trespass my heart?'

'No mother, you are wrong. This nation has been nourished on poetry. It runs in our veins. You must let the flow of your blood reach out and soothe other broken hearts. It is selfish of you to keep them to yourself. Let them fly from the prison you have created for them. It will enrich your work if other poets read them and critics write about them.'

Finally, Suri gave in. The word was stronger than the sword and her poetry crossed the boundaries of Karmanieh and travelled beyond and was read on the national radio. Using a pseudo name, she was registered in the history of Iranian women poets without ever being known who she really was.

By the late 1950s, television arrived in Iran and crept into Karmanieh a few years later. Television changed the face of the earth forever. The miracle of television brought the world into the living rooms. Radio brought people together. It was a collective joy because the instrument itself was of no significance. It could be placed anywhere as long as the voice was heard. Throughout the cold nights, people sat around the korsis and shared the glory and the romance of the heroes in the stories recited on the radio. Then they sighed with relief as the storyteller finished the episode and they prepared to go to bed, sweet dreams hanging from the edge of their thoughts. TV killed that culture. It squeezed the world into a box, like a tin of chick peas. TV changed the outfit of every family room. Everything muddled inside the walls of a single room. Cushions and chairs were rearranged to face the magic box. Curtains were drawn and dim lights installed. Evenings of excitement and nut cracking while listening to the radio were replaced by the individuality of staring at the box absorbing the events, in the solitude of one's own mind. Any outside distraction faced the strongest objections. Overnight in Iran as well as other parts of the world, broadcasters, men and women in glamorous costumes became celebrities. Role models to be copied by the young generation. The first Iranian TV channel, funded by an entrepreneur, blended the programmes with comical adverts. The vulgar language soon found itself in the popular culture. Thereafter, people's minds collided in confusion and order got out of order. Many families declared radio and television an evil instrument, which corrupted the populace. The Ulama issued orders to ban their use. Women were advised to avoid such sinful means and men were assigned to take control. There was nowhere to seek solace. Iranians were soon diluted into the magic box. Imported soft drinks and American junks added to the collection. What sucked away Suri's husband was about to swallow the whole population into his giant stomach.

As Suri saw more of the outside world, the curtain was slowly lifted from the mystery of Javad khan's yearning to get out of Karmanieh. The outside world as portrayed in the films was glamorous, grand, and magical. Books and magazines were not able to show such glories. No wonder Javad hated his confined environment and wanted to get out. Suri was on the road to forgiving him for having left his family, though she never did forget him. The future revealed secrets kept in the womb of time. Secrets which streamed out when the world was a compact village and there was no space for them to hide from watchful eyes.

* * *

Throughout the sixties, more universities were established and sending the children to higher education became the norm. Some families packed their children's bags for boarding schools in Europe and America. Sara and Shireen were urging their mother to send them to the capital to attend university. They had already wasted a few years with indecisiveness after graduating from high school. Suri had no objection to her daughters' aspirations but it was hard for her to let them go. When they pressured her for a decision, she spent months fighting with her emotions before she made her mind up. She knew that old times had passed and the world was a giant of a place once one moved outside the boundaries of small towns. Boundaries will not break by standing witness. The country was changing rapidly but Karmanieh was too small, too confined. 'Small pond will not grow big fish.' Big fish will rot in little ponds like big brains, which would be squeezed out of small skulls. Her children would have a better future if they got out of this city. For her, life was frozen as it was, but her children had to travel through time. Had her husband been around, the whole family would have emigrated at the earliest chance. Suri had no courage to set foot outside her hometown. It would be best for the children, if they went and expanded their horizons. Suri knew that she could not send them one by one and endure their departure in sequence.

184

She did not have the strength. She concluded that they must go together, leaving her behind.

So, one cool summer day, she summoned the three of them into her room and opened a rolled paper, on which she had written in big letters; 'I, Suri, mother of these lovely children, whom I love more than life, have decided to send them away to Tehran to continue their studies and become something for themselves. This decision is in accordance with their father's wishes. You have one month to prepare yourselves for the journey. I do not wish to discuss anything about it until a few days before the date. Now let us forget about it and get on with our lives.'

* * *

On the night of departure, Suri avoided her bed and spent hours walking, thinking, walking. Crying was too soft an act at that crucial moment. Walking, thinking until finally, darkness gave way to the first light as she tiptoed to her children's rooms. Suitcases packed and ready, the air of departure breathing heavily in the house. Standing at a dim corner, watching them one by one, framing them in their sleep. Those young heads heavy with dreams, their minds busy to see the unknown path they were about to take. She pushed herself in but found no way to enter. There was no place for her in the future of her children. No one knew where she had come from, what she was doing in those rosy dreams. She stood watching. Lines of concentration on Sara's forehead indicated her firm stand in life. Shouldn't worry about her. Sara had always had a head on her shoulders. Twinkling smile on Shireen's lips, moving slightly to spell a word of protest, to tell an untold story, to act the unexpected. Should she worry about the unexpected? Sasan remained abstract, dispositioned. Does she have to sow the seed of early anxieties for her only son, for whom she had banked mountains of hopes? The answer waited along the line of an unforeseen future, lurking in the horizon. Weeping.

* * *

Suri hated the ritual of farewells. Farewells claim your husband and your children. Separate your loved ones and move them away, further and farther, where they might never return. Yet she held them one by one, the shape of their young bodies carved and framed, their smell stored in her memory. Their future's shape and size remained outside her mind's reach. She wished they had never grown up, remained inside their smaller bodies forever. She was already regretting her decision. But it was too late. She put them on the bus and turned away without looking. Walked straight, stopped and paused, talked to herself, argued and reasoned. Then sent her thoughts away. Walked through town until it was sunset and fatigue took her home. Home which was home no more. Weeping had left swollen marks on her mother-in-law's thousand lined face and the aroma of rosewater splashed at the steps to wash the sorrow of their departure away. A rosy departure, they all wished it.

Now the road was long and the horizon was under the haze of the desert mirage. Soon the mirage would disappear and the road would come to an end and towns would appear out of the mist. Soon, very soon.

In the coming years, Suri was praised and admired, scorned and scolded for her decision to send her children away. Those were the years ahead.

* * *

The day her children left was a special day. Suri was left on her own as she shut the door to her private chamber. She stood naked in front of the looking glass for a long time, searching for the marks of their shapes against her, only a few hours old. Lines of worry gathered on her forehead. The marks were ageing. She was ageing. Worry and loss was taking momentum and she could hear the palpitation of her heart. Was it the right decision to send three young children to a wild city? Would she endure their absence from her daily life and not die of the loss? Would she be around to see them pulling through life, standing on their own feet? Her whole body was weeping but she put a cover on her worries and prevented the anxiety changing into depression. She looked at her firm muscles and curvaceous bust, untouched for so long. She found no urge for the touch. No one aroused any passion in her, not after Javad, who gave her so much love in the process of making it. She still had enough of it stored in her memory to satisfy herself whenever the urge overpowered her. Now her heart was beating in all directions with different pulses. The children occupied much of the beating cords. There was the fading memory of Javad and those who over the years had been close to her. Madam Brigitte, who had made Karmanieh home after the death of her beloved husband and who had given her lots of noisy, sincere and passionate French style support and was close to her as a sister. Sisters at the British missionary school, who had consoled her with their English style compassionate way, kind, distanced, cool and caring as Jesus had instructed. There was a loud beat for her lazy, snobbish Persian cat, which followed her through the house and twisted among her legs as she walked. Little, steady drums were beating for the lines of flowerbeds that kept growing at hasty pace after winter packed and left. The desert sky and her twinkling stars that each night twinkled in the Milky Way and flirted with each other as soon as the moon was hidden from sight. The desert itself, panting with secretive waves of heat and its wild storms and its undergrowth; ants, rattle snakes, scorpions, emigrating swallows, noisy sparrows. These had the courage to fight the harsh climate of sand storms and blind heat. A tiny drum was beating for the thorn bushes, which grew wild by the sudden burst of rain that moistened the earth for a short period, forcing them to wake up and rush into life. The scent of spring buds and summer heat and dry autumns and the crisp of snowy winters.

Too many things had occupied her heart for love of life. Yet a stream of tears ran across her cheeks, soaked her body, splashed over the looking glass to fill the room and overflow into the veranda and join the brook nearby. Above all, were the worries for the unknown path she had pushed her children onto, of their possible failure, of her weakness not to last long enough to witness their possible success, of them never coming back. Suri's inner emotions had all surfaced. Stripes of lonely lines were tightening round her neck. She looked in the looking glass. The looking glass looked back at her. In front of her mind's eye two roads parted in different directions. One led to a grieving mother, who had lost her children to the big city and was left on her own to rot. The other showed a woman, who has had the courage to raise her children with much difficulty in that time and age, had sent them away to become something for themselves. Either way she would miss them terribly and her house would be empty of their existence now and maybe forever. She saw the multitude of bags packed and ready, sticking out of her blurred mind. Invasion starts at the mind. If she let her mind be invaded by the melancholy of the unseen and the unoccured, it would rule over her and she would be defeated. There, she saw a woman proud of her life and her endeavours. There, she found the courage to fasten the rope round the neck of the bags, to wipe tears away and compromise with life as if her children were living close by. Close enough to hear their heartbeat. The reason she broke down after her husband's departure was the fact that he went on a no-return journey and lost contact with his family. But that would not be the case with her children. It could not be. 'Distance does not matter if love spreads its wings over space. My children will keep their contact and will regularly visit home and fill the house with their noise and laughter. I will hold them to my heart so tight that that will keep me going until next time.'

Suri let the future stay in the future. But future had hidden bags at store. Future was not all bright, and orange. Did Suri know that wars would wage, revolutions would occur and children would be swept by the tide? Did she know that she might be a silent witness alongside the fastforward pace of history to deal with her own making? Future was a multitude of colours lining in the rainbow of time. Waiting.

Part Four

Twenty Three

Sara, Shireen and Sasan arrived in Tehran with heads full of plans and one ultimate goal; to take advantage of the opportunity they had been given and make a success of themselves to prove to the world that their mother had made the right decision to send them away to study. For them, a golden future glittered at the end of the horizon. Distanced, hazy but real.

As time passed through months and into years they tried feverishly to indulge Suri's spirit in the music of their success and achievements. Yet no matter how they assured and reassured their mother of their happy lives, of being successful and having educational achievements, Suri always held on to some worries. Ever since their departure, there was a blank space in her life that never filled itself even when the children returned home for holidays. She was able to view the bigger picture of her children's life but she was absent from those details that make life pleasurable and draw one close to existence. Outside their daily routine she lived in the solitude of apprehension and loss. Constantly, she swayed between the uncertainty and the inability to have much power over their associations, hobbies and engagements. Regularly, they travelled the three days journey by bus to Karmanieh for the New Years and summer holidays and sent her telegrams and wrote letters whenever they could but they were not with Suri anymore. Among the three, Sara was the one who wrote with a feverish conviction, picturing incidents and occasions that seemed interesting to report. But it was obvious that sometimes she economised with the details. As time passed, her letters became more abstract and broad simply because Sara had less time to allow her mother with the details. Besides, there were incidents that had to be kept away. Things that would have driven her mother to near madness had she known about them at the time. Suri had accepted the situation; this generation, especially those who lived away from home went their own way and were free from parental rules and did not listen to the advice or caution of the elders. But she was not sure whether they were able to protect themselves from the dangers of life among the noise and the confusion of modern times.

By the early 1960s, the three of them were university students, busy with student life. Sara had been accepted at the medical school and Shireen at the faculty of law. Sasan started with literature but changed his mind and sat for exams at the faculty of political sciences. Sasan was the apple of Suri's eyes, the replacement of his lost father, and a rising star in the eyes of everyone. Resembling his father's handsome figure, with an air of elegance about him, he was walking out of teenage years with a spark in his eyes that would penetrate the heart and bring him close to all those who associated with him. He had grown up to become a witty, generous, kind-hearted and gentle young man with a great future in front of him. Within a short period of time and after he entered the realm of political sciences, he changed beyond recognition. No one knew how his character changed.

Gradually, as he grew older he turned into a very serious person. While other youngsters were happy and carefree, Sasan's mind strayed among a galaxy of questions. He worked his way towards adulthood with a depth that was unusual. Although he took longer than his sisters to enter the university, his aim was to complete his education and enter the world of adulthood with the best results. But above all, he found goals bigger than life. He often thought about life and the way it was lived in the 1960s Iran. At every step, his mind's vision reviewed and doubted the path the young generation was taking and whether he should follow them accordingly. He talked little as his thoughts left little space for words. He spent long hours with these serious thoughts which mingled with other thoughts and left a mark of confusion on his expression. He often walked through the streets, met with people and talked to them. But in his mind's eyes, the interpretation was always different. His expectations of life, of himself were different. He saw corners and bends that did not come to people's attention. He could not get over any incident the way his friends, the light-headed youngsters did. Sasan's thoughts travelled back and forth through the daily life of the ordinary people, into the lavish lifestyle of the upper classes back into the slums of southern Tehran back into his head. In years to come the volcano of these thoughts erupted and spread fire across the mind of this young handsome man, who was a duplicate of his father, Javad khan.

* * *

Ten years after the 1953 coup in Iran that overthrew the government of the nationalist Prime Minister Mohammed Mosadeq and smashed the communist movement and sent its leaders into exile, Iran was relatively calm due to the political repression the Shah had imposed. During this period, the Shah had established a notorious secret service and reigned with terror, intimidation on the one hand, and American expertise on the other. At the same time, unrest had started to surface as students were engaged in political activity to protest against his dictatorial policies and the clergy raised their voices against his land reform and the right of vote for women. Iran witnessed waves of religious upheavals, which took the country into turmoil. At the university level, classes were cancelled as students walked out. Opposition to the Shah's programmes worked under different banners: religion, communism, liberalism and nationalism.

By the early 1960s, universities witnessed clashes between demonstrators and the secret police. It was at this time that the main opposition figure, Ayatollah Khomeini was ordered out of Iran, first to Turkey, then to Iraq, where for fifteen years he preached the essence of a future Islamic state, away from modern times. Simultaneously, the multi-coloured, multi-faceted metropolis of Tehran swam and swayed between the rich minority and the poor majority. Those who had migrated from the villages and left their ancient habitat to find jobs in the shantytowns which orbited Tehran.

Sasan travelled through the valleys and curves that separated layers of the society and that prepared grounds for anti-modernisation sentiments. He spent hours walking through downtown, the ghettos and shantytowns, where thousands of migrant workers lived in miserable conditions, those who had lost their livelihood to modernisation. If there was a hungry stomach on the street, Sasan was not the one to throw him a coin and pass by. He looked deeper into the being, the making of him a beggar. An impulse beyond his control pushed him to sit with him, to talk to him, to absorb his sorrows and miseries and take it all into his heart. He looked into life with such intensity that often frightened his sisters, who frequently cautioned him about that: 'my dear brother, why are you so serious about life, while your peers are living their happy lives'. Shireen, though a political activist herself, was the one who would often cry out and warn Sasan of the dangers, should he continue along that line: 'I am telling you my little darling. Too much seriousness will bring trouble. Your mind is ready to cross the troubled seas and I hope you put a halt to your thoughts before they send you towards the centre of storms.'

Sara believed that Sasan was going through a phase like other youngsters and would soon walk with the mainstream. Shireen was able to travel into the depth of her brother's yearning. She was the body behind students' activities and on many occasions, students' demands were met due to Shireen's recklessness and bold suggestions. Still, there were differences between the two of them. Yet Sasan's personal life had no specific shape or size. He was entangled among many thoughts, serious thoughts, dangerous thoughts, those that might push one into losing one's head altogether. One reason for him not to speak of them to anyone.

Sasan could not decide what to do with his life. He transferred to political science, a field that suited his character and hoped to brush his thoughts off the uncertainties. Doubts about the methods used for the wellbeing of the people, of the effectiveness of social reforms and the political force behind the newly established, American backed Shah's policies of modernising Iran. Walking through that path, he was not alone. Karim, his cousin who came to Tehran at the same time and who was his best friend and confidant, and an unshaped, unorganised group of students maintained similar thoughts. In the course of time, they decided to meet over the weekends and exchange ideas, to give them meanings, to shape them and to put them into perspective. Initially, there was no aim behind their thoughts and no action beyond their words. Their untamed minds were full of aspirations and an urge to build a utopia, where all were free from fear, free to divide bread and hunger in equal share. These meetings took them beyond street demonstrations and rallies. Yet their utopia was not structured, not until someone put grown up ideas into them.

The Leader, the Messiah was a year ahead of them. He knew everything and had answers to every question. He joined the group and entered the mind and the heart of these idealists like water that finds its way into a brook. No plans were made for his leadership. Not before long, he was the leader. Not long after, they found themselves a name, a structure and a plan of action. That was when Sasan and Karim pulled away from the crowd into the solitude of an underground life. They began reading forbidden books with a frantic pace, discussing unheard concepts and joined the guerrilla movement that was the political remedy and the solution of the sixties and the seventies throughout the world.

From then on, little was known about Sasan's personal life. He seemed to have postponed the process of life. While others hastened to finish their education and enter the workforce and join adulthood,

Sasan delayed all that. He failed his second year first and then the third year but that had little effect on him. Sara and Shireen, who wanted to keep their mother's mind at peace, tried to deal with him on their own. He seldom listened, rarely talked and when the sisters forced him to sit down and discuss his aims, he gave them reassurances: 'my dear sisters, please don't worry about me. Honestly, I am fine and there is nothing you should be afraid of. I would be grateful if you give me some encouragement, instead of warnings all the time.' There seemed to be more important matters for him to deal with before he began his personal life. Matters he dared not disclose to anyone even his sisters. Alarmed but waiting, they decided not to reveal Sasan's real activities to anyone and so, for a few years, Suri and Karim's mother, Soraya were kept out of the turbulence of their sons' adventures.

Twenty Four

Customarily, Tehran University with its many faculties was the centre of intellectual thought and the heartbeat of political activity. University life and political activity have always been entwined. Traditionally, different faculties divided the task of political campaigns among themselves. Out of sheer coincidence the Engineering and Technical Faculty produced the hard core of political activists, the Law and Medical School trained the brains behind the struggle and the Faculty of Literature and Drama made poets, writers and artists who portrayed the ideals and aspirations of the young generation in poetry and plays and took them to the heart of the nation. The latter had a romantic dimension to it because poets could not produce poetry in barren lands. For this, it was called the Faculty of Flower and Nightingale. No one's heart was spared from falling in love if they were associated with the students of this discipline.

Throughout the academic year, one could see young men and women strolling hand in hand, reciting poetry, reading a play, debating Hafez and Sa'adi and other great Persian poets, along the lively corridors, on the green outside, where flowers skirted around and tall trees gave shade and sanctuary. Love bloomed and works of art came to life, sculptures were erected, dramas rehearsed and episodes surfaced and rumoured around, giving flavour to the vibrant world of student life. Students at other faculties studied in a more serious environment, yet kept close contact with the poets, writers and artists. The combination of these faculties and the mixture of students, who came from all over the country, made Tehran University the beating pulse, the Mecca for those who yearned to spend a few years of their life not to only receive a degree, which was important for their future, but more importantly to live in the atmosphere of these activities.

* * *

At the same time as Shireen was studying for her law degree, a student from a modest family with average intelligence was studying for a degree at the Faculty of Literature and Foreign Languages. Two years later, he decided to change major and moved to the Faculty of Law. He met with Shireen and over the course of time, they developed a friendship, a close relationship and then courtship, and that changed Shireen's life then and forever.

Farid was the son of a low ranking civil servant who opted for law in hope of finding his way into fame and wealth by a profession that was restructured into its modern identity. Lawyers could have their own practice after a few years' training, which was closely monitored by the powerful Lawyers' Association. High earning and the prestige attached to the profession attracted many young enthusiasts such as Farid.

Farid was much older than Shireen and initially they met at students' rallies and university demonstrations and exchanged a few words. Later, Shireen became close to Farid more as a comrade than anything else. In the course of time, he made her a proposition, which did not suit Shireen's adventurous character, yet she accepted without giving it much thought. Farid was not the type Shireen would fall in love with. At that moment in time, it was his spark of recklessness and witty character that attracted Shireen to him.

From the second year onwards, Shireen was on the forefront of political activities. Sasan was at her side for most of the time but later he changed course. Farid had the experience of dealing with the secret agents, who would mix with students and identify the activists. He would stand by Sasan and Shireen and kept vigilant to protect them from attack. On one occasion, Shireen and Farid were caught in a police raid and taken to a secret location for interrogation. Farid sat close to Shireen in the covered van and whispered jokes in her ears to ease the tension and that angered the agents, who threatened to deal with them separately. During interrogation, Farid was beaten up for mocking the agents but he kept his head high with a smirk and no remorse. His act of bravery was admired by Shireen and moved her closer to him. Later, Farid understood that further arrests and detention might damage his future as a lawyer, so he sidelined himself and stayed in the shadow until his education finished.

Not only were students under close observation, those who were detained over unimportant incidents were not heard of for long periods. Apart from detaining political activists, the tactic of spreading fear among students and deterring them from political work were the official policy. It was a tense period. The underground movement for overthrowing the Shah was coming closer to reality.

Gradually, Sasan had sidelined from public demonstrations and absented himself from the university. Finally, in the mid-1960s, he and Karim disappeared without trace. The girls searched everywhere while trying not to arouse suspicion. Had their brother and cousin been detained? Had they gone abroad to join the over-growing groups of the Shah's opponents? They were afraid that the boys might have joined the armed resistance and became guerrilla activists, in which case their life would be cut short. Not before long, they would probably be captured and sent to the firing squad. At the time, thousands were in the Shah's prisons suspicious of such activities. They did not know what to do, inform their mother? Their aunt? Maybe they should wait and give it time before taking any action. Yet life carried its course despite all the worries. It was years later that they heard from the boys and in the most unusual circumstances.

* * *

By the late 1960s, Sara and Shireen had graduated from university with good results, which were posted to Suri in separate envelopes, decorated with the Deans' signatures and their high praise of the two young girls. They were about to enter their relevant professions and become women of distinguished positions, one a successful doctor, the other a lawyer and lecturer. For them, life seemed to have travelled on its due course.

Farid had also finished his studies as well and became a partner at a law firm. By then most of Shireen and Farid's mutual friends had taken jobs outside Tehran and moved away, some had travelled abroad to continue their studies. Those who had stayed in Tehran kept their contact and met at social gatherings, or went to restaurants, cinemas, or each other's homes. Shireen and Farid had remained friends and saw much of each other. Talking of the old days, of present life, politics, gossip, agreements and disagreements kept a number of them together for a few years. Up until then Shireen had not thought of her relationship with Farid in a serious way but that was about to change.

It was an early autumn. Shireen and Farid were strolling out of a cinema heading for a restaurant. The film they had seen and its characters and the whole episode had a profound effect on Shireen. She was drowned in the music of the film and the sad ending. Wrapped in a blanket of silence, walking alongside the tree lined Kakh Avenue. She was mesmerised in her own thoughts far away from the noisy traffic and Farid's presence. The wind was blowing in the top branches, mellowing harmoniously against the cool of the night. People were walking hurriedly to reach the warmth of their homes; a group of young men were singing love songs, their voices transcending the space flying out of tune. Suddenly, Farid took Shireen's hand and squeezed it gently: 'penny for your thoughts my dear.' She sensed the touch more than a friendly attention she usually got from him and pulled herself away: 'nothing important, just these silly feelings.' He pulled her towards the dark corner of the road where they were shielded by the trunk of a cypress tree and asked her to stand still to give him the courage to say what he wanted to say:

'What do you say if I tell you that I love you and want to propose to you to be my partner for life?'

Shireen's big eyes widened with a spark and mockingly she began to laugh and replied in her usual mischievous way:

'You haven't told me yet and I have no thought about something that has not yet been proposed to me.'

It seemed that she had reacted to a comical recommendation made by Farid so as to bring her out of her melancholy mood.

Farid frowned and pulled himself away. He waited a few moments and then continued clumsily:

'I am serious Shireen. I have been thinking about us for a long time. We have known each other for years. I know that you are an independent woman and do not want to bend to any rule. But, well, people should marry one day. I love you and I know that you care about me. Please think about my proposal and do not answer in haste.'

Farid's eyes were fixed on her face. Shireen did not give her mind enough time to think. The answer jumped out of her mouth instinctively was:

'You always look funny when least expected. If you are serious about it, then the answer is yes.'

Farid was puzzled. He did not know whether Shireen was teasing him or she really meant what she said. Still, he gave himself the courage to take her in his arms and kiss her on the cheeks and lips for the first time. Sweet, scented, was the touch of her lips.

'Ok, let's go and eat now.' Shireen was light hearted about the whole matter. She did not know what else to do. They had been together for such a long time that the scene, which happened a few moments ago, had repeated itself in her mind a thousand times. Had she known that grave consequence sat between a 'yes' and a 'no', she would have declared the moment ahistorical, a milestone, a beginning to a never ending tragedy. A life ahead with many crossings, bends and curves and deep valleys hidden among one small word. Deep, dark, treacherous.

Sara was apprehensive about Farid's proposition, but saw it best not to darken her sister's mind at something she could not put her finger on. She had known Farid as long as Shireen had but he had not touched Sara's heart. There was always a layer which separated Farid from sincerity, from clarity, from what he really was and what he pretended to be and for that Sara kept her distance. Nevertheless, as the elder sister, she wrote to her mother a long letter, informing her of Shireen's decision and sent her photos of Suri's future son-in-law.

Twenty Five

'This world, which was created

by that God

is not the world

of my childhood

nor adolescence

or adulthood dreams.

I will not

I should not

I can not

sit witness

to the walls

mounting brick by brick

suffocating the breeze which is

sliding through the window-seal

so to enliven the breath of

my cherished dreams

at the gate of awakening.

I have to change

this, or that.'

This was how Sasan returned home for a short time. This poem that Sasan had written on a piece of paper torn from a yellow notebook and left inside Shireen's handbag while she was at work. Shortly afterwards, he appeared in the middle of a cold night, unshaved, tired but firm. Suddenly, he seemed grown up and distanced. Something mighty had settled his mind into a final resolution, something that had met his urge and empowered him. He tried not to alarm his sisters but told them not to expect things go smoothly in the future. He answered no questions and warned his sisters: 'my darlings, I am not in the position to give you any answers. Besides, the more you know, the more dangers it would bring to you. Please do not worry. Just keep in mind that we are doing what has to be done and that things will change for the better before the end of this decade.' They talked for a while. Shireen informed him of his eventual marriage to Farid. Sasan looked at her for a long while, then embraced his sister and congratulated her. He took some money and a few necessities, kissed both his sisters with much affection, reassured them in a voice which was not assuring and pleaded with them not to worry. And vanished from the face of the earth.

Later in the year, Suri received a letter from Sasan, informing her that he had actually gone to England to study. A year later, rumours circled that Sasan had been spotted in Europe. Three years passed, during which Sasan and Karim sent brief notes and made short telephone conversations from different places: Beirut, Istanbul, and Vienna. Shireen and Sara had a lot of trouble convincing Suri and their aunt that Sasan and Karim were well and in no apparent danger. Karim's mother was easier to convince. Being ignorant to the complexities of the world, she accepted what Sara told her. Suri did not believe her daughters' explanations. All through years, she had been a witness to the transformation of her personal life and the wider world. She had a deeper insight into life. She read continuously and evaluated the political situation and naturally lived in constant worry. She followed the world news as well as domestic affairs. She saw President Kennedy shot in front of millions of viewers, Martin Luther King assassinated, man walked on the moon, the Women's Movement expanded, bringing with it the sexual revolution, the Pill and sexual freedom. She followed the wave of revolutions in the colonial world and the sprouting of tens of small independent countries from the rubble of wars and killing fields. She witnessed the Shah's land reform and the White Revolution in Iran and women gaining the right to vote and the clergy's vehement opposition to the reforms and violent demonstrations against the Shah. The Shah's lavish festivities at his Coronation while millions of Iranians lived below the poverty line. Marginalized from life, the world strolling by, leaving her behind, Suri was a mere onlooker. A mere onlooker! She was constantly shifting between happiness, grief, doubt and fright. She had been warned not to speak to anyone about Sasan, so the avenue of complaint was narrow and at times shut. Yet somehow she believed that Sasan was about to change the world. He had taken the banner his father failed to raise and one day people would see their hero march on the street. To see their hero march through streets.

* * *

In the summer of 1970, Shireen's marriage took place in Suri's house; noisy, crowded and full of manifestations of modern times; Rock & Roll, the Twist and fancy clothes. Against overt manifestations of joy, they were deeply hurt that Sasan would not be present at the wedding. But suddenly, and as the bustle and the noise was deafening the neighbourhood, the back door to Suri's house opened and Sasan slid in, bringing a magnitude of joy and blessing to his sister's big day. No one knew how he had found out about the occasion. The ecstasy of seeing him at the door filled their hearts. Sasan sat through the ceremony silent and tense. At the end of the night, he called his mother and sisters aside, held them to his broad chest, kissed them one by one and told them that he had had great difficulties reaching the wedding. No more explanation would be given and no questions should be asked. Then he sneaked away through the night as he had entered.

Shortly afterwards, Shireen and Farid flew to London for their honeymoon. There they stayed longer than a usual honeymoon. That stretched over a period of three years Shireen lived a married life.

* * *

All in all, Sara's life had a different turn to it. The hospital where she worked as a doctor was a modern hospital equipped with the latest technology. She was dedicated to her profession and spent long hours at work, learning and at the same time assisting others. As a young doctor, Sara stood at the forefront of modernism. Young, beautiful and ambitious, she threw herself into her profession in order to gain recognition and respect, as she deserved. She worked harder than her male colleagues, manifested readiness to learn and advance. Attending to the last patient, she stayed behind when others left their shifts. Apart from the hospital work, Sara put her imprint on other areas. She travelled to the disaster areas, whenever there was an earthquake or flooding and people needed medical attention. There she would not blink until the last injured person was comforted and attended to.

A few years on, and Sara's hard work was gradually recognised though she was tired of the male-dominated atmosphere, which took women for their beauty and femininity and not their professional conduct. Eventually Sara met a doctor who had studied in America and had returned to serve his country. Sara had no thought for big romance and Ali was not the romantic type; just a good-looking, reliable guy one would share one's sorrows and joys. They were working in the same ward and became friends in the first place. Sara was glad to have a friend among the hostile atmosphere so to open her heart and take her complaints to, but gradually they moved closer towards a serious relationship. It was Sara who proposed to Ali. No great expectations on either side, no ancient rituals to deal with. Their wedding was a simple ceremony in her mother's home, with as few guests as possible. Sara continued her work in hospital and life ran through its smooth course for that moment in time.

Twenty Six

London of the 1970s was a world of adventure and exploration. The city had just settled into the upheavals of the 1960s, the era of students' demands, the feminists' second wave of revolution, the bra burning, the Pill and sexual revolution, hippies, nudists and communes. Knowing that their stay would be short and floating on the wave of excitement to explore and see, Shireen had scheduled her days to the very last minute. There they toured the city and spent much time in the museums, theatres, cinemas, dined at famous restaurants and shopped at Oxford Street and Regent Street and prepared for a happy return.

Unlike Shireen, who saw London through a visitor's eye, the city and her hot pulse had a profound effect on Farid. London entered Farid's soul like a devil that captures one's mind. Astonished at first, then hypnotised, he aimed to postpone their life back home and prolonged their stay in London. He decided to discover the extended body of this thousand-layered city. He wasted no time to explore London from every angle. Initially, he started with the art centres and cultural events, then sneaking into the forbidden territory of the mischievous underworld. Six months into their stay, Shireen had long got tired and stopped accompanying her husband. Farid frequently vanished from the flat they had rented in Kensington, leaving his young wife alone. Gradually, his mind strayed away further and farther. Step by step, he became distanced from the man Shireen had married and became a stranger in the mirror of her astonished eyes, naked, ugly, and unpredictable. She urged him to go back to their home and profession and let their child, now growing inside her, to be born in their homeland. But Farid was indulging his appetite in the dazzles of the world he had recently discovered. The second and the third year passed where by then Shireen had long lost her interest in the city and her love for Farid. She missed her mother and sister but that seemed a far reaching desire lost in constant arguments with her husband. Their money had long run out and Farid was forced to change his lavish lifestyle. Shireen was left alone to cope with the delivery and the upbringing of her daughter, Mona, while attending a course and working part time.

Eventually, as time went on, Farid changed direction. He met some people from the Students' Confederation, a powerful organisation opposed to the Shah's regime. Repentant from his sins, he suddenly redressed in the old student's costume and spent most of his time in meetings and political activities. His acceptance into the Confederation was easily approved because he claimed to have arrived from Iran recently, fresh with information. Many Confederation members were banned from travelling to the country, so recruiting new arrivals was vital to the organisation. Farid soon became a centre figure, forgetting the fact that his student life had long ended. Setting aside his profession as a lawyer and his commitment to his wife and daughter, he stepped over and passed by and moved down the road to separate himself from them. The end to their marriage was shortly declared.

* * *

In a letter written to her sister, in October 1973, Shireen confided her anguish and the ambiguity of her future with her husband by quoting one of her mother's famous poems:

Dearest Sara,

'Further down the floating road

where silence envelopes

my beating heart,

filled with longing and desire,

the mirage of a wasteland,

210

is flaring up, wheezing down.

Grey ashes of a burnt sun,

piling, heaving,

scattering, blackening

the chain of hours

into a time which elapsed

in the sunset of despair'.

'Please Sara dearest, do not whisper a word to anyone, especially to mother. I hate to accept failure. But this man is not the man I knew. We have many differences and every moment of our life is a walk away from each other by arguments or worse, silence, which sometimes takes us into months. Soon I have to decide either to return home without him, or go my own way in this cold, rainy country. I have started a diploma course at the London University to busy my mind and I also work at a department store. We live in a small flat away from the sunshine and light, far from you. Every night I shiver with cold and yearn to be folded in your warm arms. Imagine where I was, and where I have ended! This country, with the people who distance themselves from us is not meant for me. I do not like to live the life of an immigrant with no roots to stand me firm on the ground. I see no reason to exile myself from Iran. The only happiness comes from this child who is the centre of my life. Amazingly, I think less of myself and my focus has shifted towards this little beauty whose smile expands my world and whose tears torment me. I have begun to understand my mother's anxieties now that I am a mother myself. Poor mother must have suffered immensely not to have her children around. I want to spend every moment of the day to watch Mona's movements; her growing body, in her sleep and while awake, her smile and crooning while lying in bed. She is the music of love, the warmth of my heart and the centre

of my existence. Such a strange sense of possessiveness has enclosed my other senses to the point of refusing to share it with anyone else. For that I have lost my self-confidence and turned into a prey for Farid's aggressive behaviour. How awful! It is for the first time in my life that I experience fear. What can I do? I am left with no love and worse, no respect for this man with whom I share my life and my child. He has threatened to take Mona from me and punish me for putting pressure on him to face his responsibilities.

Dearest Sara, London is a great city but one has to set one's mind to settle and enjoy it in its entirety. I cannot because I have my life back home. There is no shred of interest to tie me to this country so I have to come to a decision very soon.

Yours, Shireen

* * *

Farid was spending his free time in the meetings and political rallies. He was also travelling a lot. There was no doubt that Shireen was interested in the Confederation and admired the work they were doing in exposing the Shah's dictatorial regime but the moment bore more importance in her personal domain than entering a life which for her, had already expired. She could not return to her student years. She wanted to go into the future and build her life away from demonstrations and marches and banners, especially activities that took place thousands of miles away from home. So as time passed and Farid's activities accelerated and his fascination with the students' network did not diminish, they fell further apart. Farid turned into an impatient, irrational and aggressive man, especially after their daughter Mona was born. Alarmingly, Shireen discovered that Farid's activities within the Confederation were not associated with the Left or the Nationalists, which Shireen favoured. Rather, he had entered a religious circle, which aimed to bring a religious government to power. To the best of Shireen's knowledge, Farid was not a religious person. That young, well-dressed lawyer Shireen had married was gradually turning into a slow moving, prayer whispering caricature of a clergy. He grew a beard and said his daily prayers and acted like a total stranger.

Gradually, their arguments moved from verbal to physical abuse as the curtain of respect was removed. Farid was paving the way for a final ultimatum. He was about to become a prominent figure in the hierarchy of the religious sect and Shireen's way of life did not suit his situation. Should Shireen wish to continue with the marriage, she had to become a full-time housewife and take her traditional role. He would not allow his wife to work outside the house without the veil!

Now Shireen was wondering why she had married this man, this stranger in the first place. Why did she not give it more thought when Farid had proposed to her? He had no money to seduce her, no beauty to fall for, no family background to boast about. Did she marry him because society expected her to get married, or was there love between them at the time? Whatever it was, she had shared her body, her desires and her future with this man, who had then turned into a total stranger. No teacher, no book, not even her family had warned her of the dangers on the road of choosing modern husbands without consultation and careful thought. She did not know what to do. She was locked in the institution of marriage and she knew that breaking from it would not be easy. Even if she broke the ties who would give back the years she had wasted on this man? But then she had to make up her mind and she did.

Twenty Seven

Shortly afterwards, Shireen received a letter from Sara which added to her depressed situation. Sara had decided to leave Iran and settle in England. In response to one of Shireen's letters, Sara wrote:

Dearest Shireen,

I have decided migrate to England. I will tell you the reasons once we meet. Please wait until I join you. We will sort things out. As I told you before, I have concluded that I cannot live under the wing of dictators. I think there is more to life than sitting stale giving way to despair. In my mind I see myself more successful and happy in a free country, breathing the air I want to breathe and living where one is not meant to watch one's every words as they shape into a sentence, and censor every sentence in one's feverish mind as one tries to speak it out. I beg of you to wait until I join you. Besides, I have my own problems with Ali and I do not think that our marriage will last long. Probably, Ali wants to stay in Iran and I want to take the children with me. We have talked about the matter and more or less agreed on the issue. Please wait a few more months together we wil decide what to do'

Further developments hastened Shireen's decision to return to Iran just as Sara was preparing to leave. Farid was rumoured to be dating a female student in an Islamic outfit. Was that the main drive behind his recent attraction to religion? Who was this young girl who suited her husband, the man who pretended to be modern yet ancient to the bone? She made up her mind. She could not wait any longer although she knew that Sara's arrival might ease things a little bit. She knew that Sara would be busy sorting her own life for the first few months, while she had already withdrawn from London. She evaluated her situation and her future and whether she wanted to continue living with Farid. For days, she thought and weighed the decision she was about to take. It was a wise decision but to put it into action needed courage and determination. Finally, she declared a stop to her married life. 'Damn him and his beliefs dressed in the fashion of the day. He had probably had these notions all through life. It would be best if I move away before he causes more pain. I should not allow him to ruin my life and that of my daughter. It would be best if I leave him now.'

So, one fine summer day, while Farid was on a trip, Shireen packed her suitcases, wrote Farid a brief note and left.

'I have decided to leave you and get on with my life. If you think you will be happier without me, so be it. If you were ever regretful for what you have done to me and our daughter, you know where to find us. That is in case it would not be too late'.

* * *

Shireen and Sara met in the cross road of time. Sara left for Britain while Shireen urged to build her life afresh and out-poured an energy that pushed aside the melancholy she carried with her. Initially, they all travelled to Karmanieh and stayed with Suri for a while. Shireen was heartbroken and the personal defeat caught up with her. Suri was dubious about her decision to leave her husband. She believed Shireen had given up her marriage too easily but Sara agreed with her sister and advised Shireen to move away from Farid as far as possible. Shireen assured her mother that she had given Farid enough time and opportunity to consider his position. 'I am not interested in a man who is not ready to accept responsibilities. Besides, I do not want to share him with someone else.'

In the course of time, Shireen applied for a lectureship at the newly established Faculty of Social Sciences and entered the teaching profession with much enthusiasm. The subject she chose was controversial and amalgamated with prohibitions and strict censorship but Shireen loved her career and soon became a devoted teacher and spent much time on research and her students. She was the force behind building a big library and used her personal resources to import hundreds of books from abroad and set a team of experts to translate and publish texts that were not available at the time. She established a council of teachers and students and encouraged both sides to run the faculty in co-operation and consultation. Time proved that she had not distanced from the hot-headed woman she was in the years of rebellion and revolt. Whether that would work against her in the future was a story yet to be built in the structure of an unforeseen time.

* * *

Shireen resolved that Fardi was out of her life for good. He had become a distinguished person in the circle of the religious sect and as time passed, Shireen concluded that her decision to leave him was the best she had ever made. She was still attractive and shone at parties and social gatherings. She often thought of divorcing Farid but the idea of remarrying never crossed her mind. 'One should never make the same mistake.'

Then an incident occurred. The music of love tuned and its melodies poured into her veins. One evening, in the spring of 1976, while dining at a restaurant with a group of friends, her eyes met a well-dressed, handsome man, sitting at the table nearby. She fell for him head to toe. Love at first sight and no less. Shireen was magnetised by his charming smile, the melody of his voice and the elegance of his manners. Conquered by a sense of elation, she begged her heart to stop beating so fast, so hard against the walls of her tight chest. From the style of his searching eyes, as they circled around, and stopped for a brief moment as if confirming a rendezvous, Shireen resolved that he must be experienced in spotting and hunting beautiful women. She threw herself into his arms with no effort on his part. Within the space of a few visits in the cafes, restaurants, cinemas and his secluded apartment in downtown Tehran, Shireen indulged in love and passion, as she had never experienced before. There, their bodies rolled and filled time and space. There, she experienced a world, different from any other existence. If one powerful relationship existed in the whole universe, it was theirs. If in the span of a lifetime one experiences the fulfilment of two bodies, theirs was the perfect one. The marvel of their relationship rested in the fact that they did not make much demand outside their own two handsome bodies. Josef never spoke of anything but the moments they shared. He never asked questions and did not answer any questions. Shireen was content with what she had. They did not let intruders trespass their territory and shed light on their relationship. She would rarely speak of him to anyone except her sister. Her love stood outside her daily life. In reality, Shireen did not know what was expected from this relationship. Did she want to divorce Farid and marry Josef and by that, kill the love and the passion, which had roots in no commitment to each other? She knew that the intensity of their love would not last forever. It was too complicated and too heated to stretch beyond any scope. Yet she believed that if they parted in an unforeseen future, she had lots of sweet memories clustered to her heart to indulge her for the rest of her life. Nevertheless, their love affair lasted for almost five years, during which, Shireen had to divide her time into separate compartments; her career and her students; her daughter Mona and then him. Him. Him. Her beloved Josef. A treasure in her heart, a belonging, which had to be loved on its own merit.

Twenty Eight

The road to the downfall of the Shah started like this: news broke of the acts of sabotage by the 'terrorists who aimed to turn the country back into the dark ages'. A bomb exploded at an army base, a grenade was thrown into a police station, and a gendarme's outpost was occupied by a group of so called 'guerrillas'. The gendarmes were disarmed and detained for hours before help arrived. The 'terrorists' behaved humanely towards the captured, delivered speeches to them about the corruption of the Shah's administration and the efforts to drive the country towards western capitalism. They left leaflets, propagating their aims, promised to emancipate the people from the yoke of Imperialism and Capitalism and bring 'justice for all'. The helpless gendarmes were too frightened to grasp anything out of those words. They hushed the concepts away into the wind to save their souls from corruption.

The Shah's Administration, ignorant to the scale and the number of the group and its capabilities, yet frightened of the profound method of secrecy in which it had struck, leaving no traces for the secret police to track down and above all, of the freshness of the group's tactics, was shaken to the bone. Meetings were held between the army, the police and the security forces in which everyone was trying to distance themselves from blame. His Majesty wanted a quick resolution to the problem. His country, 'The Island of Stability', where oily dollars talked and foreign investment expanded had to be cleansed from the opposition and kept intact, untarnished, unshaken. 'Act promptly and extinguish the fire, destroy the roots', were the orders, the resolution, the white card in the hands of the secret police.

* * *

Ironically, stability was waning away and the oil money could not buy it back. The Emperor was about to lose his empire by the acts of a few hard-headed, reckless enthusiasts, whose patience had run out, who wanted change no matter to the right or the wrong direction. To cool the situation down, radio and television began publicity campaigns, minimising possible harm from the acts of sabotage. Time and again, universities were attacked, suspects were rounded up and sent to jail and subsequently interrogated and tortured. Books were confiscated, suspicious elements detained, minds burnt, tongues cut, ambitions curbed. Brains were dissected to find traces of serious thoughts and then set alight and the ashes scattered across the deserts. Tongues that spoke meaningful words were cut off. But to no avail. Stability was running away. Oil money was chasing to buy it back. But it could not.

The fact was the oil was bringing money and prosperity, not for all but to a minority, who held on to power. The rest, the majority were the followers of those forces that were pulling them back into the tunnel of time. Their minds were closed to the changing world, their heads unearthed from a deep sleep, breathing the breath of bygone eras. Big brains were consuming the newly acquired wealth and small brains were getting the dust and dirt of history. A subterranean water system was penetrating through the cracks, removing the dirt, paving the path for a stormy river, fermenting under the grounds of the Iranian plateau. Stormy clouds pregnant with acid rain were in waiting to burst soon after. The world was about to witness yet another catastrophe in the guise of yet another popular revolution.

In 1978, the whirlwind of revolution was taking the state of affairs into chaos and a lawless society. The Shah appeared on TV, pale and broken, admitting that he 'heard the voice of the people's revolution' and he would meet their demands. Over a period of three months, the Shah changed three Prime ministers, imprisoned his entire administration and abolished the hated Rastakhiz Party. It was not enough. People demanded his throne. His days were over. At the international level, the G7 meeting in Guadeloupe, it was decided to stop support for the Shah and that meant the death of monarchy in

Iran. There, began the transfer of billions into foreign accounts, the flight of the Shah's relatives and the ruling elite, one by one or in groups, and an end which came sooner than expected. In early January the emperor and empress fled the country, and Iran fell into chaos. Millions marched on the streets pulling down statutes and celebrating the new era. Within days, the army, the police, the secret service, the navy and the entire state apparatus fell apart. Political prisoners, communists, socialists, the Left and the Right, religious left, religious right and nationalist, dressed in all makes; American green blazers, Che Guevara hats, Castro's beard, Lenin's sharp tongue, Mao's cunning smile and the holy man's secretive eyes, carried on the shoulders of their blind followers came out of prisons, returned from exile, came out of hideouts, to the platform of Tehran university, to the mosques, to the cemeteries, to the radio and television stations, so to deliver black, green, yellow and red speeches.

People were all hope. Hope was all that blossomed and bloomed. People marched on a daily basis, read hundreds of statements and pamphlets, listened hypnotised and waited for the events to find their way into time and materialise their high hopes. Between the space of a breath, short, brisk, discontinued, fear gathered its wings and fled only to return a few months later. No one was afraid to speak what came to their mind. Freedom was walking in full costume with hasty strides. People were freed from the dictator. Free from the arbitrary rule of fifty years. They were dreaming real dreams. Dreams that had been waiting for a very long time. Widening smiles paved the way for the aura of promises fulfilled. Everyone was kind to everyone. Old enemies were shaking hands and became new friends. The spirit of brotherhood and humanity danced in the air as freedom walked on the streets uncensored. Newspapers were flourishing, associations were forming, syndicates were establishing, women were set loose children went astray and carried guns to safeguard the newly acquired freedom. Dreams bloomed and flowered for one spring in a thousand years.

The spring of 1979 was the one and only season for the people of Iran to breathe the aromas of fresh acacia wafting across the Iranian plateau. The absence of a dictator, which had never occurred in the past fifteen hundred years, let the people taste the forbidden fruit of freedom for a very short time.

Between the revolution day on February 11, and the new order coming into power, different political groups hurried to take control of the situation, but mostly failed. The underground guerrilla movement, not knowing what strategy to take and which tactic to use, suddenly came over ground, promising the workers their share in power and the oppressed freedom from oppression. Then with the speed of sound, thunder struck the whole political system of Iran. Time, confused from its precision, ran in all directions. The political space shared by everyone for a brisk, short period was vacated in haste only to be filled by a group of hardcore zealous sectarians, who had sprung out of the thin blue sky. People never knew how they got caught in the eye of the cyclone that swept them out and away into the abyss of time. The people's movement, young, inexperienced, remained on the sideline mourning the number of martyrs it gave to pave the way for one sect to take up the power. Thereafter, heroes stood in rows, martyrs stood in rows, promises stood in rows as time was moving fastbackward to sink into its ancient plateau. An unspoken patience, tired but dignified, peeped through the cracks of the future to witness history change hands. The train of this Iranian revolution had a rendezvous with death.

* * *

Farid returned home, an Islamic hero. Immediately, Shireen filed for divorce although she had no plans to marry Josef. The delayed battle had started at the worst of times. She employed a lawyer who took her case to the court but courts were in turmoil as well. Farid declined to grant her divorce and threatened to take custody of their daughter. Yet Shireen had resolved the matter years ago and wrote Farid a brief note:

'Do whatever you want. I am not here to be ordered around. If you want Mona who is now a big girl, and the courts give her to you, I will fight you to the end but if I am defeated, so be it. You cannot force me into anything. I will not be intimidated.'

Yet the fight for divorce and the custody over Mona took her well into the early 1980s, into the abolition of the family law, which protected Shireen and her daughter to some degree. Now a serious threat was over her ten-year-old youngster. Shireen sent her to Karmanieh to stay with her mother until the dust settled. That the social and political events would affect individual's lives to such a degree was a phenomenon beyond Shireen's scope of understanding. But it did. The revolution took place and transformed the lives of every Iranian. The impact of this revolution was much harder and travelled much deeper than Reza Shah's modernisation and Mohammed Reza Shah's Americanisation policies. The majority of people overwhelmed by the religious propaganda voted the rule of religion. Slowly, meticulously but firmly, the clergy took power, held to the power, pushed aside others and invented their own system of government. An Islamic revolution meant an Islamic revolution. A one-man ideology sliced its way through the fabric of the Iranian society and was forced on everyone and everything. Otherness was a crime. Iran sank into the swamp of the past tense. The swamp swallowed and digested in its vast stomach those who were opposed to the past times. Soon, people were forced to take sides, to choose between ideologies, or otherwise leave the country or be hanged. A large number were peeling off their non-ideological skin and joined the long queue of opportunists waiting for the right moment to take opportunities. Some were caught in conflicting ideas.

One must remember that although millions had participated in the biggest event of the late twentieth century, when the Shah's regime was toppled they did not know what to do with the old apparatus, its legacy and its cultural heritage. The clergy had no idea how to shape themselves into a proper establishment, though its mighty leader preached an Islamic state.

Gradually, an ocean of raw rage was bubbling up giving way to confusion, collision and amputation of people's expectations. Soon, spring of freedom and blossoms of hope burnt among the fire lit from all sides. Had they had time in between the space, hopes might have taken shape, twined around other aspirations, and bore children of maturity. Then, children were still-born from an immature womb. History pushed herself onto a steep road. The children of revolution had no chance to re-live inside a mother who had long waited to have them delivered. Soon, the euphoria of the victory was replaced by mourning for the dead, the disappeared, the martyrs and those who were sent to the firing squad. A town was born of dead bodies. The stench of history whirled and blanketed the body of joys, the eyes of starry nights. History moved across the desert on a fastbackward train. The moon gathered its stars from the Milky Way and darkness fell upon the Iranian plateau.

* * *

By the early 1980s, as the turmoil in the country slowed the pace of life, so did Shireen's relationship with Josef. For some time, they were both preoccupied with the unexpected events. Everyone's life was in the process of transformation and people were forced to adjust and harmonise to the new order. Shireen had no intention to transform her life and conform as required but she had to fight at different fronts; her career was in jeopardy because she was branded a communist and so a threat to the Islamic society. Her divorce had not materialised and the custody of her daughter was in doubt. Her relation with Josef was hanging in the balance. By then she was aware that Josef was a married man with three children. Many things were at stake from an incident in which she had no control over it.

Josef was the first who disappeared from her life. Being a senior civil servant in the Shah's administration, rumours spread and plagued his personal life. He was in great danger. In such circumstances, his relationship with Shireen was the least of his concerns. Like thousands of others, he decided to escape to the safety of a foreign country with his wife and children. The day they said farewell was one of the saddest days in Shireen's life. Though she knew that some day their relationship would come to an end, she preferred a gradual withering of affection and passion, not an abrupt and painful departure. They embraced and became one as they painted the shape of their bodies to the last detail in the reservoir of their memories. Promised to write, to phone and to see each other in foreign lands. Knowing that future was a far-fetched horizon and distance would swallow love, kill affection, and put an end to the closeness of bodies.

In reality, their situation was no different from that of other people. In the labyrinth of a disintegrated state and in fear of persecution, imprisonment and execution by many means, of civil war as well as the imposed foreign war, children were separated from their parents, wives from husbands, lovers from love, brothers from sisters and all from their livelihood. For a period in time, the density of farewells at the airports, at the train and bus stations, at the harbours and clandestine border points choked a nation that never imagined in its wildest dreams that the cream of her society would migrate to the four corners of the world en masse. Thereafter, and over a decade, some three million Iranians, mainly the elite and the educated, who had never experienced exodus since the Arab invasion, joined the queue of refugees and had to beg foreign countries to let them in, to grant them the status of 'bogus refugee', 'economic migrant' and a 'burden on the state'. There they had to stay in migration, alienation and disintegration until the end of their time.

* * *

Change towards the formation of a religious state moved so quickly that it left no space for objection. One would wake up on one summer day, to see the music chained into the rails of ancient lamentation. One was not allowed to listen to the lyric of the highlands of Kurdistan and the coasts of Bushehr and the deserts of southern Persia and the drums of the gypsies in the eastern valleys. One would wake up at dawn, to hear on the loud speaker lamentation for the dead that had replaced lyrics that for thousands of years had sung the passion and the yearning of human nature. These were ordered to be wiped off from memory and seeped into the cavity of nothingness. Perished. The language of the human body, dance, modern dance, folk dance, gypsy dance and the dervish's dance were to freeze. Sculptures were pulled down and crushed into pieces, paintings and pictures of women were veiled and hidden in the darkness of anonymity. Iranians, who until then were famous for their love of poetry and the beauty of nature, fell into the abyss of time. Later, much later, they were known to the world as terrorists, fanatics and fundamentalists. That would come later.

* * *

The irony of history left its marks more than any other group, on the life of the Iranian woman. Iranian women were the most active group against the Shah, on the streets, in the workforce, in the underground movement, in prisons and in front of firing squads. The picture of a guerrilla woman driving a confiscated tank into Tehran University registered in the history of Iranian women's struggles for equality to men. Yet the first decree issued by the great leader targeted women and promised them oppression, humiliation and discrimination in an unprecedented scale. Did they not object to that first decree and other decrees thereafter? For days, women marched and demonstrated their objection, held sit-in protests in the ministry of justice, wrote to the newly appointed authorities and raised their voices. To no avail. Men left them alone to fight a losing battle. Men distanced from them because deep down they all agreed with what was decreed. Deep down they were all in favour of such decrees which put a halt to women's freedom and equality. Shall we accuse Iranian men of collaboration with the leader who thought nothing of Iranian women? History proved they did collaborate.

* * *

A few months into the year 1980, Shireen was dismissed from her teaching job on the grounds of instigating the students into rebellion by establishing a library and the council of teachers and students. Her crime was bigger than expected. She was threatened with imprisonment should she raise her voice in objection. Farid, the devoted, trusted lawyer, with a high position at the new administration did not waste any time. By then, he had married a young girl, half his age and was at the forefront of advocacy for new legislation, which paved the way for men to take as many as four wives and hold as many concubines as their appetite permitted. By then, the Family Law, which had given women limited rights to divorce and the custody of children were cancelled. Thousands of women were forced out of jobs, forced to wear the veil, forced to shut up and become housebound. Shireen's life was looming in the dark. She feared for her own safety and for losing her daughter to Farid. Many people had been detained without committing any crime, had disappeared, had their bodies dumped in the outskirts of towns. Personal properties were raided by thugs under false accusations and incidents of rape, murder and intimidation were rife. Shireen was on the run. She changed her address several times and hid from public for months. But how long could she continue with this clandestine life? Why should she live a fugitive in her own country?

* * *

It was the winter of 1981. Shireen had made her decision. Apart from her mother and Sara, who was waiting for her anxiously in

London, no one knew about her plan. Suri witnessed her world collapsing in all directions. She believed that life had turned its back on them but little could she do to stop what was ruining them at high speed. Fear for the safety of Shireen was very grave. Shireen travelled to Karmanieh to bring back Mona and prepare for departure. Once again the pain moved into the years ahead, as Suri held her daughter's broken body against hers and cried.

Shireen managed to buy false documents under false names. How much did she pay the smugglers to get them to the borders of Turkey by travelling through the snowy mountains and crossing under the watchful eyes of the guards, is a secret yet to be revealed. How did she manage to reach Hungary, then travel to a refugee camp in Holland, where she stayed for six miserable months before Sara got her accepted to England, is a story to be written in a separate volume. The trauma was more than the power of her endurance and she declined to talk about it, ever. Needless to say that she was ill with various nervous disorders for almost a year before she was on her feet once again. Mona, angry with her father and in protest to him, decided to abandon his surname and kept her bogus name as a bogus refugee in her borrowed home, England. Shireen could not live with a false identity.

* * *

Twenty years on, Farid, a prominent figure in the Islamic State, has twice married girls, his daughter's age. Shireen never pursued to get divorced from a man who has never been a husband to her or a father to Mona. For her, the future walks ahead under cloudy skies, over the mountains of hope and the waterfalls of despair. On sunny days, Shireen rebuilds her life, re-lives her loves reconstructs her shattered past. On the cloudy days, she mourns the loss of her lover, the country she left by force, her mother and the warmth of her students' hands. These are parts of a life, which is merged with other lives in a land which has given her sanctuary.

Twenty Nine

Sasan and Karim emerged from their hideouts, political heroes. They appeared in public hand in hand with their young and politically active wives. Until then, Suri and her sister, Soraya were not aware that their sons had married. The guerrilla organisation they belonged to did not permit any personal information to reach the families. But that was not all the story. Sasan and Karim had been away for a long time and had spent a few years in camps in Lebanon for military training and then returned and joined the armed struggle.

Now, carried on the shoulders of people, burnt-faced, hard-featured, the smile of victory on their faces and their young wives at their sides, Sasan and Karim arrived at Suri's house a few weeks after the revolution. Suri was all but a ball of happiness. Her pleas were answered, her cries no more in vain. Her long lost love had arrived. The forgotten universe, the son whom she thought was taken away from her, had his arms around her. The pupil of her eyes reflected his existence. The gate of the desert had opened and stars were falling down, pouring light over the city. Music roamed, wine was drunk, happiness danced with fresh, moist rhythms. The pair of heroes stood side by side their shining wives and their proud mothers, delivering speeches which set fire to the heart. Resembling his father on his return from Russia some four decades earlier, looking into the mind and the soul of the enthusiasts who saw a red revolution at hand, Sasan promised the paradise, the garden of equals, Adam and Eve working side by side. Suri was an ocean of joy, her feet walking above the water's surface, her mind singing, her mouth smiling. Javad had reincarnated from his deep absence.

Sasan's wife, Sima, young but mature by political consciousness, her wild beauty resembling the ancient queens of Persia, the spark of intelligence in her eyes, sat at Suri's heart the minute she put arms around her. She loved the body who shared her son with her. Sima instantly fell in love with her husband's family. As an activist of underground movement she had always declined showing emotions. Fearsome of the secret police, of prison, of torture and execution, she had moved from one spot to another, learnt the art of combat and lived with minimal luxury. All of a sudden she was showered with this intensity of attention she was not used to. In her heart she was a sensitive, poetic woman but when she entered the armed struggle, she discovered that the means of achieving her goals were far from poetic. Imagine, for most of your adult life, you have been working underground, surrounded by highly political people, who were constantly engaged in debates over strategies and tactics of armed struggle. Was there any space for personal desires while your mind was constantly directed towards such goals? For years Sima's desires were dangling along with fear, hate, death and destruction. The command to kill in order not to be killed had scared Sima's poetic feelings away into the safety of a forgotten memory. Even her marriage to Sasan and her love for him was wrapped in political decorations.

Suddenly, Sima discovered that between political struggle and real life were miles of ambiguous areas she had not walked on. Ambiguity about their roles as women with their own needs. Now, for the first time in years, she felt the tenderness of love creeping under her skin, warming her heart. Sima saw Suri, a woman who had borne the world in her womb. Sara's attention to Sasan and Shireen's deep and passionate love to her brother and his wife had astonished Sima as she listened to her husband's heartbeat, and thousands of questions lingered in her mind, waiting to be answered on their own accord. Shireen's face was radiant in the moments she spent with her brother, had him all to herself and talked the world over. She walked around him, held him in her arms and stuck to him like honey from wild flowers. Sima understood that she had to share Sasan with many women, sweet, scented but divided her love sprang back behind the limits.

* * *

Walking across the universe, picking up stars, dreaming sunny dreams, Suri wished to share her happiness with the town. In celebration of her son's safe return, she invited the neighbourhood to the biggest feast held in years. A wedding ceremony to welcome his bride, to place her on her heart. Music was yet to be banned, so she invited a famous band. Wine had yet to be declared illegal. Barrels arrived in red and white costumes. Women gathered to make sweets and cookies, to prepare the house for the occasion. It was the first time in many decades, since the disappearance of her husband, that Suri made herself a nice dress that groomed her face and coloured her hair and ordered everyone to wear their festive outfits. Across the street, around her house and in the courtyard, colourful lights glowed, flowers smiled and musicians played; three nights and four days. Troubles of the outside world waited patiently. Revolution waited impatiently. For Sasan and Sima to be wedded in style with proper processions. Intimidated by the grandeur of the event, shy at seeing all eyes on him, Sasan failed to play down his arrival. He agreed to re-marry because his mother's only wish was to be met. Turning a blind eye on the situation, Sima sat at the ceremony for the second time. The fragrance of happiness danced across the city. Condensed but short-lived. Out in the desert, wild winds were waiting to blow away from the town, from hearts, from memories, the joyous moments that could be found once in a thousand years.

* * *

Then back to political activity and mobilising people to defend the revolution, to give it shape and depth, to build their utopia. There was a lot to be done and little time left. Sasan and Sima were back

230

to business. Shortly afterwards, disagreements over strategies and tactics emerged among Sasan's comrades at the top and split up and weakened the biggest popular movement of contemporary Iran. No one could confront the ever-increasing threat from the newly established regime that aimed to oust other groups. Taking advantage of the war which imposed itself on the country by Iraq and constant fights among the opponents, the Islamic administration utilised all its might for a crackdown. Groups of organised thugs began their onslaught on the entire movement, which had helped to drive the Shah out of power.

At this time, Sasan and Sima were living with Suri. Sasan's comrades were helping Shireen to arrange her departure. A few weeks after she got out and reached Turkey and Suri breathed a sigh of relief, thugs went on the rampage through town and arrested whoever they got hold of. A common method of suppressing opposition and creating fear. Sasan knew that his days were numbered but no one knew how they decided to come for them. It all happened so quickly. One day in time, among the silent wailing of their mothers and the fearful eyes of their wives, they were both taken away by those who had appointed themselves as the law and order. Taken away into the abyss where no one could reach them for a very long time.

Suri was once again on the brink of collapse. She wanted to set fire to the world, to break it into pieces if that would help to bring back her beloved son. Then a silent fear, patience and darkness. There were no laws to prevent random arrests. There was no authority to take complaints to. Those who took Sasan away were the only law and authority. By then hundreds had been sent to firing squads or hanged from cranes or shot in the dark alleys or disappeared from sight, swallowed into the labyrinth of a lawless state springing from among chaos.

Sasan and Karim were both moved to the capital on charges of otherness. Hundreds had been thrown into the newly refurbished prisons, replacing those who were freed by the hands of these very same prisoners. The New Order had a fuming rage to persecute those who did not believe in its Order. Sima was fearful for her husband as well as herself since she knew what might happen to both of them. She advised her in-laws to keep their voices down until the dust settled and reason overcame ignorance. The women who shared one love among them were tied up in grief and just waited. There was little news from inside prisons, no visiting system, no trials, and no proof of guilt, of innocence, of crime. It was enough if your neighbour had a grudge against you. Gallows would swallow you and your footsteps would be washed from history.

It was 1981. The war was raging in the west of the country. Taking advantage of the situation, the ruling elite tried to establish what they aimed for. A one-state ideology was emerging from the onslaught. Other ideologies, right or left had to be killed, to be vanished to make way for the One and only One school of thought. That was how happiness gathered its pace and walked away. Wine and music were exiled from the land. Laughter hid among the cracks of walls. Fear imbued itself in the minds and stayed and settled until the end of the century and the birth of the new century and thereafter. Mourning for the dead, the martyrs and the ancestors became the norm. The country stood in the grip of a thousand year old curse. Occupation and bombardment of cities covered the domes with ashes of terror. Martyrs crowded the streets. Children were still born. Sima was captured. Karim's wife, Mina was captured. No one heard of them, any of them for the next five years. Short-lived, brittle, brisk was the happiness that flew over Suri's head once upon a time.

* * *

Years had arrived and passed. The end of the second millennium was near. Military dictators had been removed and replaced by civilian dictators. The world has shrunk into one tiny village, ruled by technology, lasers and soundtracks sitting at every corner, watching over everyone. Socialism and communism, once the utopias of millions, had finally been defeated and declared out of date. The oppressed have remained maimed and unable to take revenge on the oppressors forever. Star wars, militarism, terrorism, fundamentalism, ethnic cleansing, atheism, political religiosity, consumerism, vegetarianism, humanism had become the fashion of the day. Modern machines, superhighways and supersonic means of communication had replaced the age of pen and pencil. Under the very eyes of all the humanist onlookers, who cry their hearts out at the sight of a mouse being killed for medical experiments, the war and torture technology had advanced to cut tongues, to slice throats and to amputate hands. Humanists are in total agreement with their respective governments that ultimately it is necessary to create work for the workers in their home countries and shorten the dole queues and the budget has to meet the needs even if the workers produce weapons of mass destruction.

* * *

Years later, Sasan came out of prison, a broken soul. He carried the burden of a secret he could not disclose to a soul. Karim was sent, to the firing squad on that cold night. Karim, whose warm heart beats no more, whose wise thoughts are scattered in the universe and whose eyes, his bright intelligent eyes are hollow of sight and whose grave is not even marked with an unknown stone. In those days the distance between life and death was a 'Yes', or a 'No'. Karim preferred to say 'No'. Old fool! Old fucking fool! Had he known that the ideology he slaughtered himself for, did evaporate into the mist of air a few years after he was rotting under that earth, would he have said 'Yes' to the question, which had his death sentence carried in its letters? The answer would never be known.

* * *

By the end of the 1980s, prisons were full to the capacity. New prisoners were kept in the corridors for months on end before a room would accommodate them. New chambers were built in haste. Foreign experts were recruited to give consultation on torturing methods. A cemetery was filled with broken skulls, thoughtful minds and bodies saturated with desires for life. Then, suddenly, international humanists woke up from their sleep and showed an interest in the abuse of human rights in Iran. They pressed to visit the country's prisons. That was of course to visit clean prisons, empty prisons with medical facilities and the psychologists who dealt with nervous disorders. Amputated prisoners, stubborn prisoners, unrepentant prisoners were not suitable to be kept in modern prisons and be visited by modern humanists.

By then the one-state ideology was firmly in place and based on religious interpretations a One World Vision of the identity of the self in relation to the nation of Islam was formulated and put down as the new bible. Obedient citizen was the requirement of the new ideology. From the onset, the war of conformity started and continued in the media, in the textbooks, the mosques and public platforms and through individual representation. There was no space for non-conformists. So, the river of exodus roamed across time and the shadow of death spread on those who stayed inside the borders, as outsiders.

As for thousands of prisoners of conscience and who rejected the oneworldvision, prison maintained a teaching ground, a university, where all had to be brainwashed and conform. If prisoners did not learn this basic lesson, their life would always pose a danger to the state. In the wake of foreign humanists' eventual visit, thousands of prisoners were yet to have their brains washed of the past and modified into the new order. A solution had to be found to the problem. First, identification was carried out and lines were drawn between the conformist and the non-conformist. There were enough ears and eyes in the wards to identify the sincere from the dishonest. Repentant prisoners acted as those eyes. Those who had crossed the line of misery to repenting, and who knew secrets of their groups and agreed to collaborate with the authorities. It was decided to call each prisoner into the office and ask them a simple question. 'Do you believe in the regime and its ideology?' If the answer was 'Yes', so be it. If they said 'No', the state had every right to dispose of them.

Sima knew what was going on and who was going to be summoned for interrogation. Yet she kept her silence. Passing through the corridors into the interrogation centre, Karim spotted her standing at the far end of the room, nodding to the interrogator. Later, during the night, when he was preparing his final walk outside the ward and there were a few moments left, he whispered to one of his roommates but pleaded with him to keep it to himself. The wind blew the brittle words so to reach Sasan.

Seasons have changed; days have passed through darkness and emerged at dawn, and Sasan has lost his sanity in the process of time, along with his wife, Sima who was a pearl in his heart. Mina, Karim's wife had fled to America through the mountains of Kurdistan with a group of fellow comrades, where she had joined the Prozac Nation.

Yes, there is a bright side to everything. There were thousands who came out of prisons and restarted life, enjoying every moment of it. There were also many who became repentant and functionaries of the state and worked at the heart of the administration and signed contracts worth millions of dollars and at the end of the second millennium rolled in oily dollars. Sasan and Karim were not one of them.

Today, if you pass the city of Karmanieh and wish to visit Sasan, he will welcome you with a smoky smile that smells of burnt opium he smokes day and night, hour after hour and tells stories of his heroic battles against the Shah and the lost battles in the prisons of the new regime. Reclining on a mattress, propped up against pillows, he sometimes laughs uncontrollably and at times clouds gather around his smoky eyes. His stories are long, tedious but without malice. He stretches the words, puts emphasis on unimportant incidents, reveals top secrets of the underground movement and at times delivers speeches on how the world should be governed. You ask him any question he has an answer for that. But you have to give him time to smoke a few puffs, to inhale with closed eyes before he begins with the answers. If you want to visit Sasan, which is fine by me, never, ever ask him about his cousin and the comrade in arms, Karim and his own wife Sima, the pearl of Persian queens, the diamond of his youthful heart, the lost love of a lost continent. That will break his heart.

Part Five

Thirty

Days have gathered intensity and rolled into months, accumulated into seasons and formed years. Years, years. Twenty years. I have been living in London for twenty long years. In the past, exile was a concept totally unknown to us, Iranian people. Now it is the reality of our lives. I often think of this alien, yet familiar concept and wish to wipe it from my memory. But it is here under my skin hidden beneath the drums of my heart. I have been exiled from my home country. Whether it is right to have this deep sense of belonging to a territory, where one has been born and bred is a matter under much contention. There are times that I wish I could belong to somewhere else, became British not by way of a passport but in a true sense. But even if I want to strengthen my sense of belonging to this land, she would refuse me as a genuine child. A step-child, yes. But that would be all. I am the citizen of no specific place. I am a dervish, a wanderer. An onlooker to the world of belonging. I am living in exile forever, in alienation, swaying between memory and reality.

I remember my first trip to England on our honeymoon with my husband Farid and the disasters that clustered to my life thereafter. Then I blamed London for all that. Now I have washed the city of the guilt. Baptised it in the spirit of friendship. Now I love this city and the grandeur of its character. I love my street, the village nearby and the five minutes walk to the river. I love living in London, like the way I once loved Karmanieh and then Tehran. You see, you can fall in love with the place you live if you take it into your heart. My daughter, Mona and I have settled in London and consider ourselves Londoners though London is far from accepting us as one of her own. Mona has gone a step forward. She had continued her studies and became a successful professional woman, working in the city of London. She is a very happy woman. A few years ago she fell in love with and Englishman and married him and moved away from home. I have a granddaughter whom I love more than life. I have established a quiet life for myself and pursue no high ambitions because I am left with none.

Sara and I are close as ever. Sara's three children have also had their own successes. Her elder daughter, Jasmin is an environmentalist and works for the United Nations in Geneva. She is not married. Her older son, Payam is a businessman and has married an Austrian. They have two children. Sara's youngest son, Omid is an IT specialist and has married a Spanish girl and they have three children. We live in the same neighbourhood and see each other regularly. We often walk together across the English countryside, or just stay at home and enjoy each other's company. We are both on the verge of retirement. A good deal of our time lingers between the reality of life here and the past. We both have sailed through rough seas and landed ashore with more than just cuts and bruises. Sometimes, we compare and contrast our thunderous past with the dullness of the present, review the mistakes we have made and whether it was possible to prevent them. More than anything we both miss our mother, Suri, who has stubbornly refused to step outside Karmanieh. 'I have been planted to this desert soil. Go and replant yourselves wherever you want. Let me keep my roots in the depth.' She wrote to us once we were insisting she joins us here. Suri preferred her city to her children. She and Karmanieh are one soul in two bodies. Was there a secret behind her decision never to move out of the city? Maybe we will never know.

* * *

Life is a process of entwined events that begins from birth and amalgamates with the environment we live in. We often think there is no relativity between human temperament and nature. Our peace of mind and mood swings are all blended with nature. Our spirit lifts with vibrations of life when the sun penetrates the earth's womb and the light shimmers along the horizon, or the raindrops tap on the chimneys and snowflakes dance outside a window seal, or a bird croons her midday desires and crickets tune their orchestra round the edge of a rooftop.

Our temperaments change according to the seasons. It is true. Have you not noticed that everything delightful happens between March and May and sad events take place in November and December? Sometimes February sides with December, skipping January to be celebrated for the turn of the year and at other times March pulls it towards itself, lends it light, fills it with the over-spilling happiness she has in her warm heart.

On several occasions, as we have been walking on a leafy section of the River Thames, overjoyed by the sight of the weeping willows, washing their tears off in the rising tide and letting their long, green curls sweep with the breeze, and the gentle waves heaving towards the highest lines of the bank while rowers are struggling to compete and the passenger boats sail leisurely; I have discussed the matter with my sister, Sara. She has concentrated her stare at the waves, then at me with her gentle smile and agreed.

In England, nature wakes up in March but it is the month of May that splashes a sea of abundant beauty all over the land. May-time in English gardens is a heaven to be had. You drink the breath of fresh air, sweet, scented, innocent like the milk from your mother's breast, dripping, pouring and overflowing, saturated with honey. Colours and shades assemble over each other, caressing the eyes and satisfying the appetite. At times you wonder if the Garden of Eden has more to offer. In May-time, if Sara is busy at her Harley Street Surgery, I go pilgrimage around the lush park near my house and spend quiet afternoons in the presence of flowers, gathering here, scattering there. On such occasions, I walk and think, search my memory, remember and forget, walk and enjoy the enchanting vibrations of life.

Yesterday was the first of May and I was walking alongside the lake, which is in the middle of the park, surfing the waves of memories piled in my brain. Remembering those bygone eras that we celebrated the Mayday as a grand day. Gathering at the town square, flags and banners, people accelerating from all directions, loudspeakers broadcasting songs, invigorating the marchers, the group of us, vanguards of the Workers of the World United to defeat the enemy, capitalism, and hoping to conquer the world. Workers in combat costumes and red headbands, the world marching ahead to equally divide bread and hunger. Gone are those days, leaving behind broken hearts and broken banners. Now we live in a world of little hope and no aspirations.

As I reached the patchy lane, where the lake ends and the green begins, mesmerised in my dreams, a male goose agitated by my presence was following me in his goosy pace and simultaneously looking back, keeping an eye on his 'close knit' family in the middle island. Anger was flaming from his piercing eyes as he was being deprived of the privacy of living his quiet life, making love to his concubines as he wished. While pushing me away from his territory and gargling harsh warnings, his attention suddenly turned towards a group of birds who had their glares fixed on him.

A group of birds were quarrelling at a distance over unimportant matters like jealousy, and important matters such as territorial rights. The patriarch diverted his attention from the chase, to his harem. Spotting danger from a bunch of gigolos who had taken the opportunity to make advances on his concubines, who in turn had set their minds on seduction. The goose turned away from me and re-paced towards his territory in haste, sending a gale force of threats. A passer by passed, while conversing with herself, looking around without seeing. In the valley of rhododendrons, groups of

Chinese, Japanese, Mongolians and Americans, an assembly of the world population were watching, absorbing, enjoying.

Suddenly, I was filled with an urge to sow myself in the soil and sprout next May as a water lily with a purple tongue, a pink tulip with a smile, a rose bush with waiting buds in the womb and thorns to stick into an intruder's side. Invisible from sight, yet again chased by the thought of being chased, I aimed for my favourite seclusion, the forest of pine trees and cypresses. Continuing my walk along a straight line, I was all but a waiting breath. I paused and stared. I moved aside and gave way to my father, Javad khan, who was emerging from the range of handsome pines and cedars in his gabardine suit with the stripy cravat, the one he wore at the reception for the unveiling of Karmanian women, accompanied by my young, beautiful mother, Suri in her long green skirt and tailored jacket, her hat in one hand, holding her husband's hand with the other. Then I did not exist. My handsome father resembled a cedar in figure; tall, upright but handsomer than they were. The difference was that this had stood long to witness the time passing by while my father had the haze of desert roads all over his looks as he disappeared from our lives some six decades ago. No one knew how he perished from the face of earth. I speculate that he walked across new horizons, found a new life, cultivated new seeds and just wiped his footprints off the memory of his past life.

I looked at the carving of my various grief's on a tree trunk; 'In memory of a father who left his less loved-ones to serve a precious cause; and a husband who died of no natural cause; and a lover who packed his cases at the first wave of unrest, taking his wife and children out of danger without looking back at his estranged lover'.

* * *

May in English gardens is an extension of March in Karmanieh as flowers bloom in March and the New Year celebrations bathe in the air of scents and colours. Trees put on new costumes specially made for the occasion and the sky demonstrates the bluest colour one could find only in the desert. Karmanieh and her desert sky and the shimmering southern sun. Always generous, giving, spreading. When a piece of cloud, at the last stage of her pregnancy appears and bursts its waters down over the town, a rainbow then emerges from the far distance with distinctive yellow, green and red arrows whose tips are rooted, one in the valleys to the south, one at the heart of the eastern desert. Gardens suddenly give birth to the most spectacular flower buds; white daffodils with hundred petals and heavy scents, laleh abasids with diversity of colours, geraniums with crimson and sharp pink colours. The city becomes but a mixture of scents, dry, crisp, short-lived. Alleyways defrost from winter while the melting mud sticks to the shoes, begging the passers-by not to pass in such haste. Up around the domes and down inside the square courtyards winter packs its bags and withers away at the first sight of washed curtains, sheets, clothes and bedding, hanging from the washing lines and the smoke from the chimneys indicating preparations for the New Year, inviting the appetite to the coming feast. Out on the roofs, smells dance in the spring air and travel over the domes further and farther until the last line of the city ends at the feet of the desert and snakes open their yawning mouths and wake up to take their skin off and swallow their portion of the feast. Spring, well groomed and fashionably dressed walks across the city, escorted by a musical band, which roams from under the earth's womb and the city washes the dust off and defrosts itself giving way to a waking life.

But these are my recollection of the time I lived in Karmanieh, when silence had not trespassed the lines of our existence. At present and in this garden, where I take my daily walk, life is staring at me through the glassy eyes of a duckling, which is swimming under the green water, singing. My losses emerge as my memory unfolds. So many benches in this park are donated in memory of.... I have never been able to choose which one memory to sit on.

Finally, in memory of 'Dear husband John L. Downham, 1915-1980', I decide to sit at and memories of my dear father, my notorious husband and that dear, dead lover pour out of my bleeding pen. Blood drips letter by letter on the lawn and not before long, I see myself soaked in the pond, frantically splashing water over my body to wash off the blood, in case I might be charged with a murder I have not committed. And Mayday stitches itself to March with a bumpy thread, for the rainy April to sit in between. I look at the fragile figures that have their stares fixed on the gentle waves. Few words escape from their long journey through life. Silence has hoovered their memories and sentences are battling with the fatigue to whisper an expression, a remark. Happy journeys or otherwise, like me in the middle, not knowing whether I made the men of my life what they were, or made they were before I existed.

The afternoon yawns and delivers a smile to the figures who are trying to pace back and re-dream May time blossoms. Out in the open, flower petals splash their scents over my grey thoughts; pink, purple, white 'In memory of the white dress I wore at the wedding of that young girl, who then promised her husband not to leave him unless in a white shroud.' It was the husband, who left her in order to remain up-to-date for the second and the third time, in the land of honey and milk. I walk back into the past and trail my life as far as my memory reaches. I promise myself this will be the last time I journey over such a bumpy road.

* * *

March lives in my mother's fading memory of my arrival through the passage of love as she called it. Then she was sixteen. I often think of my mother at that age. When my sister, Sara was born, my mother was about fifteen years of age. It means that despite his 'modern thinking' and his strong objection to accept a child as a bride, their marriage was consummated after all. I wonder when was the first time my father slept with my mother. 'Made love' to her? Thirteen? Fourteen? Even younger? Did he or anyone else prepare her for the actual moment when he entered her tiny body? Was she frightened of him, of the act of love making? Or, did she enjoy it as well? How did she react to the sight of her body bleeding when deflowered so young? Was she in the position to raise her voice if she did not feel like having him? Could she? Was he the desired man she loved all through years, or was love, the making of my mother's mind after he disappeared from her life? After all, we Iranians are the nation of idolising the disappeared and the dead long after they have gone from the face of earth.

* * *

Walking back across the lake towards the gate, musing on the unanswered questions, I suddenly recall a joke a friend made some years ago and I have this urge to write it back to my mother to amuse her downtrodden spirit. "The people of Kashan it is said are famous for being religious, traditional yet very witty. Haji Hossein was 85, his wife, Beigum Sadat 76, old and frail. One summer they went to visit a cousin and stayed with her for a week, during which time they bathed together a few times. Whether it was a habit they had kept from youth or acquired because of practicality, no one knew. Exhausted at the effort, they sat for tea. The mischievous cousin asked a question that was wandering in her mind:

'Beigum jan, how many times a week do you normally wash yourself?'

'My dear cousin, what a question to ask! A married woman never knows how frequently she has to wash herself".

The picture of my mother not wanting to wash herself frequently and the frequency being forced on her glides in my memory, like a glider passing through a storm, safely but bruised. In this lazy afternoon I take a long shot at the greedy goose chasing the gigolos who are after his concubines. Now at the end of the twentieth century, the concubine age has re-emerged from among the rotten pages of our rotten history books in the land of forced bathing as many times as it requires. My heart sinks at the thought that my mother might have lived with the ghost of a loving man. And this question stays in my mind as I remember my childhood. 'Was my father, Javad khan, Suri's beloved husband, a man like any other man of his time?' If not, why?

A fresh breeze passes by and lifts the lid for me to exhume yet more open-ended questions. How did my mother cope with my father's absence and the emptiness, which settled and clung to her and stayed like an unwelcome immigrant who sticks to an unwanted land? If she loved him as she asserted the fact herself, it must have been a crippling feeling to continue without him, to not have him around to caress, to touch, to plant kisses on her awakened, desiring body. No wonder she tried to salvage a strand of his hair here, pieces of papers with his handwriting and small unimportant items there, with obsession. That meant she would have him for longer moments in her long, dark solitude of separation. In those years of men the bread-winners and women fertile plantations, bearers and carers of children, an extraordinary power must have disrupted my father's mind to have broken himself away from his sprouting seedlings, and left my mother to cope with the harsh circumstances of a husbandless woman. It must have been hard to stand on your feet and play the role of the mother, the carer and father, the breadwinner, to grow three children in the years of war and famine and scarcity. And we know that as time travelled into the future and he did not return, people talked and talked and the weight of gossip rained on my mother's shoulders and forced her to frantically find allies to fight back for her broken pride. Yet my mother was a fighter.

Once my mother told Sara and me in passing words that since the departure of our father, she had tried to gain her dignity and never waver with weakness. Yet it must have been hard to watch my brother, Sasan growing up, taking our father in the tone of his voice as he spoke softly and the shape and colour of his eyes as he focused on mother. Sometimes, she expressed these similarities, as a matter of fact. Would it have consoled her, I wonder if we children picked more of our father's features, or did without them, although the whole process was out of our power to diminish or strengthen? I wonder if she still thinks of him with the same degree of passion as she did so many years ago.

I remember grandfather, Haji Amir making the effort to compensate for our lost father although he was repulsed by this disabled daughter and the army of orphans for whom he felt responsible, yet was reluctant to be responsible for. Over and over again, my mother's pride was broken, as grandfather handed over money through grandmother, stained with comments and warnings. All these must have cornered my mother into the depth of despair. But it did not. My mother was a fighter.

The start of New Year visitations, as we children had our new clothes on and a feverish excitement as we reached the vicinity of grandfather's house, unaware that our mother was folding into deep apprehension. She hated and resented the ritual. From early morning, she was nervous and clumsy, walked around agitated, paid extra attention to details, changed into several outfits before she settled for one. And finally herded us out and lingered behind until we begged of her to hurry up. It did not make sense then. It makes sense now as I re-live the moments of surreal pictures that flash back into my mind. At such occasions, my grandfather's house was full of guests. Sisters who rolled their eyes and raised eyebrows and ignored my mother, while she was trying to save pieces of her dignity. We children were caught in the middle of sharp tongues, scornful eyes and pitiful hand outs, unaware that we were the orphans of a grand man who journeyed the universe to save the earth from the invasion of the Big Macs. Unaware that the Macs would one day arrive in style and would be warmly welcomed across the borders from Siberia to the Caspian Sea, to the borders of China, the Black Sea and beyond.

Years had settled between my father's departure and our minds growing to the size of understanding. Years that have replaced the loss of a lover and a husband, by the absence of a father, who should have watched over his children and educated them and warned them of the outside world and demonstrated the dignity fathers carried with them and mothers were deprived of in that time and age.

I have been searching in my mind to recollect the last time my heart was beating alongside my mother for the loss of our loved ones. And I do not seem to remember much.

Walking along the line of cypresses, remembering the past, I wonder what would have happened if I had stayed in Karmanieh, never attended the university and not walked the road I walked by leaving home 'to a better future'? Maybe I would not have seen the glassy eyes of this playful duckling staring at me in bemusement. Maybe I would have married a local rich man and settled to a quiet life away from the pollution of modernisation. In the solitude of my mind, these unanswered questions repeatedly surface and hover for days on end.

I turn my face to the breeze to wash away traces of these infectious thoughts, which have settled in my veins preventing the flow of fresh air into my body. Yet striking into each other in confusion, memories of all those years surface stubbornly. To this day, I have not been able to heal my wounds and register the death of my old scars. Difficult to de-scratch the old lines, the marks of history. They are tattooed on me needle by needle in different shapes; my daughter Mona, whose grown up shape and character is a reminder of my husband, now the great Haji Farid in the administration of the Mafia. Acquaintances who bump into me once in a while, bringing to surface a settled matter; albums whose photos stare with memories of a moment of happiness; dreams which appear in the middle of a cold night; years which reverse themselves at odd times and make de-needling the tattoos almost im-possible. Would I ever be able to cancel the history, to break it into pieces and force it into the garbage bin? No, too many memories are hidden inside those yellow pages. I have given up the job of erasing them altogether. Let them live side by side in my chest, in war, in peace. I will never sell my soul to any of them.

* * *

Every year between March and May, I cleanse my mind, bathe in the spring sun, peel off the pain, treat the wounds with a potion borrowed from life. Every year, I plant myself in the evergreen soil and hope to grow next season as a tuberose, a hyacinth, and a marigold. I review my past and keep myself up to date. As with my husband, I know that I did not marry him because I loved him, or 'was in-love with him'. I got married for the sake of getting married and forming the family institution, as others did. It was a duty to society, so I thought. In Iran, if a woman refuses to marry, she is declared 'unnatural', 'out of norm', 'outcast'. One way or the other, women are forced to ultimately step into the trap of marriage. Marriage in Iran is like pawning oneself to an institution. It confines the woman inside the letters of a one-sided contract with little way out. By consenting to marriage, women are institutionalised, sold to an institution that is unequal from the origin because men hold the ultimate power. Rules governing family derive from religion and tradition. Traditions. Traditions. Rotten to the bone, yet living eternally under our skin. We live by tradition and traditions over-shadow our freedom and independence and human rights. We might rebel against traditions once in a lifetime but at the end we all end up following the familiar route of tradition. I, for example, side tracked traditions and chose my partner but I was unaware that the institution of partnership was unequal from its root and I had no chance to have my own space for love, for being in-love. Unaware, I followed the path of tradition and pawned myself to the institution, only to discover years later that I could not buy my freedom and release myself of the debt, even when I had paid it all. A river of unanswered questions flows over my mind at odd times. Farid said he was in love with me. I accepted his declaration because he seemed sincere at the time. He ran away from his promise easy as running water. Why was it that he could catch up with his desires and I could not dissolve the partnership without his consent? Why did Josef deceive me and flee the country with his possessions, without a care for me? Why did my father leave and was never heard of? Are men's hearts made of stones? Stony-hearts, walking on a stony land?

* * *

I turn and look. My father's handsome figure is walking straight towards me. I enshrine the thought that my mother lived a short life between May and March, that her happiness had such a depth that kept her standing on her feet all through the years of famine and scarcity of love. I have lived most of my life in the coldness of November across a cavity that stretches to eternity. No depth, no weight, nothing. I have shared my life with the family of geese. Yet I believe that I have gone through the storm and passed the danger zone. I have done well and there are still a lot to be done.

Late afternoon has arrived. I shut the book of my repeated memoirs and begged the male goose to return to his concubines and be nice to them. The Park was almost empty. My heart was hollow as a balloon. Memories of husbands and lovers stayed behind to decide among themselves which direction to take. For me a straight road to peace is all that matters. Peace. Away from wars. Distanced from fights. All in peace.

Thirty One

It is summer 1996 and the end of the second millennium is close. We hear a lot about reforms in Iran and change towards a moderate state. We hear a lot about the changes that have occurred in the political and social arena and the possibility of some kind of normality. Over years, the youth have rebelled, women have taken charge, the conservative clergies have retreated from what they were preaching for years, the country has opened up to the world and there is dialogue between civilisations, as the president has declared. A president who happens to be a cleric, who has been elected by majority vote and who has promised to extract new ideas out of the ancient texts! Iranians inside the borders are excited. We, the outsiders are excited and the whole world is caught in our excitement and congratulates us. We see the name of our country on the news, not for reasons of war or terrorism but in dialogue over cultures and civilisations and hope rises like bubbles in the air.

I decide to go home. We have not seen our mother for years and I have dreamt that she has died and that prompts my decision. Maybe I will stay there for a while. I secretly promise myself. Sara is not in a position to travel. Her heart is weak and the doctors have restricted her movements. Mona is opposed to the idea without giving any reason. Sara is opposed to the idea for my own sake, though she believes mother would be over the moon to see me after so many years. Sara is afraid. She believes Farid might find out and harass me one way or the other. 'Why so, my darling, I have not heard from him for the past twenty years and I am certain that he has all but forgotten about me.' Sara looks at me for a while but then keeps her silence.

My old friend Mimi is the only one who lives in Iran and who knows about my decision and is longing to see me and narrow the gap of two decades. I did not dare ask her about mother but she said it would be wonderful if I went. Apart from common illnesses, mother is old, frail and very lonely. We, as children have been a disappointment to her. Imagine she has not seen her daughters for almost two decades! And all these years she has lived through our letters. Just letters! I know that her eyes are fixed on the road to put an end to separation and her heart is beating with hope to sit with me and talk.

In the past, I have repeatedly promised to visit my mother and was not in the position to keep my promise. Nothing is worse than a promise that is broken by forces outside one's control. I think she would forgive me, once I sit with her and hold her frail, loving body in my arms and whisper in her ear the reason I had broken my promises. Mothers are the most generous of all species when it comes to forgiveness.

* * *

For weeks, I have made preparations, renewed my passport, decided on the proper dress to wear, bought presents, bought necessities for the trip and finally said goodbyes and boarded a plane, which offered me a seat by the window but refused to board my peace of mind for security reasons. Alone by myself, I did my best to have strands of white hair under control, in case they might be put down in fear of inducing a riot or causing a revolution on board. Still, at the very first opportunity, they sent waves after waves of mysterious codes and secret messages into the cabin and jammed the air traffic control. Frantically, I pushed them in and tightened the scarf, but waves did not stay put by a weak order and before I knew the sabotage began all over again. At this time, a kind-hearted saint, who was sunbathing on a piece of cloud a few miles above the plane, saw the lines of terror in my eyes and issued an order. A stocky built guard approached and ordered my hair to stop instigating rebellion and get out of sight. Calm returned and I sat motionless until the plane landed and the doors opened.

Sealed in a long, black cloak and a big head scarf, passport in hand, rivulets of sweat under armpits and an army of butterflies crawling around my half empty stomach, I arrived at my beloved homeland. It was a long, tiring flight, after which, the long queue of passport control and security checks drained me of all emotions. At Mehrabad Airport, the men and women who were well dressed and mighty courteous at Heathrow suddenly turned into a frantic mob, pushing and shoving to get out of the cabin, into the waiting bus. I did not know then but I found out later that the long queues, which held the passengers for hours were the main reason behind everyone's rush. Still. I waited in line for almost one hour dragging my handbag along, keeping the butterflies under the guise of a faint smile, enduring the fatigue of my long journey. A journey, which took much courage and determination to take me this far.

At the kiosk, a heavily built man, with a small pointed head gazed at me for a few minutes, the began a row of tedious questions, which had nothing to do with anything.

'How long have you been out of the country Sister?' Sister!

'It must have been twenty years.'

'Why have you not returned earlier?'

'Don't know. Just happened.'

'A stamp is missing here. Do you know which one it is?'

'No, sir. I do not know what is missing. You should know it better.'

'Well, better check with the authorities in the first instance.'

'To check what?

'The missing stamp. It must have been an important one.'

'Are you going to let me through without the important missing stamp?'

'Oh, yes. It is not that important. Make sure you check it later. Otherwise, you might be stopped while returning to England.'

'Yes sir.'

'What have you been doing these years in ENGLAND?'

'Living.'

'Couldn't you live here?'

'No'.

'Don't blame you.' Next.

I must have gone mad to leave my cosy, winter warm, summer cool house back in England to expose myself to this unknown terror. I thought I was coming home but looking around, home seemed an abstract concept, transcending the boundaries of mind. Where was home at this moment in time? Any corner that gave sanctuary to my worries and calmed my tormented soul and kept the butterflies at bay could be home, peaceful and tranquil. In London, I thought my home lived in the bag of memories I carried with me all the time, while I arranged them around the corners and re-read and re-dreamt them at my own pleasure. Sometimes doubt and unanswered questions hovered in my mind and forced me to travel to the world of troubles in search of clues with an Aladdin lamp in one hand and a key to the lock of years of exile in another. Now, lined in front of me, in starry shapes, dots, triangles, and squares, worries and anxieties left no space for the joy of arriving 'home'. Now, 'at home' I felt unsafe and uncertain. Frightened of every move everyone made. Still, I yearned to visit my mother and this entity I had left behind. I wanted to see whether the people were as kind and tender as I remembered and the sun was as hot and intense as ever and whether I was able to re-organise my life and leave my adopted country behind and re-settle in the land of roses and nightingales.

* * *

Two in the morning, and I was still waiting in the queue for my possessions to be inspected by the hostile customs inspectors. The air was dense with odours of all kinds. Passengers who had arrived from other destinations had added to the already chaotic small customs hall. Two conveyors for tens of suitcases, hundreds of people, fatigue and worry all over their faces as they climbed over each other to grab their luggage. No trolley at hand. Did I have to carry my own cases all the way out of this mess? At sixty something years old, the dignity I had long kept in place was gone. I was nothing but a wrinkled cloak, a twisted scarf surrounding my drawn face, soaked in sweat, no energy to keep up my posture. I had been coiled into a miserable, little old woman, unable to get through a simple customs clearance. I, who had circled the earth so many times, attended tens of international conferences and venues, been welcomed by the hosts, who had carried my luggage into the waiting cars to take me to a five star hotel, now no more than a crippled soul. Suddenly, some foreigners appeared from the escalator, escorted by a guide. They were respectfully hushed through the customs without their possessions touched. I remembered that even in the old days, this country had much respect for foreign nationals while it kept none for her own people.

Four in the morning, and I was dragging myself out of the crowd and the building into the moistened air. Breathing a long and heavy breath and suddenly, the gate of my forgotten memory opening wide to the sense of familiar smells as rivulets of tears were forcing their way out. Earlier at the customs hall, I promised myself that if I got out of the chaos unharmed, I would send my emotions in search of the lost particles of happiness taken away from me by forces out of my control. Now the air danced in the flicker of lights from Tehran's illuminating sky and the smile on a child's face among the crowd. Finding my long lost happiness in haste I was swallowing scents of the summer night and letting strands of hair stick out, the buttons of the robe to unbutton, the breeze moving inside, touching my skin. The thought of regaining a long lost love and waves of voices accompanying that intense moment. The air moving joyously around as a dozen tall, smiling figures (toddlers as I left Iran), now handsome youngsters, waited in rows to give me their welcoming hugs. An army of relations, all smiles and with the love I had lost in years of exile.

The terror and contamination which exists in this land had not been poisonous enough to leave its marks on these fresh souls, who stood there to shower me with the warmth of their love. Standing motionless, looking and the rainfall of tears dropping and soaking me. My arms stretching horizon to horizon, holding each one of them in turn, then together. Defying the rules of not kissing and not hugging in public in fear of spreading corruption. Corruption it was said, would nurture on a little kiss and hides between the lines of a body one hugs in order to fill the gap of years. Smelling them in defiance of the official order and examining and re-examining each and one of them in turn. Toddlers no more. Grown up girls and boys who had a head on their shoulders full of ideas and thoughtful dreams. Dreams which were shattered every day and re-built every night all through the years as love was destroyed and hatred grew to nurture a utopia imported from the deserts of Arabia. My emotions were galvanised as I unleashed the feelings I had imprisoned inside the dark corners of my mind. Looking around at these cousins and friends who had come to see me first hand I could do nothing but give my gratitude to each and one of them.

On the way to Mimi's suburban home, she sat by me in her air-conditioned car and held me in her arms for a good long time. I shut my eyes in contentment. Mimi is close to me as my skin. I have kept my connection with this dearest friend of childhood as I have kept it with my mother. We sense each other's joys and sorrows even as we are thousands of miles apart. Initially, I did not notice how much

Mimi had aged. Suddenly my heart sank as I looked at her closely and tears began to run down my face. Once or twice she took out her handkerchief and wiped my tears. I looked at her from the corner of my eyes and saw tears dripping slowly down her wrinkled cheeks as well. Her wrinkled cheeks!

The driver was zigzagging madly among the noise of the traffic to the nearest highway. I wanted to look out but then I thought I needed to re-visit this route on my own without any interference. I needed to have a quiet time with the noise and the polluted air. I needed to walk across the streets in search of my old footsteps, to climb the Alborz Mountains and look at the city to embrace its size and shape now that it has spread to an immense magnitude. I wanted to sit beside the butcher, the fruit-seller, the baker, the shopkeepers and the dressmakers, to review the past, to see whether there was any familiarity left along memory lane. That, I would do later in time.

July in Tehran is a scorching sauna. When we arrived at Mimi's home, dawn had already broken. The well-wishers left me to have a few hours of rest before my first day of arrival at my homeland would begin.

The summer morning in the city of thousand colours and millions of emotions! Sleep evaporated from my eyes as I crept outside onto the balcony. In the far end of the horizon a rainbow of light has spread its arch encircling the city. A few hours left before the sun shines in full force. In the coolness of dawn, the air is heavy with scent of the tuberoses, geraniums and red roses. The sweeper has just finished the splash of water over the dust and that has lifted particles of my memory into the air, landing at my heart, driving me into madness. A wild animal has woken inside my frail body. An urge to step outside into the street and run across the town, searching, re-discovering. Yearning to walk with bare feet to touch the earth, to uncover my hair, so that it drenches in the sunlight, keeping my breast naked to the sky, borrowing milk from its blueness. Disrobing myself head to toe in celebration of my homecoming. A mad lover I became in search of lost loves and lost times. Rolling on the warm slabs, breathing the moisture of the freshly baked dust. Scents of a thousand colours standing in rows to be breathed into my thirsty lungs. If only tears loosened their grip and the lump in my throat left me a breathing space. If memories did not creep through the cracks and more years lined up ahead and the life behind was washed away by the water the sweeper has just splashed over the dust. I will compensate for the by-gone years. Will start life afresh. I have plenty of time to re-live a new life in a new age, a recycled life. I would adjust, would settle in this Islamic State and before long, gaps would fill and long lost years would wither away.

Slowly, steadily, happiness crept deep inside me as I looked down into Mimi's garden from the balcony and saw a pair of butterflies dancing over the swimming pool. I looked around and wondered whether I could indulge in its depth and search for my lost dreams and suddenly a sense of freedom was lifting me into the air. Freedom from restraining my emotions, the way I did back in England.

'Where are you from?' I have been asked time and over.

'Iran.' I have replied time and over.

Do they think I might be a terrorist, a fundamentalist? The question has hovered in the air, time and over.

'Oh, but you look very European! Have you been here long?' 'Do you ever miss Iran?'

'Not a lot. I have made my life here, no, I don't think I miss her', has always been my reply. This way I have been taken off the hook of further questioning.

But why should I tell anyone how much I miss my homeland, every corner of it at every moment in time and how intense the urge is in me to be embraced, warmed and welcomed by her scorching sun and snowy mountains and starry nights. How can I tell them that I did not leave my country by choice but I was driven out by fear of persecution and there is the difference? Sometimes I do wish I was an immigrant who leaves home by choice and puts everything in a suitcase, even her gods, and settles in a foreign land and never thinks back. But I am not.

Now in the early morning of my first day before the guests arrive and the exchange of emotions fills the air, I was free of that civilised world, concealed in this forgotten land to make peace with my emotions. I was free to wail, to tear my dress into pieces, to mourn for the friends and relatives who have passed away through natural causes and those who were killed in the futile eight years of war with our neighbour and those who were executed in prisons for thinking forbidden thoughts and the martyred Imams killed by their enemies centuries ago and those who are standing in line to become saints and be mourned a thousand years later. I did not need to hide my emotions in fear of being branded uncivilised. I was weeping for the loss and the gap in years.

We Iranians are very emotional people, you know. We come from the land of flowers and nightingales, the land of poetry, wine and love. Our emotions stem from pure sincerity and they are loud and expressive. The fervour of feelings as we talk all at the same time, take precedence over each other, not waiting for our turn in patience as one does back in England. Here, memories unleash, dreams are dreamt, poems written, the dead rise and live among people's emotions with no logical order. Here, one could be a bloody dictator buried under the rubble of history and emerge in the guise of a saint, with an innocent smile. Here is the land of a thousand and one nights with legends of her own, nightingales and gardens of Eden.

I breathed the air and my body stretched beyond the moment. My mind was hovering in the freshly baked scents, absorbing me into their concentrated aromas. I wished to be baptised in the early morning mist and as a resolution make this land my home again.

Mimi tiptoed to the balcony and smiled. I collected my thoughts, wrapped up my emotions and soon I was all washed, groomed and full of a big Iranian breakfast, Mimi had prepared and I ate with much delight. Then I had time to look around and see for the first time Mimi's new house which was tastefully decorated. Mimi is a widow who loved her husband, Mohsen dearly but lost him to the blind fury of the regime. Three years after the revolution, Mohsen was arrested on suspicion of collaborating with a group who conspired a coup attempt to overthrow the government. In the absence of a lawyer, he was tried and sent to the firing squad, leaving Mimi to mourn his loss to the end of time. Later, it was revealed that he was taken for another person, who paid millions to get out of the country. The authorities announced that those who had not been guilty and yet were killed would automatically have a place in paradise. Remembering Mohsen, Mimi laughed and said that he was eternally sitting upright on a secluded bench in paradise because he did not want to be associated with other compatriots. Mimi never wanted to have children because she believed the world was a dangerous place to raise children. So, now she lives on her own in this big house with the memories of her happy days. I sat beside Mimi and looked at the portrait of Mohsen hanging from the main wall, sitting straight as if to grant the occasion its importance but on close inspection his eyes sparkled with that mischievous wit he carried with him all the time. Mimi forgave those who had executed Mohsen in order to heal her own wounds. She has stayed in Iran and does a great deal of charity work. I told Mimi that I had no intention of forgiving anyone for any reason at any given time. I always carry the anger and frustration for the crimes that were committed in this country in the name of religion and those that sanctioned them and presented religious interpretations to let the perpetrators go free. Mimi stood up and approached me from behind and folded me in her arms and begged of me not to be hard on myself.

'Shireen, dearest, don't push yourself too far. Relax. Just take the moments as they come and avoid the journey back. It helps no one. One day, crimes and criminals will come to the open and I hope that we can have a Commission like the one in South Africa, which helped to heal the wounds of history.'

'You may be right, my dear Mimi, but I am not like you. I cannot forgive criminals, not until such time that they fall from power and answer to the nation in a criminal court of justice.'

Mimi was light hearted and took me to my room to receive her presents. I opened my suitcases to sort out the gifts I had brought for those who would visit me soon. As a visitor, I was expected to give everyone a gift, a souvenir to show that I remembered them. By midday the house was filled with the laughter of guests who arrived with bunches of flowers, delicious sweets and cakes. We hugged and examined each other and sat at conversation. Questions poured in no specific order, filling the gap of many decades. The conversation soon took over as we indulged ourselves in the aromas of brewed tea in glass teacups with silver handles that were circling around and cakes and sweets on the middle table and summer fruits, all inviting the appetite to a big feast.

History had the scars of long disruption between us all. Shallow conversation covered our separation but scars opened up once we reached a certain point and moved into depth. Nevertheless, I was soaked in the joyous moments of my first day of arrival.

* * *

In the afternoon, Mimi and I sat by the pool and shared a few hours of solitude before the next row of guests arrived. There, we dangled

261

our feet in the water and just relaxed. I was mesmerised in deep infatuation with the air and the fragrance of flowers. At times we kept our silence, suddenly whispered a memory, pointed to a subject and left it behind and moved to the depth of the moment. We talked about my mother and her situation. Mimi had visited her regularly and believed she was very lonely and fragile but still refused to leave and join us. Mimi had lost her own mother a year ago. I knew that Mimi knew all about Farid but in all, he was excluded from our conversation. She waited for me to disclose my thoughts although I knew that there was little curiosity in me to know about him.

On the second night, we moved inside at three in the morning to catch some sleep. But I was in such ecstasy and my mind had so much to deal with. I lay on the bed and looked into the void. I slept with my eyes wide open. I was too emotional to paint the picture of the first moment I will see my mother in the flesh.

Thirty Two

And a week later I was flying over the deserts of southern Persia in an ancient Russian Jet, which was rattling its way cutting the distance between my mother and I. The head-to-toe covered flight attendant offered me a package that contained a meagre portion for lunch. I looked at her politely and shook my head. She frowned in disappointment and went to the next passenger, who grabbed his share from the tray. The plane moaned and groaned as it encircled the city of Karmanieh and I looked out of the window to catch a glimpse of that enormous expanse spreading well beyond its boundaries with the desert.

I could not form the frame of my mother's present shape in my mind's eye and my heart was beating wildly. I could not describe how I felt. The ecstasy of this visit was draining me but my arms were ready to hold my mother and never let her go. My grown up memories were pushed aside and replaced by my childhood, where on the early evening of a cold autumn and in the enormous family room, beside the burning brazier, mother would wrap me in her arms and kiss me head to toe and Sara was sitting by grandmother, Ghamar khanum, while she was rocking little Sasan on her lap and told us stories of Jennies and Ghouls.

I wondered whether mother would agree to write those stories down so that I could tell them to our grandchildren. I knew that stories lose their authenticity, once they leave their natural bed, as they cannot carry their original flavour: the smell of our house, cool, calm, peaceful, caring people waiting at every corner; our maid, Sedigheh, the gardener, Abbas and our dayeh, Taiybeh, full of love and at hand to offer us sherbet as we got thirsty after hours of playing and running around the courtyard once we settled to hear an episode. I was thinking of grandmother and grandfather's graves, though my memory of them was a faint picture of the big house and the army of aunts and cousins and the Jennies and Ghouls. Now all passed away.

* * *

And all that is registered of the two short weeks I spend with my mother, Suri, is this scene that repeats itself at odd time. It is a week after my arrival and late afternoon. My mother and I are sitting on the big veranda, cross-legged. Above head, the sun is hot and dry but we are shielded by the tall cypress that had been planted when Sasan was born. Father planted a tree on the day each of his children was born. The walnut tree that has grown out of shape in the far corner of the garden belongs to Sara. My fig tree occupies the eastern corner. As a teenager I once climbed its tallest branch and registered my name on it and now Shireen has expanded sideways and looks out of the high wall that separates our house from other houses and the street. The patterns of the rug underneath us play hide and seek as we change position. A butterfly disappears, a flower blooms, half of the wineglass the young man is offering his lover hides under my toes, his head bends sideways and his eyes beg his lover to take a sip before the wine loses its original flavour.

A heap of red and yellow pomegranates in the copper tray sit between us. I can smell my mother's fragrance. Her long silver hair is tied behind by an elastic band, exposing her neck, which is marked by criss-crossed lines. Some unruly ringlets have dropped on her forehead. From under the thick glasses, her eyes are focused, her hands quick, her movements precise. She is busy cutting a round, red pomegranate's head, making lines round its ripe body soon to be opened for dissection. I see the first layer cut, the thin skin removed and hundreds of little hearts rolling into my mother's palm, then onto the bowl. I pick up a few and place them in the centre of my palm, roll them over and examine them from every angle. I begin an imaginary count of those little hearts that are

264

hidden in the layers that separates one from the other and gives them boundaries, places them in an order so they can rub shoulders with each other and live in peace. I wish I could hide my sorrows among these little hearts and forget about them all.

Mother was waiting for me to pick up a memory, to mention an incident and to bring us yet closer so that we could fill and cement the gaps. Over the past few days, we have done nothing but remembering, talking and reviewing, evaluating and judging, embracing the pains, sending them away and enjoying the company of each other. In a week's time I am gone and the distance remains as ever.

By now, mother knew everything about us, Sara and me, our children and grandchildren and the life we have lived back in England. Sara has regularly written to her since she left home some four decades earlier. But it was important to her that I told her in detail what could not be painted on the paper. My mother, Suri has changed by age but she was alert and in full control of her life. She still writes poetry, though keeps them to herself. She follows the world as it goes round. My mother is able to put things in proportion and that has helped her survive the hardships of life. I have always been proud of my mother, you know. Now more than ever.

In all, Sasan is the only one who brings tears to my mother's eyes. Sasan lives the tormented life of an addict in a forgotten part of the city. I knew about it, still I was in a state of shock to see him old beyond recognition. From early childhood, Sasan and I were very close and now in old age, we are so far apart. I went to see him and stayed with him for a whole day and we talked about everyone and everything except Sasan's past and his present situation. Every time I wanted to get close to the subject, he changed the conversation and at the end I gave up trying. I promised to visit him before I left the city though we had little to talk about.

When I left Sasan, I was like a child whose toy had been broken beyond repair. I ran to my mother and hid in her arms. She held me tight and combed my hair with her fingers until I calmed down and wiped my eyes. Then she made me drink my tea before it got cold. She is calm and in control. How can my mother stand the pain and has not gone crazy?

'My dear child, Sasan is one of the many destroyed by the political fervent that swept the world away from its orbit'. My mother scribbled. 'There were times that I thought I would go mad but then I looked around and placed him in the bigger picture. What happened to those youngsters who dared to step forward and become political activists is beyond belief. It does not matter what they believed or did not believe. What matters is the evil that destroyed so many young lives. I put my son beside that young woman who was stoned to death because she dared to love outside marriage. That teenage girl who, called on her mother right to the end, as she was frightened of the dark night that was about to fire shots at her young body. She committed the crime of reading a forbidden book. I put myself beside an old father who was summoned to prison hoping to get his child back, but instead was given the parcel of her belongings, by a stocky bearded man who introduced himself as his son-in-law, who said, 'I married your daughter the night before her execution because she was not meant to die a virgin.' You see my dear Shireen; this is how I have endured the pain of losing Sasan to the world of defeat! But in my heart I still believe he will one day come back to us, cleansed of all addiction and healthy as a bull. Just wait and see.

The next day we are sitting on the veranda and our conversation changes direction. I ask my mother whether she ever regretted her decision to never leave Karmanieh, to never be with us in Tehran and then in England. Her shoulders lower, her head bends down as she looks for her scrap book to write the answer and I already feel the hand of regret on my heart for causing her the pain she wants to forget.

By now a heap of red hearts is again forming on the china bowl as my mother cuts and peels and separates one emotion from the other, giving them proportion and sense. I never understood what power kept my mother running her life so smoothly and in good order. She would not reveal the source of her energy but now I can sense the drive behind the neat and tidy bedroom, the polished kitchen floor, the manicured garden, the locked gate at the far end with the big handle alongside the working bell and that rocking chair which faces the long pathway from the gate to the veranda to the living room, with my father's picture hanging from the main wall and our photos scattered on the mantel piece. I can see the chair, where my mother spends most of her time, writing, reading, listening but mostly waiting. The gate, the bell, the postman, the pathway and a letter to be opened to connect her to those she loves and the man she loved and is still waiting to return and bring with him a bundle of happiness and to lift her from the rocking chair into the tidy bedroom and lock the door behind for them to whisper the long gone years.

Thirty Three

I was back in Tehran and I was seriously considering re-settling there after retirement. But. If Tehran were to become my home in the near future, I had to look at it through a different lens; filtering things from the visiting guests, who are very kind to me. Tehran has a giant size and an unshaped face and above all, a depth that I had not yet been able to reach, not until I walk across and familiarise myself with its secrets, now shrouding under codes and regulations and the cloak of secrecy. Then I will be able to put things into perspective.

Everyday, I told Mimi that I was going out on my own and before she found time to object, I was out on the streets. I began touring the city, on foot, by bus and taxi north to south, east to the west. It gave me a lot of pleasure to explore the back streets and come across a familiar sign, ride the segregated buses, where men sat comfortably in the front seats and women were sandwiched in the smaller space allocated to them in the rear section. Yet segregation, whose purpose was to subjugate the female population, has rendered women much sought after freedom from the male harassment which was common in our days. In the cramped space between the two sections, a female world is born out of coercion. There, women share the space, exchange news, offer sweets to the next passenger and give advice and guidance. There, they have constructed their own free world and made a mockery of the whole system. Among the deafening noise of the traffic and polluted air, one could listen to women's complaints, jokes, ironical remarks and life stories. Their defiance of the official codes was manifested at every step at any given time. I was deeply affected by this female solidarity that has grown out of the harsh living conditions.

Whenever I asked a woman a simple question, she opened her heart to me and took me to the depth of her solitude. If I asked a man a question, he would examine me head to toe with his horrid sexual gaze before he gave the answer. Nevertheless, the city had all the manifestations of other big cities, noisy, polluted, corrupt; luxurious lives on one side, ghettos on the other. To me everything was new. A child I had become to toddle through the noise and the rush of traffic. My memory, intimidated by the passing of time, was failing me most of the time. I had forgotten the basic skills of living in Tehran i.e. criss-crossing through the cars to the other side as everyone else; bargaining with the shopkeepers; buying things in bulk even if one does not need them; exchanging pleasantries with those one does not like, yet is obliged to keep up the pretence. Everything was familiar, yet different. Had I become a non-Iranian, a foreigner in my own country?

I was finding Tehran a two-layered city, one atop the other. The first layer which catches one's eye was the Islamic gloss over everything; mosques rising from every corner, radio and television preaching and guiding the sinners, patrols on the streets to watch over one's every move so not to divert from the official guidance. Strict, bitter, harsh. The other layer was enshrouded behind and beneath closed circuits. There, indeed one finds the dress code relaxing, wine serving and music playing, men and women dancing, anecdotes and jokes circling and in all people living a normal life.

To see the first layer was easy. One has to pave the way to reach the second; the pulse of the city. I found the first layer a force-fed recipe that never met the taste of Iranians. I saw the dream of building an utopia in the land of beauty, wine, poetry and love. I saw Tehran a giant metropolis with a magnitude beyond recognition. The new order has transformed everything; people's manners, dress code, body language the vocabulary they used, the hobbies they engaged in. New freeways were curling upon each other, high rises cutting through narrow streets, modern cars alongside the old ones. Streets and squares bursting with over-population, people of different outlooks, cultures, languages, a multicultural sense Tehran had never had. Yet over-population and pollution was suffocating the city. The range of Alborz Mountains and the blueness of the sky were shielded behind hovering clouds of smog. Breathing was difficult, especially for someone who has come from a green environment.

Over the period of two decades, time seemed to have passed a hundred years backward. Latest technologies worked at the service of primitive ideas. TV channels broadcast to every household as they do in other places but programmes were inexplicable, out of touch with reality. Radio was broadcasting round the clock but I could not understand what. Cinema, theatre, galleries, universities, colleges; something has shielded the terrain of this beautiful country under the blanket of the past times. People's daily conversation was blended with expressions, idioms and exclamations belonging to the past. I have no shred of doubt that the founders of this pious fortress are aware of the fact that a painted gloss has covered the real life of Tehran as it continues under the ground. The publicity that was force-fed to the world was an illusionary vision of a non-existence reality.

A scene: Mimi and I were invited to a women only gathering in commemoration of the birthday of an Imam born hundreds of years ago. For me it was a rare opportunity. We arrived at the hallway and were greeted by a well-groomed mistress who took our cloak and headscarf. We inspected ourselves in the mirror before approaching the grand reception room. The house shimmered under the wealth and the glamour one would only see in Hollywood movies. In the middle of the reception room, a white Sofreh hosted tens of dishes and desserts, exotic fruits and sherbets and burning candles. Around the square sofreh thirty or so women and young girls, all in fashionable clothes and the latest make up, were sitting and waiting

270

for the ceremony to commence. Conversation was floating as we sat cross-legged, exchanging pleasantries.

The preacher. The bell rang and a heavily clad woman arrived in style. Removing her black chador, black robe and head scarf, changing her scarf to a white colour, feet into more comfortable designer slippers and approaching the audience in a white, well-tailored two piece suit, wrists, neck, and ears shining under the glitter of jewellery. Everyone stood to welcome her with much respect and she went straight for the only chair at the top of the sofreh designated for her. Silence fell as her presence attracted all attention. A number of young women, whose outfits resembled shoppers at Harvey Nichols, changed places where they would be closer to the preacher. Wondering what she was going to preach, mesmerised in the serenity of the occasion, I sat at a corner, an outsider within. No sooner than she had sipped her tea, she began her sermon by choosing the Imam in commemoration, depicting scenes of hostility towards him by his opponents (the infidels) and his brutal martyrdom some 14 centuries down the history line. Detailing the last moments of his life and the atrocities committed by his assailants, her voice rose from the initial gentle, low tone to a high pitch as the episode took the audience to the height of emotional excitement. Heads down in remorse, tears running across their made-up faces, the women could not be captured in more grief. Suddenly, the preacher lowered her voice and put an abrupt end to the scene and in a joyous tone announced that 'Ladies, do not forget that today is the Imam's birthday and so we have to celebrate.' Beginning to sing a jolly song, dancing with the rhythm gently, inviting the women to join in, and in a span of a moment all were but a band of merry birds, rapping on the pots and pans, bending, jumping, twisting erotically around the sofreh. Then, the preacher lowered her tone and finished the ceremony as she was given sherbet, sweets and the best portion of food. Now the room was all but a clatter of forks and knives, spoons and glasses and the humming of chatter. The pious preacher left after a while and the ceremony came to a close.

Which of these characters was the true woman in this female world? I asked myself. The one in the latest Western outfit or the woman who was weeping so vehemently for an Imam who was killed by his opponents some centuries ago in the Arabian Desert? Or the woman who wiped her tears off immediately and joined the merry dance? One has to possess a triple personality to play such different roles all at the same time. I admired their capability in playing triple roles. In the land of pretence at all times, it would be impossible to separate one from the other, simply because the player is not aware of the falsity of one or the other act. It is a land where one is taught from infancy to have multiple personalities, to hide one from the other and to feign. It is a land with a population of non-believers and zealous opportunists that have mushroomed from history and chastised in the guise of fervent believers of the faith. Opportunism is riding high on its horse. You can belong to any faith, any political group and yet pretend you have converted to Islam and then climb the ladder of opportunities. On the road up, one does not need expertise, skills or experience in order to get a position which requires one or the other. Former communists and Maoists, liberals and nationalists, non-believers, believers of different interpretations of Islam, organisers of demonstrations outside the country against the regime, attackers of the Iranian embassies and throwers of paints at their windows, distributors of pamphlets and sellers of opposition publications have now moulded into this Islamic mayhem and work at the heart of the administration and shape it as their interests demand. Here, opportunists live their small lives in the jungle of a land, which had lost its outer body to a giant stomach.

Tehran, the city of my youth had turned into an old-age disappointment. It was crowded, congested, wild and layered. It was a mixture of contradiction and harmony. These two concepts have come to an agreement to live side by side in peace and war. I had an image of Tehran, which after twenty years separation seemed totally irrelevant. When I was living and working in this city, I prided myself for being well in control of life but now I felt a stranger, the city talked a different language. There were no shared concepts and no mutual experience between me and this city anymore. Tehran was not the city I kept alive in my memory. Against its modern look, it has crumbled and aged. That natural vitality of hope and prosperity seemed to have vanished from people's daily life. Life seemed a pack of economically, socially and culturally harsh codes issued from the top without any relevance to reality. And hope was replaced by despair and uncertainty. The train of time has been derailed and coaches have fallen over each other, one killing the other; victims of an incident which pulled them towards the wrong direction. The Islamic utopia is built on the skeletons of ghosts.

In Tehran everything seemed to contradict the other; newly built mosques with newly recruited young mullahs, who in the privacy of their inner circles, watch forbidden satellite programmes and in public condemn them and issue order after order to bring the dish down in fear that corruption spreads among the populace; satellite dishes are erected above every rooftop, through which households travel around the globe and nourish their appetite watching the world going by, leaving them behind. This modern technology has been the bedrock of an ideological battle between the people and the state. Officially it is forbidden. Every once in a while, an alloutattack would pack the whole world into one's basement. There, CNN reporters, MTV presenters, Arab Sat broadcasters, Turkish junkies, Indian dancers and BBC World Service presenters scramble over each other in the thick air, taking precedence to get out. Yet it has stayed on because it is one line that has connected people to the outside world.

Tehran is not only the city of opportunists. It is the Mafia City. It is the city of men sitting around golden braziers of burning charcoal with the quality opium imported from the ravaged land of Afghanistan, concubines at their service to run their Mafia empires, buy and sell, export and import and finalise deadly deals. Their wives, frustrated by loads of money, conceal their empty brains under lavish religious parties, weep for the martyrs and give to the needy a meagre hand out to show off their wealth. Their daughters watch satellite junk and dream of the outside world. Their sons joyride across the streets in fast cars, searching without knowing.

An unusual, archaic order has put personal and political and social liberties at bay. Freedom is a far cry from reality. Modernism is rejected, yet modern technology remains at the service of the state. Controlling the mind, torture, killing and maiming citizens is carried out with modern techniques and the latest machinery imported from the 'developed' world. Ancient messages are broadcast with the fastest means of communications. The making of an utopia has been propagated for decades amongst the populace without materialisation. Tehran has turned into a sexualised city. In the lack of natural, healthy activities, a whirlwind of inter-relations is ruling the city. Sex, having it, doing it, using and abusing it rules the minds. Sex of all types, under-aged girls and boys, old aged men and women. Men and men, women and women. Women have become sex objects. Men have become sex objects. Sex and over-eating has replaced all other pleasures. Pleasures that in other parts of the world would be taken for granted; listening to the music of your choice; going to a concert, reading the writing of your choice; writing your own mind; walking on the pavement and not being on guard; going to the theatre unaware of your body and your sex; running along the river banks; running alongside life at your own pace without fear in your mind, and hope, hoping and planning for the future without fear.

Yet I must admire the efforts of a number of intellectuals, women in particular and students who are trying frantically to salvage the wreckage from drowning. But unlike our generation whose voice raised, shook the Shah's regime and toppled him, this new generation is silenced as soon as it attempts to move beyond verbal objection. But the population is young, forty five percent under thirty years of age! This means that this generation will not stand witness to see its dreams ruined at every step. Not before long, they will break out the vicious circle. Thinking of all this, the hand of sorrow for this fastbackward train is holding on to my throat. I hold to my views and do not discuss them with Mimi or anyone else.

I am certain that someone imported a dream from the deserts of Arabia into Iran and built his utopia on a sand storm. Gradually, the sand will be moving and the dream will crumble from the foundation. I am sure that I will lose my head if I speak of my thoughts aloud. However, I think my euphoria was short-lived like cherry blossoms in the month of April. Yet I am a stubborn woman.

Thirty Four

Imagine you are sitting in the shade of a passion tree, near the edge of a blue pool, with your dearest friend, on this most comfortable bamboo chair, sipping sherbet out of a tall crystal glass. The heat is taken away from the air and the onset of autumn is waiting across the street on the high branches of the ancient trees that had lined along side the Pahlavi Avenue. The leaves are loosening up to change colour and drop one by one, or in groups over the pavement, on the road, into the fast running brook that takes them away into the abyss. Against all the odds, you have convinced yourself to spend your retirement at home, here, although the whole world is against such decision. To settle or not is the unresolved dilemma between Mimi and I, my mother and I, not to mention my sister Sara and my daughter Mona, who are entirely against the idea.

Then the bell chimes and the servant walks towards the entry phone in slow pace. We put down our glasses and hold our waiting breath. Mimi makes a face indicating that she did not expect anyone at this hour of the day. Four in the afternoon of a Monday in early October! We hear muffled conversation at the door, sit upright, stand on our feet, walk towards the door to the family room and wait. Mimi walks ahead, calls on Negar and waits. Negar approaches unhurried and points to a well dressed, old gentleman, who is standing in the middle of the reception room, holding a bouquet of tuberoses. For a moment I am in total shock. Mimi's eyes widen, and then move to inspect the authenticity of the visitor. She composes herself, gives him her mocking smile and leads him to a chair. Farid looks at me for a moment and stretches the hand that holds the bouquet. I am standing where I saw him a moment ago and my mind is refusing to let me make any move. It is Mimi who takes charge:

'Come dear Shireen, sit down. This is Mr Farid, in case you have not recognised him. He has come to see you at this time of day when no one else is visiting. But I wish he let us know beforehand.'

Mimi and Farid never made peace with each other even when I begged of them to do so. She did not like him, nor trusted him. Then, she repeatedly warned me of him:

'He is not the person you should have married. He is a snake, dead or alive. One day, he would break your heart and god knows if you could bear the blow.'

I take the flowers, put them aside, sit at the edge of a chair and look in Farid's direction, avoiding his eyes. This stout figure, with the full white beard, the cunning eyes, the mouth which opens to spell a word in slow motion, as is the habit of the authorities, has been my husband in the past and present! Did I ever imagine that he would turn into this when I consented to marry that handsome young man some thirty odd years ago? What kind of life does he live now? Has he been happy living in the madness of marriages and divorces, children, concubines and politics? Poor old devil has experienced all sins! Strange, I feel a motherly, sisterly sense of pity for him as if he has been my responsibility and I have left him to stray in life. Why do I blame myself? Why do I still have feelings towards him, any feeling? Watching him while he is walking across the hallway, resembling his father. Old he has grown, older than his age. Just like his father. So much I hated Farid's father and the way he walked, the language he used; full of foul words and scornful concepts. When he died, I did not mourn his death and certainly did not turn him into a saint.

Suddenly, the clock turns back and Farid emerges from the vicinity of our tiny flat in Kensington full of rage and hatred. He is ready to throw anything at me and I am trying to protect baby Mona from his rage and myself from physical abuse. He had been my husband and I have lived with him, slept with him in the same bed. I had lived with this stranger for a period of time. Now my only wish is the suspension of history and turning back the clock to the days he was absent from my life. This urge to wipe him from my past, to wash him off my skin and erase his every trace, forces me to run to the toilet and throw up. Mimi rushes after me and begs of me to remain calm:

'Surely, he is not the same person, Shireen. Look at him. He has grown old and probably feels ashamed of what he did to you. Maybe he has come to apologise. Let's see what he wants. Try to be civilised.'

'Ok, ok in a moment. Just give me a few minutes.'

Farid explains in his slow tone that he just wants to say hello and see whether he can be of any assistance. Mimi tries to make conversation and bring the situation under some normality but I am not able to utter a word although there are millions of things I wanted to tell him. Farid leaves shortly, promising to phone! A sinister wink sparkles from the corner of his eyes. Long after his departure, Mimi and I are sitting in her bedroom, cross-legged, sipping tea and wondering how he found out about me.

Farid and I had a very short period of happy life together and many years of bitter disputes. I wondered whether he ever missed the early months of our marriage as his head rested on my arms when he went to sleep, him pressing his lips into my neck. Then we enjoyed life, sex and each other's company. Life was all a beginning and no ends. But that was short-lived. Now we have none but bitter memories, two old foes that had parted in the battleground and suddenly found each other at the bend of the road, complete strangers. I tell Mimi that I wish I could erase him from my memory once and for all.

* * *

Against Farid's sudden appearance in my life, I was still determined to buy a flat before I returned to England. I wrote a letter to my mother, informing her of my decision, promising I would visit her again at the first possible chance. I phoned Mona and told her about my decision. She was so furious that she declined to talk to me further. Instead, she bombarded Mimi with faxes and phone calls, urging her to persuade me to return immediately without committing myself to anything. In that country, she emphasised, 'everything is possible. Wars might break out, revolutions might occur, governments might change and borders close, tongues get cut, my mother's included, people disappear, she as well.' No amount of logic brought peace to Mona's frightened mind. At times, she believed I had become the victim of a conspiracy. She could not understand why after so many years and a well-established life in London, I had suddenly decided to shift to Tehran. I told her that I had not made any firm decision I was just flirting with the idea. 'Come on mum. Find something worthier to flirt with, not this crazy idea. And anyway, come back here, we will talk it over. If you convince me that you really want to move back, so be it.' Sara is as opposed to my idea as well but she leaves the decision to me. In her heart she would want me to stay closer to mother.

* * *

For almost a week Mimi and I talk about Farid's visit and his intention behind it. In all, we take it lightly and our assessment does not go beyond a curiosity that he wanted to satisfy. He was married to his third wife whom he has three children with.

Then, one day Farid is again at our door accompanied by a mutual friend, Ali, whom I knew from the old days and who is a university lecturer. This time we are more relaxed and our conversation takes us to the past. It is Ali who invites Mimi and me to dinner. I see no malice in that and without giving it much thought accept his invitation. Mimi apologises. Had I known the intention behind such a simple act I would have refused as well. But then I was not aware of a conspiracy which led to other conspiracies.

Thirty Five

Ali phones and invites me for a ride in the outskirts of Tehran, a day out, he calls it. That is a few days after the dinner party. Mimi advises me to decline but I see no harm in that. I had known Ali long enough and why would I refuse his invitation. I ask Mimi the reason for her suspicion. 'Intuition, my dear friend and living in this country long enough'.

I dress casually, take no necessities and tell Mimi that I would be back by the evening. 'Have a very nice time my dear and tell Ali to bring you back in one piece.'

'Shut up Mimi'. And just as I open the passenger door, I see Farid in the back seat. It is too late for me to back off and we drive in silence. Ali chooses the highway that leads to the northern part of town and into the valleys beyond the mountain range. I ask him where we are heading and he says Lavasan. It is fine by me. I had heard a lot about this newly orbital town in the middle of the valleys that has joined the greater Tehran. Farid is silent for most of the time and I do not try to make conversation. Somehow I find a heavy thought lingering with my other thoughts. Why did Ali not mention Farid? Why was he so dead silent?

We reach the town of Lavasan, the car turns into a road that leads into a narrower alleyway and a dead end. It stops in front of a gate. Ali presses the remote control and the gate opens its mouth and swallows us in full. Swallows Farid and me in full. I disembark, instinctively waiting for Ali to park, but he drives off before I find time to run after him. We are alone in this remote garden, with a building in the middle and no soul to hear my screams.

I find no time to gather my thoughts, to be frightened, to object, to run away or to keep calm. It all happens in a matter of seconds or minutes? I have no recollection of that. It all happens so quickly.

One minute I am happy that I am going for a ride in the countryside; the next, I find myself a hostage, being kidnapped.

I have a vivid recollection of the days that follow in that vacuum of time. For a whole week, Farid interrogates me in the style of a skilful interrogator. For a whole week, he tries to find out when and how I took Mona out of the country and who helped me to arrange the journey some twenty years back. He intrudes my personal life, asks me about Josef and my relationship with him, my other love affairs, my associations and the reason I have returned to the country. What is the purpose behind my journey? Am I a spy to a foreign country? Do I want to prepare grounds for the return of anti-revolutionaries, the agents of western countries, enemies of the state?

I am kept in one room with a single bed that is joined by a toilet and no shower. I stay in this dark prison while Farid goes out and returns time and again to repeat his questions. The tone of his voice irritates me more than the questions. His smell, his presence harms more than the act of kidnapping.

I tell him that he is a total idiot to do such a thing. I tell him that as far as I am concerned, he could go to hell, he could do whatever he wants but I have no intention of answering any of these stupid questions. And at the end I gather all my strength to keep my silence. And I keep my silence while inside me a storm was built and rising from its bed. Inside, I am in rage at myself for being such a idiot, to believe that Farid would not harm me. I sit at a corner and look at him. Carve through his mind and try to make sense of what he would do next. If he was appointed by the government to interrogate me, it would have been different. He has appointed himself to take revenge for what I did to him. I left the country and dismantled his might. Then, he was not able to do me any harm and now he has found the opportunity to do what he could not do twenty years ago.

During the whole week, which seems like a century, Farid does nothing but ask questions. Sometimes, he is kind and brings me food and begs of me to eat enough, then he would go into a state of melancholy and apologise and promises not to harm me if I answer his questions. Suddenly, he would go into rage and repeats himself time and again. I tell him that he is an idiot and he would pay for this. He has kidnapped me. Does he understand that? But he says that I would never be able to prove anything. I am his lawful wife and he has taken me here on my own freewill to spend a week with me. During my ordeal, never do I give him the pleasure to answer his questions or show my weakness. I am proud of myself although I know that my strength is fading and gradually my nerves are shattered.

Then on the early morning of Friday, I hear a car in the distance and the gate opens. Farid goes out of the room and I hear conversation. I recognise Ali's voice arguing. They raise their voices and from the distance I hear Ali saying that he is an idiot to consent to such an act. He says that he was frightened that I might accuse them of kidnapping and they are both agitated and shout at each other. Then their voices die down as they move further into the depth of the garden. I look out. The door is open. The gate is open. I step outside, look around, walk towards the gate in a slow pace, then try to run but find it impossible to do so. I am out into the alleyway, at the end of the road and suddenly a car stops a few yards ahead to let a passenger out. Instinctively, I run to it and open the door and sit in the back and ask the driver to hurry up. I tell him that I will pay him any money if he just drives me away as quickly as he could.

Mimi orders me to have some sleep before she asks any questions.

'No, Mimi, I want to take a shower. I want to wash myself off the smell of terror.' And I wash my skin until it begins to sore. Mimi brings me some sleeping tablets and I sleep for three days before I gather some energy to tell her of my ordeal. Mimi threatens to kill Farid with her bare hands. Why did he do that? What was the purpose behind this malicious act? I tell her that Farid was taking revenge because he thought of me as his wife and as his wife I was not supposed to do what I did. I disobeyed him and took his child away without his permission. I took a lover without his permission. He was allowed to take my child away and was sanctioned to take second and third wives and concubines but I was not. Mimi promises to kill the whole male population, to cut their penises and hang them from a rope, high above the roof where all can see them while drying. Her rage made me swallow mine and at times I laughed about her plots.

'I am telling you, let's get rid of all men. Some men should be cut from the source, not just circumcised. Even their balls should be given to the dogs. Castrated men are the best men. We can keep their sperm to inseminate ourselves for the children we want. Look at that bastard Ali. The only virtue you admired in him was the respect he had for you from the old times. See what he did to you. Threw you to that wolf.'

* * *

In the afternoon of the fourth day and while we are still wondering whether to inform the authorities or deal with the matter differently, I am lying in front of the fireplace, watching a film without seeing. The phone rings. Farid wants to talk to me. Mimi tells him that he has the nerves to call her number. 'Get lost you fucking old dirt. I do not want you to ever call this number again and Shireen does not want to talk to you anymore.'

The phone rings throughout the day and the night. Finally, Mimi decides to ask him the purpose of his calls. She tries to calm herself and swallows her rage;

'What do you want, you idiot? Why don't you leave her alone? You have done enough damage.'

'I will explain it to her not you, just call her to the phone.'

Something in his voice is threatening and alarms Mimi. I see her face going pale. 'I am telling you, he is up to something more dangerous. I cannot put my fingers on it but he is up to something.'

'What else can he do more than he has already done?'

I pick up the phone.

'Listen carefully. You shouldn't have run away from me the way you did. You are not in the position to ignore me. And when I tell you that I want to talk to you again, you must listen to me'.

'Otherwise?'

'You know that officially, you are still my wife. For start I can ban you from travelling abroad.'

The world circles around me, the phone drops and Mimi jumps up to help me to a chair.

'Can he really do that Mimi?'

'I'm afraid he can. Yes, he has the legal power to ban you from travelling. Wives cannot travel without their husband's permission.'

'But he has not been a husband to me for years and besides, the green stamp is on my passport.'

'He can cancel that at any moment. He does not need an excuse for that.'

Imagine, thirty odd years before, I signed a document, whose papers have rotted, whose ink has faded, whose contents have lost meaning. Thirty odd years later, at the end of the second millennium, as the world spins around its orbit and astronauts travel to the space shuttles routinely and humans are cloned; this little man is my master because of a signature I put under a document I did not even remember where I have buried! Should I ever find it from under the rubble of history, I would burn it to ashes in front of a huge crowd of spectators.

Mimi and I were on fire while talking things over, deciding our next strategy. What would Farid gain by banning me from returning to England? What does he actually want, money, his broken pride? Answers to these questions were nowhere to be reached. By then we know he is serious. If he does what he is threatening to do, it would take me months, maybe years to fight him in the Iranian courts. I have to calculate my every step.

'Courts do not listen to women'. A lawyer friend told Mimi.

'Rules and regulations are made for men. Women, regardless of their status are men's property and courts guard that fiercely. Try to deceive him and get her out of the country. This is the only way. You will never win a legal battle.'

A few days later, Farid calls again. I assure him that I will see him somewhere in town if he leaves Mimi alone.

'I do not want you to call this number again. I will see you in three days. Should you call again, I will not see you and you can do whatever you like. Do you understand me?'

He seemed to have been convinced. He had won!

'Do you promise to come?'

'Have I ever broken my promise?'

'No, never.'

'All right then, I will see you in three days although I do not know what it is that you want from me.'

* * *

Mimi is busy checking every airline that flies out of Iran. Finally, a European airline that goes straight to London books me a place. Suddenly, the memory of my first flight from Iran and others who fled in fear of persecution; through the mountains of Kurdistan, the deserts of southern Persia and the borders of Pakistan, by boat across the Persian Gulf, and those who were robbed of their possessions or drowned at sea and their bodies consumed by sharks, comes to my mind. I remember that it took me years to get over the ordeal of my first 'illegal' journey. I am not sure whether I would survive this last one.

We have to go in person to confirm my ticket. It is a terrible experience. We think we are being followed through the streets. That little, old figure is re-born in every male, chasing us through town. I know how harmful it is to be so frightened but my nerves were out of control. I have lost my marbles. It is partly rage and partly fear that drives us crazy. I am also fearful of Mimi's safety. But Mimi dismisses this last concern and assures me that she can handle the situation once she knows that I am out of Farid's reach.

Coming out of the airline offices, Mimi proposes that I do some shopping but I demand that we go home immediately. What if he finds out that we are buying time? What if someone has seen us coming out of the airline offices?

Suddenly, Farid turns into the most important person in the whole world. Farid is a US President with many detectors, the ones that at the touch of a button orders his troops to bomb Iraq because it lifts his spirit on that day. Farid is a spiritual leader with thousands of followers, who are ready to be suicide bombers and explode themselves in a busy market. Farid is a guerrilla leader whose army has taken a city under siege. Farid comes out of every taxi that stops beside our car, through every crack in the wall, in the

286

guise of every man who looks at our grey faces. Intrigued by the conspiracy, instigated by such idiot, logic has fled our minds. Thousands of plots are on display. Scattered seeds of hatred, of rage, of humiliation, of losing my dignity and respect. How dare he do that to me!

'Leave your suitcases here. I will post them to you. Go with a small case. This way you will not wait in the checking queue.'

I ask Mimi to stay behind. While we say farewell, no words come in between. Words do not need to be said when friendship is closer than your own breath. 'Listen to me. You take care of yourself, ok? Put the bastard out of your mind. He is not worth thinking about and pollute your mind with.'

I nod absent-mindedly. I do not want to further upset Mimi with my waiting tears. Mimi splashes a pot of rosewater after me.

Clouds have gathered at the edge of the Alborz mountain range. Pollution is washed away by the last night's rain and the sun is about to shimmer above the blue sky. The muezzin has just finished chanting in the nearby mosque. The devoted congregation is rushing home to have breakfast with their concubines. A few children are already playing on the street. From under my veil, I send them goodbye kisses.

The taxi races through the noise of the traffic. Mimi has instructed the driver to take me through the back streets. The driver does not ask questions and I get to the airport before the customs people are at their desks.

On the way out, my thoughts concentrate on the fact that in my own country, I have been treated a second class citizen. Besides, I am an abandoned child in the eyes of my natural mother. I have left this mother far too long and she has forgotten that I was her flesh and blood. My homeland has treated me as a stepchild. In my homeland, stepchildren are subjected to tortuous lives. Let it be. Let it be. If I get out, I would show him who is in control. England is not Iran. I would do whatever is necessary to break the ties, to tear the ancient document and throw it away. If I ever get out.'

* * *

From above, London is calm, and sunny. The River Thames is glittering under a blanket of haze. Smoke is rising from the chimneys. Women are preparing their Sunday lunch in haste because they want to go for a stroll down the market. The church near my home is preparing tea and freshly baked cakes for its congregation. God is sitting above the seventh sky, wondering what other tricks She should play to attract the runaway flock of sheep to the pasture. Competition is fierce among the churches, the Tescos, the car boot sales, the pubs, the game of cricket and lazing on the sofa, watching the film of your choice, or surfing the Net, travelling around the globe.

Finally, I am home. Peace and tranquil at every corner. My little study with the burning fire waiting, and I rest assured under in the solitude of my own world. Away from wars. Distanced from illusions and dreams. All in peace.

Thirty Six

On a drizzling night of November 1998, suddenly, peacefully, my dearest Sara died in her sleep. The doctor, who examined her warm body, mentioned a smile on her lips and a comfortable transition into death. I was in total devastation. For most part of our lives, Sara and I shared our pains and joys and coped with the harshness of life. Recently, she was complaining of her inability to cope anymore. There was no apparent reason for her depression. Yet Sara was in gloomy moods for most of the time.

'I am telling you Sheri, I have weakened. Something in me has blocked the road ahead. I sleep through the darkness and wake up in darkness; the hallucinations will not go away. I have lost my light, my guiding star. What is the use of living in total defeat? We couldn't change the world, nor were we able to gain anything significant in our small inner lives. I cannot live a happy-go-lucky life as others do.'

Once, we were walking on a countryside road, crushing the dead leaves under our feet, stormy rain dripping from our soaked hair, finding its way into our skin. Sara was talking about everything and nothing. Suddenly, she lowered her voice and questioned the world we were living in, our situation as women, our relations with men, her husband and mine in particular. 'That little creature, Farid who, possessed nothing but a penis, which in medical terms is no more than one organ in the maze of the human body, had the power to humiliate you, to over-power you. He actually had a lot of power in his hands to use them against you, Sheri. And a whole establishment stood by him and gave him support, theorised him, legitimised him, as well as baptised him. He was registered as the power. You were an invisible line that could only be read through imagination. '

I told her, 'forget about my damn ex. He does not matter any more and I have forgotten all about the episode.' But Sara was not convinced. It seemed that she had been more humiliated than I!

'The whole situation is bizarre, Sheri. Us living here in exile, our old mother over there, our broken brother gone from memory and our homeland under the control of a bunch of fanatics who have travelled on camels from the deserts to rule over us. Those men who have no respect for us women.' Sometimes, Sara's moods lifted and she was prepared to drop a joke to make us laugh: 'What if we sex-change, plant a penis on us, inject testosterone, grow a beard and find a threatening voice, men's voice. Imagine the freedom we would have; to become a holy man who would issue Fatwas; or a politician who would push his way into politics by way of deceit and false promises; or a negotiator in arms deals who would buy deadly weapons from any country for any group or nation; or a leader who would declare war and sign international agreements and immediately denies his own signature; or a mighty husband who would cheat on his wife and take as many mistresses and concubines as he would, or a state functionary who would walk over others and by that gains public respect for his manly endeavours. We might have even been nominated for a Nobel Prize like that leader whose hands were dipped in blood to the arms!'

Somehow Sara, though a successful doctor in Harley Street, felt wasted and uselessness in life and her decline was rapid. The injury to her heart gradually penetrated her soul and disintegrated that fine person. She was falling down.

'Just when you feel you have won, you fall down and break. There is no time to put the pieces together and shake the world off the dead brains in little skulls, to put fresh mind into them, and not to feel so miserable. I want to stay in the height, or leave the scene altogether.' Were her last words.

* * *

Accepting Sara's death and mourning for her, was the worst experience of my life. Burying her was unbearable. Between speaking of her in the flesh, vibrant, radiant, in full presence and her as dead, with no authority over her body, her name and her destiny, stood a flicker of a moment. In the briskness of a breath, Sara joined the line of the passed away, leaving existence behind, separating, distancing, moving into the terrain of stories. Her thoughtful brain slept to eternity, her knowledge and her life experiences were washed away and erased. As if she had been a tale once read at bedtime. As if she had never sat beside you talking, her gentle voice transcending, her loving hand warming your heart, reassuring.

In the hallucinatory world that surrounded my mind after I learnt of my sister's death, I joined her in the land of the dead and moved beyond, to see for myself where would she be residing from there on. Would it be a pasture full of milk and honey and the eternal comfort one has been promised over time? Would she settle down in the company of those she had admired during her life in this world? Would she enjoy her eternal life more than the life she spent in this material world? Wasteland, flatland, void. Nothing could be seen. Nowhere to go. Just a stop to this life and the beginning of nothingness. Sara existed from the moment of birth to the moment of departure. From then on, she would only live in the photos that lose colour over time, the letters she had written to mother, her journey through life registered in her journals and in the memory of those she has left behind. Nothing more. Nothing less.

Sara's memorial service was held at the local church, where she walked by many times a week and smiled at the handsome priest, who, according to her, desperately sought and seduced the devoted sinners. I was accompanied to the church by my daughter and my nephews and nieces full of grief. Hunched at the front row, blind with remorse and deaf to the preacher and those who spoke one after the other. The swell of tears that rained without consultation blinded the way for me to see the congregation of mourners. Tears were frantically washing not Sara's death, which was beyond grief, but the footsteps of a deeper line carved under my skin. Sara in that wooden box? Oh, dear god, someone should let the air in for her to breathe.

Shining under the glitter of chandeliers, the organ resounding, the white-washed priest, cool like a summer breeze, his funeral services' smile on his lips, welcomed the people, who were arriving in full mourning costumes. Sara was carried into the front section on the shoulders of her sons and the son-in-law, bouquets of white daffodils covering her head to toe. The priest set aside his differences with this dead person and conducted a non-Christian service suitable for the occasion. He began his sermon by introducing Sara to the mourners. His mind's eyes were searching for the proper words to not tie her to the church and to keep her at an appropriate distance, where she could be left to those who knew her to decide whether she was a Christian, a Muslim or an Atheist. He was not even sure where Sara's soul had gone after departing from her body. I admired his tolerance. He was not aware of the fact that Sara was born a Muslim and once a Muslim always a Muslim. One can never choose to become anything else. That is the order of the religion. Religion lives in our veins and is tattooed on our skin. No one can peel it off, to de-religion oneself, to become a non-Muslim. The penalty would be death by many means. Did Sara feel the necessity to belong to a faith, any faith at all? Would she decide to opt for another faith, now that she was dead and punishment could not be performed on her? Sara and religion?

The service for the celebration of Sara's life began and after a brief introduction by the priest, Sara was remembered and claimed by many as their friend and confidant, their soul mate, member of their literary group, member of the medical establishment and so on. She was reclaimed by her children and grandchildren, who looked Iranian by feature but English by language and body language. Her foreign neighbours remembered her as one of theirs.

The words that spoke of her were all but praise, adoration, devotion and admiration of Sara's personality and character as they were spoken out and travelled up into the apex of the church hall, joining the sound of the organ, touring around the hall and the chandeliers and settling on the tears which poured from many lashes. None considered Sara's consent in their affiliation, as she was too vulnerable to give consent to anything. Sara was getting tired of lying down, listening to these people who gave her reassurances of worth, of love and belonging.

Suddenly, my mind concentrated on one word. Belonging. Did Sara belong to anyone, any group or profession in an era when we are all stranded among many choices and nothing to choose from? Who did she belong to? To me as her only sister who wanted to deny her death? To our mother, who unaware of the tragedy waited for Sara's next letter to arrive in time? To her children, who adored her and now her loss would leave a permanent gap in their lives? Was she the belonging of her adopted country, England or her motherland, where she was rejected out of her womb and thrown beyond her geographical zones?

In my entangled mind I was desperate to seek Sara's consultation for the burial place. If given a choice, would she want to be buried here, in this land, which never accepted her as one of hers? Maybe it was best if I took Sara back home for an Iranian burial, where there would be plenty of mourners and a round-faced, long-robed, rose-scented Akhund, who would walk solemnly to the mosque and sit at the top of the pulpit, preaching death as a necessity, diverting attention to the death of the Imams, lamenting their martyrdom thousands of years ago.

Suddenly, I felt an urge to have an Akhund at my side, to hear his reassuring voice, his skill in making me forget my own beloved, who has just departed from this world. Yes, the Akhund would take me into the depth of the tragedies that have resulted in us having so many martyrs at our hands. Commemoration of Sara's departure should be held at home, where the male relatives would stand up during the whole procession in respect for the dead and women would wail in turn to keep the ceremony fully mourned. Strangers would pour into the mosque from every corner to mourn the newly dead and in this way grieve the loss of their loved ones, who have left them long ago. Back there the whole procession is about death. Death is praised as a necessity. Life is remembered as a passing stage into the permanent settlement. Having taken Sara back home, she would be mourned long after she was gone and settled in her shallow grave. Now in England they are celebrating Sara's Life. What about her death, the loss that has arrived and will stay eternally? What of the lacuna created by her physical absence and our inability to see her again? Ever. I was stranded among alienating feelings. I was missing the mourning procession that I have been used to for thousands of years but on the other hand, celebrating Sara's life brought some light into my mind and the mountain of sorrows lifted to give way for me to exchange few words with the congregation.

* * *

A hearse drove Sara through town. Sara was planned to be buried in an evergreen cemetery, whose entrance was concealed by a sharp bend, whose trees and shrubs have millions of stories to tell. I was not in the position to decide whether Sara should have an Iranian or an English burial. So, I refused to give any suggestions, hoping that the dread would go away and Sara would knock at my door, healthy, as she was the day before, as I saw her coming from across the green and ran to the door to open it, before she knocked and she laughed at my childish haste: 'Oh Sheri, why do you run towards the door in such haste? Do you think that I might change my mind and return home, as I am about to knock? I'm afraid one day you might fall down and break your leg. You are not young anymore, you know.'

Driving between rows of graves into the spot and the hearse tiptoeing, two women in full black costumes, solemnly walking ahead and my confused mind searching for the missing clue. In the splendour of the silence that prevailed, one thing upset my numbed brain. Did we know where Sara wanted to be laid to rest? Did she have any preference? We rarely talked about death and burial. Never thought one day we would die in this land as we have lived. Years ago, she mentioned the site of the Old Man, Carl Marx in Highgate, North London as a favourable eternal resting place. There, she said, you never feel abandoned and forgotten. The flow of visitors would stream throughout the year and flowers are laid by his giant statue in commemoration of his philosophical ideas, once the hope of humanity and their scents would waft across the cemetery, refreshing the nostrils. There, you might even find time to sit at one of his lectures and listen to him, which in the material world are imprisoned inside the shelves of libraries. He might still be regarded by his followers as a man who once brought hope to the hearts of millions. Later though it happened that keys to a more humane society and justice for all were lost in the rubbles of 'C's, and Workers of the World had long decided Not to Unite because the lines of unification with their own kind and the oppressors are blurred and so they have come to a compromise. If you cannot defeat your enemy, try to make peace with him, a civilised peace. Would Sara make a compromise and leave the selection to us? Did it matter where she would be put to rest? It did matter to me. Yet I was not sure where I wanted her to rest eternally. Now the sense of not belonging was dangling in the green air. Tears were frantically washing my thoughts from my mind but the deep shadow of fear was spreading over the church, across the streets and over the waiting ground, where the hearse stopped; Sara's final resting-place. Sara's children, dignified, mournful, with eastern features full of grief and western manner of restraint looked at their beloved mother as she was lowered and given to earth, as the priest announced.

Suddenly, without consultation, for a brief moment a woman wailed the way she would have done back home, her voice transcending across and over the stones, infiltrating deep inside the tombs. She was wailing for the loss of a beloved whom the earth was reclaiming. Then the sound of hiss and shush spread over the cemetery and she swallowed her cries as swiftly as she let them out. Skeletons, relieved by the return of silence, sucked themselves into their resting-place. Trees waved goodbye and Sara's grave stretched beyond her body by bunches of flowers that were laid at the top of fresh soil. Finished, gone, remembered and forgotten.

Part of me was buried with Sara and I saw myself laid inside the well- polished pinewood box, being remembered by the congregation, who spoke a foreign language. Didn't they know that by death we forget the adopted language and only understand our mother tongue? I was crying uncontrollably. Not for Sara, who was free of thought, as death has washed prints from her brain but for those of us, who missed her and mourned her so violently.

Living outside one's homeland for such a long time blurs the line of a sound judgement on this last earthly issue. I did not know by what standard to judge my beliefs, thoughts and emotions of death and the loss of my sister; Western or Eastern. Even the way I thought of her was caught up in the battlefield. My emotions were mixed. The words that shaped inside my mind and expressed my feeling were muddled, and above all the sense of not belonging hovered in the air. Could I, the child of a turbulent era find the magic of settlement carved on my sister's grave? Are we becoming citizens of the world with no specific land to claim us? Could I call Sara an Iranian by nationality, a Karmanian by ethnicity and English by residence? Now that she is dead and gone, what would be carved on her grave: Here lies a heart full of love, a beloved who was born in a desert city, educated on the tracks of a fast moving era and lived and died in this cloudy, cold land, in which she lived most of her life and accepted her as her adopted homeland, although this land considered her a step-child to the end. Maybe justice would be best served if she was cremated and her ashes were divided into three equal portions and scattered across her triple homelands. Silence sat between my thoughts as I tried to reach a decision, as doubts were lurking overhead and remained in the distance. In the secret of my mind I was not certain of any resolution. In the depth of my heart I yearned to sit beside my mother so that we mourn our loss together. I knew that I had to remain in the grey area before I could land on a possible option. A frozen smile on the lips of the priest showed that he had set his mind to a peaceful settlement.

* * *

Civilised. Someone said Sara's funeral was. Now the dilemma solved itself. I imagined myself dead and my daughter was about to decide on my type of funeral. Alas, I forgot to remind her that I did not want my funeral to be civilised. I wanted my funeral to be mine, to identify with me, not just civilised. I wanted to see the lines of women, who sit at the top of the service hall, head to toe in black, wailing, if they may. This well-dressed congregation who swallow their tears in fear of being portrayed 'uncivilised' suit other funerals but not mine. Shifting from East to West, becoming 'civilised' is ahistorical process that takes its own course to ripen. I don't want borrowed funerals, or borrowed weddings in borrowed lands. Maybe I would settle for a service free of all rituals: 'let the wild-eyed, long haired gypsy girl dance with the merriest highland songs, reminding me in my borrowed coffin, of my homeland and her snow-covered mountains, her stormy rivers with mad waters and the rain in its scarcity. Let the congregation attend with any dress code they like. Let them bring the food they like and plenty of wine, if they may. By passing away into the other world, getting to know my new neighbours, if I find the bunch of them, as is claimed one might find, I want to share a glass with each of those sinners; Bernard Shaw, Khayam, Hafiz and that wanderer, womaniser, whom I have loved all my life, Sa'adi of Shiraz. Before you lower me down, splash the earth with particles of that everlasting sun that barely sets in my homeland. No prayers please. And keep your fingers away from my grave, reciting prayers for me. I want to adjust without the interference of your prayers. I will choose my own prayers if I may. The music must not be forgotten, the best of the Iranian Tar and Scottish highlands Pan Pipes and Rodrigo's guitar. You are free to wail or dance but just to the music. If you wish to invite an Akhund to the ceremony, make sure he gets quite drunk and dances with the music. You are free to remember me whichever way you like, or forget me the day after, or speak of me in any language you like. One last piece of advice and I will move on. Do not talk of me as if I had been a saint all my life. I hate it. If you talk of me, talk as if I had been a woman with goodness and badness, with mountains of blues, and rivers of joys, and vineyards of loves and stretches of losses. Do not blanket me with hollow praises and do not give me a Noble prize just because I am dead. It is pathetic when you attend a funeral and the dead suddenly turn into a saint. If saints have turned into saints the way we portray our dead, then we must know what type of saints we have had at our hands.

* * *

Silence sits between my thoughts and me. For no apparent reason and in middle of my worse melancholy, I see happiness dripping from a glass of wine which is served outside the wine bar and the sun comes out and a warm hand pats me on the shoulder and offers me a glass. Sara is standing at the distance her hair is dancing with the breeze, the patterns of her skirt, waving an oceanic colour. She is about to join me for the occasion, after which we will walk on the river bank hand in hand, thinking forbidden thoughts. That is if the weather stays warm.

Part Six

Thirty Seven

Time has passed slowly, steadily, leaving the dead behind. Time has travelled uphill, reaching its destination, the end of the Twentieth Century. The old century is reaching its end. One hundred years old; puffing, panting, tired of the burden of thousands of incidents, accidents, inventions, innovations and wars. The birth and the growth of socialism and fascism, the expansion of capitalism, then the gradual death of socialism. The emergence of existentialism, surrealism, modernism, postmodernism, feminism, post feminism, environmentalism, humanism, fundamentalism, terrorism, globalism and village of the world.

Leaving these aside, a new century is waiting at the bend of time, ready for a fresh beginning. The scent of the new era is travelling across the flatland, encouraging the earth's inhabitants to distance from the past and to celebrate the new millennium. Soon, at the tip of a sharp bend, the old century will put her weight down to deliver it to the next millennium, fresh, young, and virgin. Whether the peoples of the world who had passed through the turbulence of the old century would have learnt a lesson to live in peace and harmony in the coming millennium is in the womb of the future. For now one must remain optimistic.

Twentieth century constructed itself by and over two major wars and hundreds of regional battles and ethnic conflicts which kneaded, fermented and prepared grounds for a huge leap towards the geopolitical transformation of the world. Muddled in her bloated womb, the First World War, the October Revolution, the Second World War, wars of independence, Cultural Revolution, the Vietnam war, genocide in Cambodia, Rwanda and Zaire, apartheid in South Africa, the creation of the Zionist state of Israel and the occupation of Palestine and tensions in the Middle East, the emergence of puppet dictators in Latin Americas, the Islamic

Revolution in Iran, the disintegration of the Soviet empire, the Balkan wars and the might of the United States of America as the only super power.

Leaving this aside, the advancement of technology and communications left a hallmark on the twentieth century. Within five decades after the second war, which in the span of time is less than the blink of an eye, the globe has shrunk into a small village, watched and controlled over the waves of electronic devices from the earth and above. The twentieth century turned the earth into a flatland with the possibility of seeing everything through its thin air. Apart from the advances in the natural and human sciences, the expanse of communication broke lines of secrecy and made it possible for us to excavate our past and find treasures buried in the depth of history. Now, there is nowhere to hide and nothing to hide from curious eyes. Our exposure to information, our ability to learn and discover has gone beyond imagination. Now time is ripe to re-read history, to retrace footsteps, to find clues to the mysteries that have been kept away from us throughout past time. Now one can press a button and travel back into time within seconds.

There are incidents or tragedies that knot one's life in the maze of unsolved questions. Sometimes, time renders the opportunity and puts one in a position to unravel a secret. On such occasions one can release pressures from the mind as these might clot into a malignant tumour. For my part, I am glad that I have passed through the turbulence of the twentieth century. Being born in another epoch, there was no guarantee that I would have witnessed so many ups and downs.

Thinking of these, led to other thoughts, which made me to take an unprecedented decision at this stage of my life. A few months after Sara's death, these thoughts surged in my mind and swayed for a considerable time. Most of my thoughts were polluted by the painful memories that lingered around and made me miserable to the point of a black depression. But among all this, I came to the conclusion that to shake hands with the new century required clean hands that were washed off the crimes, dirt and secrets of the old one. I did not want to transfer the germs of ancient wounds into the body of the next millennium, since it is yet free of pain, pollution and viruses that humans have carried over time.

Maybe it is time to trespass the memory lane, to illuminate the secret that has tormented my family for so long. Maybe it is time to lift the seal from the mystery that has haunted us for most part of the twentieth century, for almost six decades. I must admit that I am settled with the grotesque fact that Sara has actually joined the line of history and turned into a loving memory everyone talks about. Sara lives in the past tense although I see her at every corner and keep her inside my bereaved heart. Now that Sara is gone and I am left alone to cope with her loss, I have to find a project to focus on. So I decide to position the last pieces of the jigsaw in place and find out what really happened to our father as he left home to help his socialist comrades to win the war against fascism. What happened to a man whose love has remained untarnished and undiminished in his wife's heart, now eighty years old and still waiting? Why didn't he ever contact us to let us know of his whereabouts? Why didn't he return home like many others when the war was won and Soviet Russia became the victor? For these to unfold, I have to make a journey back through the ageing century, the most turbulent, most intense and disastrous and yet amazing of all centuries. I was making preparations.

Shortly after Sara's death, I retired from my teaching job and lived the life of a pensioner with no future to look forward to. I decided that I must put my wandering thoughts into action and step out of this state that has nailed me down and walk into the world of adventure by tracing my missing father. It was at the suggestion of a friend who was persistent to push me into action that I decided to set off for the journey of discovery. Should I write to my mother, informing her of my intention? Would that add more pain to her broken heart knowing that I might find the truth about her husband? I decided to wait until I obtained some information. Nevertheless, I wrote a letter to my brother Sasan and informed him of my decision. I never got a response.

* * *

It was the end of the 1990s. The old Soviet Empire had long disintegrated into small states and Russia was heading steadfastly into yet another capitalist state. The era of Perestroika and Glasnost have lived their time and were replaced by a steep rush towards capitalism. Russia has opened herself to the information that is travelling through superhighways and is in a rush to catch up with time. The era of Communism and Socialism has been hastily replaced by manifestations of capitalism and deep corruption, where everything is on sale and everyone could be bribed for a reasonable price. Russia is entering the 'free world'.

I set off to trace my father's footsteps. Initially, I began the painstaking job of gathering information. According to the data that were sixty years old, Javad khan had left to join the international communists against the German invasion. No one knew at which front and in which country. Yet he had reached Russia some time after he left home. I decided to find my father's former comrades and speak to them. But my attempts failed from inception. I could not find anyone. If they were alive, they must have been about ninety years old. As old as the century herself. I wrote letters to the remnants of the disintegrated pro-Soviet communist party of Iran. No answer came. The party did not exist any more. I searched the archives and history books, reviewed all papers and magazines, spent weeks in the British Library. But I understood that information lay at a far distance; the birthplace of the trouble. I contacted some of the Communist parties left from the Old Soviets, where Iranians had traditionally woven ties. The secret service in eastern Germany, where I understood, had stored the bulk of information on migrant Iranians in the former Soviet Bloc, and the Republics of Azerbaijan, Georgia, and Tajikistan. A matter that seemed easy at the beginning became more complicated in the twists and turns of the bureaucracies.

In 1999, I was preparing to travel to the region. It was a tour through the Silk Road. A road that began from the farthest parts of China and stretched to Russia and beyond. It was not an easy task. It was a mission impossible. My daughter Mona and Sara's children were more excited than I and helped me all the way. My English friends were sceptic and warned me of the dangers and the possibility of failure. During preparations I thought a lot about Sara. Her absence cut deep into my heart. If Sara was there to be consulted upon! If only Sara had said no, I would give up my mission. Oh, Sara, dearest how much I miss you! Finally, I boarded the plane.

I knew that the regional communist parties in the old soviet republics were under direct command from the Kremlin. Socialist parties throughout the world were also under the wing of the ruling Soviet Communist Party and financially supported by the soviets. Soviets supported these parties hoping they would take the power in their respective countries and eventually establish a socialist state. Over decades, socialism and socialist ideology took hold of almost a third of the globe, from Cuba to China, Vietnam, Africa and beyond. In this respect, neighbouring Persia was a strategic point for the Russians and with direct assistance from the soviets, the Iranian communist movement grew into a substantial size and at some stage, were a threat to Reza Shah and later his son, Mohammed Reza Shah. But both dictators managed to crush this movement by persecution and the imprisonment of the party's cadres as a result of which, a large number of them fled Iran and made the northern soviet republics their home. I hoped to get some information through these expatriates who had been living there for years.

In April 1999, I boarded a plane destined for the Republic of Azerbaijan, which was then an independent state. I had gathered enough information to guide me towards my expedition. I set foot on the Azerbaijan soil, expecting to see a modern city made of promises of seventy years of socialism, enriched by equality and justice. Instead, I saw a country that had not touched the twentieth century and was yet to recover from the bloody regional war with her neighbouring Armenia. The aftermath of the collapse of the Red Empire resulted in regional wars and ethnic conflicts and ravished the former states, now independent and yearning to embrace capitalism, trying to gain recognition by the West. Baku, pregnant with the biggest world oil reserves at the edge of the Caspian Sea was waiting in patience to be invaded by capitalism.

Staying at a hotel, whose windows opened to the Caspian Sea, I almost forgot my mission for the first few weeks. So much similarity between this city and its sister region of northern Iran drowned me in yearning. Sitting and staring through the haze of the early morning, my old country illuminated on the other side in the blue horizon like an old flame from a forbidden love. A few hours sail and I would be at port Anzali. Just a few hours separated me from that beloved land. I had no immediate plan to start work on my project and so nostalgia invaded my mind. I was disoriented. I spent hours walking on the shore, painting pictures of the people of northern cities and villages, fishermen returning from the sea, their vessels loaded with the fish whose swollen bellies were full of caviar, singing in their native dialect, lyrics soothing to the ear; of women in the rice fields, a sea of colourful bodies, sowing seedlings in the mud, their children tied on their backs; of the crowded early morning vegetable and fish markets, where men and women put their products on display and the moist air, smells and scents, the noise and the crowd of shoppers and errand people all wafting across the space. I sat on the balcony, crying loudly, walked through the streets of Baku amazed at the resemblance. I was drowned in a feverish urge to take a ferry back home. I cried, for the loss of my sister, the disappearance of my father. And above all, I missed my mother, whom I knew had imprisoned herself in a dark room and refused to come out to life. I knew that at such hard times we both needed each other.

Spring went by, giving way to the season of hot and humid weather and fresh melons and the juiciest grapes on earth. Finally, the fountain of my tears ran out and my heart sank deep to watch me drowning. Despair was about to overcome my willpower. I needed all my determination to pull out of the Caspian shores into the reality of my purpose, into the smoky rooms of the state buildings, ruins of the old Soviet might.

Slowly, I managed to get over my depression. Yet similarities between Baku and Iran were intense and that satisfied my yearning. The Iranians whom I befriended during my stay in Baku gave me ample advice and helped me to start from the files and archives, buried under the dust in the basements of the buildings of the old communist state. They also arranged for me to talk to some statesmen from the Party. It helped me a little and I got some background information about the operations during the war. But that was all. Nevertheless, I learnt to approach from a different angle not known to many. The disintegration of the Soviet Empire left a vacuum where no one knew what to do. There was no authority over the country's assets, nuclear arsenal and cultural heritage. The top KGB officials hand in hand with the newly grown entrepreneurs took a grip on these assets. To begin with everything was put on sale. One could travel into the country and return with a component for making a nuclear bomb, paintings and sculptures held in the museums, files, archives, personal accounts of well known statesmen and old spies. I could use this opportunity to my advantage. Finally, I saw light at the end of the tunnel. It was a tunnel indeed. Long dark, torturous, stretching over a period of sixty years.

Thirty Eight

Hitler's troops had had severe setbacks in the Soviet fronts, especially around the city of Leningrad, which was under siege for a long time but did not fall because the red army and the people were defending it against months of blockade and fierce assault. As a result, millions died of starvation and cold. Thousands of the Nazi soldiers also died before Hitler recognised that victory at this side was an impossible task. He planned to penetrate Russia from the southern borders with Iran. This plot was aborted because the Allies acted promptly by removing the pro-German Shah of Iran, forced the country to expel thousands of Germans and thus secured Iran's northern borders with the Soviet Union. It was during this severe assault on Leningrad that internationalists were called in to join forces with Russia to defeat the Nazis.

Comrade Javadov and his counterparts started their hazardous journey to the Russian fronts through the Caspian Sea. They boarded a ship in port Anzali and reached Baku in the middle of a dark, stormy night, where they reported to the Communist Party's headquarters. The Iranian brigade aimed to join the contingent of volunteers in Azerbaijan. But there seemed to be chaos everywhere. No one knew who they were and what was the purpose of their journey at such time of great danger. Fear of espionage and the spread of war to this side of the Soviet empire had created an atmosphere of suspicion to every one who entered the country. Under intense interrogation, which lasted for days, they were separated from each other and bombarded with questions. This was a situation they had not prepared themselves. They believed they had left their families and their country to help in whatever way possible, to save the land of revolution but instead, they faced the unexpected. Their experience of the Soviets went back to the old days of comradeship after the October

Revolution and the first few years that followed before Stalin had established his dictatorship and they knew little of the political situation within the Soviet Union and their knowledge of the war was limited. The diplomacy to deal with the Party officials was non-existent. Now the Party had an official bureaucratic ruling body with its own discipline and code of practice, along with a deep fear and suspicion in everyone's mind. Fear of thinking their thoughts, of speaking their minds, of criticising the state and each other. Gone were the days when comrades held sessions of criticism and self-criticism in order to improve their morality and those of the people they represented. Now a group of bureaucrats had clawed to power in order to climb the ladder.

However, later Javad and his comrades were released and a guard was appointed ho accompany them everywhere. The first code of discipline came as they met a number of Iranian comrades and Javad complained about their treatment, the present situation and the role of the Party. Suddenly, they silence fell across the room and people crept out cautiously. Javad and his friends were confused and astounded as nothing had yet been explained to them. Finally, their guide, comrade Abutalebov told them briefly that, 'they better keep their thoughts to themselves.'

'Try to remember, comrades, you are in the Soviet land. We owe everything to Comrade Stalin. In this country, Comrade Stalin thinks for everyone and speaks for all.'

So for that period in time, comrade Javadov and the others kept themselves to themselves and followed orders and were placed at the bottom of the line, until such time that they could prove their loyalty. Thereafter, for one whole year they lived a silent life, invisible to the outside world behind the Iron Curtain. They had chosen a one way road, where their footsteps were washed the minute they paced a step forward. No one outside the borders was aware of their existence. Ever.

It was hard for them to understand the reason behind their isolation. Later, the puzzle was solved. The problem stemmed from the fact that Javad and his comrades were not affiliated to any group, rather, they were an ad hoc gathering of idealist-socialists, whose ultimate goal was to get justice for the oppressed. They were unaware that socialist ideals had gradually been replaced by a bureaucratic system that was the state apparatus. Those Iranians, who had settled there before, benefited from their loyalty to the Party and its rigid ladder of hierarchy. Right from the start, antagonistic sensations and rivalry began between the two, one experienced and familiar with the system, the other, an idealist number of men who had left home to contribute to the struggle. This rivalry over gaining the confidence of the officials polluted the air of comradeship and ended in constant battles as the bigger war continued and ravaged, and fear of being branded unfaithful and then dispatched to the remote parts of the Soviet for 'training and rehabilitation' remained in place.

Javad and his comrades had no time to think of home and their families. Ironically, their presence in the Soviet soil did not make any difference to the war. Rather, they were a burden to be housed, fed and dealt with in the presence of shortages and famine. The Iron Curtain shielded the horrors that the mind could not accommodate at that moment in time.

* * *

It was 1945 and the war was coming to a close. Soviet troops had walked into the ruins of Berlin as victors and returned home over the bodies of millions and the destruction of cities and towns. Stalin's strategy to industrialise the Soviet Union went on without interruption. More and more people were called in for reconstruction projects. Thereafter, Stalin rebuilt the war-torn country and at the same time expanded his socialist empire into Eastern Europe and beyond, conquered new territories and built an arsenal of armouries which competed and took precedence over the West.

By then, comrade Javadov and his friends had managed to move to Moscow, away from the confinement of Azerbaijan. It was in Moscow that they realised the great mistake they had made in coming to Russia, but the road to return was shut. No one was allowed to travel out. Comrade Javadov had no choice but to integrate into the system and settle into some kind of normality. He was lucky enough to enrol in the Academy of Political Science to study Communism, Socialism and materialist dialectic. He managed to get a job at the education department with a salary, which was barely sufficient to feed him. He was given a room in an apartment block along with hundreds of others who lived in such crowded and cramped conditions. No one knew who he was and how he coped with loneliness and alienation. Did he ever write to his family over the years to tell them of his situation? Did he keep his faith to the soviet system or did he regret his decision? No letters arrived home. Ever.

* * *

Day by day, piece by piece, I was learning of my father's mystery. But I discovered that I had to go to Moscow to reach the source of information. Under pretext of doing a research project, I managed to get hold of the most secret documents and files in the archives. These files were rotting in the basements of the old KGB buildings. I thought it would take years to scan and read them all. My interpreter, who was intrigued by my project, reassured me that we will soon get the result. 'Wait until I get permission to go through these files.'

And so, for the next six months, we went through official letters and circulars related to Iran and the Iranian nationals who had lived in the Soviet Union in the forties and fifties era, with the purpose of finding those crucial files that revealed the truth about Javad's fate. We found a system that would separate each section. Suddenly, one day by sheer coincidence, we came across a cabinet that held clues to the mystery.

Due to his previous stay in Russia in the early 1920s, and the fact that Javad khan knew Russian language, his promotion had arrived sooner than expected. He had been appointed to a senior post as teacher at a boy's school in the upper parts of Moscow and was given a bigger room with some pieces of furniture. By then their group had disintegrated into individuals and each had moved away though their friendship remained intact. Over years, some had found partners and moved in with them but comrade Javadov lived on his own.

These pieces of information would have been interesting enough for any one to finish her mission and went home. But for me it was just a beginning. I had to reach the bottom of my father's final stage. The pile of documents that needed screening was beyond handling. But I did not want to leave any of them unscreened. I was keen to return home to celebrate the new century with my daughter and Sara's children, but not empty handed. It was very frustrating. What on earth was my father doing in this country, when he was most needed by his family? Was there no way for him to get out and reach Iran?

Suddenly, we came across some files, which were a breakthrough. We found an address where comrade Javadov had lived between 1948 and 1950. By then, some kind of normality had returned to the Muscovites. Schools had reopened. Buildings were renovated and more apartments were built. Jobs were created and those who had stayed in the city during the war were re-housed in the newly built apartments.

We set out for the neighbourhood, where my father had resided for three years. I talked to some elderly people in the estate and showed them my father's old photo taken from the archives. I was jubilant when a round-faced, good-humoured old woman focused on the photo and shouted: 'Oh, this is that kind-hearted man who had a sad smile on his face! Yes, I was young at the time and remember him living next door to us. My father and brothers had been killed in the war and my mother and I lived in the worst living conditions. This man used to say hello to my mother and ask whether we needed anything. We knew that he was lonely and sometimes invited him for a simple meal and a glass of vodka which he drank with much elegance. He was such a peculiar man!'

The old woman stopped while I saw father coming down the stairs, exchanging pleasantries with the population of women and children and no men, going down the dark corridors, thinking his own thoughts. I stopped my wandering thoughts concentrating on what the old woman was remembering. 'On sunny days, he would take his canvas and brush to the nearby park and paint until dark. We often watched him while playing in the park. The next day, he would go to another spot and paint over his original painting. He was polite to everyone but rarely talked to any of us. A heavy burden seemed to have fallen over his shoulders. He walked with the weight on him. Sometimes we saw him awake until late at night, writing. We never knew what he wrote but neighbours believed he was an artist who liked to remain anonymous. Pity he disappeared all of a sudden and was never heard of. We all thought he was dispatched to a mission. You know what I mean. Then, on an early morning of a cold day, we woke up by the footsteps rushing up the stairs. My mother got out of bed, trembling. She thought they had come for her although she had not committed any crime apart from being a loyal party worker. They broke the door and his possessions were taken away in boxes; books and paintings etc. Well I am sorry that I can not help you more.'

I was standing at the doorway of the apartment block C, listening, something rushing inside my brain. Suddenly, I felt my knees weakened and I sat on the stairs and began to weep. The interpreter sat beside me, and the old woman just looked. By then she knew too well the pain I had endured coming this far. Finally, she asked whether we wanted to have a look inside 'his' room?

'I can ask the present tenants to let you in', she said.

Trembling, I climbed the stairs and as the tenant opened the door, I almost collapsed before going in. 'Come in. Come in please.' A red-haired, well-groomed woman was grinning at us. I stepped inside. 'Nothing much has changed since we occupied the apartment. We have been living here since the early 1950s. I was a young bride at the time. We were told that the man who lived here before us had been assigned a job at a collective in the south, so he took his belongings with him. Most of the stuff was gone but those two paintings on the wall have been here since then.'

I looked up and from under my cloudy vision saw a clear blue sky, barren mountains in the background; an orange grove with plenty ripe oranges that had lowered their branches; three little children, two girls and a boy sitting at the edge of the garden, watching the sky. A waiting look spread across their faces. A beautiful woman stood at the side of a tree, wearing a flowery dress, her hair blowing in the wind, her smile spreading across the garden. My head turned to the second painting, a more sophisticated one; a crowded city with factories on one side, a cemetery with no greenery across the road. A coffin over the shoulders of four men, the head of the dead man rising from inside the coffin. His wide eyes looking across the road into the factory. The skeleton of hundreds of workers bent, frowning, walking out of the factory. At the top of the factory a sign glowed: 'Workers of the World Unite.' Further down the road, a man with a big belly, smoking a cigar looked at the crowd. A mocking grin painted over his face.

This was my father's world, this apartment, these people, his paintings! Where were his family? His old country? Us children? Where was his young bride whom he trained to do so well? I was taken into the unknown world of my father. I saw my father sitting on the balcony gathering his thoughts and then walking his way to the park to paint them down. I saw him back to his apartment waiting for the woman next door to invite him for a meal. I saw him everywhere, felt his presence beside me. I did not know that he

313

painted so well. I saw him sitting at the edge of the bed, frowning while writing. What was he writing? Letters? To whom? I even heard him crying out our names.

The woman took my arm and led me to a chair. 'Oh my dear. What can we say? It is such a long time and you are still looking for him.'

'Can I have these paintings?' I pleaded with the woman. 'Of course you can. After all it has been your father who painted them. These might be the only items that would remind you of his life in this country.'

I did not know how to thank these kind-hearted women but the interpreter advised me to give them some money. 'These people are not in the best of financial situations, inflation and price rises are breaking their backs.' I had to insist until they finally accepted a few thousand roubles. And we left the building and the ghost of my father which I was sure wandered in the forest nearby. I wept the whole night, holding the paintings to my chest. My father was around, watching. I felt his presence. I sensed him close to me.

* * *

A big break-through. Inside a tiny file at the far end of a dusty cabinet laid a bunch of letters with an indexing system. The date read October 1949. On the first page there was a letter that read: 'By the orders of the authorities, comrade Javadov, who has been suspected of propagating corrupted materials, has been detained and taken to a Camp in Siberia for rehabilitation. Comrade Javadov has recently criticised the education authorities and especially the party managers who ran this part of the city and has spread rumours about their incompetence. He had even tried to put the blame on the Great Leader, Comrade Stalin. Since such outrageous behaviour cannot be tolerated, the head of the local committee has recommended rehabilitation. Comrade Javadov's case would have begun with a caution and possibly suspension from service, had we not discovered his strange behaviour in the neighbourhood and the letters he has written to his family, which are all kept in a separate file, and also his paintings, which are reactionary and outside revolutionary norms.'

In a separate note, the location where Javad khan was taken mentioned a camp, designated to the intellectuals who had to be rehabilitated and proletarianised. A remote camp in the farthest parts of Siberia, where no one had ever returned from the winters of 50 degrees below zero. Rehabilitated. No more explanation and no further reports in that file.

I could take no more of the discovery of the final chapters of my father's life. I ran out of the building, across River Volga and wept in despair. Tania ran after me. She was deeply worried about my state of mind. She strongly advised me to wrap up the operation and do away with further search. 'What is the use, my dear? You have discovered the mystery. Why do you want to torture yourself? There is nothing more to know. Go home. Go to your family and let the matter rest in peace.' Something in my heart told me that I would unravel further if I continued with my search. So, scanning the files, searching and reading went on for another month.

Meanwhile, my daughter, Mona having understood that my health was deteriorating, begged of me to return but I refused: 'my dear, don't worry about me. I am certain that I will find more about my father and until such time, I will not leave this place.' And finally, at the end of a tiring day, we opened a file that read 'Personal' letters. There it was! Hundreds of letters that Iranians had written to their families over many decades buried in the basements of this rotten building. In a frantic attempt to see my father's handwriting, I dropped the file on the floor. Suddenly, words of love, of despair, of longing and far-reaching affections fell down, spread, banging their heads on the floorboards. Scattered through the musty air. Words that at last had found their freedom and declined to return to the old boxes, were running in every direction. Letters written in many languages, Persian, Russian, Turkish, Kurdish flying from their enclosure. The interpreter and I sat on the floor, collecting them one by one, among which, many belonged to my father. Frantically, we organised them in one pile. These were precious to me. I wanted to possess them, to take them home and to read and re-read them at my own pleasure. I wanted to post a few to my dying mother, so patiently waiting to hear the last words about her husband's fate. Would the authorities permit me to take them out? Could we smuggle out a few? These had endured the imprisonment of many decades. It was time they were set free. It was time Javad khan's journey through life in the Soviet Russia and his longing for his family which was painted in these series of long, agonising letters, dated back to the early 1940s right after his departure from home, returned to their lawful owners.

* * *

Finally, I was able to set a few of the letters free, to let them out of the confinement of their long detention and let them be read by the whole world. Whether my mission ended or just began is left to the readers to decide. For now, I have done what I thought should have been done. I put down the pen, close the book, put on a nice flowery dress, take my keys and step outside to walk across the green into the vastness of this dewy morning. Sara is lingering behind. I can hear her footsteps. The sun will soon gleam over head.

Thirty Nine

It is a month before New Year 2000. I left London a week ago and arrived in Karmanieh the night before. This is where I have decided to celebrate the new century and maybe stay for a while. I managed to divorce Farid and get him out of my life at long last. The weather is crisp and the dust is taken away by a persistent rain that has knocked at my window all night. Today the sun is in full swing and there is no shred of a cloud on this blue sky. My mother and I wrap ourselves in shawls, bring the samovar and the silver bowl of oranges to sit beside us on the veranda and lean our backs on the cushions. I promised my mother to let her read all the letters in time, one by one at her own pleasure. I have already read them a hundred times and memorised most of them. It is time for my mother to know the whole story and wrap her memories in the crimson past and let the remaining part of her life live without waiting. She looks at me and smiles, puts on her glasses and looks at the yellow papers for a good long time, gives her breath time to turn normal and begins in earnest. Then the bell rings, the door handle bangs and the maid opens the door to my brother Sasan, who looks handsome, healthy and in full control. I get up to embrace him and place him beside me. The letter slips from my mother's shaking hands as she tries to move aside to make a space between herself and me for him to nest. Sasan does not say a word. His eyes focus on me; turn to mother to ask her to begin what she had started. Soon he drifts away in the second letter as his shoulder leans on me. I am all but a heart full of love. I am in peace, content.

* * *

Letter one

August 1942

To my dearest mother and my wife,

If you can find a space in your heart for forgiveness please spare it for me. My darlings, I know that by leaving you I have done both of you a great injustice. I will not defend my decision but there is nothing in the world more precious than the two of you and the children. The force that separated me from you and sent me this far was a burden on my conscience that had occupied my mind since I had returned to Iran years ago. It is hard to explain but it is as if I had an unfinished business, a debt to pay. Although my love of socialism and its birth place is second to the love I had for you, I could not live in peace had I not returned to fulfil my duties. I will promise when all this is finished and I return, I will compensate for the lost times and the pain I have caused you all. I am certain that you, my dear mother and beloved wife, are strong enough to take care of the children until my return. I love you all very much.

Javad

PS: I think I should tell you what happened after I left. En-route, I joined other comrades, and then we set off for the northern borders and took a ferry to Baku. It was difficult to get out of port Anzali. We had to hide in a cargo ship by paying the captain extra fare. The sea was rough and at some stage, we said our prayers because we thought we would all die in the middle of wild waters. Fortunately, the captain was an experienced man and led the ship out of danger in no time. When we reached Baku it was as if we have arrived home but it was not before long that we were dispatched for interrogation on suspicion of espionage. We were kept in separate cabins in the worse living conditions during this period. At first, it was hard to convince these border guards that we were not spies or had not travelled this far to work for a foreign country; rather we were a group of enthusiasts, who came to help the Soviets to win the war. I never forget the look on the face of a high ranking officer as I told him this simple truth. He stood up, walked round me and repeated what I had just told him. Then he pushed the chair from

318

*under me and kicked me so hard that I thought I was going to die.
Then he left me in that situation until another interrogator opened
the door the day after. During this period we were almost starved to
and one of our comrades got ill and died a painful death. The coast-
guards had no sympathy for any of us and no matter how much we'd
beg of them to call a doctor they just laughed and ignored our
pleas. At some stage, things were getting out of hand and I thought
we would be tried as spies. But fortunately, we were released but
kept under constant surveillance.*

*But darling don't worry. Everything is going to be fine. I can
understand that in war situation, there is nothing wrong with being
suspicious. And besides, these were only a bunch of coast-guards
doing their duty. I have no hurt feeling towards them. Hopefully, we
are free now and in contact with the authorities. We will be
informed of our duties in no time. Baku is not what I remembered
from the old days. There is chaos everywhere but I suppose it is
because of the war. The Party leaders are very different from those
comrades we used to know. We have met a lot of fellow Iranians and
hope to tie bonds with them. The Iranian communist party is very
close to the Azerbaijani leadership and lots of politics go on but I
would not want to bore you with that.*

*Here, life is very different from Iran. Apart from the war and
shortages, there is a nice side to everything. There are good schools
and academies. There are theatres and music halls. Of course, there
are more facilities in a big city like Moscow. When the war ends,
one of my aims would be to take you, my dear wife and the children,
to this blessed land and live in peace and happiness for the rest of
our lives. I am sure that you would like it here because you know
the language and people are so friendly. The children would love it
here. They will become something for themselves. I cannot wait to
take you to the opera house.*

I will try to write to you whenever I find time. Please darlings forgive me and kiss the children one by one; Sara, Shireen and my little Sasan.

Dearest Suri, take care of my mother. I know that the two of you get along well. Darling, I hope you write to me. Forgive me if I have hurt you so badly.

* * *

Letter two hundred and one

Spring 1948

To my dearest wife,

I have almost lost hope of receiving any news from home. Over years, I have written you tens of letters but received no reply. I am living in hell. The pain and torment is unbearable. I miss you, the children and my mother so very much. Above all, I regret the decision I made in the first place. Is there any way to turn the clock back and start afresh? Would you ever forgive me if I came back and asked clemency? Would I ever see you again?

My darling Suri, as you would know from the address, I have long moved to Moscow, hoping life would be easier than Azerbaijan. There, we were constantly under observation and surveillance by the authorities and members of the Iranian communist party. We came to the Soviet with great aspirations to free the socialist state from the Nazis' invasion and make it home for ourselves and our families, which we hoped would join us at some later stage, but that never materialised. Not only did we find ourselves a burden on the system but lost our souls in the process. Our spirit is lost in all the control, rivalry and intimidation. Here I am a schoolteacher with no power to influence anyone at anything and contribute to nothing. I have to confess that I have become a miserable creature, full of fear and void of those high hopes, which took me this far in the first place. I am reaching a point where I sometimes think of taking my own life.

My dearest Suri, you and the children are my only bright stars in this gloomy sky. By day I live with the hope of getting news from you, knowing that you are well and I will see you some day. At night, I live in my dreams, sweet, scented, full of you and the children. They should have grown up by now. God knows how much I miss them. In the face of every child at school, I see Sara, Shireen and Sasan. I hear their voices and long to hold them tight to my chest. I know the post is very slow but sometimes people receive letters from their families. I yearn to be with you, to touch you and see you smiling. Oh my darling, please forgive me for the pain I have caused you. I have had my punishment. I ask for pardon and hope that you grant it to me. It is so many years that I have not heard from anyone back home. What I did was horrible and I am paying for it. I hope that upon receiving this letter you write a few words and let me know how things are. Please give my regards to my mother and the rest of the family. I love you all very much and hope to see you soon.

With all my love,

Javad

PS: After many years of communal living, I have been given a small room near the school I am teaching. It has a balcony to the rear that opens up to a deep forest. In winter, snow covers everywhere and wild animals appear on the edge, asking for food, not knowing that we do not have enough to feed ourselves. When the weather is nice, I walk under the shade of the trees, as they never let the sun reach the ground. I hear voices in the silence of the dense forest. A lot of flowers and plants bear similarities to the flowers back home and that drives me to the point of madness. Their scents wake the urge in me to rush and embrace you, my dear beloved, and my longing stretches to eternity, to the edge of horizon, where hope is waiting, where bright stars glitter in the sky. If I were able to follow those stars to take me out of this enclosure and throw me into your arms! If I could walk across the steppes and swim the rough seas to reach home! If.

My neighbour next door is a widow, who is as unfortunate as I am. She has lost her husband and her only son in the war. She is left with a daughter. Not knowing of the pains that are crushing me under, she sometimes wonders why I stand on the balcony and follow the shadows into the forest. What can I tell her? That once upon a time, I had a beautiful wife and three lovely children; that I left them to help a cause which did not need me in the first place; that I miss them very much and have not heard from them since I left home so many years ago? Sometimes I see her crying in silence, in desperation for her loss and the miserable life she is living. I ask her if she needs any help. She looks at me with tears and replies: 'Yes comrade. I want my life back. I want my husband, my son. Can you give them back to me?' The neighbours are all very kind and sometimes invite me to their tiny rooms for dinner and a drink, but I know that I am a burden on the meagre rations they receive from the state.

Darling, I have recently started painting. It gives me a lot of satisfaction and relief. I wish I could put everything on the canvas, an impossible job for different reasons. When I see you and if I see you, I want to paint your lovely face with those searching eyes that talked your language louder than words. I want to immortalise your smile, that beautiful smile that was the backbone of my strength. At the moment, I am painting my thoughts, my dreams and fears, alongside the beauties of Moscow. Future is very uncertain. I am not sure if I will be able to paint those dreams in totality. Pray for me. Wash me in the kindness of your heart, in the love we shared and do not let me drown in despair. Pardon me.

* * *

Letter three hundred

October 1950

My dearest wife,

Winter has arrived at the camp sooner than expected. Snow, ice and the cold nights have entombed us. This enclosure they call rehabilitation camp is dark, damp with long corridors, hard beds and few blankets. No heating and no place to hide from the wild winds that howl constantly through the cracks as we shiver every moment in time. Stormy weather brings snowflakes and the wind cuts through our bones as we are covered from head to toe labouring in the open. Every morning, the line of icy humans stretches on the road, staggering, bending, falling, rising, struggling. Everything is covered under the blanket of whiteness, the cruelty of the guards, our bruised and falling bodies, human being stripped of their humanity. Here, mountains are high; forests are wild and the camp authorities beyond description. In this world of madness and violent behaviour, the camp population fluctuates all the time. It swells by the new arrivals; it deflates a few months later. Most of the time the balance is kept. The same numbers die by the time new people have arrived. The mixture always differs. Sometimes we have more poets, at other time writers of various genres prevail. A year ago, we were hosting a large number of art enthusiasts and critics, who turned the camp into a debating society for the first few months before their energies died down. In that short period, nights stretched into dawn with whispers of approval and disapproval. Inmates reading poetry, a piece of writing, a philosophical issue. We all sat on our beds, wrapping the only blanket we had around us, listening. Darkness sheltered sharp tongues of those who were criticising the system; those who believed it was a betrayal to the humanistic ideals that socialism stood for. Then suddenly, silence fell over the camp. Illness followed, despair prevailed and many began the long and painful process of losing their hopes, thereby driving themselves into the trap of death.

Here, death means humiliation of life. When someone dies, they do not bury him with ceremonials; music band, officials walking behind, red roses and medals of honour covering the red coffin. They are not mourned and their names are not carved on a white stone; 'Here lies a Comrade, who was a patriotic writer of the Socialist Soviet'. No. Their death, which is always caused by hard labour and disease, is not investigated and lessons are not learnt to prevent other deaths. Why should they? Prisoners are forgotten the moment they are detained and dispatched to this forsaken land. As one dies, his bed is quickly assigned to a new arrival, who knows nothing of his predecessor and his own destiny a few years later.

My destiny passes through the same route, although I have not been an artist, nor a poet or a writer. This schoolteacher must be proud that he was assigned the same mission as those of his honourable comrades in this horrifying gulag. I am proud that if I lost my precious possessions, I ended up dying among the most learned of all, those who make a mockery of death. Their lives short as it becomes, would stretch beyond time. Some day, they will be remembered and their honours restored.

In the years to come, as these precious lives come to an end and history moves on, passing through this part of Siberia, I hope someone reminds the people to walk slowly, quietly with respect. On the grounds of this camp, men of fine brains, full of burning love, mindful thoughts, knowledge of the world and the wildest dreams, men of poetry and prose are laid side by side, bumper to bumper, waiting for the judgement day, which will come to unearth their souls, not in another world, which is nowhere to be found but in this same earthly world that has produced the good and the bad, the criminal and the poet, out of the same soil but has given them different souls. I do not know who will be the judge and the jury and who will be held responsible for these crimes. I only understand that as times go by my urge to live diminishes among the hardship of life itself.

I am bewildered at the extent of my ignorance a few years ago, and the knowledge I have gained of the scope of the holocaust that humans bring to other humans. In a far-reaching future, someone should pay for these crimes. Some day people should ask themselves; if these were the ideals, which led in their name for people being separated from their homes and their loved ones, and sent to the death camps, shame on the ideals and the ideology. Damn the evil conscience of those, who led these fine people to their death trap.

Throughout the long winter nights, awoken by the cold and the pain that reigns all over my body, I have circled the world, round and round, to find a bright star, to find solace but have returned to point zero. I have not found peace of mind since I was taken to this camp, for a crime I have no knowledge of. Some say that my tongue spoke my mind. Should it be the reason? Others suggest the letters I have written to my family have revealed my true doubts about the system. Could that be counted as a crime?

It is true that I did not obey the flock of sheep to the slaughter of schools, of colleges, of factories. Doubt and Thought were my biggest crime. For that I am paying the price. A heavy price it can be said. Rehabilitation has not rehabilitated me. I still think my own thoughts and use my own judgement among doubt and reason. So, I believe my freedom is far to come. Will possibly never arrive. Not in living. Surely in death. Living in this remote part of the world, fighting with the wild weather and the wilder guards, who are as much prisoners as we are, has not bent my determination, though crushed my health. My body is giving way to fatigue, to hunger, to ailment. My lungs can no longer stand the cold. Coughing is unbearable and my blood drips out of my mouth slowly, painfully, emptying my body of the red substance. It colours the flag that flies at full mast above our camp. The flag is red with my warm blood but my love has withered away along the river of despair, across the shores of disillusion.

Once upon a time, I had a heart full of colourful loves, for the people, for a cause I believed was just, for the pain and suffering of the oppressed. Now I am hovering in the air above the branches of the tallest forest trees, looking at the crowd of people who depart from the factories, out of the farmlands, bewildered. Their hungry stomachs ache, their empty minds tingle, their fears walk ahead of them. Thought is taken away from their minds, locked up in the laboratories for scientists to do experiments. Ideology needs no thinking soldiers. Ideologies require armies of obedient soldiers for their dictators to rule. Dictators have the power to dictate ideologies. Power talks. Bees do not talk and surely do not think. I thought. I talked. I ran after concepts that made no sense in reality and in the process lost everything that was dear to me.

My dear Suri, hold on, from a distance I can see you walking bare foot on the snowy steppes towards my direction. I have to hold on to my breath now trying to slow down. I focus on the movement of your feet as they dance an inch above the surface. Your figure is transparent in the clear distance. Now your hair is blowing away from the moonlight of your face and your beautiful eyes are searching for me. I am hanging from the clouds, up in the sky. I am trying to stand on my feet and touch the surface of your skin to make sure of your existence. Suddenly, all is white. Something in my brain sets free the wires from the extra burden of thought. Slowly, meticulously, without much effort my memory is white-washed as my mind is emptied of joy and pain. My experience and knowledge of external and internal existence is wiped out and clean as a new born, I stand in the middle of this white vastness and my eyes catch a glimpse of your silky shade, twirling, twinkling in the wind. I hold my last breath to call on you. Snow turns into hail. Snowstorm and gusty winds are blowing you away. Darkness falls. My wide-open eyes glitter in the dark like two shady candles. I fall down from the edge of the torn cloud; your eyes look at me in anguish. My beloved, hold me tight. Hold me tight.

Glossary of Persian words

1. Andaruni, inner section of a harem, where women and children lived and only close male members of the family were allowed to enter.

2. Biruni, outer section of a harem, where the male members of the family worked and socialised.

3. Akhund: a Muslem clergy.

4. Attar: traditional herbalist.

5. Banu: the lady.

6. Chador: a wrap that covers the woman's body head to toe. The style of chador is different from country to country.

7. Charghad: a long scarf that is tied by a pin under the chin.

8. Dayeh: wet nurse. Women who lived in the premises and breast-fed the landlord's babies.

9. Dudul: slang for penis.

10. Ghaout: mixture of seeds, roasted, grounded and mixed with sugar and served in special silver bowls when people came to visit the newly born baby.

11. Ghelyan: hubble-bubble. In Persia, before the arrival of cigarettes, women used to smoke ghelyan, mostly in social gatherings.

12. Ghouls: imaginary giants that frighten the children.

13. Hamam: Public baths, where women bathed collectively. It was in the mid-twentieth century that the idea of building private baths at home arrived in Iran.

14. Hedjleh: bridal chamber.

15. Hojreh: traditional office mainly in the bazaar, where merchants sit all day, doing business.

16. Howzkhaneh: a shaded and airy chamber where people spent hot summer days.

17. Huris: the most beautiful angels who reside in Heaven and tend to men's needs eternally.

18. Wine House: a place in the outskirts of towns, where wine was served by women or young boys.

19. Korsi: in the lack of other heating methods, a low table would be placed in the centre of the family room, covered with a huge cotton quilt. Under the table a brazier of charcoal would burn steadily. Family members would sit around the korsi, leaning against cushions, stretching their feet to keep warm.

20. Laleh abasi: a type of plant that grows in Iran and some other hot countries. It blooms purple or pink flowers.

21. Muezzin: a person with a loud and nice voice who chants prayers from the town's minaret, inviting the devotees to go to mosques for prayers.

22. Payab: a system of long passages with many steps, going deepdown to reach the subterranean water systems which ran through gardens.

23. Rubandeh: a piece of gauze or muslin that covers the face.

24. Saghi: a woman or young boy who served the customers in the Wine Houses.

25. Sofreh: a piece of cloth that is spread on the floor, where food is placed and people sit around cross-legged it to eat.

26. Sorkhab: a kind of red powder used for make up.

27. Sormeh: traditional eyeliner.

28. Talabeh: a student Muslem clergy.

29. Ulama: high ranking Muslem clergies.

30. Zaifeh: females were called by this title because it was widely believed that women were weak and not capable of taking care of themselves.

Acknowledgments

I would like to thank many friends who persuaded me to complete my manuscript and send it for publication. Special thanks to my friend Mary Wright, who spent so much time to read the manuscript and comment on it. I thank my dear friend, Dr Shadab Vajdi for reading the manuscript, as a literary critic of Iranian women's writings and commenting on it.

A special love goes to my son Parham Donyai who read the manuscript meticulously and without whom this publication was not possible. My unconditional love goes to my daughter Parastou Donyai who spent time to go through parts of the manuscript. I love both of them for helping me all the way.

I would also like to thank my long-term friend Ali Mahvelati for the beautiful calligraphy of Pomegranate Hearts in Persian, which has gone into the cover design.